"A wonderfully joyful ode to good food, best friends, tough choices, and great love. *Off the Menu* = one delicious [...] complete with recipes! So much [...]

—Alison Pa[...]

"Smart, sexy, and delightfully bu[...] scrumptious. Stacey Ballis has [...] happiness between the covers of a book."

—Quinn Cummings, author of *Notes from the Underwire*

Good Enough to Eat

"*Good Enough to Eat* is like a perfect dish of macaroni and cheese—rich, warm, nuanced, and delicious. And like any great comfort food, Stacey Ballis's new book is absolutely satisfying."

—Jen Lancaster, *New York Times* bestselling author of
If You Were Here

"Witty and tender, brash and seriously clever, Stacey Ballis's characters are our friends, our neighbors, or, in some cases, that sardonic colleague the next cubicle over . . . Her storytelling will have you alternately turning pages and calling your friends urging them to come along for the ride. And in Stacey Ballis's talented hands, oh what a wonderful ride it is."

—Elizabeth Flock, *New York Times* bestselling author of
Sleepwalking in Daylight

"A toothsome meal of moments, gorgeously written, in warmth and with keen observation, *Good Enough to Eat* is about so much more than the magic of food; it's about the magic of life."

—Stephanie Klein, author of *Straight Up and Dirty* and *Moose*

continued . . .

The Spinster Sisters

"Readers will be rooting for Ballis's smart, snappy heroines."

—*Booklist*

"A laugh-out-loud hoot of a book. Jodi and Jill are amazing characters. They are challenged by balancing their business lives with style, charm, and grace. A must-read." —*A Romance Review*

"Filled with characters so witty and diverse yet so strong in their passion for friends and family that they could easily be our best friend or favorite aunt . . . Women of every age will relate to Ballis's clever yet unassuming story." —*RT Book Reviews*

Room for Improvement

"For those who say 'chick lit' is played out, all I can say is think again. Stacey Ballis proves the genre can be funny, honest, clever, real, and, most importantly, totally fresh." —Jen Lancaster

"More fun than a *Trading Spaces* marathon. One of the season's best." —*The Washington Post Book World*

"Rife with humor—always earthy, often bawdy, unwaveringly forthright humor." —*Chicago Sun-Times*

"A laugh-out-loud novel that will appeal to HGTV devotees as well as those who like their chick lit on the sexy side. One of the summer's hot reads for the beach." —*Library Journal*

"In her third outing, Ballis offers up a frothy, fun send-up of reality TV. Readers will have a blast." —*Booklist*

Sleeping Over

"Ballis presents a refreshingly realistic approach to relationships and the things that test (and often break) them." —*Booklist*

"*Sleeping Over* will have you laughing, crying, and planning your next girls' night out." —*Romance Reader at Heart*

Inappropriate Men

One of Chatelaine.com's Seven Sizzling Summer Reads for 2004

"An insightful and hilarious journey into the life and mind of Chicagoan Sidney Stein." —*Today's Chicago Woman*

"Ballis's debut is a witty tale of a thirtysomething who unexpectedly has to start the search for love all over again." —*Booklist*

"Stacey Ballis's debut novel is a funny, smart book about love, heartbreak, and all the experiences in between."

—Chatelaine.com

"Without compromising the intelligence of her readers, Ballis delivers an inspiring message of female empowerment and body image acceptance in her fun, sexy debut novel."

—*Inside Lincoln Park*

Berkley Books by Stacey Ballis

ROOM FOR IMPROVEMENT

THE SPINSTER SISTERS

GOOD ENOUGH TO EAT

OFF THE MENU

Off the Menu

STACEY BALLIS

BERKLEY BOOKS, NEW YORK

THE BERKLEY PUBLISHING GROUP
Published by the Penguin Group
Penguin Group (USA) Inc.
375 Hudson Street, New York, New York 10014, USA

Penguin Group (Canada), 90 Eglinton Avenue East, Suite 700, Toronto, Ontario M4P 2Y3, Canada
(a division of Pearson Penguin Canada Inc.) • Penguin Books Ltd., 80 Strand, London WC2R 0RL,
England • Penguin Group Ireland, 25 St. Stephen's Green, Dublin 2, Ireland (a division of Penguin
Books Ltd.) • Penguin Group (Australia), 250 Camberwell Road, Camberwell, Victoria 3124, Australia
(a division of Pearson Australia Group Pty. Ltd.) • Penguin Books India Pvt. Ltd., 11 Community
Centre, Panchsheel Park, New Delhi—110 017, India • Penguin Group (NZ), 67 Apollo Drive,
Rosedale, Auckland 0632, New Zealand (a division of Pearson New Zealand Ltd.) • Penguin Books
(South Africa) (Pty.) Ltd., 24 Sturdee Avenue, Rosebank, Johannesburg 2196, South Africa

Penguin Books Ltd., Registered Offices: 80 Strand, London WC2R 0RL, England

This is an original publication of The Berkley Publishing Group.

PUBLISHER'S NOTE: The recipes contained in this book are to be followed exactly as written.
The publisher is not responsible for your specific health or allergy needs that may require medical
supervision. The publisher is not responsible for any adverse reactions to the recipes contained in this book.

This is a work of fiction. Names, characters, places, and incidents either are the product of the author's
imagination or are used fictitiously, and any resemblance to actual persons, living or dead, business
establishments, events, or locales is entirely coincidental. While the author has made every effort to
provide accurate telephone numbers, Internet addresses, and other contact information at the time of
publication, neither the publisher nor the author assumes any responsibility for errors or for changes that
occur after publication. Further, the publisher does not have any control over and does not assume any
responsibility for author or third-party websites or their content.

PUBLISHING HISTORY
Berkley trade paperback edition / July 2012

Library of Congress Cataloging-in-Publication Data

Ballis, Stacey.
Off the menu / Stacey Ballis.
p. cm.
ISBN 978-0-425-24766-2 (pbk.)
1. Administrative assistants—Fiction.   2. Celebrity chefs—Fiction.   I. Title.
PS3602.A624O34 2012
813'.6—dc23
2012008568

PRINTED IN THE UNITED STATES OF AMERICA

10 9 8 7 6 5 4 3 2 1

ALWAYS LEARNING   PEARSON

This book is dedicated with my whole heart to my extraordinary husband, Bill, my true b'shert, who showed up right on time and made everything in the world bright and beautiful and possible. You are the magic in my life every day, and I am the luckiest girl in the world. Thank you for everything you are, and everything I become when I am with you. I love you more than Pamplemousse.

*For Payton and The Lucky Dog,
and in loving memory of Willy and Otis*

Acknowledgments

As always, my work is made possible only because of the support of my amazing family, now supersized! With much, much love to Moms and Dads—both Ballis and Thurmond—Jonnie, Deb and Andy, Jamie and Steve, Rebecca and Elizabeth, Oliver, Kalie, and Quincy. A merry group recently made much merrier.

And since blood doesn't make it better . . . the Schayes and the Schnierows are all in my corner, and I'm always grateful. Ditto all generations and iterations of Gault, Adelman, Srulovitz, and Heisler.

Nothing works without my friends, and I am so blessed that you are all way too numerous to mention by name, but you absolutely know who you are, and if you are wondering if I mean you, I totally do.

Special mention necessary for the inspiration and support of my Wonder Twin Jen Lancaster, and our lunch girls, Gina and Tracey. Some of the characters in this book would not exist without Harry and Penny and Scott; thanks, guys, for letting me co-opt your witty turns of phrase and charming personalities. And for all of my dear and talented writer gal pals, thank you for help with titles and talking me off ledges!

To my very dear friend who just happens to also be my agent, Scott Mendel, thank you for everything, always.

To Wendy McCurdy, editor extraordinaire, who believed in this book as much as I did, it was great to have you with me.

To everyone at Berkley/Penguin, especially Leslie Gelbman and Melissa Broder and Katherine Pelz, and the entire sales team, thank you a million times for all you do.

To some of my favorite chefs—Michelle Bernstein, Stephanie Izard, Gil Langlois, Susan Spicer, Allen Sternweiler, and Michael White—thank you so much for letting me mention your names and reprint your recipes and, most important, for all of the delicious.

1

Through the fog of those last ephemeral floaty moments before I fall into deep sleep, I suddenly feel a stirring in the bed next to me. I smile, knowing that as delicious as sleep is, there is something unbearably wonderful about the need for tenderness and contact. I roll over and let my tired lids open, forcing myself back from the brink of the sleep I desperately need, to attend to my sweetheart, who I need more. He looks at me with what can only be described as a perfect combination of love and longing, and tilts his head to one side, dark chocolate eyes sparkling wickedly in the darkness.

"Yes? Can I help you?" I say, my voice slightly roughened with exhaustion.

He lets his head tilt slowly to the other side and he reaches for me with a tentative teasing touch, then stops and just waits.

"You are very demanding, you know that?" I can't help but laugh.

But what can I do? He is the love of my life. A smile appears on his face and he reaches out again, this time more assuredly, tapping my hand with gentle insistence.

"Okay, okay!" I give up. I can deny this boy nothing.

As soon as he hears that word, he pounces, all twenty-six pounds of him landing with a thump on my chest.

This dog will be the end of me.

"I know, I know, boy, you need some extra-special love time, because you were at doggie day care all day while I was working to put kibble on the table."

Dumpling rolls over in my arms so that I can scratch his oddly broad chest. He is, to say the least, one of the strangest dogs anyone has ever seen. Which of course, is absolutely why I adopted him. I don't really know for sure what his lineage is, but he has the coloring and legs of a Jack Russell, the head of a Chihuahua, with the broad chest and sloping back of a bulldog, wide pug-ly eyes that bug out and are a little watery, and happen to mostly look in opposite directions. His ears, one which sticks up and one which flops down, are definitely fruit bat–ish. And when he gets riled by something, he gets a two-inch-wide Mohawk down his whole back, which sticks straight up, definitively warthog. He's a total ladies man, a relentless flirt, and the teensiest bit needy in the affection department, as are many rescue dogs. But of course, he is so irresistibly lovable he never has a problem finding the attention he desires.

He is also smart as a whip, and soon after I got him my dear friend Barry took him to train as a therapy dog so that the two of them could work occasionally in hospitals and nursing homes and with disabled kids. He has the highest possible certification for that work, and was one of only two dogs out of fifty to pass the test when he took it, proud mama me. Barry is an actor and cabaret performer, and on the days when he is not in rehearsal he often volunteers to "entertain the troops" as he calls it, singing standards for the elderly, doing dramatic readings of fairy tales for kids with cancer, and teaching music to teenagers with autism. He'd seen someone working with a therapy dog at Children's Memorial Hospital, and when he found out how meaningful that work can be, he asked if he could borrow Dumpling and see if he was the right kind of dog. Dumpling turned out to be more than the right kind of dog; he turned out to be a total rock star, and has become a favorite at all of their stops. The fact that Barry has snagged many dates with handsome doctors and male nurses using Dumpling as bait is just a bonus for him. Dumpling loves the work and I love knowing that he spends at least one or two days a week out and about with Barry instead of just lazing around and getting too many treats from his pals at Best Friends doggie day care.

Dumpling is the kind of dog that makes people on the street do double- and triple-takes and ask in astonished voices, "What kind of dog IS that?!" His head is way too small for his thick solid body, and his legs are too spindly. His eyes point away from each other like a chameleon. One side of his mouth curls up a little, half-Elvis, half palsy-victim, and his tongue has a tendency to stick out just a smidgen on that side. He was found as a puppy running down the median of a local highway, and I adopted him from PAWS five years ago, after he had been there for nearly a year. He is, without a doubt, the best thing that ever happened to me.

My girlfriend Bennie says it looks like he was assembled by a disgruntled committee. Barry calls him a random collection of dog bits. My mom, in a classic ESL moment, asked upon meeting him, "He has the Jack Daniels in him, leetle bit, no?" I was going to correct her and say Jack Russell, but when you look at him, he does look a little bit like he has the Jack Daniels in him. My oldest nephew, Alex, who watches too much *Family Guy* and idolizes Stewie, took one look, and then turned to me in all seriousness and said in that weird almost-British accent, "Aunt Alana, precisely what brand of dog *is* that?" I replied, equally seriously, that he was a purebred Westphalian Stoat Hound. When the kid learns how to Google, I'm going to lose major cool aunt points.

Dumpling tilts his head back and licks the underside of my chin, wallowing in love.

"Dog, you are going to be the death of me. You have got to let me sleep sometime."

These words are barely out of my mouth, when he leaps up and starts barking, in a powerful growly baritone that belies his small stature. The third bark is interrupted by the insistent ringing of my buzzer.

Crap. "Yes, you are very fierce. You are the best watchdog. Let's go see what the crazy man wants."

Only one person would have the audacity to ring my bell at a quarter to one on a weeknight.

Patrick Conlon.

Yes, *the* Patrick Conlon.

Owner and executive chef of Conlon Restaurant Group, based here in Chicago. Three local restaurants, Conlon, his flagship white tablecloth restaurant, housed in a Gold Coast historic mansion, which recently received a coveted second Michelin star. Patrick's, a homey high-end comfort-food place in Lincoln Park, and PCGrub, his newest endeavor, innovative bar food in the suddenly hot Logan Square neighborhood, dangerously close to my apartment. He also has Conlon Las Vegas, Conlon Miami, and is in negotiations to open PCGrub in both those cities, and a one-off project looming in New York as well.

But even if you have never eaten in one of Patrick's restaurants, you have probably seen him on Food TV, where he has two long-running shows, *Feast*, where he demonstrates home versions of his restaurant recipes and special menus for entertaining, and *Conlon's Academy*, which is a heavily technique-based show for people who really want to learn professional-level cooking fundamentals as they relate to a passionate home cook. Maybe you have seen him guest judging on *Top Chef*, snarking and sparring with Tom Colicchio, Padma getting all giggly and tongue-tied in his handsome presence. Or judging on *Iron Chef America*, disagreeing charmingly with Jeffery Steingarten at his curmudgeoniest. Or on a booze-fueled tour of the best Chicago street food with Anthony Bourdain. Or giving his favorite foods a shout-out on *The Best Thing I Ever Ate* or *Unique Eats* compilation shows. Or maybe you have read one of his six bestselling cookbooks. Even more likely, you have seen him squiring an endless series of leggy actresses and pop princesses and supermodels on red carpets, and read about his latest heartbreaking act in a glossy tabloid. And yes, before you ask, that latest angry power-girl single by Ashley Bell rocketing up the country charts about "settin' loose the one who cooked my goose" is totally about him.

Why, you might ask, is a world-famous chef and gadabout television celeb ringing my bell at a quarter to one in the morning on a weeknight? Because I am his Gal Friday, Miss Moneypenny, executive culinary assistant, general dogsbody, and occasional whipping post. I help him develop his recipes for the shows and cookbooks, and travel with him to prep and sous chef when he does television appearances and book tours. I also choose his gifts for birthdays and holidays, order his apology flowers for the Legs, as I call them, listen to him bitch about either being too famous or not famous enough, and write his witty answers to the e-mail questionnaires he gets since few journalists like to do actual note-taking live interviews anymore. I let the endless series of the fired and broken-up-with he leaves in his wake cry on my shoulder, and then I write half of them recommendations for other jobs, and the other half sincere apology notes, which I sign in a perfect replica of his signature, practiced on eleventy-million cases of cookbooks and glossy headshots that he can't be bothered to sign himself.

And on nights like these, when he has a date or a long business dinner, I drag my ass out of bed to make him a snack, and listen to him wax either poetical or heretical, depending on how the evening went.

I quickly throw on a bra and my robe, while Patrick leans on the bell and Dumpling hops straight up and down as if he has springs in his paws, and joyously barks his ill-proportioned tiny little head off, knowing instinctively that this is not some scary intruder, but rather one of his favorite two-leggeds.

Cheese and rice, why are the men in my life so freaking demanding tonight?

"I. Am. Coming!" I yell in the vague direction of the door, turning on lights as I stumble through my apartment.

I open the front door, and there he is. Six foot three inches, broad shoulders, tousled light brown hair with a hint of strawberry, piercing blue eyes, chiseled jaw showing a hint of stubble, wide grin with impossibly even white teeth, except for the one chipped eyetooth from a football incident in high school, the one flaw in the perfect canvas of his face.

Fucker.

I gather up all five foot three of my well-padded round self, with my unruly dark brown curly hair in a frizzled shrubbery around my head, squint my sleepy blue eyes at him, and step aside so he can enter.

He leans down and kisses the top of my head. "Hello, Alana-falana, did I wake you?"

Patrick doesn't walk as much as he glides in a forwardly direction. Most women find it sexy. I find it creepy.

"Of course you woke me, it's one o'clock in the good-manned morning, and we have a meeting at eight." I cringe at my accidental use of my dad's broken-English epithet. A lifetime of being raised by Russian immigrants, who murdered their new language with passion and diligence, has turned me into someone who sometimes lapses into their odd versions of idioms. The way people who have worked to get rid of their Southern drawls can still slip into y'all mode when drinking or tired.

He turns and puts on his sheepish puppy-dog face.

"Oops. So sorry, sweet girl, you know I never keep official track of time."

It's true. Bastard doesn't even wear a watch. It would make me crazy, except he is never late.

"It's okay. How may I be of service this, um, *morning*?" He'll ignore the emphasis on the hour, but I put it out there anyway.

Patrick reaches down and scoops Dumpling up in his arms, receiving grateful licks all over his face. Damned if my dog, who is generally indifferent to almost all men, doesn't love Patrick.

"I had a very tedious evening, and a powerfully mediocre dinner, and I thought I would swing by and say hello and see if you had anything delicious in your treasure chest."

"Of course you did. Eggs?"

"Please."

"Fine."

Patrick follows me to the kitchen, carrying and snuggling Dumpling, whispering little endearments to him, making him wiggle in delight. He folds himself into the small loveseat under the window, and watches me go to work.

Between culinary school, a year and a half of apprentice stages all over the world in amazing restaurants, ten years as the personal chef of talk show phenom Maria De Costa, and six years as Patrick's culinary slave, I am nothing if not efficient in the kitchen. I grab eggs, butter, chives, a packet of prosciutto, my favorite nonstick skillet. I crack four eggs, whip them quickly with a bit of cold water, and then use my Microplane grater to grate a flurry of butter into them. I heat my pan, add just a tiny bit more butter to coat the bottom, and let it sizzle while I slice two generous slices off the rustic sourdough loaf I have on the counter and drop them in the toaster. I dump the eggs in the pan, stirring constantly over medium-low heat, making sure they cook slowly and stay in fluffy curds. The toast pops, and I put them on a plate, give them a schmear of butter, and lay two whisper-thin slices of the prosciutto on top. The eggs are ready, set perfectly; dry but still soft and succulent, and I slide them out of the pan on top of the toast, and quickly mince some chives to confetti the top. A sprinkle of gray fleur de sel sea salt, a quick grinding of grains of paradise, my favorite African pepper, and I hand the plate to Patrick, who rises from the loveseat to receive it, grabs a fork from the rack on my counter, and heads out of my kitchen toward the dining room, Dumpling following him, tail wagging, like a small furry acolyte.

"You're welcome," I say to the sink as I drop the pan in. I grab an apple out of the bowl on the counter and head out to keep him company while he eats. I'd love nothing more than a matching plate, but it is a constant struggle to not explode beyond my current size 14, and middle-of-the-night butter eggs are not a good idea.

Patrick is tucking in with relish, slipping Dumpling, who has happily returned to a place of honor in his lap, the occasional morsel of egg and sliver of salty ham. Usually I am very diligent about not giving the dog people-food, but I don't have the energy to fight Patrick on it, especially since I am feeling a bit guilty about how little time I have had to spend with the pooch lately. Barry is out of town playing Oscar Wilde in a Philadelphia production of *Gross Indecency*, so it has been all day-care all the time for the past three weeks, and another three to go. So a little bit of egg and prosciutto I can't argue with. Patrick manages to inhale his food and pet Dumpling nearly simultaneously with one hand. With his other hand, he is fiddling with my laptop, which I left open on the table when I went to sleep, after a night of working on new recipes for his latest cookbook. He pauses, and looks me right in the eyes.

"Damn, girl, you make the best scrambled eggs on the planet." Patrick is a lot of things, but disingenuous is not one of them. When he lets fly a compliment, which is infrequent, he makes eye contact and lets you know he means it very sincerely.

I let go of my annoyance. "I know. It's the grated butter." I can't stay mad at Patrick for longer than eighteen point seven minutes. I've timed it.

"I know. Wish I had thought of it."

"According to the *Feast* episode about breakfasts for lovers, you did," I tease him. I'm not mad about this. It's my job to help him develop recipes and invent or improve methods. And since I am petrified at the idea of being on camera or in the public eye in any way, shape, or form, he is most welcome to claim all my tricks as his own. Lord knows, he pays me very, *very* well for the privilege.

"Well, I know I *inspired* the idea." He's very confident of this, thinking that I came up with the technique to enhance his dining experience when he foists himself upon me in the middle of the night, which I also think he believes I secretly love.

He is enormously wrong on both counts.

I came up with it for Bruce Ellerton, the VP of show development for the Food TV Network and senior executive producer of our show. Bruce comes to Chicago periodically to check in on us since we are the only show that doesn't tape in the Manhattan studios, and he and I have been enjoying a two- to three-day romp whenever he is here or I am there for the past four years. We are, as the kids say, friends with benefits, and I like to think we enjoy a very real friendship in addition to an excellent working relationship and very satisfying sex. We have enough in common to allow for some non-bedroom fun, and easy conversation. We also have a solid mutual knowledge that we would be terrible together as a real couple, which prevents either of us from trying to turn the relationship into more than it is. We stay strictly away from romantic gestures; no flowers or Valentine's cards or overly personal gifts. If either of us begins dating someone seriously, we put our naked activities on hold.

Or, I'm sure we would, if either of us had time to actually date someone seriously.

Bruce's favorite food is eggs, so I developed the recipe for him one evening when bed took precedence over dinner and by the time we came up for air, take-out places were shut down for the night. Patrick is blissfully unaware of the special nature of my relationship with Bruce, so I just let him think they are "his" eggs.

"You inspire all my best ideas. Or at least you pay for them. So was tonight business or pleasure?" I crunch into my apple.

"Biznuss," he says around a mouthful of toast and egg. "The New York investors want to push the opening back a few months. Michael White is opening another place around the same time we were going to, and everything that guy touches is gold, so we don't want to end up a footnote in the flood of press he will get. Mike is a fucking amazing chef, so I don't want to invite any comparisons. Let him have a couple months of adulation, and then we'll open."

Patrick, to his credit, is a chef first and a television personality second. He keeps a very tight rein and close eye on all of his restaurants, develops all the menus in close consultation with his chefs de cuisine, who train the rest of their staff in his clean and impeccable style. For all his bluster, and as much as he has the vanity to enjoy the celebrity part of his life, the food does come first, not the brand. He is at the pass in each of his Chicago restaurants at least once a week, and checks in on his out-of-town places once a month or so. And he is secure enough to recognize when someone else is really magic in the kitchen and to not want to muddy the media waters. Having eaten at almost all of Michael's restaurants over the years, I can't blame Patrick for wanting to bump his own stuff to let the guy have his due. The words *culinary genius* come to mind immediately and without irony.

"So, late spring then?" I'm mentally adjusting my own schedule, since whatever Patrick does inevitably impacts my life not insignificantly.

He takes the last morsel of toast and wipes the plate clean, popping it in his mouth and rolling his eyes back in satisfaction. "Yup."

"I'll go through the calendar with you tomorrow and we can make the necessary changes." Crap. I have eight thousand things to do tomorrow, or rather, today, and this was not one of them.

"Sounds good. You just tell me where to be and when and what to do when I get there!"

I wish. "How about you be at *your* house in ten minutes, and go to sleep . . ."

He laughs. That is not good. That means he is choosing to believe that I am joking so that he can stay longer. There is not going to be enough caffeine on the planet to suffer through tomorrow. Er, today.

"So guess what started today?" He smirks at me, pushing his empty plate aside and moving my computer in front of him.

"I can't begin to imagine."

"EDestiny Fall Freebie Week!"

Oh. No.

"Patrick . . ."

"Let's see what fabulous specimens of human maleness the old Destinometer has scraped up for our princess, shall we?" He chuckles as his fingers fly over the keys, logging into the dating site with my e-mail and password, settling in to see what new profiles the magical soul-mate algorithm has dredged up for me. It should be the last thing I would ever let him do, or even tell him about, but my ill-fated brief stint as an online dater somehow became part of our business practice. And it is my own damn fault.

Dumpling nuzzles under Patrick's chin, another betrayal, and I clear Patrick's plate and flatware, and go to wash dishes, while my bosshole in the other room yells out that there's a very nice-looking seventy-two-year-old bus driver from Hammond, Indiana, who might just be perfect for me.

2

I should go to bed, but the computer is taunting me.

RJ. 49. 6'0". Lives in Chicago. No kids and doesn't want any. Internet media consultant. Likes wine, cooking, travel, art, music, reading, his job, his family, and his life. About twenty-five words that say nothing, and yet, all hit me where I live. No profile picture. No hobbies or favorite films or inspirational quotes. Really, the bare minimum of information you can put online and have your profile accepted by EDestiny. But something about it has haunted me all day, ever since I spotted it during Patrick's assault on my account last night.

It is nearly eleven p.m., and I have just gotten home after a brutal day of meetings, six hours of recipe testing, and a long after-work therapy session with the latest casualty of Hurricane Patrick, a new show prep cook just out of culinary school who was on the receiving end of the famous "Fifteen Minutes on Knife Skills" rant. Patrick asked for carrots in batonnet and celery root in allumette, or large sticks and small sticks, and got everything in fine julienne, or very small shreds. Easily remedied, and a classic newbie error, but Patrick is nothing if not precise, and since this was a test run for an upcoming shoot of a stir-fry episode of *Academy*, where size and shape of ingredients is paramount, he just lost it.

"Are you FUCKING KIDDING ME?" Patrick swept her

station prep onto the floor in one wide swipe of his arm, sending little bits of carrot and celery root shreds flying in the air like confetti, and equipment clattering to the floor. "Exactly what mail-order culinary school did you graduate from? Incompetent Twat U? This is unfuckingacceptable. You might not have noticed, but I have a few things on my schedule. One of them is NOT supposed to be looking over your sad little schlumpy shoulder to make sure you know how to CUT SHIT UP. There are only two options here. Either, one: you actually don't know the difference between batonnet, allumette, and julienne, in which case you are desperately underqualified for this job, and whoever hired you is going to need both a proctologist and a podiatrist to get my foot out of their ass. Or, two: you DO know and just don't give a crap, and you figured I wouldn't notice, which makes you both a dumbass and about half an inch from fired." Her lower lip began to tremble. But when Patrick gets on a roll he makes Gordon Ramsay seem maternal.

"So, let's all gather around and have a lesson this afternoon, shall we? Because obviously we have lost our passion for precision around here. Someone get me a fucking knife and some goddamn carrots." They magically appeared at the station in half a second, and for ten minutes he turned a pile of carrots into perfect, even batonnet, allumette, julienne, fine julienne, large dice, medium dice, small dice, brunoise, and fine brunoise like some sort of human food processor. Each piece in each category was identical to all its compatriots, as if made by a machine. Minimal waste, station clean, every little pile complete and perfect. Patrick trained under both Marco Pierre White and Thomas Keller. He got his temperament from the first and an almost OCD level of perfectionism from the second. I often wish it had been the reverse.

The whole time he was cutting, he muttered maniacally to himself about what a waste of time this was, mentioning, as he loves to do, that his time was worth approximately twenty-seven-hundred dollars an hour, and that everyone should be paying him for the lesson. When he finished, he picked up a leftover carrot, pointed it at her face, telling her to, "Get it right, or get gone," biting the tip off viciously for emphasis, and then headed to his office and slammed the door.

She sniffled for the rest of the day, and I had to take her over to Nightwood after work and let her vent. Twentysomething angst is enormously tedious, but some oversight of the culinary underlings is part of my job, so this comes with the territory. I don't do the hiring; Food TV and Patrick's executive assistant do that, so it wasn't really my ass on the line for bringing her on. And Gloria runs the test kitchen, so she is in charge of training, and I don't doubt that she was very forthcoming about how important precision is to Patrick. But I do try to keep an eye on show prep as it is going on, and am usually able to spot a potential problem and get it fixed before Patrick is aware of it. I try not to get attached; the show is a meat grinder, and by the time you learn someone's name, they are out the door. I mentally call them by their most obvious attributes. At the moment we have Neck Tattoo, Geek Glasses, Orange Clogs, Bubble Butt Bike Boy, and little snifflepuss whom I've been thinking of as Sad White Girl Dreads, who sat across from me sweating chardonnay and asking me if she shouldn't just quit. To their faces, they are all just "Chef." They think it is a mark of respect and honor, but it really just saves me wasting mental space on name retention.

Six months into my "tryout," I had been on the receiving end of my own first Patrittack. I hadn't had time to caramelize onions the way Patrick had asked for them. He started cooking, reached for the onions, and then abruptly stopped the shoot. He came around from behind the stove and towered over me.

"Miss A-la-na here seems to think that my pork medallion with caramelized-onion pan sauce is a little heavy-handed, that the onions need a lighter touch, a less intense flavor. Do you think the recipe needs altering? Hmmm? In your INFI-NITE wisdom and experience?" His voice dripped with sarcasm, smug and smooth and utterly contemptuous. And I was not in the mood.

"In my HUMBLE opinion," I began, equally quiet and calm, and no less scathing, "the recipe indeed needs some lightening. And since you *ostensibly* hired me to help make you look good and ensure that the recipes you put out in the world can actually be successfully produced by the general population, you should trust that I am going to take your recipes and make them better, and leave it at that. I do things the way they should be done, and you cook your dishes like a good little boy and STAY OUT OF MY ASS."

You could have heard a pin drop in the studio. No one moved, no one breathed, no one made eye contact. Patrick took the world's longest inhale, and while I braced for venom or violence, I refused to unlock my gaze from his, standing as tall as I could manage, spine straight, full of piss and vinegar. He threw his arms around me, braying with laughter. "Ladies and gentlemen, I am officially just the face. Meet the boss." He backed up, bowed deeply at my feet, and began applauding. Slowly, cautiously, the rest of the crew began applauding too.

I sighed, and my ass unclenched. "Well, if I'm the boss, can you shift your sassy self into high gear and get this shoot done? It's my niece's first birthday, and if you keep fucking around and whining about onions, she's going to be headed off to college before I get to her party."

"You heard the lady. Let's get this done already so we can go home." And while it wasn't the last time I ever caught hell from Patrick, it set the tone for the rest of our relationship.

I look at the sniffling girl in front of me.

This is not my first time at this rodeo. If she had been angry at how she had been treated, called him names, told me she hated him for humiliating her and making her feel small, I would have told her to tough it out, get through the whole season and then she'd be able to write her own ticket. It would have shown an instinctive awareness of the insanity we all deal with, and an ability to cope.

But the ones who dissolve in soggy emotion, they don't last, and this one had completely gone off the rails into self-loathing-how-could-I-disappoint-one-of-my-idols mode, so I assured her that no one would blame her if she didn't want to return, and that I would be happy to write her a recommendation for a new job; food television is not for everyone. She drank way too much wine and picked at her salad and by the time we were done I had gently led her to decide for herself that it would be best to tender her notice in the morning.

By the time I got home, I couldn't focus on work; I just needed to veg out. I put on one of my Julia Child DVDs for happy background noise, grabbed my laptop for perhaps a little online retail therapy, and let Dumpling plop on the couch beside me.

I scritch him behind the ears, and he puts his little head on my knee. "You know the difference between batonnet and allumette, don't you, boy?" He lifts his head, licks my knee once, decisively, as if to say, "Of course I do, silly two-legs," and then puts his head back down and closes his eyes. When I open the computer, it shows the last page I was looking at.

EDestiny.

RJ. Wonder what that stands for? I shouldn't care, I know. Online dating just doesn't work for me.

When EDestiny began doing their freebie events, I would log in, just to amuse myself with all the *terrifically perfect* guys I was missing out on. They apparently really missed my monthly contribution to their bottom line, and stepped up their game volume-wise, sending me the very young, the very old, and the very scary. The recently released and the practically deceased. The stamp collectors, coin collectors, and, for all I knew, body part collectors. They sent me not only my COUSIN Sam, who we all think is gay anyway, but then one of my sister's chiropractic partners, who is not only also most likely gay, but so deeply closeted that he is currently married.

It became a game. The more I didn't pay them, the more often I was offered free weekends and special deals, and peeks at new matches, not one of whom was remotely someone I would want to meet on the street, let alone become romantically involved with. They sent me four guys with more tattoos than skin, three spectacular mullets, a classic Jheri curl complete with "Thriller"-era pleather jacket, and one guy who called himself Metroman and described himself as a modern-day superhero. I got matched with a guy in medium-security prison, who swore that getting caught embezzling was the best thing for him, since he was able to kick his cocaine habit in prison. A guy who bred chinchillas in his basement. And one of my former professors from Northwestern, who had given me a C, made shitty comments on all my papers, and whose expression behind his bushy Claus-esque beard always looked as if he had recently smelled something unpleasant. Which he probably had, because I would not have been in the least surprised if that face fur contained morsels from a decade's worth of school cafeteria meals.

A good 80 percent of my matches lived anywhere from fifty to five hundred miles away. At least 50 percent of them were ten years older or younger than my requested limits. And 100 percent of them were not remotely dateable, at least not by me. I started actively booing at the TV anytime I saw the happy spokescouples on the EDestiny commercials.

My three best friends from high school, Mina, Emily, and Lacey, had turned our monthly Girls'-Night-In date into Official EDestiny Night. They would come over for snacks and cocktails and we would go through my new profiles for the sheer hilarity of it. Emily is a ghostwriter for a *New York Times* bestselling chick lit author, and would take the opportunity to make up little impromptu stories about each guy and what our life together would be like. Some of which were so hilarious that you can now see them played out rather painfully by the likes of Katherine Heigl in the big-screen adaptations of the novels she writes. Somewhere in the middle of each get-together she sneaks away to call her husband, John, to tell him how much she loves him and how lucky she is to have him, since she is reminded of what else is out there.

Lacey, the VP of marketing for a local chocolate manufacturer, and herself an experienced online-dater, would just hand over another peanut-butter-bacon bonbon and shake her head. Lacey is a serial monogamist, who dates an endless series of men in uniform—firemen, policemen, servicemen— each for about six to nine months before taking a few months off to be alone with her dog, Jaxie, and then start all over again. And Mina, head recruiter for a Chicago-based executive consulting firm, would try once again to convince

me to let her recruit a boyfriend for me. After all, the boyfriend she recruited for herself was pretty fantastic, why
wouldn't she have equal success on my behalf? But I had
learned long ago that you actually probably don't want to
know what kind of guy your besties think you ought to be
with. It always says as much about what they think of you as
what they think of him, and I find a certain comfort in being
ignorant of what my pals might envision for me.

My favorite EDestiny offering was the guy we call "Tiny
Furniture Man," whose profile picture showed him oddly
posed, leaning on a dresser from behind. At least, we assumed
a dresser until Emily pointed out that since EDestiny loved
to send me the little ones, it might in fact be a nightstand.

"Look at me! I am this much taller than this piece of
furniture!" Emily said, wiping tears from her bronzed cheeks.
Emily is an unapologetic tanorexic with thick, wavy blond
hair that is always perfectly coiffed.

"I'm totally bigger than this nightstand," Lacey piped up,
folding her long legs underneath her, and tossing treats to
Jaxie and Dumpling, who had collapsed in a pile of panting
fur at her feet after an hour of playing.

"The fact that I am leaning on it from behind to hide an
enormous goiter should not deter you in the least," Mina
chimed in.

No one at Whitney Young High School would have thought
we'd end up friends. I matriculated as an unapologetic band
geek, playing an adequate if uninspired second-chair flute,
dating other band geeks for the convenience of it. I was short
and overweight, with frizzy curly hair that was waiting impa-
tiently for the invention of mousse, which was still a year
away. Mina was a gorgeous almond-eyed African American
girl with killer cheekbones, who simply decided she was in

charge, got elected president of the freshman class (and sub-
sequently sophomore, junior, and senior, the only student in
school history to serve for four years), and eventually led the
debate team to three consecutive city championships and two
state titles, while handily maintaining a solid A average and
one besotted boyfriend per annum. Emily was a cheerleader
of the whip-smart and snarky (but not mean girl) variety. She
was also head of the Young Republicans (a shockingly big
club during the Reagan era), always perfectly put together,
and dated the quarterback of the football team, whomever
that happened to be at the moment. Lacey was an athlete,
five eleven, strong as anything, played varsity softball and
basketball, ran track, and tended to always be dating friends
of her older brother, who was in college ROTC.

But there we were, freshman year, sitting in first-period
biology, hating life and crushing on Adam Ant, having
snagged the four chairs in the back of the room. And when
the super-popular blond bombshell in the front row misread
"organism" as "orgasm," the four of us made eye contact, and
before the end of the period, little folded notes were flying
back and forth along that row like we had invented the
method. By October we were completely inseparable—thank
god everyone had two-way calling for group discussions, and
for Lacey's parents being so generous about allowing
sleepovers. Despite losing one another for a bit during college
and immediately following during the era before e-mail and
cell phones, we reconnected at our five-year reunion and discovered that we liked the women we had become just as much
as we loved the memories of the girls we had been. So we
agreed to make a once-a-month date so that we didn't lose
each other again. And for the past fourteen years, we have
kept that date pretty sacred. We don't talk on the phone or get

together much beyond that one night a month, except for big parties and the occasional birthday and random girls' weekends. But we are the kind of friends that don't need to spend all our time together, as long as we keep the connection alive.

"Okay, seriously, where the fuck do they *find* these guys?" Lacey asked, incredulous.

"Um, are you really one to talk?" Mina raised one perfectly threaded eyebrow. "Didn't your last date from Match take you to *Hooters*?"

"He did, but just for the wings," Lacey said, smirking.

"Yeah, and he subscribes to *Playboy* for the articles." Emily snorts.

We all convulsed in laughter, poured another round of gimlets, and I got up to answer the door. That was the night Patrick showed up unexpectedly in the middle of our entertainment. And I'd been drinking just enough to let him in, and let him participate.

"Wait a minute," he said, swigging a gimlet and finishing the last piece of beet bruschetta and pointing at me. "Has she ever once met any of these guys?"

"Hell, no," Emily said. "None of these guys are even worth the free drinks."

"She might be missing out on her soul mate." Patrick dipped his finger in the hummus and let Dumpling lick it off.

"Nah, I'm reasonably sure her soul mate isn't a card-carrying member of the Tea Party!" Mina said.

"Or related to her by blood," Lacey offered

"Or a little person," Emily added.

"Or older than her dad," Mina says.

"Or living in the Upper Peninsula," Lacey pipes up.

"Besides, she is not going to settle, ever again," Emily assures the room.

"Yeah, she is not going to just date someone to date someone. It is going to have to be the right someone," Mina declares.

"She's waiting for The One. As well she should," Lacey says.

"But she better not be *too* picky, or she will be alone forever," Patrick says.

Oy. "*She* is right here, and *she* would prefer you not talk about her as if *she* were not present." It was more than a little irking to watch Patrick win over my girlfriends. I knew that after he left I would be attacked for saying snippy things about him and be told that, generally, I was too hard on him. Patrick had an amazing ability to seduce everyone in my life, so unless I was going to make all of my friends and family members come hang out with me at work to witness the consistent insanity and occasional cruelty that he possessed, I was destined to have everyone in my private life love him.

Ever since that night, he has looked forward to the EDestiny freebie events and checking out my possible future lovers with a vengeance. The girls and I got bored with the game nearly a year ago, shifting our monthly evenings to focus almost exclusively on catching up with the antics of whatever current batch of Unreal Housewives are facing divorce, bankruptcy, wardrobe malfunction, or the release of an auto-tuned dance single. But every two or three months, Patrick will remind me that "the game is afoot!" and I have to suffer his opinions of the profiles the Destinometer sends my way.

But last night, this profile, this RJ . . . something just struck me about it.

Forty-nine. So, age-appropriate. Lives in Chicago, geographically desirable. Six feet tall, so I presume, you know, legs. Not that one should have to ask net or gross with such things, but history makes us wise. Likes all the things I like. No picture, so probably a troll. Minimal info, so perhaps not so good with words, could be looking for a green-card marriage. Then again, could already be married. Probably ultra-conservative Tea Party Republican. Or just a liar, plenty of those out there in cyberspace. Most definitely not my soul mate.

But despite the litany in my head, and the instinct to just log out and go to bed, I do something I have not done on this site, not ever.

I click the "Invite Destiny" button, which sends this mysterious RJ a preset list of three questions that I picked so long ago I don't even remember what they are.

From the other room I hear Dumpling flop off his perch on the couch and come clicking purposefully down the hall to find me. He licks my ankle and then sneezes three times in quick succession, which is his sign that he needs to go out. I look at the screen.

"Congratulations! You have initiated contact with RJ from Chicago! Good luck, and remember, your Destiny is right here!"

My stomach turns over, and I close the computer quickly.

"C'mon, Mister Man, you know *you* are my real soul mate. Let's go out."

As much as I love Dumpling, I always do remember Maria's sage, if scatological advice. "The man in your life, 'e should not require you pick up 'is poop, hmm? A dog, that is a good frrrriend, a *companero*. But not a man. You get a rrrrreal man, and then 'e picks up the poop."

I clip on Dumpling's leash, and grab a blue bag and some treats from the bowl by the door. And before I get completely out the door, a brief thought flits through my brain.

I wonder if RJ likes dogs?

3

That's a wrap, people. Thank you all. We'll do it again next week." Bob, director extraordinaire of both *Feast* and *Academy* finally gets the ending he wants for the "Win Over Your In-Laws" brunch episode of *Feast*, the third show we've shot today. We do anywhere from three to five half-hour shows on a shooting day, three days a week, shooting the entire seasons of both shows for the following year in a whirlwind five months at a frenetic pace and with minimal sleep. The shows are not scripted, but rather lightly outlined. Patrick is a natural, so as long as he knows his talking points, he can work off the cuff. We generally tend to do four recipes per episode, two three-minute, one six-minute, and one eight-minute, which leaves room for an anecdote or two. Nearly clockwork. Crazy to some, but it frees Patrick up to run the restaurants and do personal appearances and work on the books and show planning six months a year, and for us both to have the full month of August off to recharge our batteries. No one can work effectively in Chicago's August heat and humidity anyway; it makes us all mush-brained.

It became clear early on in our working relationship that the usual vacation schedule does not apply to Patrick's personal team, and while other employees can grab a week here or there for trips with family, or plan ahead for getaways with friends or lovers, I am only on vacation when Patrick is on vacation. Sometimes I get lucky and he gets a bee in his bonnet about a mini trip, and makes the time for himself (or the Legs of the moment) and I get a spontaneous bit of freedom. I have become adept at snagging last-minute deals for spa getaways with Bennie, cheapo airfare for long weekends in wine country or Montreal with the girls or Barry, or quick zips into New York to see friends and play with Bruce and eat expansively. But usually it is just a day or two of freedom, which I will spend holed up in the little cabin I bought a couple of years ago just over the border in Wisconsin. Just a ninety-minute drive, so close enough to get home quickly if there is a Patrick-related emergency, but far enough away to relax and breathe fresh air. It is Dumpling's favorite place on the planet, where he can run around in the woods, chase chipmunks and rabbits that he never catches, and laze around being a warm puppy in the sun while I swing in a hammock or float in the Lilliputian pool, an in-ground so small that no more than four people can float in it at any one time. Emily, who often borrows the cabin to write the last few chapters of her books, calls it the Puddle.

August is when I can really decompress. Whole weeks at the cabin, where I can host barbecues with friends, spend quality time with the family, catch a Cubs game, sleep in, and take luxurious afternoon naps. Go to the farmer's markets and get excited about canning, pickling, and making jam. Unfortunately, as today is the eleventh of October, I have 312 days to slog through before my next long break.

I meet Patrick in his dressing room-slash-office as I always do after taping.

"That was okay, right?" he asks, while taking off his makeup with cold cream and a hand towel like some 1930s film diva. I tried to turn him on to the new makeup remover wipes, but he insists they goop him up so much for the camera that if he doesn't really "deep down clean up" he gets foundation all over his eight-hundred-thread-count Italian linen pillowcases. Poor baby. So hard to be him. But even someone as pretty as Patrick can't get away without makeup these days; HD is a bitch. Look at poor Bill Maher. I know he's smart and funny, but when I watch his show all I can think is that the man needs spackle. In regular definition? Not a bad-looking guy. In high-def? He looks like his face caught fire and someone tried to put it out with a golf shoe. I'm not saying, I'm just saying. Lucky for Patrick, his skin is smooth enough, and he usually just needs to hide the dark circles under his eyes or the occasional blemish.

"It was great, as usual, Margot Channing. I think it will be your best season ever." Patrick hates it when I use old movie references, as he is allergic to black-and-white. But watching him take his makeup off is so very *All About Eve*, I just can't help it.

"And I'm not going bobblehead yet, right?" Patrick is very aware of what we call the bobblehead phenomenon when it comes to food television. The networks hire people with real, genuine personalities, endearing quirks, and charming ways about them to host shows. And somehow, the more time they spend doing their various projects, the more overexposured they become, and the more they are turned into weird and annoying caricatures of themselves. Initially cute phrases become overused tag lines. The anecdotes get more far-fetched. The special episodes become more heavily costumed and thematically insane. The joy and passion for cooking become forced, the smiles wider, the eyes more dead. Odd guest stars are trotted out. Veneers and hair extensions and plastic surgery rear their heads, making everyone look like the Madame Tussauds wax version of who they used to be. There are more and more competition shows devoted to finding new hosts, the casts of which mostly range from mildly annoying to Machiavellian. The solution seems to be to just keep adding shows, perhaps in an attempt to keep the hosts themselves interested, but really just further diluting their appeal.

People who were easy and entertaining their first couple of seasons, now a decade or more in, are painfully unwatchable. Very few have escaped becoming bobbleheads. Nigella Lawson is one, and she is one of the few I still TiVo. Especially since she did an event with Patrick, and I got to spend half a day with her. She is luminously beautiful, and just as smart and funny and humble as she appears to be on television. Plus, all her recipes actually work, which is rarer than you might think for people who make a living cooking on TV. Jamie Oliver is another, although he walks a fine line sometimes and I don't hold great hope for him in the long run. Some of the new faces on the Cooking Channel are hanging in there, although some of them started full-on bobble and aren't getting better. And as far as I'm concerned Tom Colicchio can do no wrong, and I wish someone would give him a cooking show—I can't imagine him going bobblehead. But the Food Network as a whole has pretty much completely jumped the shark, and at least 30 percent of Patrick's colleagues on Food TV are bobbling, and the network is only five years old. Which is really troubling, since they are looking into launching a sister network themselves, because what America really needs is four channels devoted to twenty-four-hours-a-day food television.

Patrick is very easy on camera, and has so far been able to just stay himself, at least the fun, happy, nice, competent television version of himself, which makes his shows still relevant and is why all the talk shows love him. The daytimes love his ability to banter and do a cooking demo simultaneously, and the nighttimes love his quick wit, willingness to laugh at himself, and the fact that he is up for anything. Letterman especially loves to have him on, even occasionally having him do a "man on the street" segment. I've always been enormously grateful to a certain Italian mama's-boy chef whose on-camera cringe-worthy devolution and subsequent need to completely resurrect his career and re-form his face have meant that Patrick has both turned down all offers of reality shows and stayed far away from the Botox.

"Thanks, Alana-banana. I felt good about it, especially that last episode. And I love what you did with the French toast, the brûlée-ing idea was a genius move."

We wanted to do French toast for the brunch, but acknowledged that it is a dangerous item for a special event where people might be dressed up. Patrick had an awesome recipe for the toast itself, using day-old Challah, melted vanilla ice cream as a main ingredient in the soaking liquid, and just a hint of sea salt. I had come up with an alternative to the sticky drippy-down-your-front maple syrup problem by mixing equal parts maple sugar and demerara sugar, and having him sprinkle this on top of the already-cooked French toast and doing a quick brûlée under the broiler, giving the toast a thin crackly maple sugar shell. All the sweet and smoky taste, nothing ruining your mother-in-law's favorite silk blouse.

"Glad you approved. But even gladder that you finally managed to do it without setting it on fire." Three takes of smoking, blackened bread, because Patrick was waxing poetic about his ex–mother-in-law and forgot to get the pan out of the oven.

"What can I say; Dora means the world to me." It's true. Patrick's ex-wife, Sharlene, would not piss on him if he were on fire. But her mom secretly stays in touch, and Patrick takes her to a special lunch once a year, and still sends her Mother's Day cards, and fairly lavish birthday gifts, which I agonize over choosing for him. I think this has less to do with genuine affection for Dora and more with it being a wonderful way to send a big fat middle finger to his ex.

"Yes, I know."

"Change of plans for the weekend. I'm going to head to New York to check in on the new place, and have some meetings."

Crap. I was so hoping to have a life this weekend, maybe brunch with the girls, some doggie-park time with Dumpling. My disappointment must show on my face.

"No worries, pumpkin, going solo. You are off the hook for the next three days."

I can feel my entire spine relax. "Sure you don't need me?" Please don't need me please don't need me . . .

"I always need you, you are my right arm and my left lung and my middle testicle, but I'll be okay for one little weekend in New York." The little smirk playing around the corner of his mouth tells me all I need to know. In New York will be a new set of Legs, making my presence both unnecessary and unwelcome. Which is fine by me.

"Well, you and your testicles behave yourself and leave the city standing. Stealth me if you need anything." Patrick and I have a private instant-messaging system on both of our iPhones, which he calls "stealthing." The messages don't get stored on any system and cannot be hacked. It is almost CIA-presidential. But when you are a celeb and *Us Weekly* pays a bundle for text messages and e-mails of a private nature, you get a little paranoid.

Patrick wipes the last of the cream off his face, and stands up, with his traditional kissing of the top of my head. I know he thinks it is a big-brotherly type of affectionate display, but frankly it always feels a little condescending. And reminds me that I am only five three. It doesn't bother me enough to ask him to stop, since I've experienced the alternative, which is his signature kiss on the inside of the wrist. He takes your hand and then turns it over, kissing you right where your hand meets your arm. It makes you all tingly in your girl parts, completely beyond your conscious control, which utterly wigs me out. It's like having a random sex dream about Dick Cheney. You know consciously that it doesn't mean you actually find him attractive in any way, but you still feel like you want to take a Silkwood shower when you wake up.

"You put some weekend in your weekend, kitten. We have a big week next week."

"We always have a big week. Do you need me to make any arrangements?" Patrick's executive assistant, Andrea, usually does travel booking, but she has been out all week with a horrible flu. The one unbreakable rule on Team Patrick is that the moment you feel like your health is going round the bend, you call in and stay away. We work too closely together, for too many hours, with too little ventilation to let anyone sick, even with just the sniffles, come in to work. If you are able to be available on computer and phone, great, but keep your in-person germs to yourself. There is an industrial-size pump jar of Purell around every corner, Airborne and Vitamin C lozenges and zinc tablets on the craft service table, and our crew washes hands like the set is an operating theater. But with this kind of diligence, we have not had the kind of crud that so often sweeps through a whole team. And because Patrick insists on contracts being very generous about paid sick days, including days to take care of spouses or children who are sick, no one takes advantage.

"I was a big boy and made my own arrangements, thank you very much."

Which means that he is staying with whomever she is, and doesn't need a hotel room.

"Great. Well then, have an amazing trip, eat something delicious for me, and we'll hit this again on Monday."

I scamper across the hall to my little office, wall-to-wall cookbooks, and piles of recipes in progress. It should take me less than twenty minutes to finish up some e-mails, and approve the shooting schedule for next week, and then I can head out. Barry is freshly back from his star turn in Philly, with a pile of excellent reviews and a Barrymore nomination, and he and Dumpling are celebrating at an after-school program for autistic kids and their nonspectrum siblings. If I hurry, I'll have plenty of time to stop and see my folks for a real decent visit before heading home. I flip open my laptop.

RJ from Chicago has answered your questions at EDestiny! Special free weekend starts today, log in and see what he has to say. Your destiny could be right here!

Oh. My. I had forgotten about that. It's been nearly a month since I hit that button, and we've been so busy it didn't occur to me to remember that I had reached out, or to be annoyed that he didn't reach back. But apparently, here he is.

And the fact that it is another freebie event is not lost on me—he grudgingly gets extra points for probably not wanting to pay them anything either.

I click the link, and log in to my account. I can't help but notice that the first thing on my profile is a notification that I have a new match. Jerry is sixty, five four, with an obvious Grecian Formula dye job, including his neatly trimmed beard, and apparently makes his living as a magician. I always wanted to date a man in a cape.

RJ has not added anything to his profile, including a picture. Likelihood of him being Trolltacular increases exponentially. Ditto married. I open his response.

1. If you could have a dinner party with any three people, living or dead, who would you invite and what would you serve?

Hmm. Very good question. As an aside, having taken some time with your profile, you are a very good writer! So, that puts me in the mind of writers for this little dinner party. . . . Oscar Wilde for certain, no lulls in conversation and he's British, so anything I serve would be an upgrade to his diet. George Sand, since that gives lots of flexibility in boy/girl seating arrangements. And you, naturally. For me, this kind of meal starts with wine, and wine means Burgundy. So, besides laughter and entendre, expect some combination of gougères, quenelles, mushrooms and birds with lots of really good Burgundy from the cellar.

2. Looking back on your life, of what are you most proud?

That I'm a go-to person for my family and my good friends. My parents and sister are accomplished people who have touched a lot of people's lives, but they still depend on me for thoughtful advice. I'm very proud of that. Same for my closest friends, who tend to be very successful in a variety of fields, although when I think of it, with my pals it is often mostly about food and wine.

3. What is the one dream for your life you most look forward to having come true?

Accepting that my life is really good and that my dreams aren't all just over the horizon. That being said, one dream is to be able to answer these questions and not have it be all about just me.

Oh. My.

Oscar Wilde, my favorite non-food writer, whose famous quote "I can resist everything except temptation" is my slowly scrawling screen saver. And gougères. Wonderful gougères. The first thing I taught myself how to make in my tiny apartment in Paris during my semester abroad, which was the impetus for my returning home, dropping out, and going to culinary school. My first duty during my stage at an auberge outside of Lyon, filling endless baskets with the hot, crispy cheesy puffs for the better part of my first week. Gougères are my own personal soul food. He likes his family, so I assume he will understand and respect my connection to my own crazy brood. And he dreams of a life that isn't about him, rare for someone his age who is single; most of them are *all* about themselves. Now I am totally sure he is either deeply unattractive or married, or even both.

I pick up the phone and call Bennie, and read her his responses.

"Oh, HONEY! He sounds dreamy. What did you send back?"

"Nothing yet. I mean, do I even want to? Hitting the button the first time was just some strange impulsive move. But this seems, I don't know, real. What if he's actually great? Do I have time to meet someone great? Look at my schedule! Look at my life, what there is of it. Is it even fair to him to respond?" I can hear Bennie's deep, warm laugh.

"Do you hear yourself? You're already worried about disappointing your *boyfriend*. How about you just reply like a good girl and see what happens before you imagine yourself ruining your relationship."

I can see her point. "Fine. I'll respond. But it will all end in tears." We both laugh.

"Send me a copy of what you send him," she demands.

"Will do. Talk to you later."

I stare at the blank EDestiny e-mail screen. I take a deep breath. It has been so long since I bothered to do this that I feel almost like I don't know how.

It's like bread baking. Get into the habit and you can do it by feel and sight and smell; no recipe needed. You know by the amount and quality of bubbles if the yeast has proofed enough. The dough will tell your hands when it has had all the flour it needs. You can smell the moment it is perfectly cooked, crust firm and crisp, insides pillowy and cooked through but still elastic. Get out of the habit and your dough doesn't rise, your crumb is too dense, the middle is gummy and raw-tasting, your crust pallid and the taste insipid. Flirting, communicating, reacting, and generating reactions are all muscles long atrophied in me. My "on the DL" thing with Bruce keeps me perky enough, no pressure, no strings, no complications, no expectations.

Thing is, deep down, maybe a complication or expectation or two wouldn't be so bad.

Dear RJ—

Thank you for your response to my questions, and the compliment on my writing. I don't know that I have shown any particular skill thus far, but I'm most appreciative of the kind thought. I am, however, far more appreciative of your own talents in expressing yourself, the fact that you use complete and grammatical sentences, do not use text-message abbreviations, and seem to actually have things in common with me. These attributes make you exceedingly rare on this site, at least in my experience, and for that I am profoundly grateful.

The fact that you would invite Oscar Wilde (one of my favorite writers) to dinner is a definite bonus. That you even know what a gougère is, let alone possess the ability to successfully produce them, seems an embarrassment of riches. And as I am a devout fan of Burgundies both red and white, we are off to a lovely start.

So, what can I tell you? I'm a first-generation Chicagoan. Mom and Dad married in a little town outside of Moscow and emigrated instead of a honeymoon. I have two older brothers and a younger sister. My brothers each have three boys, and my sister has two little girls, so family events have eight kids under the age of nine, which may be a big part of why I have chosen to remain childless. Also? Children are sticky. So I'm both utterly devoted to my nieces and nephews, and always very grateful to hand them back to my siblings when I am done spoiling them. I am embarrassingly passionate about the Bears (despite current performance level), and the quest for the perfect roasted chicken.

I think most flavored waters taste like furniture polish, and yet cannot stop drinking Pamplemousse LaCroix, and go through a case every other day or so. I do not really know if this is because I genuinely love the light grapefruit flavor that much or if it is because *pamplemousse* is my favorite word in French.

I like college basketball better than pro, lard over butter or shortening for piecrusts, and I choose to believe that Shakespeare wrote Shakespeare.

I don't think there is ever a wrong time to drink champagne, unless it is plonk. I don't believe there is ever a right time to watch *Jerry Springer.*

I'm never sure what is relevant information in these situations, so if there is anything I haven't covered already, feel free to ask.

Tag, you're it.

Alana

I copy and paste a version to send to Bennie, and then, before I lose my nerve, send it out into the ether in the direction of RJ. And grab my bag and head out before someone hands me something that needs attending.

4

I jump into the Honda Accord Hybrid that Maria gave me
as a parting bonus gift when I left her employ, and head
over to Gene's Sausage Shop in Lincoln Square. My mom
has wanted to make pelmeni with me for a while, so I figured
with my little gift of time this afternoon we can knock out a
big batch while catching up. I have Gene's coarse grind beef
shoulder and pork butt in equal parts, throwing a couple of
onions and a few garlic cloves into the grind for me to
save us chopping. My mother has not removed the Cuisinart
food processor I bought her for Mother's Day seven years
ago from its box, preferring to use her double-bladed chop-
per and a battered wooden bowl that were part of the dowry
she schlepped here from Russia fifty years ago. But while
I have time for pelmeni, I don't have patience for doing
everything by hand, and this will save us a world of mutual
annoyance.

I park in front of my parents' small bungalow on Karlov
just off Milwaukee Avenue. Every time I come here I am
astonished that the six of us managed to live here together;
it seems impossibly tiny. And yet, here we were, Mama and
Papa; my brothers, Sasha and Alexei; me; and my little sister,
Natalia. Three bedrooms, one and a half bathrooms, fifteen
hundred square feet. About half the size of my current condo.
My Realtor thought I was a little insane when I bought my

place on Francisco, the first floor of what was originally a Victorian mansion on a double lot, complete with the original built-in hutch in the large dining room and a butler's pantry. All for a single woman who has no intention of starting a family. But after spending most of my life elbow to elbow with not only my immediate family, but also my aunt and uncle and five cousins who lived two doors down and were in and out of our house like it was just the south wing of their own, I have always craved expansive space and deep, glorious quiet. My place is a three-bedroom, two-bathroom sanctuary, and someday I plan to finish out the portion of the basement that is part of my unit to create a master bedroom suite of ridiculous proportions.

My father is raking leaves in the postage-stamp-size front yard, wearing a thick wool sweater my mom knitted for him. The sleeves are too short, but the torso is three sizes too big, dwarfing his ever-diminishing frame. Papa used to be five nine, is now closer to five seven, and retains his wiry strength even at the age of seventy. He was a cabinetmaker and union carpenter, particularly good with intricate work, and made his living mostly on custom built-ins and special-order original commissions through designers, taking general-contractor work when things were slow. His hands are gnarled with arthritis and still callused from decades of hard work, but he would never let me hire someone to help out with things like yard work.

"My leettle baba romovaya." He grins widely and opens his arms to me, letting the rake fall where it may, and calling me by the endearment of my childhood, a reference to a yeasty cake soaked in cherry juice and plum brandy and covered in a creamy sauce—round and plump and pink and sweet, which is how he saw me. "Come give Papa a kisseleh."

I put my arms around him, and kiss his cheek, smooth-shaven and smelling of bay rum. "Hello, Papa."

"How you are doing, eh? No work meedle of day?" He shakes his hand up and down. "So fancy!"

"Got done early, thought I'd come make pelmeni with Mama."

He smiles even wider, closes his eyes and inhales deeply, as if he can already smell the little meat dumplings, swimming in butter and onions and dunked in rich, thick sour cream. "Then I not keep you. Thees is important work, for you and Mama. Not for hens to laugh at."

I laugh. Russian idioms never translate particularly well. "Yes, Papa. Very serious work."

He kisses my forehead and smacks my ample bottom. "Go. Make pelmeni. I do leaves."

He turns away in his voluminous sweater, wrists exposed and somehow dear, picks up the discarded rake from the ground, and returns to meticulously and laboriously making piles of fall foliage. I know my dad; he will not come in for dinner until every leaf is gone from the yard; he is passionate and proud about keeping his home immaculate. We moved in here when I was a baby, and he and Mom paid it off by the time I was in high school. It might be small, but it's in perfect condition, everything kept in good working order by Dad, and impeccably clean by Mom.

I open the door, and call out. "Mama! It's Alana."

My mom's head pops around the corner from the kitchen. She is wearing her usual pale blue cotton kerchief over her gray curls, which are as unruly as my brown ones. Over her housedress she is wearing a crazy hand-painted WURLD'S BEST GRANDMMA apron that Sasha's boys made her for her birthday last year. It leaves a little sprinkling of silver glitter behind her when she walks, like she is the Wurld's Oldest Strippur, but she loves it and wears it religiously. Whenever I bring Dumpling over it takes me a week to get the sparkle out of his paws.

I head for the kitchen and kiss her cheek, wordlessly handing off the package of ground meat as she reaches out for it, like a delicious drug drop.

She squeezes the package, and sniffs it appreciatively. "Pelmeni or cevapcici?" she asks seriously—dumplings or Serbian sausages—one recipe from her Russian paternal grandmother, one from her Romanian maternal grandmother.

"Pelmeni, please."

"Goot. Come. Tea first, then cook." My mother turns to the stove and puts a flame under a kettle. She reaches above her head for two thick glasses from the cupboard. She takes the jar of syrupy sour-cherry jam from the counter, and puts a healthy dose into one glass, knowing how I love the old traditional tea sweetened with the preserves. I get much of my economy of motion in the kitchen from her, every gesture practiced and simple. Coasters and squat, heavy glasses from the bottom shelf of the middle cabinet. Tea leaves from the old tin delivered in a fat pinch into the battered white china teapot, painted in an intricate netting of cobalt blue, its gold accents chipping off. She catches the water just as it starts to steam, but before it hits a full boil, tells me, "Boil makes bitter," for the gazillionth time in my life. She brings glasses and spoons to the oilcloth-covered table, along with the teapot. I stir the thick, purple-black jam until my tea is clouded and little pieces of cherry float and spin. My mother takes a dense sugar cube from the bowl on the kitchen table, and places it delicately between her teeth, sucking the hot tea into her mouth through the cube, a sweetening method I have never been able to master without eating about seven sugar cubes per cup of tea.

We don't talk while we drink our tea, but my mom reaches over and pets my hand while we drink. I love this about her. She always gives you room to breathe and be, without needing noise all the time. I think after the barely controlled chaos of my siblings and me growing up in that house, she, like me, loves the quiet. She knows we will talk while we cook, but for now we can just drink tea and hold hands. It is enough. Our sips are measured, and we finish within seconds of each other, my mom crunching the last morsel of sugar in her teeth while I shake the final cherry morsel from my glass. She smiles.

"Pelmeni." It is a statement, not a question. She gets up and I put our tea things in the sink while she gets the big bowls out. "I make dough, you do meat, nu?"

"Yes, Mama."

She dumps flour into her bowl, adding eggs and salt and milk, mixing by hand until she has smooth, plastic dough. I put the ground-meat mixture into mine, seasoning with salt, black pepper, and ground caraway seeds, an unusual and delicious family addition to the traditional recipe. She begins to roll thin rounds with a small wooden dowel, flours them and stacks them on the table between us so that I can fill them. She'll finish the dough well before I finish pinching the fat dumplings closed, her hands a blur.

"Zho. Why you no bring my Dumpling to make dumplings, eh?" She loves Dumpling like another grandchild, and adores dressing him up and taking pictures when I leave him with them when I travel. She especially loves theme pictures for holidays, and while I would never in a million years dream of dressing him up myself, I secretly love the photos she takes with the ridiculous outfits and props. My favorite so far is the Dumpling Lama, draped in an orange scarf like a monk's robes, in honor of Chinese New Year.

"Dumpling is working today."

"Ah, zho busy, zho hard to be dog een America, have to have job. Pull up by paw straps." Her eyes twinkle as she teases. She once ran into Barry and Dumpling while she was visiting a sick friend in the hospital, and got to see them in action. She was very proud.

"Everyone has to contribute," I joke back. "How are you guys doing?"

"Goot, goot. Sasha and Alexei brink all boys over Sunday to watch Bears." She sighs deeply, shaking her head in disappointment, remembering the spanking our beloved team got. "Like throwing peas against the vall." She throws her hands up and sucks her front teeth disparagingly. "Tsssk. Monday we go recital for ballet for Natalia's girls. Lia, she is goot, graceful like Natalia. But leetle Racheleh. Not so goot. Not maybe supposed to do the ballet. The dancing, ees like small elephant putting out fire in own shoes. Like you, remember?"

Of course I remembered. I took ballet for one session when I was six. I spent four months clomping around, spinning the wrong way, endlessly pulling my leotard wedgies out of my little butt, stepping on the teacher's feet, accidentally kicking the girl in front or back of me, knocking over the portable barres, and, on one memorable occasion, pirouetting with as much force as I could muster and clocking the lithe little princess next to me right in the face. I had never seen a nose expel that much blood in that short a time. They politely said to Mama that they did not think there was a place for me in the next session, and that was the end of my dance career and the beginning of flute lessons. There is no bloodletting with the flute. Mama continues listing her week of activities. "Tuesday mah-jongg, I win. Today, pelmeni with you. Plehnty busy."

"Good for you." I roll small balls of the meat mixture, and cover them with the thin dough, pinching carefully to seal, making sure there are no air bubbles. The first time I made pelmeni with Mom, I was about nine. I was careless with the dough, and when we boiled them, the air pockets I left made the dumplings explode, ejecting their fillings with little muffled pops, like edamame squeezing out of their pods. Mama strained out the mess, winked at me, dumped some tomato sauce over it and called it pasta kerchiefs and meatballs. Ever since that day, I have been very diligent about air bubbles.

"And Patreek? You bring him pelmeni, nu?" My mom is not immune to the charms of Patrick. My dad is more leery, especially since he believes that Patrick is in love with me. Of course, my dad believes that every man I ever meet is in love with me, including Barry. But Mama, she thinks Patrick hung the moon, especially since he praises her rustic cooking and always takes leftovers home when he comes to family events. It should be noted that after the first time I brought Patrick, at his own insistence, to a family Shabbat dinner, which we try to do once every other month with the whole gang, my mother began inviting him directly to most other family occasions. I think my parents are hilariously split in their views on the whole Patrick thing. My mom would like me to marry Patrick, so she invites him to every birthday and Chanukah party, sure that spending time together away from work will push our relationship to the next level. And my dad, who is positive that Patrick is after me romantically, is scared that I will cease to resist the endless advances he imagines I fend off every day. So when Patrick is at a gathering, my dad works very hard to keep him busy, showing off his tool collection, talking sports, inviting him outside for one of his rank greenish cigars, which take forever to smoke and smell like an ashtray full of manure.

"Yes, Mama. I will bring him pelmeni." And I will. Because if I don't, when my mother calls him and asks if he liked them, they will both kick my ass. "He is out of town for the weekend, but we will freeze some and I will give it to him on Monday, I promise."

Mom, finished with the wrappers, nudges me aside with her hip and we shift, I roll the meat mixture into little balls and hand them off and she swiftly covers them with dough, pinching them perfectly closed, setting them aside on trays.

"You veel come next week, nu? Shabbat dinner?"

"Of course. What should I bring?" It is only in the last few years that my mother has allowed me to bring food to the family dinners. It both thrills and saddens me. I'm delighted that she finally trusts me to make some of the family recipes, and that she genuinely seems to enjoy when I tweak them slightly to make them new while still honoring the flavors we are all used to. But sad, because I know that, in part, her acquiescence means that she gets too worn-out by taking on the whole menu herself. My aunt Rivka, Mom's younger sister who lives up the block, is a terrible cook, so she is not allowed to make anything. She buys the challah from the bakery near the Russian community center where she volunteers, and brings the wine. But the food is on my mother's shoulders, and they are beginning to stoop slightly with age. I hate seeing my parents show the signs of getting older.

"Tssk." My mom sucks her teeth, a habit she has when she is thinking, or annoyed, or very pleased. "Borscht maybe?

And carrot salad?" And then a pause. "And Patreeck, of course." A little smile plays around the corners of her mouth.

I ignore the last bit, and decide to take a major risk. "How about I do a brisket? Patrick just got a gift shipment from a local farm, and gave me a huge one. It is taking up so much space in my freezer; I would love to cook it so I can make some room." Mom will never let me do the main dish unless she thinks it is somehow helping me out of a jam.

She tilts her head at me and squints, trying to see if I am implying that she is no longer capable of making the family meat. I keep my face impassive, and a little imploring, and she buys it.

"Well, yes, eef freezer is too much full it no work well. Things go bad, get freezer brunt. You brink brisket. I make kugel."

Whew. "Thank you, Mama, it will be a huge help."

"Pish. Is somsink the cats cried out."

I smile. "Well, it is a big deal to me." I lean over and kiss her. She grabs my nose between her knuckles and gives a gentle twist.

And we set back to making pelmeni.

By the time we're finished, my mom asks me to invite Barry to bring Dumpling here for dinner instead of dropping him off at my house. He is thrilled, and promises to bring wine, knowing that as delicious as almost everything is at my folks' house, they drink wine so awful that it is impossible to choke down. They buy it in large unlabeled gallon jugs. I believe it is Polish in origin, those famous wine-making people, and the grape varietal seems to be a blend of concord and petrol. It is simultaneously horrifically sweet and yet has an astringency that sucks all the saliva out of your mouth.

He arrives with an excited Dumpling, a bottle of Bordeaux, and an endless series of charming stories about his recent stay in Philadelphia.

"So the young man playing Bosie, Oscar's lover, comes onstage dressed in Victorian underwear and in the back of the house one of the women in the audience says, 'Damn, baby!' as loud as anything."

My mother laughs, and my dad slips pieces of meat filling from his pelmeni to Dumpling, who rests at his feet under the table.

"Right out loud?" my dad says. "So rute."

"It was pretty funny actually. And better than the night before." Barry is in his element, telling funny stories to people who think his life is endlessly glamorous.

"Vat happent night before?" my mom asks, rapt.

"Well, there is a very quiet scene when Oscar knows that he is going to jail. Very poignant, very sad. And a gentleman in the front row, well, he just . . ." Barry looks at me for approval to continue, having already shared the event with me the evening it occurred. I nod.

Barry pauses dramatically. "He passed wind. Very loudly. Twice."

Both of my parents convulse in laughter, wiping tears. Fart jokes transcend all cultural differences and language barriers. But Barry is not done.

"And a minute later, up on stage, we could *smell* it. And it was *awful*. You could practically *taste* it. And you could just see everyone onstage as the smell would get to them, I mean it was *so obvious*, they would start to walk away, like it was *chasing* them, and then we all started trying not to laugh."

My dad is smacking the table with his hand, and my

mother is wiping her eyes with the corner of her apron. Barry is leaning back in his chair, puffed and proud. Dumpling wanders over to lick my ankle, and I think that whatever else goes on in this crazy life of mine, it is a good life. A very good life indeed.

5

Dear Alana—

So let's get the excuses out of the way in terms of my waiting so long to answer your questions—consumed by work, lost track of time, loathe to actually subscribe, inside knowledge of the freebie-weekends schedule, fill in the blank. What's wrong with being a remora on the great white EDestiny shark, I ask you? By the way, nothing like having someone who is obviously a very good writer compliment one's writing to brighten the day. Considering that I was born and educated in Tennessee, I exponentially thank you. Oscar Wilde, gougères, and Burgundy—what are the odds? Obviously you are some sort of goddess . . . or siren. Once you work through that Bears problem, you might want to sell shares in you. Let's not overlook that, being from the South, I know a little bit about hoops and piecrust. I think I just wrote a Nashville hit. And you had me at *pamplemousse*. What do you say we consider being grown-ups and cut the EDestiny apron strings? You can reach me at rjmanor@comcast.com.

Hope to hear from you again soon.

RJ

I'm glad he acknowledged the near month that had passed between my reaching out and his reaching back, and even gladder to know that he too was not paying EDestiny any money. And he continues to be witty and smart. Baffling. Now I am quite certain that he must be covered in warts and smell of old cabbages. Or is entrenched in a marriage he will never be free of. Probably both.

But that doesn't prevent me from replying.

RJ—

I too tend to only pay attention to the freebie weekends at ED, and have been pretty busy myself, so your radio silence is understandable. And I'm a fan of being grown-up enough to guide my own communications.

I've actually never been to Tennessee, but I hear it is beautiful. And that the pie and hoops are always worth the visit. I have met a few people in the country music business and they rave about Nashville. Keep meaning to go check out the barbecue.

Other than buckets of work, and projects around the apartment, and the demands of one small dog, I've mostly been trying to hang out with friends and family, testing new recipes with a couple new ingredients I am playing with, and helping one of my best pals prepare to host her first Thanksgiving.

What's been fascinating in your world?

Alana

I shoot this off trying not to think too hard or edit too much. I've finally gotten to an age when it is tiring enough to just be me; trying to be some super-duper-special uber-desirable version of me to attract a guy is just a game I don't have the energy for anymore. This is who and what I am, and if you are the guy, you will get that and be fine with it. So I don't try to be any wittier than I actually am, and instead make a conscious decision to just be completely myself and let the chips fall where they may. I mean, I do spell-check and reread a couple times to be sure I don't sound like some mouth-breathing idiot. But I don't overthink or overedit content.

"This is very exciting," Bennie says when I call her to share the latest on the RJ front. "You are getting your birthday wish, I can feel it."

"We'll see. That was a tall-order wish." Last year, when I turned thirty-nine, I looked at the universe and essentially had a heart-to-heart. I said I was grateful for the blessings in my life of good friends, and loving family, and a mostly great if insane job, and my health, and Dumpling, and a pretty good sex life. And I said that I did have faith that "the guy" was coming, and that I would not spend my life without a real partner. But, if the universe wasn't too enormously busy, might it be possible for whoever he was to hurry up a bit, because I did not relish the idea of waking up on my fortieth birthday alone.

"That was not a tall order. That was a perfectly reasonable wish. You are entitled to a real guy, and you are entitled to want him to show up in time to usher in a new decade. And who knows, this might be him!"

"This might be a married guy looking to play around. Or one of the endless 'love to e-mail doesn't ever pull the trigger on a date' guys that linger around dating sites. Or we'll meet and I won't be attracted to him. Or he won't be attracted to me. Or we'll both be attracted and then the sex will be bad . . ."

"Stop."

"What."

Bennie sighs. "Just stop. Why is it so hard to believe that he might just be a great guy who seems to already sense that you are a great girl, and you will meet and be great together?"

"When does *that* happen?" I laugh. My actual dating life over the years hasn't been that much of an improvement on my online theoretical dating life, and the older I get, the less patient I get and the more jaded and cynical.

Bennie chuckles. "Okay, you're right. He is a fundamentalist Mormon who wants you for his seventh wife, and will expect you to breed at least eleven children and be in charge of hand washing all your sister wives' sacred undergarments."

We both giggle. "Okay, okay. Maybe he will be totally normal and he and I will have a very pleasant first date and take it from there." I say this, but deep down I'm thinking it is much likelier that I am headed for the sequel to *Big Love, A Jewess in Juniper Creek*.

"Much better. Now, more important, is my room available the weekend after New Year's?"

Bennie always stays with me when she comes to town. "Your room is available whenever you would like to come inhabit it. Did Maria summon?"

"Yep. She wants to totally redo the workout room now that she has dropped the strength training and treadmill in favor of pilates, yoga, and the elliptical. So we're shifting from bad-ass gym chic to soothing and spalike."

"Wonderful! How long will you be here?"

"Probably three or four days."

"Can I throw a party? Everyone who has met you wants to see you again, and everyone who hasn't, wants to."

"Of course! Sounds wonderful. We'll make plans as we get closer. Hold on. Driver, please take a left on Fourteenth Street. Yes. Just pull up here on the left. Alana . . . got to go, love you! Call you later!"

Bennie always calls me from taxis between appointments, or late at night. Which is perfect for me, since the taxi calls are quick catch-ups, and the late nights can be really good chin wags. Dumpling rises from his fabulous little teak and leather bed that Bennie designed and built for him, stretches strangely long for such a small, squat dog, and comes over to hop up on the couch next to me. I rub him under the chin, or rather chins, one of his favorite things, and take a small treat from the bowl on the windowsill behind me.

"Who's my good boy?" Dumpling barks. I give him the treat, which he wolfs down and then he snuggles against me, making a strange guttural noise. In the months he spent at PAWS before I adopted him, he got very close to some of the cats, who apparently made a big impression on him. When he is very happy, he makes a noise that almost sounds like choking, his way of trying to purr.

"Should we go visit Maria?" She has invited me over for brunch, says she has something she needs my help with, and she requested that I bring Dumpling with me to have a play-date with her two brindled French bulldogs, Abrazos y Besos—Hugs and Kisses. Maria's signature sign-off at the end of her show. The three of them are BFF, and hilarious to watch when they visit. Just hearing Maria's name makes Dumpling jump off the couch and spin in a circle. "Okay, okay, let's go!"

Dumpling goes over to the door and pulls off the leash I keep hung over the knob. He does prefer to walk himself. I grab my bag and keys and we head out.

Maria greets us at the door and grabs me in her expansive embrace. "*Mi amorrrrrr!* I am so 'appy you arrrrrrre her-rrrrre."

Dumpling tears into the living room like a (fruit) bat out of hell, where Abrazos and Besos tackle him from two sides like a couple of tiny linebackers. The three of them tangle into a pile of loving play, until Maria comes in and says firmly, *"Perros. Silencio."* The three dogs immediately stop what they are doing, and sit in a straight line, Dumpling flanked by Maria's dogs, all three of them with their heads tilted to the left waiting for further instruction. It never ceases to be hilarious to see them together, Dumpling's head way too small for his body, and Maria's dogs with their heads way too big for theirs. They look like seconds from the dog-head factory.

"Gigi?" Maria calls, and in two seconds her personal assistant materializes in the entryway. "Can you please take these thrrrrrree *ninos* to the dog park for an hour so we can 'ave some peace?"

"Of course. Hello, Alana, how are you?" Gigi has been with Maria for more than a decade, a quiet girl from downstate who landed an internship at the show while still a student at Columbia College, and turned out to be the perfect replacement for Maria's first assistant, who got engaged, married, and pregnant with twins in quick succession, leaving Maria for a life of diapers and bottles. Gigi is amazing, and truly keeps Maria on schedule and organized. She leans down and asks the dogs very seriously, "Should we go to the park?" The three of them hear the word *park* and go nuts. "Well, then, troops, let's go!" and the four of them head for the door. I love Gigi.

"You arrrrre 'ongry, *sí*? Comer?" Maria reaches for my hand, and we head for the kitchen.

Laid out on the rustic farm table that sits to the side of Maria's enormous kitchen island is a lovely spread of fresh-looking salads. Wheat-berry salad, what looks like a Greek salad, asparagus, a platter of beautifully arranged fruit, and some cooked tuna steaks. "This looks amazing!" I've been mired in fall comfort foods for work, all braised and hearty, and it is very exciting to see such fresh and light fare for a change.

"My Melanie, she is a mirrrrracle."

Melanie is a local chef who runs healthy gourmet take-out restaurants and a food delivery service, and it is her light and delicious food that has helped Maria lose weight and get healthier. They met when Maria did a segment on midlife career changes. Melanie used to be a lawyer before she left to go to culinary school, and then opened her first place in Lincoln Square. Since then she has opened three other locations, one near me in Logan Square, one in the Gold Coast and one in Hyde Park. I often stop by on my way home from work to pick something up if I am too tired or lazy to cook for myself. The cobbler's children have no shoes, as they say, and no one eats more takeout than chefs. When Maria and I parted company, she went through an endless series of diets with prepackaged food. Nutrisystem, Seattle Sutton's, Jenny Craig, Weight Watchers, The Zone . . . She tried it all. She'd lose ten pounds and gain six. She hated the food with a passion. Up and down, forward and backward, minimal successes and maximal annoyance.

After the career-change show aired, she called Melanie, who worked with Maria's doctors and nutritionist to come up with a food plan, and Mel began both delivering meals and occasionally catering Maria's events, ensuring that Maria could continue to entertain without derailing her program. And for the first time, Maria began to have serious sustained success, because first and foremost, the food is delicious. Appropriately portioned, restricted in all the ways Maria needs it to be restricted, but very, very tasty. And they have become good friends and colleagues with a common cause. Melanie and Maria have launched a program in five of the local charter elementary schools in some of the food desert neighborhoods, to support healthy options in the school cafeterias and nutrition education as part of the science curriculum. Maria is pushing the Chicago Public School system to adopt the program for all of the elementary schools in the city, which is a long and difficult process, but I don't doubt that she will eventually succeed.

"It all looks amazing." We fill our plates with small portions of all the dishes, and sit at the other end of the table to eat.

"'Ow is *la familia*?" Maria asks, picking up a spear of asparagus in her fingers and munching on the tip.

"*La familia y un poco loco en la cabeza*, but very good. Mama wants to know if you are coming for Thanksgiving this year?"

"Of courrrrse! And my doctorrrrr says I can have little bit of everrrrrything, but no seconds." She says this both as a way of guaranteeing her own smart eating, since once she has told me what the doctor said she can't cheat and pretend otherwise, and as a way of knowing that I will warn my mother about not pressing her to eat more food. My mother, who has stood in line for two hours for a loaf of bread and one orange, thinks that nothing is more satisfying than filling people to eight times human capacity with rich food. Hence the size of my ass.

"Fantastic! Everyone will be very excited." This is exuberantly true. Maria is just herself, all day every day. She doesn't have a "television persona." All that warmth and wit and nurturing spirit that make her fans so rabid is genuine. Which is why the more famous she gets, the more secluded she becomes. Because she is the kind of person who would never deny someone access or reject someone reaching out to her, being in public can be exhausting for her. I know that famous people choose that fame, and so does Maria—she is not one of those celebs who bemoans the fact that she can't go out in public without being recognized. She is resigned to the fact that in order to do what she feels is her calling, she has to give up some of the things she used to love, like shopping and eating out. I've seen her spend more than six hours in a bookstore after a reading, signing copies of her memoir, taking pictures with everyone who asks, kissing babies and soothing the people who become so overwhelmed by her electric presence that they break down in tears. She would never dream of leaving unless every person there has what they came to get, regardless of how exhausting it is or how much time it takes.

When she comes to Thanksgiving, which she has now done about eight or nine times in the years we have known each other, she makes special time with everyone. She admires my dad's antique woodworking tools and reminds him how many compliments she gets on her custom closet, which Bennie designed and my dad built for her. She praises my mom's cooking, telling her that it is no wonder I am such a good chef. She consistently refers people to Sasha's law firm, Alexei's accounting office, and Natalia's chiropractic service.

She actually wants to hear about all six of my nephews' sporting events and science fairs and my two nieces' recitals, math competitions, and spelling bees. She's a mean hand at Wii bowling, which the kids love, and loves football, which wins points with the rest of us. She brings stacks of signed books from famous authors for my sister and sisters-in-law to take to their book clubs, and CDs and DVDs for the kids, and sports memorabilia for the guys. She is like Santa Claus and a fairy godmother and your favorite aunt all rolled into one.

"Good. You let me know what I can bring. In the meantime, we 'ave a new prrrroject I need your 'elp with."

I finish my bite of tuna. "Of course, what is it and how can I be of assistance?"

"You know the school prrrroject, it goes verrrry well, *sí*?"

"Of course. You must be so proud. I think it is fantastic."

"*Sí*. Of courrrrse. Verrry 'appy. So good for the little ones. But the teenagerrrrs. We 'ave nothing for them."

I know this has bothered Maria for a while, the fact that all the programs are limited to younger kids, and not available in high schools. But the initial research indicated that teenagers would simply opt out of any cafeteria food that they didn't want, especially since most of Chicago's public high schools are open-campus for lunch and surrounded by fast-food joints. Home Ec hasn't been taught in Chicago since the late 1960s, and the standard science curriculum just doesn't have room in it to do more than touch briefly on nutrition. They try to sneak it into PE a bit, but never very successfully. And PE is tricky because any student participating in an active extracurricular like a sports team or marching band gets PE credit and doesn't have to attend the class.

"Well, if you can continue to get your program out there

with the grammar school kids, they will eventually bring that knowledge with them into high school."

"Trrrrrue. We think this also. But we do still want to do something for high schools. So we think, what about an after-school program, like an internship or job? They learn cooking, with nutrition and food safety, and maybe the best ones get scholarships to culinary school?"

I think about this for a moment. "It seems amazing. Not every kid is cut out for academic colleges, but there are many jobs to be had in the food-service industry, especially in a city like ours with so many hotels and restaurants and catering companies and even colleges and universities. And there aren't that many scholarships available for culinary school."

"This is what we arrrrre thinking. We 'ave permission from Clemente High School to do a pilot prrrrogram, eight students, all seniors, one semesterrrr. Once a week cooking class after school, with a full week during spring break for intensive work. The Cooking and Hospitality Institute of Chicago, Washburne, and Kendall colleges have all agreed to save two places in their fall class for students, so we can give six scholarships."

"Maria, that is fantastic. Do you want me to ask Le Cordon Bleu if they would save two places there as well?"

"That would be wonderrrrful. That way we know that we can offer scholarships to all participants, if they qualify. And I want you to be on the advisorrrry committee."

I think about this for a moment. "How much of a commitment is that, time-wise?"

"Does it matter? This is rrrrright up your alley. It won't be too much." This is not a question or a request. This is a mandate. And Maria has asked very little of me over the years, so there is no way I would ever deny her.

"Of course I'm in. I'd be delighted."

"Good. I will send you the inforrrrmation for the meeting next week. Now. Enough business. 'Ow is your love life? Still with the Brrrruce?"

I love that Maria calls him the Bruce. Like Robert the Bruce. "Yes, I am still with Bruce, such as it is. He is coming in next week for a couple of days while we are shooting."

"And anyone that is *not* the Brrrruce?"

I hesitate. She and Bennie are close, but I know Bennie doesn't share confidences. Then again, I didn't say that my correspondence with RJ was a secret. I have to err on the side of honesty, because if Bennie did mention something and I hide it, Maria will be hurt.

"I have someone else that I am e-mailing with, but it is very new and we haven't even spoken on the phone yet, so I am not really thinking anything much there yet."

"But you like him?"

I think about this. "I like the very little I know about him so far, and the way he expresses himself. We seem on the surface to have a reasonable amount in common. But until it is more than just a few words exchanged on the computer, I can't really say if I like *him* or not."

"Good. You like him." Another mandate.

"I suppose I am hopeful in the liking him direction."

"Excellent, *mi amorrrr*, excellent. You know I never really like this thing with the Brrrruce. Sex is fine, but you need boyfrrrrriend. And good sex makes you lazy."

"I know you think that. Bennie says the same thing. I prefer to think that good sex makes me smart and clear-headed to make decisions about who I date and why. If I am being taken care of in that way, I never will rush a new relationship or try to make someone the right someone just

because I want sex. I can take the time to get to know someone, and trust them, and then decide if they are the right
person for me to be with." It is my standard response for the
handful of people who know about my current arrangement.
I try to ignore that it sounds a little bit like a justification.

"Hmm." Maria looks at me pointedly. "And exactly 'ow
many men have you taken the time to get to know while you
sleep with the Brrrruce?"

Gulp. "Um, none really, but . . ."

Maria puts up her hand, one finger pointing in the
air. "No 'but.' You 'ave no buts to give. You arrrrre busy with
work, spend all your time with friends and family at people's
'ouses, you arrrrre cooking for Patrick at all hourrrrrs of the
night, and you have sex with the Brrrruce. No dating. No new
men. No going out to meet people or have blind dates. I am
glad you meet this man online. Do not let the Brrrruce dis-
trrrract you."

I laugh. She is right, of course, as always. "I promise, I
won't let Bruce distract me."

"Or Patrick."

"Patrick is not a distraction."

"He crosses lines." Maria is as leery of Patrick as my dad,
but for different reasons.

"He is fine. He is the same as he ever was."

"Ay, this is what I am afrrrraid of!" Maria spears a grape
tomato and piece of feta with purpose, and pops them in her
mouth, wagging her fork at me.

I suppose I should probably mention that I did actually
once sleep with Patrick, much to my embarrassment, and it
is essential to my whole existence that we both pretend he
doesn't remember it.

6

After Maria reached a level of fame that made eating out an exercise in fending off fans, she frequently asked both superfamous and up-and-coming chefs alike to cook for her and a few guests in her home. That way she could partake of their wonderful skills without anyone asking for pictures or autographs or hugs or advice or money. On these occasions, I would serve as sous chef, helping the chefs find their way around the kitchen, and assisting in any way I could. Usually they would provide recipes ahead of time, so that I could shop for ingredients and do prep work before they arrived. It was an amazing time for me. I cooked with so many of the greats: Tom Colicchio, Eric Ripert, Wylie Dufresne, Grant Achatz. Rick Bayless taught me not one but two amazing mole sauces, the whole time bemoaning that he never seemed to know what to cook for his teenage daughter. Jose Andres made me a classic Spanish tortilla, shocking me with the sheer volume of viridian olive oil he put into that simple dish of potatoes, onions, and eggs. Graham Elliot Bowles and I made gourmet Jell-O shots together, and ate leftover cheddar risotto with Cheez-Its crumbled on top right out of the pan.

Lucky for me, Maria still includes me in special evenings like this, usually giving me the option of joining the guests at table, or helping in the kitchen. I always choose the kitchen, because passing up the opportunity to see these chefs in action is something only an idiot would do. Susan Spicer flew up from New Orleans shortly after the BP oil spill to do an extraordinary menu of all Gulf seafood for a ten-thousand-dollar-a-plate fund-raising dinner Maria hosted to help the families of Gulf fishermen. Local geniuses Gil Langlois and *Top Chef* winner Stephanie Izard joined forces with Gale Gand for a seven-course dinner none of us will ever forget, due in no small part to Gil's hoisin oxtail with smoked Gouda mac 'n' cheese, Stephanie's roasted cauliflower with pine nuts and light-as-air chickpea fritters, and Gale's honey panna cotta with rhubarb compote and insane little chocolate cookies. Stephanie and I bonded over hair products, since we have the same thick brown curls with a tendency to frizz, and the general dumbness of boys, and ended up giggling over glasses of bourbon till nearly two in the morning. She is even more awesome, funny, sweet, and genuine in person than she was on her rock-star winning season on Bravo. Plus, her food is spectacular all day. I sort of wish she would go into food television and steal me from Patrick. Allen Sternweiler did a game menu with all local proteins he had hunted himself, including a pheasant breast over caramelized brussels sprouts and mushrooms that melted in your mouth (despite the occasional bit of buckshot). Michelle Bernstein came up from Miami and taught me her white gazpacho, which I have since made a gajillion times, as it is probably one of the world's perfect foods. Those nights, cooking in Maria's kitchen, were some of my favorite.

But one of them I'd prefer to erase.

When Patrick first began getting rave reviews, Maria asked me to set up one of these dinners for a few friends. Patrick had not yet built his empire, wasn't on television, and was just a young hotshot chef making waves on the Chicago culinary scene. He sent over his recipes, with complex and obsessively complete instructions. A half-dead platypus could have cooked his dishes from those recipes. They practically listed the number of grains of salt.

Which was a good thing, because Patrick was in no condition to cook them.

He arrived two hours later than we had agreed upon, suffering from a hangover so powerful that I thought he was going to gag every time he opened his mouth. Deciding that he was essentially useless, I made him a large glass of *sangre del tigre*—"blood of the tiger"—a lethal Bloody Mary that I had picked up in Mexico City. Tomato juice, clam juice, raw egg, fresh horseradish, hot sauce, ground white and black pepper, salt, the juice from pickled jalapeños, orange zest, and a large slug of mezcal. He drank it down, put on his headphones, and immediately fell asleep on the couch in the back of the kitchen. I prepared the meal for him, making every one of his recipes, seething at his arrogance and inappropriateness, and mentally writing him off, while he snored away across the room. He might be hot shit for the moment, but you can't be a party boy while you are supposed to be working and maintain the necessary standards to keep a fine dining restaurant running. I don't care what you do after or before work, how hard you party after the people go home, but you had better be up to speed while on the clock. I know plenty of chefs who will have a snoot or two during service, a few more who rely on some unconventional pharmaceuticals to get them through the day. But I don't know anyone who can maintain a serious party habit that infringes on the work who gets anywhere. The fact that he had been so unprofessional to Maria, of whom I was always enormously protective, potentially putting her in a difficult position with important guests, made my blood practically boil.

But damned if his recipes weren't spectacular. A chilled pea soup of insane simplicity, garnished with crème fraîche and celery leaves. Roasted beet salad with poached pears and goat cheese. Rack of lamb wrapped in crispy prosciutto, served over a celery root and horseradish puree, with sautéed spicy black kale. A thin-as-paper apple galette with fig glaze. Everything turned out brilliantly, including Patrick, who roused himself as I was pulling the lamb from the oven to rest before carving. He disappeared into the bathroom for ten minutes and came out shiny; green pallor and under-eye bags gone like magic. Pink with health and vitality, polished and ridiculously handsome, he looked as if he could run a marathon, and I was gobsmacked. He came up behind me just as I was finishing his port sauce for the lamb with a sprinkle of honey vinegar and a bit of butter, the only changes I made to any of his recipes, finding the sauce without them a bit one-dimensional and in need of edge smoothing. He leaned over me, dipped a spoon in the sauce, tasted it, and then kissed the side of my neck right below my ear.

"You're amazing. Perfect fix, it's been eluding me for weeks."

I hated the way my nipples got hard when he did that. Down girls. We hate this smug fartweasel.

He followed the plates out to the dining room, where I soon heard both laughter and applause. I rolled my eyes, and turned to plate the galette. He returned, wordlessly helped get the plates together, and as soon as the waitstaff took them, turned to me and said, "I'm going to need another one of those magic concoctions." Whatever bit of respite he had

gotten from his condition had started to wane, and I was still
so shocked by his behavior, I could do nothing but make him
another drink and hand it over.

It revived him almost immediately, and he was summoned
to the living room to join the guests for coffee and cognac.
I cleaned the kitchen, packed up leftovers, and made Maria's
lunch for the next day. In the guest bedroom that I used on
nights like this when the act of driving home was a recipe for
disaster, I changed out of my chef whites and into the pajamas
I kept there, taking my hair down from the severe bun I favor
while cooking. I headed to the kitchen, suddenly starving,
and in need of a little snack and a glass of wine. Patrick was
sitting on the kitchen island, waiting for me.

"My little savior." He oozed off the counter, sidled over to
me, put his arms around me and literally bent me over in a
dip and kissed me firmly and a little wetly on the mouth. He
tasted of cognac and chocolate. He smelled like freshly mown
grass. He was a really good kisser. I'm not really sure to this
day why I took him back to that room. Probably a little of it
was that it had been a long time since I had slept with anyone.
Maybe a little of the cachet: bagging the hot-stuff pretty boy.
Some of it was that in the moment I simply couldn't come up
with a good reason not to, which in and of itself should have
been the reason, but I was in my twenties and didn't know
better yet.

The sex was brief and, frankly, unmemorable. I was too
tired and he was clearly suffering from some diminished
capacity. We didn't really speak. Patrick got up soon after we
finished (or I should say, after *he* finished), to go to the bathroom, and I fell asleep while he was gone. When I woke it
was morning, and there was no trace of him beyond whisker

burn on my chin, a condom wrapper on the floor, and a sinking feeling of mortification.

When I went to the kitchen to rustle up breakfast, I found Maria getting ready to head out to the studio.

"Good morrrrrning," she said with a smirk.

I must have blushed the color of cabernet. "Good morning."

"And how did you sleep?" She was enjoying the heck out of this.

"Fairly well, thank you."

She raised one eyebrow at me, and then we both burst into laughter. I told her the whole story, she thanked me for saving the meal and the night, and we promised never to speak of it. Flash forward eight years, and she was recommending I work for Patrick. "You go meet him. 'E needs a new assistant now that 'e is adding a second show."

"Um, Maria. I don't think that is such a good idea."

"Why not? The job is perrrrrfect for you. You cannot stay with me, you will be borrrrrrred of the salads and steamed vegetables and you hate the sad diet chicken brrrrrrrreast."

It's true. I think boneless, skinless chicken breasts are the devil. The idea of cooking them with any regularity makes my spine lock up. But not enough to leave Maria, and especially not enough to work for that smug, drunk fucksack. Especially after what had happened. Which was essentially nothing. He sent Maria a huge floral arrangement with a gushy card to thank her for allowing him to cook for her, which made me throw up a little in my mouth. He called and told her that anytime she wanted, he would open his restaurant on their day off to entertain her and her friends. He did not ask her about me, acknowledge me in any way, did not call or send me flowers. Which said to me that he was either as embarrassed as I at our little assignation, which pissed me off, since there was nothing at all embarrassing about sleeping with me—I'm adorable. Or it meant that he was so accustomed to any female within arm's-length falling into bed with him, that there was no need to even pretend that it was necessary to follow even the basest bit of postcoital politeness, as if sleeping with him once was reward enough for some nothing like me.

"Maria, perfect or no, how could I ever work for him? After what happened?"

"To be 'onest, and don' be mad, I don' think he remembers. When I talked to him, 'e says anyone I would recommend would be welcome, and that he looked forward to meeting you. 'E did not say that it would be good to *see* you *again*, but to *meet* you. It was so long ago, and you said 'e was verrrrry dronk. I know it is not the best, but you would rather it 'ave not 'appened. If 'e does not rrrrrrememberrrr, it did not 'appen! Clean slate."

I thought about that for a moment. And she was right. Whatever blow it might be to my ego that the arrogant bastard could actually have sex with me, even minor, quick, drunken sex, and completely not remember it, it did free me up to consider the job.

"Okay, I'll meet with him."

And I did. And much to my relief there was not the slightest flicker of recognition on his face. Or at least, he made sure there was not the slightest flicker of recognition on his face. If he had twinkled the tiniest bit, smiled in the wrong way, said anything the tiniest bit double entendre, I would have walked right out. But he either genuinely did not remember our night together, which I hoped and prayed, or at the very minimum, he was working very hard to make it appear that he didn't remember, and, frankly, either was fine by me. He explained the job, the duties, said he would match my current level of salary, and if I passed the tryout, would meet my current benefits package. If I wanted the job, it was mine to try to hopefully keep.

I went into the job with Patrick thinking I knew what I was getting into. Excited by the challenge. Assuming I would do it for a year or two until I could find the right person to get me back into the personal chef business. Assuming that he would chew me up and spit me out like so many before me. When he promoted me to executive culinary assistant, I made him put in a severance clause that some Fortune 500 CEOs would have envied. Or rather, I asked for something ridiculous, presuming he would have the lawyers bring it down to something rational that would make me feel like I had the smallest bit of security. But he didn't balk. He just laughed. "You must love me an awful lot to make it so expensive for me to get rid of you." And signed the papers.

The thing is, as much as he makes me crazy and I hate the way he treats 99 percent of the population, as much as I get creeped out by his pursuit of fame, and his treatment of women, I do, I suppose, love him in a way. Some days I would prefer to love him from afar, but at the end of the day, he has been good to me. In an overly demanding, obliterating-boundaries, twenty-four-hours-a-day sort of way.

But if I'm honest, I also have to admit that I've never suggested any other way.

It's a slippery slope, being needed and depended upon, especially when the person who depends on you is notorious for never letting anyone get close, never trusting someone else. And Patrick has earned his independent nature. His dad left when he was a baby, and his mom resented him fairly openly for what she perceived as his driving away her husband. When Patrick graduated from high school she effectively threw him out—he was eighteen and had a diploma; her work was done. He had a job flipping burgers, and jockeyed the couch at a friend's place for a few months, living on pilfered food from the restaurant, saving every dime he could get his hands on, knowing that all he really wanted to do was cook. At nineteen, he got a cheap ticket to London, where a friend from high school was doing a semester abroad. He befriended a bartender at a classic chef's after-service dive hangout, and eventually met Marco Pierre White, who took a shine to him and hired him as a dishwasher. Within six months Patrick was working garde-manger and absorbing everything he could from his cantankerous mentor. After eighteen months with Marco, they had a falling-out and even though they both apologized, it was agreed that Patrick should move on. He used Marco's connections to do some stages in Paris, and then he moved to San Francisco, working in several restaurants, always moving up the line, until eventually he landed a stage at the French Laundry. He stayed eight months, and then, with Thomas Keller's blessing, he moved to Chicago to take over a failing old warhorse of a restaurant, his first gig as executive chef. A year later, the restaurant flush with good reviews and a renewed clientele, he landed investors to help him open Conlon, and has never looked back.

There is obviously more, as most people have seen from the *Chefography* documentary on him, or, will see in his new memoir *(Not) Saint Patrick*, which is due out next fall. The short version is fairly typical. Pretty much everyone he has ever relied upon has left him. His mother died before they ever really got close, and well before he opened his first place. His dad, unsurprisingly, reappeared shortly after he began doing *Feast*, and it was not a warm reunion, resulting in some nasty tabloid headlines, one restraining order, and a hush-hush settlement, after which his fair-weather father disappeared again never to return. After the one brief marriage to Sharlene, which lasted less than two years and little of it happy, he became an unrepentant playboy. Legs last anywhere from one weekend to a maximum of six months, and I have never ever heard him refer to one of them as a "girlfriend."

Bob has been directing the shows since the beginning; Gloria has been running the test kitchen. I'm third in seniority, Patrick-wise, and everyone else he works with has been in a reasonable state of perpetual motion. Even Andrea, his current personal assistant, is the fourth person to hold that position in the six years I have been working with him. She's lasted just shy of two years so far, and we have high hopes that she might just stick around.

But I am the only one whose lines have gone past blurred into nonexistent. He and Bob might go to a ball game now and then or grab a beer after a shoot, and Gloria does any on-air support when he does shows like *Chopped Masters*, or when he beat Bobby Flay on *Iron Chef America*, so they have had the after-work travel adventures that come with that territory. But neither of them get the late-night drop-ins, the invasion of family gatherings, or the complete lack of separation between church and state.

"I think you like it more than you claim," Bennie said one night when I was complaining about how Patrick had shown up the previous night wanting to hang out and not taking no for an answer, requiring that I surreptitiously cancel a long-anticipated romp with Bruce. "Or you wouldn't let it continue," she pointed out.

"I feel bad for him. And yes, I do appreciate that he does trust me so genuinely considering that he doesn't really trust anyone. But that doesn't mean I wanted him to come over and twat block me, and make me listen to him whine about not getting the Beard Award for best chef *again*."

"Methinks you doth protest too much," she said.

"Because, what? I *wanted* to spend the night babysitting him and not getting laid?"

"Because I think if getting laid were more important to you than being Patrick's go-to girl, you would have faked a case of explosive diarrhea, or told him that Barry was having a crisis that needed attending, or you would have just put on your big-girl panties and told him that it wasn't a good night for you and that you would be happy to deal with it tomorrow."

"That's not fair. You know I'm a terrible liar. And he would have either stayed to take care of me, or wanted to accompany me to Barry's, or put on his sad, needy face and convinced me to stay anyway."

"Full. Of. Shit. You are so full of shit I can smell you from HERE. Why is it so hard to admit that you LIKE when he just needs his special Alana time? It feeds something in you."

"I am not full of shit, I just, it, um . . . I dunno."

And truthfully, I didn't.

And don't. And I prefer not to think too deeply about it.

7

So this is how it starts.

Hello, Alana—

Free at last, free at last! With our own guidance we are free at last.

I think of Tennessee as a pleasant enough place to drive through on your way to a place you want to be. I hope you aren't having to talk your hostess friend off any ledges. Just tell her she's cooking a big chicken, make people bring their favorite childhood side dishes (green Jell-O and Cool Whip where I'm from), buy lots of wine from Howard Silverman at Howard's Wine Cellar, and it will be spectacular. I have a great recipe for the world's most versatile dish—Banana Salad. It's an appetizer, a salad, a side dish and a dessert. Oh, yeah. It requires three ingredients and a willing suspension of disbelief.

So what new ingredients do sirens play with?

Looks like I'm talking your eyes off.

RJ

Hello, RJ—

I am intrigued by this Banana Salad of which you speak. It sounds either very Southern or otherworldly. Possibly both. Or possibly that is redundant. My latest culinary playthings have been very unique and inspiring. Korean black garlic, which is whole heads of garlic that have been aged until the cloves inside turn black and chewy. . . . They taste like a combination of mild roasted garlic, dates, and balsamic vinegar. And Mugolio, which is Italian sweet syrup made from the sap of pinecone buds. I also recently was given some truly outstanding red grapefruit marmalade from Sicily. My toast has never been happier; it tastes like chunky Campari. It must be that whole *pamplemousse* thing again. . . . Anything in the grapefruit family is thrilling to me these days.

Sounds like your work has been busy, which must be both a bless- ing and a curse these days. Hopefully it is something you enjoy. Running to a meeting—we are voting on lasagna recipes. At nine in the morning. I have a very strange job.

Alana

———————

Alana—

Looking at the thread, I appear to be running off at the fingers, so I'll try (probably unsuccessfully) to self-edit. My father is a Lutheran minister, and we moved around a lot in Tennessee when I was very young, mostly around Nashville. I managed to finish my grammar school education in Nashville, and then he was hired at the University of Tennessee in Memphis to teach classes in comparative religion, and to serve as the minister and counselor for their Lutheran chapel on campus, so I went to high school there, and my folks have been in Memphis ever since.

I will visit them there for a few days prior to Christmas when my only sister and her kids will be visiting from Atlanta. Couldn't get out of the near South fast enough, so left for Chicago eleven minutes after graduation to attend the University of Chicago, where I majored in art history, and then went to the School of the Art Institute to do an MFA in visual and critical studies. Every time I move away from Chicago (three years in NY to get it out of my system, two years in Kalamazoo, Michigan, to make a lot of money and be miserable), I return, so I consider myself a Chicago Guy. Learned that NY is exhausting and expensive and much better as a vacation destination than a home, and that Michigan is Kentucky with crappy weather.

Banana Salad does not truck with modern fussiness or strange sci-fi machinations. Thin, vinegar-y mayonnaise, whole banana quartered lengthwise, crushed Spanish peanuts. Dunk banana in mayonnaise. Dredge in peanuts. Voila. Everyone cringes when they hear about it; nobody eats just one.

And let's get to a key point. *Pamplemousse* is not only truly my favorite French word, it may be the best single word in any pronounceable language. I beg every person I know who gets a dog or has a child to name the animal Pamplemousse. You can confirm this at some point. Your latent urges aren't about grape-fruit. They are about a primal connection to all things *pample-mousse.*

RJ

RJ—

I'm a native Chicagoan, so I know how addictive this city is. I might have mentioned already that my parents emigrated right after they got married, so I was born here, but my dad, like you, loves his adopted city with a fierce passion. I may have mentioned that I too have only one sister, two years younger, and she is married with two little girls. But I also have two older brothers, both married, and both with three boys. All the kids are under the age of nine, which makes family gatherings loud and messy. But luckily they are all really great kids, smart and funny, and generally well-behaved. Which is how I like my kids . . . smart, funny, well-behaved, and belonging to someone else! I started at Northwestern as a business major, which was what my parents wanted. The trade-off was that if I stayed home for college I could do a semester abroad. I spent the first half of my junior year in Paris, came home and promptly dropped out and enrolled in culinary school. I am the executive culinary assistant for a TV chef, so I spend my time developing recipes, testing techniques and products, coauthoring cookbooks and the like. The work is interesting, the hours are weird, but I love what I do, and am grateful to be able to make a living at it, despite being a college dropout. ☺

I have a small, weird-looking dog who is letting me know that I have to take him out before we have a problem, which is good because apparently I can't *Reader's Digest* my e-mails either! Do you have any pets?

Alana

A—

May I call you A? As in A'int you grand, and A-List, and A for effort
and any other positive thing you can associate with A's. I do have
one cat. His name is JP (for Jackson Purcell). He is fifteen years
old, and in sprightly health, much to my chagrin. He is a devil in
a cat suit and I let him loose in the neighborhood every day In
hopes he won't return, but he keeps coming back. My ex went out
to the farmer's market for broccoli one day and came home with
him instead. I would have preferred broccoli. When we split it was
decided that he was too old to move to a different home. I mentioned that she was a lot older than the cat and she was moving,
but that did not go over terribly well. I have reluctantly come to
love him in spite of his horrible personality. I will miss him when
he is gone. But not for long.

I wish you a lovely evening whatever your plans, and hope that I
get to meet this dog of yours one day, as I have always preferred
canines as furry companions. (See what I did there? Because if I
get to meet the dog, then I get to meet YOU, which is rapidly
becoming a major focus of my day and a serious distraction from
my work.)

RJ

"Barry, this guy is IN MY HEAD."

"He sounds fabuloso. What on earth are you worried
about?"

I chew on the end of my pen, a horrible habit I picked up
when I stopped biting my nails. All chefs are orally fixated,
we suck straws and chew toothpicks and smoke like fiends

and bite our nails till the cuticles bleed. I'm down to just pen chewing, which I find the least offensive of the chefly jawing, and is only bad when I occasionally get too aggressive, which you can tell by the stain of ink in the corner of my mouth. "I am worried about his fabulosity. No guy is this great right off the bat, no red flags. And he is COMPLETELY un-Googleable. I can't find one thing online about him, no Facebook, no MySpace, no articles or references. And you know, in this day and age, if you can't Google-stalk someone, it is because they have taken great PAINS to not have an online presence. So what is he hiding? Is he using a fake name so that I can't find him? Witness protection? What?"

"Do you even HEAR yourself? You sound like an insane person."

"Because I am having a really hard time being calm and casual about this, and we know what happens when I get too excited about a situation with POTENTIAL."

"Oh, yeah. That isn't so good historically, is it?"

No. It isn't.

8

The movies have ruined me. Don't get me wrong, I love movies. But as someone who spent my formative years watching an endless combination of John Hughes teen flicks and early Meg Ryan romantic comedies, I'm sort of broken when it comes to dating. My expectations aren't just high—they're stoned out of their gourds with one hand on the Mallomars and Pink Floyd on the stereo. Deep down I sort of have always believed that my Mr. Right will appear outside my window, boom box akimbo, blasting Peter Gabriel. That he will come running to find me before midnight on New Year's Eve to tell me that when you realize you want to spend the rest of your life with someone, you want the rest of your life to start right away. That we will "meet cute," that he will woo me in some silly and utterly romantic fashion, and that, despite a setback or two, we will eventually live happily ever after.

When I met Andres in Barcelona during the last month of my fellowship and he wooed me in a way that only a Latin man can, I completely got caught up in the amazing movieness of it. The late nights spinning around the city on his classic Vespa. His murmured passionate endearments, in softly purring Spanish. Taking me home to meet his family, a raucous group so like my own, that it made me deeply homesick and powerfully nostalgic. My parents met at the wedding of a mutual friend, and were married themselves within weeks. When we fall, we fall hard. So when Andres begged me to marry him three weeks later and said he would move home with me, I said yes, and we wed in a tiny judge's office, with a family-dinner celebration at his parents' home, and had a three-day honeymoon in Majorca en route back to Chicago, where I had to try to explain him to my family and all of my friends. Once he had successfully learned English by watching a lot of daytime television it became clear that language had not really been our barrier to communication, and that we had nothing in common. He refused to find work, was indifferent to my family and dismissive of my friends, and began to spend late nights out, coming home smelling of booze and sickly sweet perfumes that I tried to ignore. Once he had gotten his green card and completely ruined my credit rating, we divorced, and I was thrust into a dating scene that I was ill-prepared for.

One of the problems with loving all those classic rom coms, is that it puts me in a constant state of observing my romantic life with an eye toward "the story." And frequently, it backfires. I'm so convinced that I'm supposed to have some sort of adorable first meeting with the soon-to-appear love of my life, I forget that I am not Meg Ryan, circa 1987, and I am just a normal girl and that it might not be guaranteed. I had not really considered when I decided to pursue this odd career of mine, which keeps me in a fairly small social circle and is rife with weird work hours, that there are not, in fact, a whole lot of single men wandering aimlessly around my apartment on any given day. So meeting guys has always been, to say the least, difficult.

A couple of summers ago, after a wine-soaked lunch with Barry, I hailed a cab to take me home. And when I got in, I

sat on something uncomfortable. A BlackBerry. Not *my* Black-
Berry.

I put the treasure in my purse, arrived at my destination,
and took Dumpling for a walk. While wandering the neighborhood, Dumpling managing to mark every tree on the
planet, I thought of the BlackBerry and my pulse quickened.

This was it. This was the way it happens.

I will call the first name on the call-back list, explain that
I have someone's phone, and give my number. A voice like
honey over gravel will call me back, thank me for saving his
life, and take my address. And then a tall, handsome, salt-
and-pepper gent with a confident bearing will arrive at my
house, tell me I'm amazing, and offer to take me to dinner to
thank me for my Good Samaritan ways. We will talk easily
until the restaurant closes, head somewhere for a nightcap,
and fall madly in love. For his birthday I will order a cake in
the shape of a BlackBerry. He'll propose on the corner of
Michigan Avenue and Washington, where I got in the cab.
At our wedding we will toast Yellow Cab number 1472 for
bringing us together.

I pressed redial, and got a gentleman named Robert, who
announced that he was a colleague of the phone's owner at
Rush University Medical School . . . so now I know that not
only is my *innamorato* a doctor, but a professor type as well.
He praises my good nature, takes my number, and promises
to get the info to my future hubby.

I head home, chuffed. The phone rings. A voice like honey
over gravel thanks me for saving his life, takes my address,
and announces he will be by around six. He jokes that he
would call me from the car to tell me when he was close, but
I have his phone. Sigh.

I primp. Not excessively, but I spruce up. Change clothes,

add some makeup, tweak the hair, floss. At six fifteen I hear the gate unlatch, and Dumpling begins his fearsome barking. I peek out the window. The gentleman heading up my walk-way is tallish, handsome-ish, salt-and-peppery. I take a deep breath.

The bell rings. I go to answer it. He smiles broadly and hands me a small gift bag. "For you. For renewing my faith in people." As he hands the bag to me, I catch out of the cor-ner of my eye a glinting sparkle.

Of his wedding ring.

Fuckety fuck fuck FUCK!

He left with his phone, and I came inside to unwrap my consolation prize.

A pound of chocolate-covered raisins. A pound of Swedish Fish. A pound of salted cashews. Three of my favorite food groups.

So now, not only don't I get a husband, I have to sit home alone and listen to my ass grow. Great.

Second on the list for us hopeful romantics, in terms of finding love, is the inevitable return of a lost love or a past crush. A while back, I joined Facebook. Shortly thereafter, I received a "friend request" from Marshall Jordan, who noted that we "went to high school together."

Oh. My. God.

Marshall Jordan was my personal (it should be mentioned, totally unrequited) Jake Ryan. He was a senior my freshman year and, due to some academic glitch, was in my algebra class. He sat behind me. I was madly in love with him. I was also, at the time, madly in love with about six other guys, but during third period at least, my love was only for Marshall. Emily, Lacey, and Mina all had Spanish that period, leaving me alone in the class with Marshall, so I spent my time trying to be winsome and mysteriously appealing, giving him the rare but fraught-with-meaning look. In retrospect I am sure he probably thought I was either lightly damaged or gassy. But, he was sweet to me, totally uninterested in romance, but at least friendly.

I looked at the friend request, from a man I had not seen in twenty years.

This was it. This was how it happens.

I will respond, we will reconnect, we will meet up, and it will be easy and fun, and soon we will fall madly in love and he will propose to me on the steps of Whitney Young High School, and we will live happily ever after.

We began an e-mail reconnection, during which he reminded me that I had written a mushy poem about him. I remembered the poem, but not that I'd had the chutzpah to give it to him. Mortifying. We found out that a friend of mine is a favorite author of his, and planned to meet up at the launch party of his latest book. He hadn't changed at all, and we fell easily into conversation, reminiscences of days past and talking about what was going on for both of us now. He was charming with my friends, and four of us ended up leaving the party and heading for a late supper and cocktails. He suggested, when I dropped him off well after midnight, that we should "hang out."

This is not a good thing for a forty-year-old man to say to a woman. What does that mean? Hanging out? Hanging out like playing PlayStation with a buddy, or hanging out like naked with the Sunday crossword before pancakes?

I invited him to join me for a soft opening at a new local restaurant. I dressed up. Okay, I brought all my cleavage with me. My friends on the staff told me I looked fantastic, and were duly entertaining, praising me in front of Marshall, and

winking at me when he wasn't looking. The food was amazing; we were invited to hang out after closing with the chef
and owners, offered free booze and great food, and I got to
introduce him to a bunch of big-name people on the Chicago
culinary scene. Our conversation continued to be easy and
fun and we laughed a lot. We left the party and went to a bar,
and ended up closing the place, talking until nearly two in
the morning about everything and nothing. We made a date
to "hang out" again, to watch a movie at my house.

He came over in the afternoon. I bought his favorite beer.
We watched the movie. And when it was over, he said he had
to go.

Because he had a date.

Guess that "hanging out" thing means the same thing to
a forty-year-old as it does to a fourteen-year-old. Probably
wouldn't have shaved my legs if that had been clearer.

You would think that after the Marshall debacle, I would
be more careful about how I Facebook. But even the smartest
girl, it should be noted, can be tricked.

A few years ago, a gent named Seth came to the studio for
a meeting about some media stuff, and how his company
might be of assistance with a project Patrick was doing. He
got there early, and I gave him coffee and fresh muffins and
we chatted a bit. I thought he was cute, but didn't think much
beyond it.

A few months later, as this was during my horrible online-
dating phase, JDate sent me his profile as someone I might
be interested in, and I sent him a note saying essentially,
"Ha-ha, JDate thought we were a good match . . . isn't that
funny?" figuring it was up to him to say, "Maybe they are
right!" and ask me out if he was intrigued. He replied that it

indeed was funny and a small world and that he hoped I was well and that he would probably see me around one of these days. Message received: not interested. No biggie. We have bumped into each other here and there, always very sweet and friendly, but never sparky.

So about a year ago he "friends" me on Facebook. I checked out his profile, saw a couple things that I thought were interesting and I sent him a note. It was totally innocuous. He replied immediately and we began catching up via Facebook messages.

Two days later I got an e-card for Chanukah. Sweet. I sent him a thank-you to his regular e-mail. The next day he sends me an application on Facebook inviting me to find out Which Shakespeare Play Are You? and telling me that he is *A Midsummer Night's Dream*.

The following e-mail correspondence ensued:

Seth—

So apparently, I'm *Romeo and Juliet*.

I'm not sure how I feel about that, always felt more *Much Ado*, myself. . . .

Alana

————————

Alana—

Hey, you could have turned out to be *Titus Andronicus*, and no amount of therapy in the world would have undone that one!

I figure as long as you don't engage in double suicide at the end of a date, you're okay being in the R&J category. Plus, you get swordfights and sex; I get a donkey head.

Seth

_____

Seth—

I could have been *Richard III*, and lord knows it is a bitch to accessorize a hump, and Manolo does not make a clubfoot stiletto. . . . I have never engaged in double suicide at the end of a date, but have been frequently tempted to commit justifiable homicide on a date. :)

You also get swordfights and sex AND you get fairies and magic. I get whinging, spotty teenagers, and Hatfields-McCoys in pumpkin pants.

Alana

_____

Alana—

Yes, but as *Richard III* you also get a horse. Sure you have to give up a kingdom, but you get a horse. That's pretty cool. And yes, it's a bitch to accessorize a hump; but I've also read it's quite a hump to accessorize a bitch, or so they say at the Westminster Kennel Club dog show.

I guess I do get swordfights and sex, but it's very PG. Plus, depending on your perspective, being surrounded by fairies and magic might not help (I had that experience when I went to see *Xanadu*!).

OK this is now the least politically correct e-mail I have sent in recent memory. Thank you for bearing with it.

By the way, I bet you look hot in pumpkin pants.

Yep, definitely the least politically correct e-mail I've sent in a long, long time.

Seth

—————————

Seth—

I think politically correct is boring, feel free to be un-PC with me anytime you like.

And while I look hot in many things, I don't think pumpkin pants are on that particular list. But I thank you for the sentiment.

Ah, witching hour, a smart girl would go to bed, but I think I may have to watch *Battlestar Galactica* instead . . .

Alana

—————————

Alana—

Hang on, you're staying up late to watch *Battlestar Galactica*? Be still my heart! Amazing, amazing, AMAZING show.

Of course you've ruled out pumpkin pants but left me to imagine all the things you DO look hot in. NOW how am I supposed to get to sleep?

Seth

_____

Seth—

LOVE BSG, totally addicted. Have been rewatching it from the beginning. And yes, I do own all the DVDs. 'Cause that is the kind of slick bitch I am.

And don't feel bad for not liking something the masses like. . . . I frequently find myself in the position of thinking the emperor is naked.

Mmm. Naked. Sleep on that. :)

If a girl didn't know better, she'd think you were flirting with her.

Alana

_____

Alana—

Flirting? Online? Is that even legal here in Illinois? Dare we live so dangerously and on the edge?

Well . . . let's review . . . hmmm . . . I refer to you looking hot in pumpkin pants and other outfits . . . you mention being naked and invoke that key phrase "mmm."

Yes, it appears there's some flirting going on here! (Although if a boy didn't know better, he'd think it was mutual.)

Seth

_____

Seth—

I think online flirting is still legal, provided both parties retain counsel in advance, and sign a preflirting agreement indicating that the intention to flirt and anything that comes of the flirting is mutually consensual.

But a couple of outlaws like us can't be bothered with such technicalities.

And I thought I wasn't getting anything good for Christmas.

Alana

At this point, I happened to change my status on Facebook to *Alana is* . . . waiting for an offer. Which I was. From my friend Denise, who had dropped hints about she and I team-teaching a special Valentine's Day menu, and what with all the online percolating that was going on, I was starting to think about romantic food, and daring to imagine that I might in fact have someone for whom to cook this year.

Alana—

So regarding that offer . . . Is that a professional offer you're waiting for? Or perhaps a social one?

Not sure what I can do about the former, but perhaps with all this rampant flirting and references to pumpkins and nudity and all, one of us should get bold and make an offer.

So . . . Wanna go hunting for naked pumpkins?

Or perhaps a drink first would be better form?

Now to sign off I need an outlaw name . . .

Seth the Kid

_____

Kid—

Guilty of playing up the double entendre . . . I am waiting for an offer for a cooking-class gig, and waiting for you to ask me out.

But hunting for naked pumpkins sounds like a lovely way to spend an evening with you. Drinking while hunting naked pumpkins even better.

Alana

Then, there is nothing. Nada. Radio silence. One day goes by. Then two. On the third day I ask two straight guys on the crew what the deal is and they say, don't worry. By the fourth day, I cannot stand it so I send this:

Seth—

I think you're in NY, and hope you're having some fun here and
there between what must be an insane amount of work. You are
missing a glorious day here in Chicago.

Can't remember if you get back Thursday or Friday, but if you were
thinking about trying to get together next weekend sometime, let
me know.

Have a great trip, and I'll look forward to seeing you when you get
back.

Alana

On day seven I begin getting weird messages from Facebook, repeats of stuff I already received days earlier, notes
from people that messages I sent haven't been received . . . so
I send this to his regular e-mail:

Seth—

Sort of confused as to why I haven't heard from you . . . but have
had a couple people tell me that Facebook messages I have sent
have not been received, so just in case, thought I'd try to catch
you here. So, if for some reason my notes didn't come through,
was just checking in to see if you still wanted to get together. And
if for some reason you'd prefer not to be in touch, let me know
that too.

Alana

Two MORE days go by and then FINALLY I get this:

Hi, Alana—

Sorry to have disappeared! Been in some work semi-hell, with a devious employee (now ex) making life very difficult and requiring me to be in New York this week. Ah, the joys of running a company. Will be back this weekend to regroup and then I will get back to life in general—thanks for understanding!

S

This is the last thing I heard from him. It would have been totally fine if he had taken me out once, told me there was no chemistry, and wished me a happy life, like any mature, normal guy in his MID-FREAKING-FORTIES would do. But friending me, flirting with me, asking me out and then falling off the face of the flipping earth after I say yes is simply inexcusable. Nearly two months went by, and every time he posted on Facebook it just made me seethe. I made excuses to go to New York to spend time with Bruce, just to remind myself that I am desirable company. I read back over the e-mails we had exchanged eight million times wondering what exactly had turned him off. I overindulged in late-night baking, bringing endless brownies and cookies and sweet breads into the studio so that I wasn't left home alone with sugary treats, but still managed to gain five pounds. Barry and the girls dutifully made noises about what a shit he had been, what shits men were in general, and reminded me that I was lucky to find out what kind of guy he was before actually getting involved with him. And I got over it, I thought.

And then I got a brief e-mail from him asking if my schedule was busy. Shocked and annoyed I replied simply that yes, it was. He said that was a bummer, and did I want to try to see if we could find some time for an afternoon coffee.

And I? Went off the freaking deep end.

Seth—

So, to be clearer than perhaps I was in my last note, yes, my schedule is entirely my own, yes, it is busy, and no, I am not particularly inclined anymore to create space in it for you.

I have far more lovely people in my life than I ever have time for, and these days, only make room for two kinds of new people. Either people who seem to have romantic potential or people who seem to have good friendship potential. You clearly lost any interest in the former sometime around my acceptance of your date back in December, and have not exactly shown yourself to be terribly worthy of either in light of your overall inconsiderateness.

Most people would have written you off completely once your initial ardor cooled, but since everyone I know who knows you thinks you are this great guy, I figured I'd still try to give you a second chance to see if we could be friends. (Why I would want to be friends with someone who behaves in a manner I'm fairly certain his mother would find horrifying, is a different issue, and one I should probably explore.)

I even suppose if your note to me the other day had indicated the slightest bit of remorse on your end, the tiniest acknowledgment that you have been deeply and importantly rude to me, even a modicum of "mea culpa, wait till you hear why I've been such an asshat, and wait till you see how I'm going to make it up to you," I probably would have been still open to getting together. But "afternoon coffee"? That famous audition-meeting of the noncommittal? The event you don't really look forward to, and create firm plans to get you out of in a definitively brief time frame? SERIOUSLY? That I REALLY don't have time for. I don't even drink coffee.

Despite your behavior, I certainly wish you no ill will. I assume at some point that you and I will, by virtue of the small world in which we live, be in a room together, and interact in the way acquaintances do. Making time to be in a room with you for the express purpose of spending time together? I'm hard-pressed to imagine why on earth I would do that. Sounds like an exercise in futility to me.

Bummer, indeed. The whole thing.

Alana

HA! Take that you supreme fucksnort. That will teach you to be so careless with the emotions of someone of my caliber. Coffee indeed. Kiss the fattest part of my ass. I forward my letter to Barry and the girls, who are unanimous in telling me that I showed him and struck a blow for women everywhere, but I get the sense they think I might have gone a little overboard. Bennie suggests I might have been able to get my point across with fewer words. Barry says he is going to steal it for his next audition. I reread it a few times, and do agree that perhaps I could have edited, but then my pride comes back and I think that he should not have been spared one bit of my ire. As my dad would say, he is neither fish nor meat, not remotely worthy of attention or respect.

I am all kinds of sassy and self-important for about three hours. Then I get this.

Alana—

Feel better?

Good. I'm glad you got that off your chest. You're entitled to whatever perceptions you want to have, and I won't argue with you about them. I'm sorry both that I disappointed you, and that you feel that much more disappointed on top of that.

Since we began those chats, more than you know has gone on. In addition to a very stressful and time-consuming employee issue that's cost much time and much money, I've had two serious health scares and a death in the extended family. All serious flirting and social activities more or less came to a halt during that time. I'm sure you would have appreciated an explanation, but, frankly, a series of e-mails saying, Hi, Alana, forgive the silence, but I'm afraid I might have cancer, followed by Hi, Alana, well you're not gonna believe this, but I came down with a flu that's gotten into my muscles and I'm having trouble walking—well that seemed burdensome to both writer and reader alike.

I was just genuinely trying to reopen contact, at which time I would have been happy to tell you what's happening. I didn't have to do that, but I did, out of sheer interest in getting better acquainted.

Life gets in the way sometimes, Alana, as I am sure you know. Apart from a few other times of intense personal losses, the last year has been the most challenging of my life, and I'm sorry that it coincided with the opportunity to get better acquainted.

As for behavior that my mother would find horrifying, I think right now she's more focused on being happy that her son has a healthy prognosis and is likely to live a good long time, and be able to walk straight and breathe easily while doing it.

I can't really apologize that you weren't among the first on my list to notify, because frankly I didn't really notify many people in my inner circle. The anxiety was intense.

How much of the anger in your note should be placed solely on my shoulders or not is up to you to reflect on, but I certainly hear your frustration and I'm sorry my circumstances added to it. But can I just say that someone suggesting getting together for coffee, while perhaps not the dream date you'd prefer, is hardly a slap in the face; and next time, before you invest yourself in such an eviscerating diatribe (incredibly well written though it is), you might ask some questions first. I'm not saying you're not owed explanations; I'm just saying there are better ways of getting them than acting as if you've been the victim of one of the year's more astonishing emotional atrocities.

Can I suggest letting cooler heads prevail, allowing some dust to settle, and meeting sometime for, perhaps, a friendly tea?

Seth

Crap. So much for my finding my inner strength and representing with the power of the pen all of the women who have had time and energy wasted and then been blown off by stupid boys on the interwebs. I go back and reread my letter again, and for some reason cannot find any of the cleverness or strength I thought it contained forty minutes ago, and instead see an overly reactive, whiny, sad letter that reads like the desperate ravings of someone who is going to remain single for a very, VERY long time.

Sigh.

Seth—

Well how on earth am I supposed to feel better without my righteous indignation? The whole thing isn't really fun unless YOU'RE the asshole. When I'M the asshole it takes all the enjoyment out of it.

And since you have been so forthcoming, which you certainly had no responsibility to do in light of my vitriol, I will attempt to reciprocate.

You were sort of an unexpected and delightful surprise. Someone I had found to be smart and funny, someone who turned out to not just share the interests I already knew about, but several that I was thrilled to discover. And during a time when (for many reasons I am sure you can guess based on my previous missive) I have essentially left all dating in the hands of fate and fix-ups, you appeared out of nowhere and engaged in delicious badinage, and brought a little bit of hopeful life into a dating dry spell. Just enough that you put a little spring in my step. And then you disappeared, making me wonder exactly what the hell was so wrong with me that the very act of saying yes to a date sent you fleeing.

Bad criticism, to paraphrase one of my favorite movies, is fun to write. You hurt my feelings, made me feel small, and while I get that it wasn't your intention, it struck a much deeper nerve than I had a right to attribute to you alone. And when it has happened in the past, I have never really indulged my desire to call someone on their bad behavior, and often regret sucking it up and keeping mum. Clearly I picked the wrong time to decide to let it all hang out.

Thank you for your honesty, and the rightful scolding, which obviously I needed. And I am sorry for what you have suffered, and only wish that things had been in a different place, one where you might have thought to lean a bit, even just for an ear to vent to. I talk too much, and write a hundred words when ten would suffice, but I do listen.

And I happen to like tea very much. Although under the circumstances, I think something a little stronger might be more appropriate. (Scotch, not hemlock . . .)

Be in touch or not as your head leads you. It's either the best or worst possible beginning to something, and, frankly, I am at a loss as to which. But I am delivering a ball into your court for you to do with as you choose. I personally am a big fan of the total rewind/do-over. Your mother isn't the only one who is grateful that you have a healthy prognosis. And now I must go buy a hair shirt. Do you think they have them at Target?

Alana

"I'm still proud of you for standing up for yourself," Bennie said about the whole affair. "You had no way of knowing he had all that going on. I still think he is a schmuck."

"Of *course* he is still a schmuck. He could play the woe-is-me health card all he wants; he was Facebooking all over the place every day, posting links and commenting on people's walls. If he could play fucking Mob Wars, he could have takes ten seconds to just get in touch. Even if he didn't want to tell me the specifics, a short e-mail that just said things were completely off the rails and stay tuned would have done the trick. It's just that I am a *worse* schmuck, and I come off like a completely desperate idiot."

"Well, you never know. You did leave the ball in his court, maybe he will get back in touch." She didn't sound convinced.

You can imagine the rest. He did not get back in touch. And to his credit, the one time I ran into him at a restaurant, he was lovely and chatty and did not give any indication of his secret personal knowledge that I am an insane person.

Which is why I am trying with limited success not to hope too hard about RJ. I have been here before, with the meet cute and the sense of possibility and the great e-mails and the greater disappointment.

Then again, I can't help but fess up that deep down, I know that this is usually when the heroine convinces herself that she is okay alone, that she has a great life that she is proud of, that she doesn't need a man to complete her or make her days have meaning. That she vows to focus on any new person coming into her life as a potential new friend, nothing more, and that she is going to just let whatever will be, be.

And then it *really* happens.

She *really* meets the *real* love of her life who *really* will woo her and will be handsomely and affectionately at her side when she runs into Seth-who-doesn't-have-cancer at some event. Or who will answer her phone in his deep, commanding voice when Marshall calls, thinking maybe he made the biggest mistake of his life. Or open the door in his bathrobe when Dr. BlackBerry leaves his wife and comes back to see if the girl he couldn't get out of his head all these years is still living in the same place. He will be everything she never knew she'd always wanted, and this time, he will fall in love with her, and she with him, and they will live happily ever after.

At least, that is what I want to believe, even if I don't want to admit it to anyone, especially myself.

9

Saturday morning is prime doggy time in Logan Square. Dumpling and I have a routine. First, we head up to the boulevard, Dumpling marking every possible vertical surface, greeting his friends as we go. There is Ollie, the bloodhound, all ears and jowls, who gently places one huge paw on Dumpling's diminutive head like a benediction. Dumpling delicately nibbles his ankle in return. The black Schipperke from around the corner does some intense butt sniffage before indulging in a little WWF maneuver that flips Dumpling over with ease. They bark joyfully while they romp, but the schipperke becomes focused on the need to poop. We head up to La Boulangerie at the corner of Milwaukee and Logan to pick up a crepe for breakfast, and a baguette for later, running into Sweetness, a yellow lab so gorgeous he looks like a painting. Sweetness is the king of the high five, and I give him a treat when he obliges me.

On our way back home we run into a boxer, which is always a problem. Dumpling hates boxers. His secret Mohawk pops straight up, and he hunkers down, growling low and glaring intently. I put myself between him and the offending creature, shrugging at the twentysomething hipster boy who is walking him, all ironic facial hair and skinny pants. Once the boxer is gone, Dumpling stands up and shakes, his back fur returning to normal.

"Really? What is it with the damn boxers? Huh?"

I could swear he shrugs.

We are almost home when Dumpling finally decides to get down to business, producing a poop literally almost larger than his head. He stands over it pridefully.

"Yes, good boy. You are such a good boy." Dumpling spins in a circle and barks. I toss him a treat, and quickly manage the blue-bag duties. We wander down to drop the package in the garbage can on the corner, where Dumpling automatically sits, so that we can cross the street safely together. I tie him up outside New Wave Coffee and zip in to get a hot chocolate, my weekend treat. By the time I am finished, a small crowd has gathered.

"He is so *cute*, Mommy!" A little girl in a Hannah Montana shirt is on one knee receiving loving kisses all over her face.

"He's weird-looking," says a boy I presume is her older brother, his head tilted to one side and squinting at Dumpling. "His head is *way* too small."

"Is he yours?" The girl looks up at me.

"Yep, he sure is." I lean down to untie the leash.

"He's very sweet," the mom says. "C'mon, Ella. Time to go. The doggie has to go too."

"What's his name?" Ella asks, rising slowly.

"Dumpling."

She smiles, front teeth missing. "That's a silly name."

I smile back. "He's a silly dog. Just look at him!"

"Bye, Dumpling. I love you!" Ella leans down and kisses his head, before turning to walk away with her mom and brother. Just like that. I love you. Love at first meeting. Pity it doesn't happen after you are six.

Dumpling and I head home. I give him his breakfast and, in order to feel a tiny bit productive, mix myself a small tester bowl of the latest granola with fruit and yogurt. I finally seem to have nailed a delicious low-fat, low-calorie version that is high-fiber and healthy but doesn't taste like a bowl of twigs. Only took eleven attempts. But I think it works, and make some notes to send to Patrick.

The phone rings promptly at eleven.

"Hi, RJ. Nice to finally speak with you!" Don't sound too eager, Alana, it is just a phone call. RJ's e-mails are consistently witty, charming, self-deprecating but not self-loathing. Flirty but not lascivious. Grown-up e-mails. *Courting* e-mails. He replies promptly, but not immediately. He has started to feel like a when and not an if, and I find it exhilarating and terrifying.

"Indeed. You're a busy lady."

"That I am. And you can't stay in one time zone."

He laughs. I like his laugh. It is genuine, and makes me wonder for the millionth time what he looks like. He laughs handsomely. I'm in major freaking trouble.

"Guilty as charged. Q-four is our biggest, busiest quarter, and I am running around like a headless chicken trying to keep the clients happy and gear them up for a great end of this year so that I can hit them up for increased business in Q-one next year."

Okay, Alana. Just be honest. "RJ, I know you have said a little bit in your e-mails, but can you explain to me exactly what it is that you do?" Because I? Am an idiot about most things, and director of Client Development for an Internet media consulting company sounds like bladdity bladdayblah blah bippetty boppetty boo to me.

He chuckles again. "Really? I'm a schlepper. I'm a salesman. I just don't sell physical products. What I sell is an ability for an online retailer to target their potential clients with very specialized Internet advertising, and I package both the advertising hits themselves with the functionality to manage how it is delivered. But at the end of the day, I'm just a seller. I go to my clients and I sell them the ability to increase their reach, to up their direct sales."

My Call Waiting beeps. I can see it is Patrick.

And for the first time in six years, I ignore it.

"Okay, that actually makes sense to me. Sorry, I'm just technologically completely inept."

"So am I. We have a whole floor full of twentysomethings who deal with the actual technology. I just find out the needs of the clients and try to translate that for the guys who do the programming."

Beep.

"Do you need to get that?"

"Nope. Not at all. You'll forgive me, but um, how did you get into that business?"

"You mean because I have a degree in art history, and then went to art school, the whole time singing in a punk pop band?"

"How do I say this? Yes, in a nutshell. It just seems like such a leap from musician-slash-artist to corporate guy."

He laughs again. I could jump into that laugh and paddle around like a happy duckling. "I can guarantee you that I'm the only one from my graduating class that is working in my industry."

Beep. Fucker. I am IGNORING YOU.

"What about the art and the music? Not following those dreams?" Not that I'm sad about it. I've dated guys who never got over not becoming the rock star—slash—pro athlete—slash—movie star. They are endlessly resentful of the life they think they had to settle for.

"Preempted by a need to live indoors and feed myself. I turned the passion for making art into a passion for collecting and being a spectator, so I love to go to museums and galleries and occasionally buy something if it's within my ability. And I took up the electric guitar again, mostly just noodling around at home, but my company has a house band that we put together for all the events and parties, and I sing and play with them so that keeps me feeling connected to the rock 'n' roll in my heart. In the meantime, I fell into a job that I really love and happen to be reasonably good at, so I get the best of all possible worlds." Thank goodness. He seems very secure in the choices he's made and, even better, seems really content and happy with his life.

Beep.

"Someone is mucho popular. I really don't mind holding."

Sigh. "I'll be right back."

I click over. "What?"

"Someone is cranky. What're you doing?"

"I'm on the other line. What do you need?"

"Oh, can you do one thirty instead of one? I want to get a massage."

"Fine."

"Okay."

I click back over.

"Hi, sorry."

"No problem. Everything okay?"

"Completely fine. That is very cool, what you were saying about your work. I feel the same way. Although most people who do what I do did go to culinary school, so that isn't so incongruous. But I got into what is probably the most specialized segment of the food industry accidentally, and just got very lucky."

"It's very refreshing to meet someone who loves what they do."

"I agree. But I'm lucky, most of my friends are pretty happy in their careers."

"Most of your friends are rich and famous."

Now it is my turn to laugh. "I suppose I do run in something of a rarified crowd," I say in my fake hoity-toity voice.

Beep. GODDAMNIT. I am ignoring you, Patrick Conlon, you complete crapbucket.

"Don't downplay. Let's see, from what you've told me so far, your crowd includes the talk-show host most likely to fill Oprah's stilettos, one of the world's most recognizable television chefs and restaurateurs, and a *New York Times* bestselling author."

"Ghostwriter," I correct him.

"Okay, so her name may not be on the books, but isn't it cooler to know the person who actually wrote the books that sell all those millions of copies rather than the faker whose name is on them?"

Emily is going to love him. "I've always thought so." We're allowed to say that Em is a ghostwriter, and even that books she has written have been on the list; we just aren't allowed to say which actual books she has written or for whom. Between us, the woman for whom Emily writes such witty and wonderful material is a spoiled, bored trust-fund baby whose daddy got her the book deal to begin with, ignoring the fact that his precious baby got kicked out of fourteen prep schools, never went to college, and cannot string four words together coherently when she is sober, which is rare. We all just refer to her as Princess Drunkypoo.

Beep.

"Same person, or is it a movie star or head of state?" He doesn't sound at all annoyed.

"Same person. I'll be back in one second."

I click over again. "WHAT???"

"Are you still on the phone?"

"Yes, I am still on the phone. What is it you want?"

"My masseuse can't take me, so we are back to one o'clock."

"Great. See you then."

I click back over to RJ. The conversation flows insanely easily. We find that we have a ridiculous amount in common: obscure bands we both love, old movies we can't stop watching. We are both crazy for L'As Du Fallafel in Paris. When I mention the name of the tiny town in the South of France where I spent a week with a local chef, it turns out that he has a friend there. Who just happens to live in the house I walked by every day on my way to the market, dreaming of a life where I could buy the house and open a small café in one of the outbuildings. We talked about our families, his upbringing in Tennessee and mine in Chicago. And then, as it always does in these situations, the conversation turns to how we met.

"So, how is EDestiny working out for you?" he asks.

"Um, that is sort of an interesting question."

"Because?"

"Because I really wasn't on there for dating, per se." I'm going with honest.

"Intriguing, oh woman of mystery. Do tell, why were you on there?" His voice sounds as if he is smiling.

So I explain about the history of online dating and horrible matches, and the game of checking in on the free weekends for the fun of it, hoping that he will be flattered that

I reached out and not offended that I'm dissing his dating site. Instead, he listens, chuckles where appropriate, asks about some of the more egregious bad matches, and is generally charming and sweet and completely understanding about the whole thing.

When I get to the end of my saga, I ask him, "How about you, are you having good success with the old Destinometer?"

"Well, it is interesting that you admit you weren't really there looking for a date, because neither was I."

Hmm. "Well, that is equally intriguing, oh man of mystery. And why, pray tell, are *you* on EDestiny not looking for dates?" Here it comes. The married thing. I can just feel it, the bastard.

"You know that whole Internet media consulting thing I do?"

"Yes?"

"EDestiny is one of my biggest clients. I was there to test the functionality of the site. That's why there is no picture, and so little information. I just put in the minimum stuff so I could effectively see how the site operates and how I can help them maximize the way they interact with their current and potential clients."

"You're not married?" I can't believe I just let that slip.

"Not since 1998."

"That is an enormous relief."

"Did you really think I'd be married?"

"It wouldn't be the first time. How long were you married?"

"Seven years. Have you ever been married?"

Oy. "Yes, once, very briefly, just over a year. Divorced in 1996."

"Sounds like there is a story there."

Boy, he said it. "I think I'll save that one for when we have a decent bottle of wine." Presumptuous me.

"Even better. What are the chances we can get that on our calendars? If it isn't too forward or fast, I would love to take you to dinner if you'd be ready for that."

My heart melts. Not afternoon coffee, or "Let's meet for drinks." No tester date just to be sure you can escape without risking too much time or laying out too much cash. A real, live dinner date. I frankly can't remember the last time a guy asked me out for one of those. "I would love to have dinner with you."

We check our calendars and realize that, despite it only being the first week of November, the first weekend night we can schedule our date for is the Saturday after Thanksgiving. Which he also gets huge points for, not booking a weeknight dinner, when an early morning at work is a good excuse to cut things short. A real, live, Saturday-night dinner date. Be still my heart.

"Well, I'm glad we got that on the books!" RJ says. "I'm tempted to ask you to schedule a second date now, just to make sure the rest of your year doesn't fill up!"

"Not fair, you have six business trips yourself, mister."

"Guilty. I should probably admit that while I would of course rather see you sooner than later, the distance doesn't really make me nervous. I feel like you and I are going to be friends, real friends, even if the in-person chemistry isn't there for romance. So I don't feel like there is pressure to move faster or try to squish in some short little first meeting. I hope you don't mind my saying that."

I love that he feels comfortable expressing that feeling, because it is what I have been feeling the whole time we've been talking. "I don't mind at all, because I agree completely."

Beep. I am going to FUCKING KILL HIM.

"Do you need to?"

"No. I don't really."

"I would like to keep talking between now and our date if that is okay."

Beep. "I'm counting on it."

"Well then, can I call you again tomorrow?"

I look at my schedule. "I should be home by nine thirty, latest."

"So I'll call at ten? Give you time to walk the dog and get settled?"

Beep. "Wonderful."

"Good-bye, Alana. I look forward to continuing this tomorrow night. Go tell your other boyfriend that he can have you back now."

"I'm looking forward to talking again. Bye, RJ." I purposely don't deny that it could be another man. After all, it's okay to retain some sense of competition with guys.

I turn and look down at Dumpling, who sits up to look back at me. "Oh. My."

My phone rings. "WHAT. DO. YOU. WANT. NOW?"

"I was going to say that my masseuse has an opening at three, and I can't take it, but you seemed sort of tense, so if you want the appointment, it's my treat."

I check my watch. Forty-two minutes. I have blown the record for staying annoyed at him out of the water. "That is very sweet. I'd love a massage. Thank you."

"All righty. I'll set it up."

"Thanks, Patrick. I'll see you in an hour."

"And, Alana?"

"Yeah?"

"You really have to try to relax, nothing is that serious."

I hang up the phone. "What am I going to do with that man? And more important, is it possible to lose twenty pounds in three weeks before I have to meet RJ? And what on earth am I going to wear?" Dumpling sighs, stands up, spins once, and then flops back down as if to say, "Don't get your hopes up, Crazy Pants. You have no idea what he even looks like; he's still just theoretically good. Don't set yourself up for disappointment."

Which, while logical, is looking like it is going to be much easier said than done.

My meeting with Patrick at Uncommon Ground coffeehouse is brief, and basic. I hand off the drafts of the first twenty-five recipes I've done for the new cookbook, so that he can play with them and make them more Patrick-y. He gives me a bunch of ideas he has been toying with, jumping-off points for me to play with for the next set of tests. We chat about the upcoming week of shooting, go over the ten shows we have scheduled, and I talk him through a couple interesting new gadgets I found that he is going to be using on-air. The person writing his blog for the Food TV website has agreed to freelance write a blog for his personal website as well to keep the same voice, but will need some help pulling the right recipes together. Just one more little thing to add to my plate.

"So. I think that is all I have. Do you have anything for me, Alana-cabana?"

"Um, I think that is probably it. Bruce says the network is planning on a Grilling Week around Fourth of July, so we might be on deck to shoot a special extra episode. I've pulled together an initial menu based on some of the better grilled stuff at PCGrub, thought you might want to do the shoot there, I know your PR team would be delighted."

"Yeah, that sounds like a plan. It hasn't been featured since last year's 'Check, Please!' episode, so it will make the media whores happy."

"Okay, I will see what I can do to get that in the works."

"Great. And now you should go for your soothing forty-twenty."

"What the hell is a forty-twenty?"

He grins. "A massage. Forty minutes of relaxation, and twenty minutes of trying not to fart."

I can't help but laugh, because the man speaks the truth. "It's why I stopped doing yoga. My sphincter couldn't take it."

"Exactly. Have a good rubdown. What are you doing tomorrow?"

"Dunno. Dog park, laundry, some work, try to check in on the folks. You?"

"I have a meeting."

"Anything fun?"

His eyes twinkle in a mischievous way that chills my blood. "Maybe. We shall see. I'll let you know soon."

Aw, crap. This is going to bite me in the ample behind sometime in the near future, I can just feel it. "Okay, well, I hope it goes well, whatever it is."

"I'm sure it will." He gets up, kisses the top of my head, and leaves. I sigh, and pay the bill. Patrick may be generous with health insurance, but he is a notorious skinflint when it comes to the nickels and dimes, and I am forever paying for his lunch and coffee and snacks, grabbing him a paper, picking up bottles of water. Andrea finally told me to just save the receipts and give them to her, and she expenses them and gets me reimbursement checks from the production company. I love Andrea. But even though I'm no longer personally out-of-pocket, it still ticks me off.

Lucky for me, I now have an hour-long massage ahead in which to become unpissed. I am a little concerned though . . . that extra granola breakfast followed by coffee doesn't exactly bode well for getting through it without possibly perforating my colon from gas suppression.

10

I'd like to propose a toast!" Patrick raises his glass from the head of my parents' dining room table. Or tables. My parents have cobbled together from the regular dining room table, the kitchen table, and three card tables of various shapes and stability, a place for the family to gather for Thanksgiving. Eighteen of us, including Maria and Patrick.

It is the first time Patrick has joined us for Thanksgiving. Usually he gets adopted by another local chef, but this year one of his New York investors had invited him for a Hamptons Thanksgiving, so he turned down all other invitations. And then Chicago got slammed with a snowstorm, and his flight got delayed and delayed and delayed and delayed and then cancelled. Of course, because he was bored hanging out at the Admiral's Club all day, he called me every ten minutes. Nothing more convenient when trying to help your family cook Thanksgiving dinner with six children tearing through the house, than your boss calling to ask, "What are you doing *now*?" forty-two thousand times. Then when his flight got cancelled, he called to say he was on his way. Not to ask if he could come, or if there was room at the table, or if we wouldn't mind. Just called and said, "Tell Mama the prodigal adopted Irish son is en route!" Fanfreakingtastic.

Mama was, of course, thrilled. "So goot to have my Patreeck for Thanksgiving."

Maria showed up early to wrangle kids and keep them out of the kitchen, bringing the one dish she cooks better than anyone I know, a truly spectacular flan. "Don' you worrrrry, *mi amorrrrr* Patrick will behave 'imself. With all these *ninos*, no one will notice him!"

I was surprised by how annoyed I was with him, at the presumptuousness of it. My sister, Natalia, called me out on it.

"What's the big deal, Lana?" she said, extricating her slim leg from the grasp of Alexei's youngest, eighteen-month-old Jon, and pushing him toward the door to the den where Maria and the rest of the kids were watching *Toy Story 3*. "Wouldn't you have invited him anyway if he hadn't invited himself? I mean, what? Were you going to just let him go home and be alone?" Nat is the opposite of me, tall and slender with bone-straight light brown hair, and a clavicle to kill for. I know I have a clavicle by virtue of my neck not flopping around like wet spaghetti, but I'm pretty sure no one has ever actually spotted evidence thereof. Nat's clavicle is like a little poem.

"Who's going to be alone?" Sasha's wife, Jenny, wanders in and sneaks a piece of crusty stuffing from the corner of the casserole dish, while Nat slaps her hand away. Jenny is short and round, like me and Mama, but with the creamy fair skin and water-blue eyes that come with her English and Swedish background. She looks like a milkmaid, and is about the calmest, most patient person I have ever met. Which is good, because her three boys are darling, but high-maintenance. The oldest, Benjamin, has some really weird food issues, and there are only about six things he will willingly consume, making Jenny play magic chef, constantly trying to sneak nutrition into things that look and taste like the handful of things he likes. Their middle son, Jacob, is about the smartest kid I've ever met, and as a result is endlessly curious, asking eight million questions a minute with machine-gun precision. And their youngest, Adam, has discovered a passion for taking things apart, so if Jenny turns her back for a minute, the phone is in sixty pieces all over the floor.

"Patrick invited himself to dinner and Alana is pissed." Alexei's wife, Sara, like all accountants, is brief and to the point. She and Alexei met in a study group for their CPA exams. She does a little bit of freelance tax work from home for a couple of her friends, and occasionally helps Alexei with larger projects from his firm, but mostly she manages their boys' schedules. Alex, the oldest, and David, the youngest, are both athletes, so there are endless games to shuttle to and more stinky laundry than any one person should have to wrangle. Joshie, the middle son, seems to take up a new passion every three months or so, mostly in the sciences, and loves all the local museums. He knows his way around the Adler Planetarium, Shedd Aquarium, and the Museum of Science and Industry better than some of the staff, and is always begging someone to take him to one or another. Last week I picked him up from school and we did the Field Museum of Natural History. Joshie regaled me with the life of Australopithecus Africanus as casually if he were describing an episode of *SpongeBob*. I know aunts aren't supposed to play favorites, but Joshie holds a very special, quirky place in my heart.

"I still don't understand," Nat says. "Would you or would you not have invited him to dinner once you found out his flight was cancelled?" Nat is solo today, her husband, Jeff, took their girls to the burbs to have dinner with his family, and will hopefully get back here in time for some dessert. Nat and her in-laws do not really get along very well. And Jeff isn't

Jewish, so she gets stuck with extended command performances for Christmas and Easter. Jeff and the girls alternate Thanksgiving between our family and his, but for the sake of Natalia's sanity, she gets excused from Thanksgiving in Winnetka, ostensibly to help Mom. Anytime they get pissy about it, he reminds them that they get their grandchildren every Christmas and it shuts them up.

"Of course I would have invited him."

"So what's the problem?" Sara asks.

"He didn't give her a chance to invite him; he invited himself, which takes away Alana's ability to feel good about inviting him. It was presumptuous and a little rude, am I right?" Jenny says, sort of nailing it.

"Exactly. There is just something that irks me about his not giving me the chance to be generous. And what if it would not have been a good idea for him to be here? He also didn't give me a chance to apologize for *not* being able to accommodate him, if that had been the case. He just made a pronouncement, and the rest of us have to obey His Majesty."

"I think you are wasting too much time and energy on it. The bottom line is that he is welcome; there is no reason for him not to be here, so either way, Patrick was going to be coming to dinner. So why on earth would you let your day get ruined? If the answer is nine, does it really matter if you get there by adding five and four or multiplying three by three?" Sara, turning everything into a black-and-white math equation.

Mama comes into the kitchen. "Table for eighteen, now. Goot luck. Chai." Eighteen is a sacred Jewish number, since the word *chai*, or life, adds up to eighteen. I got at least two dozen checks for eighteen dollars when I was bat mitzvahed. Mama is beaming, and I know that it makes her very happy that Patrick is coming. And Sara is right. I love this holiday, and letting something as stupid as the way Patrick weaseled into it bug me only hurts me. I vow to shake it off, and turn to take the cranberry sauce out of the fridge to take the chill off.

The last half hour before Thanksgiving dinner is an exercise in true brigade cooking. Sara takes on the mashed potatoes, which are really only perfect if made at the last minute, and lucky for us all, her potatoes are *killer*. Full of butter and cream and sour cream and chives, perfectly smooth and creamy and addictive. Jenny transfers cooked and cold dishes to pretty plates, garnishing as appropriate, and makes sure proper serving pieces are attached. Nat arranges the buffet dishes as she receives them while I carve the turkey and Mama makes the gravy. I am just putting the last slices of breast meat on the platter and basting the whole platter with a bit of butter emulsified into turkey stock, and spooning the juices that have gathered in the cutting board over the meat so that it all stays wonderfully moist, when I hear the doorbell, followed by loud, happy noises of greeting in the front room. Himself has arrived, and made some sort of entrance.

I bring the platter of turkey out, place it at the head of the buffet, and Mama follows with the old pockmarked pewter gravy boat. Patrick makes a beeline for my mom, kissing her on both cheeks. "Mama! Do you believe I had to order this horrible weather just so I could come be with you for Thanksgiving?" Give me a break. He surveys the room and the buffet. "You did not strike the mud with your face, Mama." I hate that he now knows enough parent-speak to throw her own weird saying at her like an expert. She laughs, blushes, and slaps his arm.

"Eet is Alana. By myself? It would be to break up some

firewood." I know it is in English, but frankly I have no idea what the hell they are saying to each other. He turns to me after I put the cranberry sauce next to the turkey.

"Alana-chicana." He kisses the top of my head, and then looks me up and down, taking in my chocolate brown corduroy skirt, pale blue cashmere V-neck sweater, and brown boots. My hair is down, and due to lack of humidity is actually behaving, settling into ringlets instead of frizz. I have my contacts in for a change, and am wearing a little makeup. "You look adorable. I forget that you're a girl." Great, thanks. "It's nice to see you out of the cargo pants and ponytail! And who knew you had those blue eyes under those glasses?" He's such a shit. We have been to more black-tie events than professional prom chaperones, and he always says the exact same thing. Usually right before he disappears to put his hand up the designer skirt of some set of Legs.

"I clean up okay," I say, biting back the "Fuck you" that is rising in my throat.

"You do, at that." He tugs my elbow and pulls me into the little nook between the kitchen and hallway. "Hey, honey, I just wanted to really thank you for letting me crash your holiday. I know it is probably a pain in the ass, and not what you were hoping for, but it really means a lot to me that you let me come."

I can feel myself soften. "It's okay. We never would have let you spend it alone."

"Well, alone isn't the issue, my phone was blowing up with offers all day, but I really needed to be somewhere I knew the food would be good. You know how it is with Thanksgiving. If the meal is disappointing it just sticks with you till Christmas! Remember when I went to Bob's house that year and they didn't have mashed potatoes? Or that ghastly deep-fried turkey? Plus, you know how crazy I am about food safety. Thanksgiving is a hotbed of potential food poisoning. Undercooked turkey, stuffing cooked in the bird just breeding bacteria, children of unknown hygiene touching the yams with their germy fingers. I knew you'd have everything perfect, delicious, and e-coli free." My neck spasms. He's here because of the flipping food. Not because he wants to spend the holiday with warm and welcoming people who have always treated him like family. Not because my sweet mama always calls him *zeen*, the Yiddish word for "son," and tries to be a surrogate mother to him, knowing he never really had one. Not because I am probably closer to him than any human being on the planet, and who else would he turn to on a day like today. Nope. Sir Conlon just wanted to guarantee he didn't end up somewhere with dry turkey and gluey gravy, or a serious case of the shits. Unbelievable.

"Glad to be of service. Want to grab a plate and we'll get you fed?" I give up.

My siblings get their gaggle of munchkins settled at the kids' end of the table with their plates, cutting things up into bite-size pieces, and filling glasses and sippy cups with milk and apple juice. Maria and Patrick are sent through the line as honored guests. I always go last; it is the nature of the chef to want to stand back, watch people pick and choose, hear the people who are already tucking in moan and groan in delight. In my pocket, I feel my phone vibrate. I have a text message.

Hope u r having a wonderful day with ur family, full of delicious & happy. I just wanted u 2 know that I'm thankful 4 having begun 2 get acquainted with u, & that I'm very much looking forward 2 Sat. nite. If u get home at a reasonable hour & r inclined, feel free 2 give me a call. RJ

And suddenly, every ounce of ick I was feeling melts away. I quickly text back.

Just getting ready 2 eat, all is good. Hope your day is quiet & happy. Am thankful 4 meeting u 2, & also looking forward 2 Sat. Will call when I get home. A

"To this wonderful family, who are so generous and special." Patrick is standing, glass raised, and everyone is quiet, even the kids. "I am very blessed to know each and every one of you, and I am very thankful for your company and your hospitality. And I am especially thankful for Alana, without whom I wouldn't be half the success or half the man that I am. Alana, I love you and want you to know that I am infinitely better for having you in my life, and I thank you for all you do for me personally and professionally. Cheers."

Everyone clinks glasses, Patrick makes important eye contact with me, and my mother beams and my father glowers suspiciously. Maria winks at me, takes a mouthful of stuffing, and rolls her eyes in ecstasy. The next forty minutes are a festival of soul eating. I know many immigrant families incorporate their traditional dishes into the Thanksgiving feast, but not my folks. Our menu is Norman Rockwell on crack. Turkey with gravy. Homemade cranberry relish and the jellied stuff from the can. Mashed potatoes, sweet potatoes with marshmallows, green bean casserole. Cornbread stuffing and buttery yeast rolls. The only nods to our heritage are mustard-seed pickled carrots and dill-cucumber salad, to have something cool and palate-cleansing on the plate. A crazy layered Jell-O dish, with six different colors in thin stripes, looking like vintage Bakelite.

Jeff and the girls show up just in time for desserts . . . apple pie, pumpkin pie, pecan bars, cheesecake brownies, and Maria's flan. He and Nat share a long hug and deep kiss, which tells me that he has had a long, clenched sort of day, and is ready to finally relax. Their girls, Lia and Rachel, are in matching pink frilly dresses and black patent Mary Janes, and the way that Nat is admiring them through gritted teeth tells me that this is not what she dressed them in before they headed to their grandparents' house.

We believe that Thanksgiving is as much about leftovers as the meal, so the extra fridge in the garage is already filled with bags prepacked with smaller versions of the complete meal already set to go. Mama and I roasted a second turkey yesterday, and we made double batches of everything, filling endless disposable plastic containers and making up the bags for everyone except me, as I will pack my own bag from the actual leftovers from tonight's meal.

After dinner, Patrick insists on being in charge of cleanup, and dons Mama's apron and a pair of yellow rubber gloves, much to the delight of the kids, whom he recruits for drying and putting-away duty. Mama and Papa relax in the den, a little worn-out from all the tumult, while my siblings break down the massive table arrangement, and get the folding chairs back into the attic. Maria and I pack up the rest of the food.

"'E is funny with the *ninos*," she muses. "Verrrrry much on their level! Maybe he would come do a guest class with the after-school prrrrrogram."

I think about this. "It's actually a good idea. I'll ask him this week. Did you find a teacher yet?"

"Yes, Melanie's partner, Kai, is going to teach the first group. 'E has been with her since the beginning, so 'e knows all about the nutrition."

"I've met him, he's amazing. And I think his energy will be perfect for the kids. Very smart. When do the classes start?"

"Januarrrrry. Thursday afternoons. Patrrrrick can do any class he wants from Febrrruary on."

"I'll get it on his schedule."

Patrick starts to chant like a deranged drill sergeant. "And, WIPE the front until it shines! Then WIPE the back like your own behinds!" Patrick is singing and conducting the six kids who are old enough to wield dish towels, all of whom are collapsing in laughter at his naughty song. "Make sure it's dry, or I'll tell you what! Your aunt Alana will kick your butt!"

I shake my head, and Maria laughs.

"You 'ave to admit, 'e has his moments!" She puts an arm around me and squeezes. I squeeze back.

"He certainly does." Pity they are few and far between.

Once things are cleaned up, the crowd disperses quickly. The kids are all punchy and past their bedtimes, Maria is determined to go home and do an hour on the elliptical before bed, and Patrick whispers in my ear that a certain young actress with whom he had a brief fling at the South Beach food and wine festival is apparently also stuck in town, and in need of entertaining.

But it doesn't faze me. I am eager to get home and walk Dumpling, and call RJ and hear his voice. And that eagerness is something I find that I am actually thankful for, and for the first time, not nervous about.

When I get home, Dumpling is sitting in his little bed, looking sort of odd, and not jumping up to greet me the way he usually does. As I get closer, I can see that all of the white fur sections on his little head are a strange orange color.

"Dumpling . . ."

I see a small spot on the rug. I lean down and touch it. It

is damp and a little sticky, and leaves an orange smear on my finger. I gingerly sniff it.

"Tomato?! What the?"

Then I see it halfway down the hallway. The large box of Pomi crushed tomato puree I had left on the counter. "Dumpling! What did you do?" I walk down the hallway and find the box, neatly chewed open and emptied of its contents, every corner of the silvery inside of the box licked clean to a mirrorlike finish. I suddenly realize that not only did he have to do a vertical leap of well over three feet to grab the box, but he would have had to stick his whole head into the box to eat it. No small feat, even with a miniature head. And after a quick look around, I also realize that the orange fur and that one spot on the rug are the only bits of evidence.

The dog has managed to eat twenty-eight ounces of crushed tomato puree out of a box and not make a mess in my apartment. I don't know if I am more pissed or impressed. And then I hear Dumpling get off his bed and come down the hallways toward me.

"Dumpling." I put on my serious unhappy voice. "Bad dog. BAD dog." And then I see the look on his face and realize that the after-effects of eating a twenty-sixth of his body weight in tomatoes is going to be punishment enough. No sooner do we get out of the front gate, than Dumpling makes a beeline for the space under the tree halfway up the block where he prefers to make his evening toilet, and befouls it in an explosive manner, made worse-looking for being highlighted by the accumulated snow. Poor pupper. I have a feeling it is going to be a long night for both of us. When he has completed his unfortunate business, complete with a little snowy butt scoot for good measure, we head back inside. I give him an Imodium, put some long-grain white rice in the rice cooker, and take some ground white-meat chicken out of the freezer to thaw. He'll need a day or two of a rice and chicken diet so that his tummy can settle down. I'll make enough to get us through the weekend. I change out of my skirt and sweater, and get into a pair of knit lounging pants and matching hoodie, from the Target Cashmiracle collection . . . feels like cashmere, but melts if you get too close to the stove. Don't ask how I know. I have four sets in black and charcoal gray, and they are my uniform when I work at home from November through April.

Dumpling sloppily drinks his bowl dry, and looks at me imploringly to refill it.

"More sodium than you are used to, huh?" I fill the bowl with water, and float two ice cubes in it, one of his favorite things, chasing the cubes around the bowl with his nose, slurping them up and spitting them back out until they are gone. When he is set, I grab the phone and check my messages.

"Alana, you are our *hero*!" It's Emily, and I am presuming her first Thanksgiving has been a success. "Everything worked like magic. Well, except for when I opened the cabinet above the stove and a glass fell out and shattered in an explosion sending shards of glass into the pumpkin soup, but don't worry we threw it out and made a new batch that wouldn't shred anyone's intestines. And everything was delicious. And everyone loved it. And everyone wants to come back next year. We have FLIPPED THE SCRIPT, and it is all due to you. Love you, John loves you, Mina and Lacey love you. . . . We are all SO DRUUUUUNK! And full of yummy. Call me tomorrow." Emily and her husband are estranged from both of their families, and have always ignored the holidays, sort of holing up and pretending they aren't happening.

But this year I suggested to her that Thanksgiving is right up her alley, a holiday all about food. Since she and John love to cook together and are trying to entertain more, I told her to host it herself and see if she could turn it back into a holiday she could like. Mina came with her dad. Lacey's folks are in Florida, and no way was she traveling Thanksgiving weekend, so she was available. A couple of friends of John's without local family. A true orphans' Thanksgiving, and apparently a wildly successful one at that. It makes me happy to think that Em and John have reclaimed the day, and hope it becomes a new tradition for them. I check my watch—nearly ten. I pick up the phone to see how RJ's day has been.

"Blissfully quiet and uneventful. I made myself a rolled turkey breast, some yeast rolls, steamed green beans, and a baked sweet potato. Had a day of football, rocked out a little on my guitar, took a long nap, and then made little turkey sandwiches on the leftover rolls. Indulged in some Chips Ahoy cookies, which for some reason hold a special place in my heart for no rational reason. Spoke to my folks and my sister and her family. And now I've just been watching TV and hoping you would call." There is nothing calculated or creepy about him saying this. He is matter-of-fact, and impeccably genuine. "And how was *your* day?"

"Mostly lovely. We ended up with Patrick last-minute, after his flight got cancelled, all the food was great, the kids were hilarious, and I am stuffed to the gills."

"Sounds lovely. Share the menu, please, I need to live vicariously."

And in this moment, I suddenly regret that I didn't invite him. Even though it would have been way too weird—who has a first date at Thanksgiving with your whole family? But we have spoken on the phone almost every day for the past three weeks, and every conversation flies by, no lulls, no awkwardness. I feel like we actually *know* each other. And I sort of hate that we couldn't figure out a way to meet in person sooner, because as much as I resented Patrick horning in on my family's day, I am equally sad that RJ spent his day alone, and for some reason, I feel like it would have been much more natural for him to be with us than it was for Patrick.

"Well, we roasted a turkey, of course. . . ."

I share the whole meal, we compare brine recipes, he tells me about the yeast rolls he made and they sound amazing. I cook up Dumpling's chicken meat while we are talking and pack it up with the rice. He tells me about his mom's pehic pie, essentially a pecan pie with half the pecans replaced with hickory nuts. I admit I've never tasted a hickory nut and he promises to rectify that. We talk about vacations we've taken, and places we are dying to go back to. I tell him about Dumpling's Houdini Tomato Adventure. He asks me to e-mail a picture of Dumpling, which I do, and love the sound of his laugh when he opens the attachment.

"You'll forgive me saying, but that dog looks like a parts bin!"

"I know. He's a little odd-looking."

"He seems to have quite the collection of dog feet." It's true. In the picture he is lying on his side, all four of his feet are gathered in front of him, and it doesn't look like they match at all. "But cute. And if they are ever going to make *Men in Black Four*, he's a shoo-in."

Before I even notice, it is nearly midnight.

"I suppose we should probably save something to talk about Saturday," I say, suppressing a yawn.

"I don't worry for us finding things to talk about. I was thinking one last meal at Terragusto on Addison before it closes for good, does that work for you?"

"I've heard good things, but haven't ever been. Perfect choice."

Dumpling and I take one more quick visit outside after RJ and I say our good nights. He still is showing signs of being a little poorly, but not as bad as it could have been, and I am hopeful we might make it through the night. When we get back inside I climb into bed, and Dumpling climbs up beside me, pawing aside the covers and settling himself with his head on the pillow. He smells like graham crackers. I rub his side.

"Dumpling, my love, you'll take this the right way, I hope . . . My fingers are crossed that in the near future, you might have to start sleeping in your own bed for a change."

Dumpling makes a noise that sounds very much like "har-rumph."

"You're right. I won't count my chickens."

But I can't help it. The chickens, they are begging to be counted, and the strongest, most self-reliant girl in the world would be hard-pressed not to at least indulge a little.

I lay in the dark, listening to Dumpling snore softly, full of good food and warm feelings and a pervading sense of potential and possibility. And I am thankful.

11

What are you wearing?" Barry asks.

"I'm wearing a black swishy skirt, that charcoal sweater I have with the matte beading around the collar and cuffs, and my black kitten-heel boots."

"Hair up or down?"

"Up in the front so I'm not moving it out of my face all night."

"Good. Nervous?"

"Nope."

"Really?"

"Not really, my tummy is all aflutter, and I'm praying that it behaves itself and doesn't pull a no-gallbladder moment during dinner. I mean, mostly I'm excited. I feel like I'm going to meet an old friend. We've been e-mailing and talking for like a month and a half. And we've both been really honest about wanting to be actual friends, so I feel like this is just meeting a friend for dinner. I don't feel any pressure on the romantic side, I think we are both just figuring if there is chemistry there is chemistry, and if not, we still have met someone fabulous and interesting that we genuinely want to know. On the other hand, that of course makes me really want there to be chemistry. And I know that he can't be as perfect as he appears to be, but then again, neither can I. So what if he really is fantastic and then I'm not his flavor?"

"Or what if you are just what he has been craving?"

"I'm just trying to focus on the friendship thing and to be myself and to hope that he is as honest about who he is as I have been about who I am, and let the rest of it be what it will be."

"Which is about the most romantic thing you could possibly say," Barry says, sighing, as he is currently between paramours. "Que sera, sera. Of course, I'm sure your upcoming trip this week is helping keep things in perspective."

I am headed for New York on Monday for three days; the James Beard Awards are on Monday night and Food TV is having a big party Tuesday for their five-year anniversary. Patrick has more secret meetings that he is dealing with, still playing all mysterious and teasing me about telling me when it is time for me to know, and I can just sense that there is a big bucket of shit dangling over my head, and I'm just waiting for it to fall on me. But despite a lovely room that they have booked for me, which I will use as a Midtown pit-stop location, I am actually staying with Bruce in his Chelsea apartment, so there will be three nights of great sex, a fancy dress-up party, and with Patrick off in his meetings, some time to hang out with Bennie.

"It's not hurting."

"And what happens with Bruce if this RJ person is hot in addition to being full of friendship?"

"Bruce knows that our thing is casual. If a miracle happens, and in addition to our intellectual chemistry, RJ and I are mutually attracted to each other, and that chemistry is realized in a way that makes us want to eventually be together exclusively, then Bruce and I will be friends and colleagues with no naked. But let's be frank, that is a lot to ask. I'm going to have dinner tonight with a new pal. I'm excited to meet him in person, and I have to try to have every faith that we will have a good time, that the food and wine will be delicious, and that I will be glad that I went. Beyond that, as my mother would say, it is written with a pitchfork on the water."

"Which means?"

"Nothing is certain or defined. Not RJ, not Bruce, not me."

"Well, I hope you will be okay with my hoping that RJ turns out to be as handsome as Cary Grant and twice as charming."

"I'll put on my best Rosalind Russell if he is, you can be certain."

"Okay. I'm going to bed early, as I have to pick up your pooch tomorrow morning to head to Children's Memorial and no kid likes a hungover storyteller. Don't forget to hang a sock on the door if you have company!"

He is so silly. "How about I just do the chain on the inside."

"Probably more subtle."

"Indeed. I'm not going to sleep with him. If he is amazing and there's spark, I'm taking it slow. My ho days are behind me. I'm back to being a third- or fourth-date girl. So I will see you in the morning."

"Okay, princess. Have a wonderful time tonight. I can't wait to hear all about it!"

"Smooches."

I check my watch. Seven. Terragusto is only about ten minutes away; I'll give myself twenty in case of traffic and parking issues, especially since I have never been there before. I'd always rather be early and wait in the car than late and frazzled. Especially since I am one of those people whose sweat glands hate to stop once they start, so if I am rushed, I get all schvitzy and that is not a good look. I do one more check in the mirror. The outfit is a favorite, nice enough, but also comfortable. Hair is staying fairly manageable; makeup is there but not overdone. I'm wearing the diamond studs Patrick bought me three years ago, and my watch, but no other jewelry. I look like a pretty cute version of myself, but I don't look like it took me forever to get ready. Which, as any girl knows, means it took me forever to get ready. One more slick of lip gloss, and I throw my coat on. Dumpling gets up and starts hopping in place.

"Uh-uh. You already went out. I'm going to have dinner with a nice man and you are going to stay here and behave yourself. No parties. No girls. And no looking for doggie porn on the Internet. If I get charged for *Debbie Does Dalmatians* one more time, you are in trouble, bud." I lean over and rub his head, and head out.

I find a parking space right in front, and check the clock. Seven twenty. A little early, but not enough to hang out in the car. I open my purse and take out my phone. Patrick is not invited tonight. I put the phone in the glove compartment, get out, and head into the restaurant, a small space with maybe twelve tables, all full. That nice buzz you get in a place where people are eating and drinking well, but not shouty loud. Amazing smells. The owner is closing it soon to open a new place, and even though I have just walked in, I'm a little sad. About three tables into the dining room, a man stands up.

He is tall, broad-shouldered. He has light hair buzzed very short, cool rectangular glasses. He is wearing a sport coat over a black turtleneck sweater, black slacks. His face is youngish, boyishly cute, and he is looking at me and smiling warmly, hazel eyes crinkled up and sparkling. RJ. I walk over and he greets me by taking both my hands in his and leaning in to kiss me on the cheek.

"Well, hello there," he says, in a voice that has become as familiar to me as those of my best friends.

"Hi." I smile back at him. He helps me off with my coat, and pulls my chair out for me before sitting back down across from me.

"Can I just say, you are even more beautiful than your pictures."

"Thank you. So are you!" I tease him, since he never did post any pictures on EDestiny, and by the time we were speaking it seemed really shallow to ask him to send me some. I tried doing some more in-depth online stalking with Mina's help, but he didn't have any pictures on the web anywhere, and when I finally figured out how to find his Facebook profile, listed under RJChiTown, there was a picture of him when he was six, cute and impish, but as we know cute at six doesn't guarantee cute at forty-nine.

"I am the least photogenic person you will ever meet. I promise, you should be happy you never saw a picture before tonight. I always look like I'm in gastric distress or should be living under a bridge with some goats."

I laugh. "It can't be that bad."

"Oh it is, trust me. I hope you don't mind, I took the liberty." He points to a champagne bucket on the table, reaches in and pulls out a bottle of Pierre Gimonnet Premier Cru. I'm a sucker for good bubbles, and this is one that a sommelier recommended to me last year for a dinner party, but it was more than I wanted to spend. Generous, this RJ.

"These are my favorite kinds of liberties. I've wanted to taste this one for a while."

RJ pours a glass for me, and one for himself. He has big, strong-looking hands, but they move with smooth grace. He raises his glass to me. "To what I believe is a wonderful new friendship, and what I hope might become more."

"I'll drink to that."

"I'll drink to you." We both sip the wine, and I am blown away. Perfect balance of mineral stoniness and fruit at the back. Tiny bubbles that are gently tickly. I feel like the champagne is kissing me.

"This is delicious."

"It's a good one. I always believe in starting with bubbles, and then thought we'd switch to red with dinner if that's okay with you." He gestures toward the other bottle on the table, a 1993 Barolo from a producer I am not familiar with.

"I'm in your capable hands. As long as it's okay that I'm not going to be able to drink half of both these bottles, I'm kind of a lightweight." What I am is a girl with acid reflux and no gall bladder who is pushing forty, so I just can't party like I used to. More than three or four glasses of wine and I'm a sad girl in the morning, not to mention I'm driving.

"The kitchen will be glad of whatever we send back; don't feel like you have to drink a lot, frankly I much prefer someone who doesn't overindulge. Especially someone who drove here."

"We're in agreement about that. Have you looked at the menu? Anything exciting?"

"Well, we can order a la carte if you like, but they do a nice dinner for two here where we order two appetizers and two pastas and then share a main and a dessert. Sort of like a tasting menu."

"Oh, let's do that! More fun that way."

We look at the menu, which is simple and lovely rustic Italian. He asks which items appeal to me most and when I tell him, he laughs. "Those are all the things that were speaking to me as well."

"Well, we're going to have to stop being surprised that we have everything in common eventually."

"Something tells me that you are never going to stop surprising me." And while out of any other guy's mouth it would have been a little much, and out of Patrick's it would have been nauseating, when RJ says it, it makes me feel just wonderful.

The waiter comes over and RJ orders for us. The more I look at him, the cuter I think he is. He has such a sweet face and a great smile, and even behind his glasses his eyes are just twinkling. And he looks at me like he can't believe his luck. I can't remember the last time a man looked at me like that while still clothed. And my whole spine relaxes and we start to talk.

I know that the food was amazing, a salad and some other antipasti. A couple great pastas. A braised pork shank that I made a mental note to try to replicate. A light-as-air hazelnut mousse. I know that the Barolo was the perfect thing with the meal, and that the chef came out to thank us after we sent a third of the bottle back to the kitchen along with the rest of the champagne. I know that we lingered over cappuccinos. That we seemed to talk about everything and nothing. And that when we looked up, we were the only people left in the place and it was after eleven.

"I think we had better let them close, huh?" I said, looking at the staff gathered at the other end of the room.

"I had no idea it had gotten so late. We should definitely go."

I stood up and he was right beside me, helping me on with my coat. We walked outside into the freezing air.

"I'd like to walk you to your car, if that is all right."

"I'd like that." He offered me his arm, and we walked two steps. "Here I am."

"Ha-ha. Very funny."

"Sorry, couldn't resist. Thank you, RJ, this was such a wonderful evening."

"It was more than wonderful, it was extraordinary. I can't believe we were here for four hours. It just flew by. I'd really like to do it again, if that would be okay."

"I would love that. I am back from New York Thursday."

"So, maybe next weekend?"

"Absolutely."

"We can firm it up tomorrow when we can look at our calendars. Will you do me a favor? Call me when you get home so that I know you're safe?"

"I will, promise."

He walks me around to the side of my car, and opens my door for me. "Thank you for a lovely evening, Alana." And he leans in and kisses me softly on the lips. No tongue, the lightest of pressure, sweet and simple and not insistent.

"Thank you. Good night." I sit down and buckle in.

"Drive safe. And don't forget to call," he says, and closes my door.

As I wend my way home, I'm blown away by how simply perfect the evening was. The restaurant had been the ideal choice, the food delicious, the wines extraordinary. But frankly? He could have taken me to McDonald's, and if he had smiled that smile and twinkled those eyes at me, we would have been there for four hours too. I can't process how comfortable I feel with him, like I could tell him anything, and what is more, that I never once the whole night felt the need to edit, pretty up, or in any way manage what I told him. I was 100 percent myself, and he made me feel like that was more than fine, it was spectacular. He complimented me consistently, but I never felt like he was feeding me a line.

He laughed at my jokes and funny stories, with true delight. I feel like I just spent the last four hours in a deep hug. Which scares the bejesus out of me. I can't just blindly trust that he was as into me as I was into him. I can't assume that the spark I felt was mutual. We spent so much time being so open about the idea of making a new friend, I don't have anything to hang my feelings on. It is entirely possible that he is just pursuing this on the friendship tip, and now that he is real and not theoretical, disappointment is out of my hands.

I pull into my space in the back, grab my phone out of the glove compartment, and walk up the gangway to the front of the building. It shows I have new messages, but I'm not in the mood. As soon as I get to the front window, I can hear Dumpling bark twice, to let me know that he knows I'm here. By the time I get the door open, he is spinning and barking and sneezing all at the same time.

"Okay, okay, I know, let's go!" I stand aside and Dumping shoots out the door. While he is peeing, I grab my cell and call RJ. He answers on the first ring.

"Are you home safe and sound?"

"I am home safe and sound, and walking the dog, who is peeing so much I feel like he is going to start to deflate."

"Good boy, him have to pee a *lot*," RJ says in a silly voice that makes me giggle.

"Now he is walking up and down the block marking every tree and bush and gate post he can find. This is apparently Dumpling's world and we're all just living in it."

"As it should be. I just have to say, Alana, tonight was just one of the best nights of my life. The hours just flew by, and even though my expectations were very high, based on how great our phone conversations have been, tonight just exceeded them. And I know we said that no matter what, we will be friends, and I hope and trust that is true, but I also want you to know that I hope there's a possibility we're headed in a different direction. Because I could look into your eyes forever." My breath practically stops. And I want to jump up and down a little bit.

"I know. Tonight was really sort of magical. Probably the best first date I've ever had. Maybe the best first date anyone has ever had. And I'm hopeful about where we might be headed, but also I feel like tonight I had dinner with someone I am going to know and enjoy forever, and that is just as important to me."

"Good. So, I'll call you tomorrow and we'll find a time next weekend to get together again?"

I take a deep breath. Every dating book would tell me to stay cool, play coy, make him work for it. But I don't want a relationship that is work. I like that I feel I can be honest with him.

"We can talk tomorrow and figure it out, unless maybe you would want to meet for brunch?"

"I like the way you think. What time and where?"

Whew. "How about eleven at Four Moon Tavern?"

"I'll see you there. Good night, sweet Alana."

Dumpling and I head inside, and I change into my pajamas. Just as I am settling in on the couch, my phone rings.

"Tell. Me. *Everything.*"

"Hey, Bennie, was just getting ready to call you."

"How was it, start at the beginning and DO NOT STOP."

So I do. I tell her everything. Every sip, every bite, every laugh. And when I finish, she is quiet for a moment and then she says the scariest, most wonderful thing.

"You're going to marry that man." She is very matter-of-fact. And not in that supportive, "Yay, girlfriend, you had a good date" way. She says it as a basic statement of reality. She says it like she is telling me that the sky is blue, that the earth is round, that cheesecake is a perfect food. And even though I know I am about to deny it vehemently, there is a little nugget of joy in my heart that I don't even want to acknowledge.

I force myself to not just agree with her and start planning the happy ever-after. "Let's not jump to any big conclusions. We had a great first date, maybe even the greatest first date since the beginning of time, and I am looking very much forward to a second date, and maybe more. But I can't let myself get too excited about this. You KNOW how I am. I turn everything into some stupid movie in my head, and then I'm disappointed."

"Well then, don't overthink, but don't deny yourself the pleasure of the fantasy either. We're all waiting for the great happy-ever-after, and anyone who says different is a liar. But mark my words. There are two things I can predict with frightening accuracy. People who are about to get pregnant and people who are about to get married. You listen to me, baby girl; you are going to marry that man. There is something different in your voice tonight, something has changed, and I happen to believe that it means that you have found the person you are supposed to be with. You can choose to believe it too or not as you like, but I know what I know."

"Okay, then, I'm glad that's settled. If it's all right with you I'll still do the whole dating thing for a while, though. You know, unless he proposes at brunch tomorrow."

"Good girl. So, more important, what are we doing this week?"

We make some plans to go to some galleries and do some shopping and eating. It is after one when we finally hang up, and I crawl into bed exhausted. My phone is blinking, reminding me that I have messages. I hit my voice mail button and enter my password.

"Alana, it's Patrick. We have a problem. Andrea fucked up the New York plans, and now I don't have a room, so it looks like we are bunking together in some tiny closet. I'm not really sure what to do about her. I mean, this shit just cannot happen."

Beep. Fuck.

"Hey, it's me. I'm thinking that I have to have a come-to-Jesus meeting with Andrea, I mean, it's the little stuff that can just add up to not really fulfilling your job, you know? What do you think? Should I give her a good talking-to on Monday before we leave?"

Beep.

"Where the fuck are you? Seriously. The more I think about it, the more I think that Andrea just doesn't have what it takes. Might be time for a change. Call me back."

Beep.

"Okay, here is where I am. I think I'm going to have to just fire her. I don't have time to constantly be after her to do the most basic things. How hard is it to book a fucking hotel room? She booked YOU a hotel room. She called to confirm YOUR reservation. I mean WHAT THE FUCK? Call me."

Beep.

Sniff. "Alana? It's, um, Andrea. Patrick just called me." *Sniff.* "And, um"—*sniff*—"I'm fired. Which, you know"—*sniff*—"shouldn't really surprise me, you know?" *Sniff.* "It *is* Patrick. But um"—*sniff*—"I'm not really sure what to do now. I don't want to bother you"—*sniff*—"especially on a weekend, but can you um"—*sniff*—"call me tomorrow? I really need to talk." *Sniff.* "Okay, bye."

Beep. Godfucking damnit.

"Hey, Alana, don't really know where you are or what you're doing, but seriously, wouldn't hurt to check your phone now and then. Andrea is out. You'll have to pick up her stuff till I find someone new. Emergency meeting tomorrow. I'll come to your place around ten."

Beep. Shit. Shitshitshitshitshit. Can't I have ONE NIGHT? One night where I get to go out to dinner and have a lovely time and come home and dish with a girlfriend and just go to sleep happy with nothing crappy hanging over my head?

I reach for my laptop. I send Andrea an e-mail telling her to sit tight and not panic, that I will try to smooth things out with Patrick, and that if I can't, I will help her find a new job. I send RJ an e-mail explaining that a work emergency has come up and asking if we can make our brunch a late lunch instead, or even an afternoon coffee, figuring that I'm going to need at least two hours to deal with Patrick. I send Bruce an e-mail saying that it is looking like our plans are going to have to change, since Patrick and I would now apparently be sharing a room, which will make it impossible to not sleep there. There is a teeny part of me that doesn't really mind things getting blocked where Bruce is concerned. Not that it wouldn't have been fun, and no sane woman would purposely skip three nights of great sex, but even though RJ and I are a long way from exclusivity, jumping into the bed of another man this second is just not where my head or heart are at. Although, it would maybe help me keep myself a little realistic.

It is well after three before I can finally shut my head off enough to sleep, and even then, it is fitful. I feel like I spend the whole night checking the clock.

Andrea wakes me at eight, still weepy, and explains that

the hotel screwed up the reservation in the insanity of managing so many famous food people and their entourages. And that she has copies of the e-mails she sent clearly booking him a suite and me a room, but only the room got booked. She had found two other suites for him in different hotels, and the hotel promised that the first cancellation would be his, but that he was adamant about having to stay in the same place with everyone else. Patrick hadn't even listened to her; he had just railed about her incompetence and told her to have her stuff cleared out before he got back from New York. I had her forward me the e-mail and asked very pointedly if she wanted me to get her unfired or not.

"I don't think so, Alana. I'd never be able to relax and just do my job. As upset as I was last night, and I'm still weirdly residually emotional, I also feel like a weight has been lifted. I need a job where I am appreciated and treated with respect."

Crap. I really like Andrea, and she's been good for Patrick, whether he knows it or not. This is going to suck for me. "How would you feel about assisting a writer?" Emily has finally reached a place in her career where she actually needs help, since she is writing a book a year for Princess Drunkypoo, freelance magazine articles, and just signed her first book deal for her own work under her own name. That on top of the huge mansion she and John just bought and are renovating. She is in need of someone to manage her life and take a bunch of stuff off her hands.

"Anyone sane."

"One of my best pals. You'll love her. And she has never had a personal assistant before, so you'll be able to train her to treat you right."

Andrea laughs. "I'll send you my CV; feel free to give it to anyone you think would want me."

"Will do. And when I get back from New York we'll go to The Violet Hour and have cocktails."

"That's a date."

I e-mail Emily telling her I just found her the perfect assistant, and to call me later for details. I get an e-mail from RJ saying that he hopes nothing is too tragic, that he is just doing life maintenance stuff today, and that I should just call him when my work stuff is done and he will be delighted to meet me whenever. And Bruce e-mails to say that he feels like he has a head cold coming on anyway, so maybe it is better if we don't try to make private time. I try to ignore how relieved I am at the contents of both of these e-mails, and get ready to spend the next few hours managing the world's biggest petulant infant, and hope that the shitstorm that is likely on the horizon is brief and easily survivable.

12

Hey, how is the work going?" RJ asks, his call a welcome break from my work fog. It's been a Sunday morning full of playing catch-up, not at all weekend-y, and deeply annoying, so hearing his voice is a wonderful distraction.

"Fine. I've got about five or six more hours I want to try to get done today. But I think I have found a new assistant for Patrick, so if they have a good meeting tomorrow, I might be able to get back to just enough work for three people instead of five. What are you up to?"

"I was wondering if I might convince you to take a break for precisely two hours and twenty minutes."

"Do tell!"

"So remember that movie we were talking about the other day at lunch? *Out of the Past*?"

"I do."

"Well, a copy arrived yesterday from Netflix, and I have a lovely bottle of bubbles, so I thought you might let me come over for afternoon champagne and snacks and a movie if I promise to leave right after it is finished and let you get back to work."

He is so dreamy. "That sounds perfect, and I could use a break, my head is all fuzzy."

Normally, this would be my cue to frantically primp and prep and try to get super cute while crazily tidying the apartment. But not with RJ. I'm in one of my Target outfits, hair in a ponytail, glasses on, no makeup, and the house is what the house is. And I don't feel one bit of pressure to change any of it. Not because I don't want to impress him, or because somehow he isn't worthy. But because RJ won't mind, and I love that I know this about him, and I love even more that I feel so comfortable with him that I don't feel the need to go all tornado on myself. I know that he would feel bad if he thought that I would waste time and energy on stuff like that; he likes me just the way I am.

It's been a lovely couple of weeks. We had a delicious late lunch after my insane Patrick meeting, where he listened to all my work bullshit like a trooper and was completely understanding. And was equally understanding when, after three whirlwind days in New York, I returned completely swamped by work, limiting us to one brief date at the Art Institute, which was interrupted and cut short by another of Patrick's manufactured emergencies.

"Studio. Right now," he said when I answered quickly, my phone shockingly loud in the middle of the Modern Wing Fischli and Weiss exhibit.

"Patrick, I'm at the—"

"You're at the STUDIO in FIFTEEN MINUTES."

"Fine." I turn to RJ. "I, um."

"Work thing?"

"Yeah. I'm so sorry."

"It's okay, things come up." But I could tell he was disappointed.

"Things should not come up like this, but you are very kind to understand."

"You're worth it."

He had said it with conviction, making me feel even worse,

and not worthy of the sentiment. This is going to be one of the reasons he eventually decides I'm totally not dateable.

Patrick's frantic emergency at the studio? Paint color. Over the weekend the set and props people repainted the studio kitchen. Just a freshening up of the same color it has always been, a deep, saturated, slightly greenish brown that reads great on camera, and makes everything in front of it really pop. But Patrick was apparently convinced they had switched the color on him.

"It looks like shit. Actual shit. I took a shit this very color this morning."

"Patrick, I can't speak to your bowels, but this is the same color it has ALWAYS been."

"Nope. They switched it."

"No, they didn't. And even if they did, exactly what do you expect I should do about it tonight?"

We went back and forth, and finally I grabbed an old still from his office where he was posed in the kitchen with Michelle Obama, who had come on the show with a box of produce from the White House garden to promote her healthy eating campaign. I held it up to the wall. Same color.

"See?"

"Something is off. I just know it."

"Your brain is off. And you ruined my evening, by the way."

"You were at a museum." He says the word with utter distain, as if I were somewhere unfortunate. I haven't told him about RJ yet, especially since we met on EDestiny. He'll just give me crap about it, and I'm trying to just be mellow. I also haven't told my family. No need to get everyone's hopes up; its hard enough not to get my hopes up.

"I was having a nice evening, and had reservations at Terzo

Piano, so you get to call Tony and tell him why I blew him off
when I'm pretty sure he had Meg ready to make it special for
me." Tony Mantuano is the executive chef at the elegant restaurant in the Art Institute Modern Wing and both he and his chef
de cuisine, Meg Sahs, are friends.

"I'll do you one better, we'll call them up and go over there
now, my treat."

Which is how I ended up enjoying my romantic dinner
with my idiot boss instead of RJ.

Lucky for me, RJ just let it slide. We have continued to
talk every day, and the more time I spend getting to know
him, the more I like him and the more attracted to him
I become. So far our passion has been limited to just kissing. He is a perfect Southern gentleman, and is not applying
any pressure on me. And I'm finding that the slow, luxurious
pace of true courting suits me to a tee. My desire for him is
building alongside my trust and our friendship, and I really
hope that when we do take that step, that it is as good as
I want it to be. Which, of course, makes me pretty sure that
it will be horrible and disappointing, or he will turn out to
have weird fetishes, or we'll just be out of sync and the whole
thing will lead to our breakup.

I tidy up my computer a bit, and clear the detritus off the
coffee table. Dumpling starts barking, not his traditional bark
of greeting, but deeper and more growly, with a tinge of actual
menace. "Stop that, boy, it's just RJ."

I walk to the door and open it. "Hello, beautiful." RJ leans
over and kisses me. Yum.

"Hello, you." I kiss him back.

He looks deeply in my eyes, holding me to him with one
arm. "You look adorable and cozy. Perfect for a Sunday afternoon movie. And I have . . . What the—?" he says, looking

down. Where Dumpling is casually and proudly taking a piss on his leg.

"DUMPLING! BAD BOY! GO. TO. YOUR. BED. RIGHT NOW! Oh my god, RJ, I'm so sorry, he's never . . . I mean, I just . . ."

Then we both start to laugh. "Well, that is some greeting."

"That is just the worst thing ever. RJ, I don't know what to say." Dumpling turns with a sniff and walks over to his bed and flops down, glaring at RJ with what can only be described as contempt. "Dumpling, you are a VERY BAD BOY." I have never been so mortified.

RJ touches my arm. "It's really okay. Dogs don't necessarily love me on first meeting." He hands me a large shopping bag. "Any chance you have an extra pair of sweat pants lying around?"

"Of course." I am gobsmacked. I put the bag on the kitchen counter, and go to fetch him a pair of pants. I bring them out to him, and motion him to the front bathroom so he can change. While he is gone, I unpack the bag. On top, a small bouquet of flowers, deep pink peonies mixed with pale pink tea roses. A bottle of Vilmart pink champagne, already chilled. Smooth chevre, sharp cheddar, caramel-y aged Gouda. Three kinds of sausage. Two kinds of olives. Cornichons, those tiny puckery pickles that I am addicted to. Marcona almonds. A pear, an apple, and a small bunch of grapes. A bar of dark chocolate.

And a bag of organic dog treats. I look over at Dumpling, who is pouting on his bed. Dumb dog. And with RJ so excited to meet him and bringing him treats.

I get out a platter and some small bowls.

"Well, I don't think this is going to be my most fashionable day," RJ says behind me. I turn and can't help but laugh. My sweatpants hit him mid-calf.

"Heather gray manpris are all the rage."

"Well, I guess I should be grateful that my jeans are so absorbent, saved the shoe. Don't suppose you have laundry?"

"I do, in fact. Please allow me." I reach for the pants. He hands them over and I head up the hall to the washer-dryer, and toss them in. By the time I get back RJ has managed to arrange the nibbles artfully.

"Thank you for all of this, especially the flowers. They're so lovely."

"Well, they made me think of you. I seem to remember you said something at some point about peonies." This man remembers everything.

"They are my favorite flower." I slide my arms around his waist and tilt my head up, and he obliges me with a deep and thrilling kiss.

We bring all the goodies to the living room and arrange them on the table. I put the DVD in the player, while RJ pours the champagne.

"To making you play hooky, even just for a couple of hours."

"If this is how you make me play hooky, I'm in whenever you like!" We sip, and the bubbles go straight up my nose in the best possible way. "I really do want to apologize about Dumpling, I have never seen him do anything even remotely like that. I don't know where it came from!"

"Really, don't worry about it. I had a friend bring her old dog to my house once, and while we were looking at something in the garden, he somehow got locked in the bathroom and totally panicked and pissed everywhere and shat himself, and then got even more panicked and was apparently just running in circles in the bathroom peeing and pooping. By the time we came back in the house and heard him, my bathroom looked like a sewer line had exploded."

"Oh NO!" I am laughing at the very thought.

"Oh YES. And I? Only have ONE bathroom. In retrospect, a little pee on the leg is not so bad."

"Shh. Don't give him some challenge."

"Hey, he's adorable. And if you were my person, I'd be sure that any interloper who showed up was made perfectly aware that he was being watched, and that you would be protected at all costs."

"You keep saying things like that and plying me with champagne and flowers and delicious snacks, and I could be persuaded to be your person."

He leans over and kisses me deeply, sending shocks of electricity right down into my toes. "I'm counting on it."

By the time the movie is over, we have decimated a good percentage of the platter, the bottle is empty, and RJ is back in his freshly cleaned pants, smelling of the dryer.

"Is the dog still on lockdown, or can I try to make up with him?"

"You are welcome to try."

RJ walks over to the kitchen and picks up the bag of treats he brought, opening it up and taking a couple out. Then he comes back over to the living room and sits beside me on the couch. "Dumpling, c'mere, boy. Get a treat." He pats the couch next to him and holds up the treat. Dumpling rises from his bed, stretches a bit, and walks over to the couch. "Good boy. Let's be pals." RJ holds the treat down to him, and he leans over and sniffs it before taking it in his mouth. "Good boy, that's a good boy. Want another?" Dumpling takes the second treat and wolfs it down, allowing RJ to pet his head. Then he jumps up on the couch and wiggles his weird little misshapen self right in between us. RJ laughs. "He's just jealous. And that's fine by me."

"Oh really, why is that?"

"Because it means he thinks there is something to be jealous of, and I hope he's right."

RJ gets up, pats Dumpling one more time on the head, and I stand to walk him to the door.

"So, I'm sure this is either early or late or presumptuous or something, but I was wondering if you had plans for New Year's."

"Well, I do have plans for New Year's Day with my family, but no firm plans for New Year's Eve yet." Which is a lie. I am supposed to spend New Year's Eve at Patrick's annual party, to which I was going to invite RJ, but if he has other ideas, I'm more than willing to blow Patrick off. He usually ends up luring me into the kitchen and I spend the whole night whipping up extra food in uncomfortable shoes.

"Some friends of mine are having a small dinner party, and I would love it if you would come with me."

YAY! "I would love to come with you."

"Good. So I've got the last of my work travel stuff this week, and then I head to Tennessee to see the family for Christmas, but I'll be back on the twenty-sixth. Maybe we can sneak in another date between then and New Year's?" My kiss is all the answer he needs on that, and I watch him walk down my front steps and out to his car.

Sigh. I turn around and look at Dumpling, who is preening on the couch as if he has done something to be proud of.

"You're still on my list, buddy boy. And make no mistake. At this point, if you challenge that man, you just might lose."

He looks at me as if to say, "Bring it."

I take the platter over to the kitchen, and discover a card sitting on the counter. I open it. On the front is a picture of a heart and the words *From the bottom of mine.*

Alana—

Just a little note to thank you for coming into my life. I'm romantic enough to want to believe in magic or "it" or whatever describes a priori rightness, but pragmatic enough not to bank on it. I do know that I've never felt more naturally comfortable with or attuned to anyone else. So, whatever eventually transpires between us, I don't ever want you to not be a part of my life. Call it luck or effort or both, but we each have pretty good lives independent of each other. And I don't ever want to impinge on that for you. I do know that you take me to another level of happiness, and for that, I thank you. I hope you have a great year coming and I hope to be a part of it.

RJ

P.S. My handwriting is TERRIBLE! I write like the unabomber!

And he does, sort of, but I don't care. I hold the card to my heart. And I try to focus on the deep-down broken part of me that does still believe in happy-ever-after, and no shoes dropping, and think, *yes.*

13

"What time is your future husband picking you up?" Bennie asks, continuing to claim that her premonition about me and RJ is going to come true.

"About seven, so I have three hours to get ready."

"Are you so excited?"

"I am, but also a little nervous."

"RJ never makes you nervous. What's up?"

"I'm more nervous about meeting his friends, and you know how I get about dinner parties with people who don't know about my stupid food stuff."

Bennie laughs. "For a chef, you do have some serious limitations."

"I know."

It should be mentioned that I am very oddly picky about my food. I've never been one of those chefs who would just eat anything, and some of my issues can be enormously problematic.

Without putting too fine a point on it, there is a lot of food that I don't eat. A list the existence of which I hate to acknowledge, a list of things widely touted as so delectable that people think of them as the pinnacle of perfection. And I'm not allergic to anything, and I don't have political agendas against how the foods are attained or prepared, and I'm not restricted by religious beliefs.

I just don't like 'em.

Now, I don't think you need to be Andrew Zimmern to effectively fit yourself into the foodie category. I know plenty of serious chefs and gourmands who aren't going to tuck into insects and four-year-old putrefied shark. But despite having once eaten two live termites (a story for another day), my issue isn't with extreme eating. It's with stuff that most people find delicious, and I'm always afraid of that moment with someone who doesn't know me when I have to tell them the stuff I don't eat.

It would be like having to tell someone that, while you happily acknowledge your sex addiction, you aren't interested in S&M, porn, toys, erotica, threesomes, and will only do half of the positions in the Kama Sutra. Your street cred would suffer significantly.

Same for me. I'm a trained *chef* for the love of Pete. I have more than seventy herbs and spices stocked in my cabinets. I have fourteen kinds of vinegar in my pantry. I am prepared, by virtue of a good stock of staples, to make a hearty, delicious meal at the drop of a hat. I believe in making homemade stock, in using top-notch ingredients prepared to best heighten their natural goodness, and that good food made with your heart is one of the truest forms of love. I subscribe to eight cooking magazines. I write cookbooks with Patrick, and collect other people's cookbooks and read them like novels. I have been all over the world cooking and eating and training under extraordinary chefs. And the two food guys I would most like to go on a road trip with are Anthony Bourdain and Michael Ruhlman, both of whom I have met, and who are genuinely awesome guys, hysterically funny and easy to be with. But as much as I want to be the Batgirl in that trio, I fear that I would be woefully unprepared. Because an essential part of the food experience that those two enjoy the most is stuff that, quite frankly, would make me ralph.

I don't feel overly bad about the offal thing. After all, variety meats seem to be the one area that people can get a pass on. With the possible exception of foie gras, which I wish like heckfire I liked, but I simply cannot get behind it, and nothing is worse than the look on a fellow foodie's face when you pass on the pâté. I do love tongue, and off cuts like oxtails and cheeks, but please, no innards.

Blue or overly stinky cheeses, cannot do it. Not a fan of raw tomatoes or tomato juice—again I can eat them, but choose not to if I can help it. Ditto, raw onions of every variety (pickled is fine, and I cannot get enough of them cooked), but I bonded with Scott Conant at the James Beard Awards dinner, when we both went on a rant about the evils of raw onion. I know he is often sort of douchey on television, but he was nice to me, very funny, and the man makes the best freaking spaghetti in tomato sauce on the planet.

I have issues with bell peppers. Green, red, yellow, white, purple, orange. Roasted or raw. Ick. If I eat them raw I burp them up for days, and cooked they smell to me like old armpit. I have an appreciation for many of the other pepper varieties, and cook with them, but the bell pepper? Not my friend.

Spicy isn't so much a preference as a physical necessity. In addition to my chronic and severe gastric reflux, I also have no gallbladder. When my gallbladder and I divorced several years ago, it got custody of anything spicier than my own fairly mild chili, Emily's sesame noodles, and that plastic Velveeta-Ro-Tel dip that I probably shouldn't admit to liking. I'm allowed very occasional visitation rights, but only at my own risk. I like a gentle back-of-the-throat heat to things, but

I'm never going to meet you for all-you-can-eat buffalo wings. Mayonnaise squicks me out, except as an ingredient in other things. Avocado's bland oiliness, okra's slickery slime, don't even get me started on runny eggs.

I know. It's mortifying.

And beyond dreaming of a road trip with Tony and Michael, it makes situations like tonight fraught with potential for disaster. It's bad enough that so many people get freaked out by the idea of cooking for a chef, thinking we are going to judge them or be disappointed, when in fact, any chef is usually thrilled that someone wants to cook for them for a change. But the idea that I could sit at someone's lovely and thoughtfully planned dinner party pushing things around my plate like some picky child, it knots my stomach. At least RJ was very cool about it when I fessed up during one of our marathon phone calls. He told me that I should never be embarrassed or shy about liking what I like, and anyone who would think less of me because of it wasn't worth my time. I'm sure eventually he will say or do the wrong thing, we all do, but so far he is batting a thousand, and despite the fact that we have only actually seen each other in person a few times, I just feel entirely wonderful whenever I think of him.

Bennie continues to stick by her story that he is The One and that my forever after is around the corner. And she continues to talk me off the ledge about my own varied and ridiculous insecurities. Like now.

"You have nothing to worry about, silly girl. It's New Year's Eve. I'm sure there will be either prime rib or rack of lamb, with traditional sides. No one is making broiled kidneys with blue cheese sauce stuffed into a green pepper on New Year's Eve."

"Okay, that just made my whole stomach turn over."

"Sorry. But aren't you probably more nervous about after the party? I mean, aren't you thinking that tonight is the night?"

"Yes, I'm thinking that tonight might be the night I ask RJ to sleep over, if it feels right."

"It will be fine. You like him. You trust him. The kissing, etcetera, has been great. Don't overthink."

"Yeah, um, are you new? Have you met me? I overthink EVERYTHING."

She chuckles. "True enough. Look, lovely girl, go indulge in some New Year's Eve primping and dreaming, have a wonderful night with your man, and we will chat tomorrow. And I hope you don't mind, but I thought maybe I'd stay with Maria when I come next week."

"How come?"

"Because I think you are at a place with RJ that your busy lives are going to have to stop preventing you from spending more time together, and having me in your guest room for four days is not going to be conducive to that."

"Hey, you know I'm not one of those girls who abandons her girlfriends in favor of boyfriends."

"Wouldn't have dreamt of suggesting such a thing. I just mean that you guys are about to be in the best phase of your new relationship, and you both have enough barriers to time together without having a houseguest for the better part of a week. Not to worry, we'll still have quality time, and there is the party to think of. I just want the two of you to be able to get all wrapped up in each other without any impediments."

"Have I told you lately how much I love you?"

"Yes you have. Go have a wonderful night, and happy New Year my sweet friend. I love you."

"I love you, and I can't wait to see you next week. Happy New Year, Benlet."

"Mwah."

I'm just getting out of the shower when my phone rings. "Help." Patrick sounds urgent, but then again, when you are the center of the universe, things are always urgent.

"What? What's wrong?"

"Fridge died. All the food has gone off. Fifty people imminent. I need you."

This cannot be happening. "Slow down. Exactly what happened?"

"Did all the food prep yesterday, platters set, everything ready. Then I open my fucking fridge and the light doesn't come on and it's totally warm and it smells like a corpse someone pulled out of a swamp. Fifteen hundred fucking dollars' worth of shrimp and oysters and stone crab claws and lobster and cheese and caviar and all the little sliders I made that just needed reheating and the pot of chili . . . The damn thing must have died in the night and now I have fifty people coming in four hours and NOT ONE FUCKING THING TO FEED THEM."

Goddamnit all to hell. "Patrick, I have plans, I—"

"YOU cannot have PLANS when I NEED YOU. This is a catastrophe."

"Patrick, I have a date . . ." This is the first time I've ever said these words to Patrick in all the time we've worked together. He doesn't notice.

"So what? I have a CRISIS. Get it together, Alana. What the fuck are we going to do?"

I stand in my bedroom, hair dripping, trying to pull something out of my ass that won't totally screw up my night.

"Pick me up in ten minutes. We'll go to the test kitchen. You've got me till seven, and not one minute later, Patrick, I mean it."

"I love you, my little Alana-guanabana. I'll see you soon."

So much for primp time. I throw my wet hair in a loose bun, slap some makeup on, and put on a pair of cargo pants and a work shirt. I bring the black wrap dress and boots I am planning on wearing tonight, and call RJ.

"Hi, slight change of plans. Would it be okay if you picked me up at work instead of at home?"

"Of course, but why are you at work?"

I briefly tell him about Patrick's disaster. "I told him he had me till seven, and not a minute more."

"Of course. Don't worry. Did you want me to meet you there early? Can I help in any way?"

ACK! Cannot let Patrick at him yet. "You are the sweetest man on the planet, and no, we'll have it under control. Call me when you are getting close to the studio and I will meet you outside. And thank you so much for understanding."

"Of course, honey, just do what you have to do."

Patrick picks me up in his new Hummer, which I think is probably the single most unnecessary and obnoxious car on the planet, and we go to the studio. Once we get into the test kitchen, I look through the walk-in and get a handle on what our options are. And then it hits me.

"Flatbreads," I say.

"Flatbreads?" He looks at me like I am insane.

"Flatbreads. You've got four ovens in that kitchen of yours. You'll set up a DIY flatbread station. Everyone gets a round of dough, you set up all the toppings on the island, and they make them up however they like. They only take twelve minutes to cook, and you can do four sheet pans per oven, so sixteen flatbreads at a time. We'll make a big salad, and some easy pasta to fill in, and steal all the nuts and olives and cheese to put out for antipasti. Everyone ends up in the kitchen anyway, this way they can participate. One step up from ordering pizza."

He pulls me into an embrace. "You're a genius. I'll do pasta, you work on the dough so it can rise, and then we can knock the rest out."

In a frenetic whirlwind we chop and dice and mince, turning anything we can think of into a possible pizza topping, and packing them all in small hotel pans in the rolling coolers we use for field shoots. When the dough has risen, I roll out fifty twelve-inch rounds, separating each with sheets of parchment, and stacking them in sheet pans, and putting them into Patrick's car. He whips up two pastas, a rotini with a creamy sauce with ham and peas, and a simple rigatoni with vegetables in a light tomato sauce. Patrick discovers a big bowl of leftover risotto from Friday's testing, and heats up the deep fryer, yelling at me to set up a breading station so he can do some arancini. While he is frying the little rice balls, I grab a huge prep bowl and fill it with romaine, shaved Parmesan, croutons and crispy capers, and I mix together a quick peppery pseudo-Caesar-style dressing. By the time it is nearly seven, Patrick's car is filled with the makings of a fine party, and I am a limp, sweaty mess.

I go to the ladies room to change into my dress, and find that my hair is a frizzed Jew-fro, my makeup has melted off, and I am flushed from exertion and the heat of the kitchen. I know it is going to take me at least an hour and a half before I stop sweating. I put on my dress and boots, try to fix my hair, fairly unsuccessfully, and get the runny mascara mostly out from under my eyes. I am presentable. But I am not fabulous. And I so wanted to be fabulous. I'm exhausted. I smell of the kitchen. I have prosciutto under my fingernails. I want a hot bath and a cold, clear, high-proof adult beverage and my pajamas.

My phone rings just as I get back out to the kitchen. "How is it all going?"

"We just finished."

"Perfect timing, I'll be there in five minutes."

"Thanks, RJ. See you soon."

"That the guy?" Patrick says behind me, making me nearly jump out of my skin.

"Yes. That was the guy."

"Who is he?"

"He's a guy. A nice guy. You wouldn't know him."

"You like him, this nice guy I wouldn't know?"

"Yeah, Patrick, I like him. I like him a lot."

"But not more than you like me!" He grins, very sure of himself. "I'm still your favorite."

I have neither the time nor the inclination to engage with him. "Patrick, you should get going, you still have stuff you have to get set up at your house, and you have people coming in an hour."

"Right you are, my sweet. You'll close up here?"

"Of course. And you'll have to explain to Gloria what happened here. She is going to kill you for decimating the stores."

"She loves me too. I'll fix it, no worries."

"Okay. See you later."

"See you later."

And then he leaves.

No "thank you," no "happy New Year." No mention that I have just saved his ass. Not even the tiniest acknowledgment that I had done anything above and beyond the call of duty. Because with Patrick, there is nothing above and beyond his expectations. I'm so angry and hurt I can't even think about it, and I feel tears prick my eyes. I put my whole day on hold, dropped everything to help him out of a jam, even though he KNEW I had other plans, KNEW I had a date. It is New Year's Fucking EVE, and he doesn't even have the common courtesy to THANK ME.

I will not let myself cry over that ass. I blink back the tears and swallow the lump in my throat. I shut down the kitchen, locking up as I leave, and head out the front door, wishing Jimmy the security guard a happy New Year.

RJ is waiting, standing next to his Acura MDX, looking very handsome in a long black cashmere overcoat with a gray scarf and a black fedora. He is having a Cary Grant/Gregory Peck/William Powell sort of night, and my heart skips a beat. His whole face lights up when he sees me.

"Hello, beautiful girl. Happy New Year." He leans down and kisses me, and I can feel my disappointment begin to melt away. "Shall we?" He opens my door, and I get in, mentally readying myself for a party.

"So, did you get everything done?" he asks as we head north toward Ravenswood Manor and his friends' house.

"We did. It was insane, but once we knew that make-your-own-pizza night was the way to go, we just had to make the dough, and prep a lot of toppings. Patrick made a couple vats of pasta and some little fried risotto balls, we threw together a salad and some impromptu nibbly bits. We pretty much ransacked the walk-in and storage, so Gloria is going to be pissed, but at least his precious party will go off. Which means he might not even call me again tonight, which would be a blessing."

"Well, it's good you were able to help him."

"Comes with the territory, unfortunately."

"Can I ask a silly question? Doesn't he own five restaurants in this city?"

"Yup."

"Why wouldn't he have just called one of them to help him out? I mean, I'm sure the fancy place is booked with some special dinner for the holiday, but surely those casual places could have knocked out some food for him, especially since he knew in the afternoon before they would be opening for dinner. I mean, I know if I had a crisis I would want Alana with me, but it seems a little weird that he wouldn't have just had his people take care of him."

I'd never even thought of that. Why didn't he call the PCGrub near his house and have them prep burgers and stuff for him? The menu isn't any more casual than what we put together; they would have been fully stocked for the weekend. He could have gone over there and had six people help him get something together. Six people who were *already* working that day. Instead of just me. "I have no idea. But I wish I had thought of it."

"Well, no harm, no foul, I suppose. At least you guys were able to finish in time so that we could still have our evening."

"Thank goodness for that." I sniff the air. "What is that I smell?"

He grins. "Gougères. My contribution to the party."

"Rascal. I thought you said we weren't going to bring anything? I would have cooked something."

"We weren't going to, but um . . ."

"What?"

"Well, see, I asked about the menu and she is doing her famous spicy tuna tartare for an hors d'oeuvre, and I know you can't eat raw fish, especially spicy raw fish, so I asked if I could bring gougères. My baby can't just sit there with nothing to nibble on."

I love that he just called me his baby. I love that not only does he know me well enough to know about my food bullshit; but that he ensured that I would be taken care of. "You are so sweet, thank you for doing that for me. I am very touched." I reach over and take his hand.

"You're very welcome. And I think it's about time someone was making sure you have what you need in life for a change."

"You are a very wonderful man."

"I'm not really, but you make me want to fake it as best I can manage."

He squeezes my hand and we sit in companionable silence, listening to the radio and winding through the city.

The evening is wonderful. There are four couples total, all very nice and interesting people. RJ's gougères are delicious, and everyone makes me feel very comfortable. They are all foodies and wine people, so I get to win some points by sharing some gossipy dish about a few of the famous TV chefs. Dinner is a perfectly cooked rack of lamb, and I smile, thinking about what Bennie said earlier. There is a gorgeous chocolate cake for dessert and some excitement when the host's Lab-mix pooch, Harry, does a little counter surfing, nearly knocking over the cake, and scampering off with a pilfered lamb bone. Everyone makes fun of her for sounding surprised, when in fact it appears that Harry is a veteran food sneak from way back. RJ tells the Dumpling-Pomi story, almost pridefully, and I love hearing him tell a cute tale about my dog. There are spectacular wines, and a brief countdown, and then it is the New Year and RJ is kissing me and every

bit of my frustration and annoyance from earlier in the day
is just a distant, faded memory.

"I was so proud to be with you tonight," he says in the car
on the way back to my place. "They all loved you."

I look over at him, and my whole heart just swells. "They
were so nice. Thank you so much for including me. It was a
truly lovely evening."

"Yes, it was."

"I don't really want it to end."

"Me, either."

I take a deep breath. We've been taking things slow, and
he is such an old-school gentleman, I don't want to sound like
a harlot. "Would you like to stay over tonight?"

He turns to look at me, and smiles as if I have handed him
a present he has always wanted. "I can't think of anything
I would like more." He reaches for my hand, and we both grin
and hold hands all the way home.

14

O uch!" I wake to the bed shaking and the noise next to me. I turn over to see Dumpling standing on RJ's chest, glaring down at him. RJ reaches up to pet him. "Hey, boy. You are shockingly heavy for such a little guy." Dumpling grudgingly accepts a few pats, and then schlumps down, landing squarely between us. He wriggles around until he is on his back, splayed out like a spatchcocked chicken. His tongue is sticking out on the palsied side of his face, and he has a little smirk that seems to imply that everyone present is now aware of who takes precedence in this scenario. I rub his chest, and meet RJ's eyes.

"Good morning, you."

He smiles. "Good morning, beautiful. How bad was the snoring?"

I can't help but laugh. "Spectacular. Deep and resonant with an occasional nose whistle. Musical." I would have assured any other man that he hadn't snored in the least. But RJ's snoring didn't bother me at all. I was just so happy to have him there, it was a welcome racket.

He shakes his head. "Excellent. Nothing sexier than sleeping next to a wildebeest with a sinus infection."

"I'd sleep next to you anytime. Snoring doesn't scare me."

"Good."

I push Dumpling forcefully off the bed and scootch over

into RJ's embrace. "Happy New Year." I can hear the dog sigh, and click down the hall. If he isn't getting snuggly bedtime, there is no need to stick around. I'm sure he is off to chew on something.

"Happy New Year."

He kisses me and we pick up where we had left off early this morning when sleep finally became a serious necessity. I will not share the details. For once in my life, we're going to go all Doris Day, and insist on the meaningful closing of the bedroom door and just a soft focus fadeout. We are tangled and sated when I hear, spoken into the depths of my hair, "I love you, Alana."

Uh-oh. On the one hand, I'm happy and flattered, and I think he is so brave to share what he is feeling in this moment. On the other, it feels soon and scary and even though I've spent the last few weeks afraid that he wouldn't like me enough to stay, I'm a little suspect of the timing, and I also know that I'm not quite in the same place.

I sit up a little and look at him, stroking his cheek. "Thank you. I have very, very strong feelings for you too, and even though you might be one or two exits ahead of me, we are very much on the same road. You make me extremely happy, and I thank you so much for sharing that with me." I'm fonder of him than I have been of anyone in a long time. But I know my heart, and while I can feel myself falling for him, I'm not totally there yet, and I care about him enough to want to be able to say it without hesitation and with my whole heart.

"You're welcome. And I know that I'm a little ahead of you on this, but I also know that I have to be honest with you about what I feel. I'm glad you don't feel pressure to say it back. Just know that I hope you do feel it someday, and when that day comes, you will take me from being the happiest man on the planet to being the luckiest."

We kiss again, and he rolls over on top of me, stroking my face, and kissing my eyelids.

"WHOA!!" he yelps, and jumps off me.

Dumpling is standing on the foot of the bed, with a bully stick in his mouth. The dried bull tendon chew stick is mangled and slimy. And has apparently recently made intimate contact with RJ's bare tush. "DUMPLING. Take that nasty thing off the bed RIGHT NOW."

"Now that is a wake-up call," RJ says, laughing.

"RJ, I think Dumpling is clearly having some issues with you being the man in my life, and I'm just so sorry. He has never acted out like this before. I hope you'll be patient with him."

"Of course, my sweet. He's part of the package. And nothing makes me happier than hearing you say I am the man in your life. He's a good dog, and I genuinely like him, and I'm sure we'll be friends eventually. I do think maybe we should think about closing the door next time, though."

"I completely agree."

We get up, and get dressed. I make coffee, and we finish off version six of the banana bread recipe I've been working on, with white chocolate chips and toasted pine nuts. And when I can no longer ignore that Dumpling needs walking, we get him organized and RJ heads out with us.

"Have fun with your family today; call me when you get home?"

"I will. You have fun at your party." RJ is going over to a friend's house for a day of chili and football.

He pulls me in for a kiss. "Thank you for being the best start to a New Year that I could have ever imagined."

"Thank you for the best New Year's I have ever had."

Dumpling and I head off for a long walk around the boulevard, enjoying the crisp air.

He clips along next to me, with his odd little gait. I have no idea how he manages to have all four of his feet headed straight, and yet his little warthog potbelly ribcage swings side to side as if on an independent suspension system. Passersby do double takes and whisper to each other as they watch him. I have always talked to Dumpling like a person, and today is no different.

"Seriously, dog. You have got to get it together. This jealousy thing is going to get old fast. RJ is a very, very nice man and I am very, very fond of him and probably falling in love with him and he is in love with me, so he is going to be around. And he wants to be friends with you, but you have to be willing to share and be nice." He snorts at me, and wanders over to a grass patch to dig up a grub. We run into Ollie and exchange some pleasantries with him and his dad before heading home.

Back at the house, I pack up the snacks I made for hanging out with my family later, sweet-and-sour meatballs and an awesome cheese dip that Denise taught me.

My phone rings. "Hello?"

"*Mi amorrrrr.* 'Appy New Yearrrrr. 'Ow are you?"

"Happy New Year to you! I'm very well, Maria, how are you?"

"Verrry good. Verrrry good. 'Ow is RRRRR Yay?"

It tickles the crap out of me that Maria cannot pronounce his name to save her life. "He is good, he just left."

"Ah-ha! 'Appy New Year to *you*, yes?"

I laugh. "Yes. A very happy New Year."

"Mmmm," she says lasciviously. "'Ow 'appy?"

"Let's just say that the last possible thing that could have gone awry did not. We had a very lovely evening with his friends, and an even lovelier evening when we got home, and I'm not giving you any dirty little details except to say that I am a very, very glowy girl today."

"Good. Verrrrry good. When do I meet him?"

"He'll be at the party for Bennie next week, so you can meet him then."

"Wonderrrrful. So, we 'ave a small prrrroblem, I 'ave to impose on you." Get in line, I think.

"What's up?"

"Kai 'as the mono."

"Kai has a monkey?"

"Ay, *dios mio*. Not mono, MO-NO. The sickness."

"Oh no, that sucks. Poor guy. I had it once in college, knocked me out for over a month."

"This is the prrrroblem. 'E is supposed to start classes with the kids next week."

"Oh crap."

"*Sí*, crrrrrrrap. So, you 'ave to teach until 'e is betterrrrr."

Maria is not asking. She is telling. We've been meeting and planning for the pilot program for a couple of months, and everything is in place. A teacher from the school came to talk to us about how to deal with their students, and part of what she shared with us is that these kids have major trust problems. You can't blow them off. You have to be consistent and present and solid for them. It is as important as the content, maybe more. Two weeks ago we got to finalize the eight participants, reading their personal essays and watching the video interviews they did. They seem like a really great group, and the process of developing this program has been the second best thing in my life lately, after meeting RJ.

"Okay. Thursday? Four o'clock at CHIC on Orleans, right? In demo kitchen two?"

"You arrrrre an angel. Probably at least three weeks, maybe more depending on 'ow 'e is recoverrrrrring."

"No worries, I've got it." I'm not really worried, Kai and Mel and I wrote the curriculum together, and the whole program is pretty well laid out. And it is just for a few classes. I find I'm actually a little excited at the prospect.

"*Muchas gracias.* Now go, and tell that RRRRRR Yay that 'e is *de perlas*, and I am so 'appy forrrr you."

"The pearls?"

"*Sí. De perlas.* Just what you need. And if 'e hurts you, I'm going to cut 'is balls off."

"I think I'll skip that last part. Can you have Gigi send me the packet of info on the kids so I can study up before Thursday?"

"We will messenger it over tomorrrrow. And maybe you and I 'ave dinner with Mel afterrrr? To see 'ow it goes?"

"Good plan. Your house?"

"*Sí.* Just come over when you arrrrrre done."

"See you then."

Dumpling and I head over to my sister Nat's house. She always has an open house on New Year's Day, with football on all the televisions, plenty of food, and people come and go as they like. Mama and Papa are already here. They like to come early and leave early.

"Come, Alana," my dad says, patting the couch next to him once I have deposited my offerings on the buffet. "In the feet there is no truth."

I sit next to him, snuggling up. "Hi, Papa. Happy New Year."

"And to you, my goot girl. Happy New Year."

We sit and watch some television. Various grandchildren arrive to flop themselves on the floor around our feet, begging to turn off the football and turn on a movie. Eventually we are way outnumbered, and we get up to find the rest of the adults. Not surprisingly, they are mostly gathered in the kitchen.

Nat is arranging raw veggies on a platter, and my mom is stirring a big pot of solianka, a traditional Russian soup full of meats and bright flavors like capers and olives. My brother-in-law Jeff gives me a kiss on his way to open the door for the next wave of revelers. My dad stands next to Nat, eating veggies almost as fast as she can get them on the plate.

Natalia squints her eyes at me. "What?"

"What?"

"Something is going on with you. I can see it. You're all sparkly."

I can feel the blush rise in my face.

My mom turns around and looks at me, still stirring. "Yes. Is somsink. Do not hang noodles to the ears, you tell Mama troot. Is man, yes?" She grins, I assume because she thinks that perhaps Patrick and I have consummated our love.

"Yes, Mama, it is a man."

"Vat man?" my dad asks around a mouthful of carrot stick, clearly afraid that Patrick has seduced me at long last despite his vigilance.

"His name is RJ."

My mother narrows her eyes at me. "Jorge? Another Spaniard, nu? Did I need to make a notch on your nose? You forget what that Andres did?"

"Mama, not Jorge, R-J. For Ronald James. And he isn't Spanish, he's from Tennessee."

"There are Jews in Tennessee?" my dad asks.

"Well, yes, there are, but RJ isn't one of them. He's Lutheran. But not religious."

"Mama, Papa, just wait," Natalia says, turning to me. "This RJ, he's a nice guy?"

"Very."

"And he is making you twinkle like this?"

"Yes."

"And he's normal? Straight, single, employed, has all his limbs?" Nat is privy to the whole EDestiny problem.

"He is the most normal man I have ever met."

"Vere you meet him, thees Are Jay?" my mom asks.

"Online, Mama, but not the way you think."

She looks at me over the tops of her glasses. And I can't avoid it anymore. I take a deep breath. "So a while ago I was playing around on EDestiny, and I saw this profile. . . ."

I tell them about RJ. The *Reader's Digest* G-rated version, of course, but I also don't pretend it isn't a big deal. I tell them that things are going well, that we really like each other, that I am hopeful.

"Ven we meet him?" Mama wants to know.

Oy. "Maybe Shabbat dinner in a couple of weeks?"

"Eet vill be okay, ziss Lootran, at the Shabbas?" My dad is always concerned about people being comfortable.

"It's okay, Papa, his first wife was Jewish, he's very familiar with the customs." Might as well get that out in the air.

My mother looks perturbed. "First vife?"

"Yes, Mama, first wife. It isn't some sin. Alana has a first husband, remember?" Nat always has my back. "I think it's great. I think it's a long time coming, and it will be lovely to meet him."

"As long as he makes you happy, bubbeleh." My dad pinches my cheek between his knuckles and gives a little twist. I know he is just happy that I'm with anyone besides Patrick.

"Eef you like him, we like him." My mom says this as a statement of fact, lord help anyone who might argue.

I kiss her cheek. "Thanks, Mama. I think you will like him very much. And I think he will love all of you."

"Goot. Now, Alana, psschht, stir soup." My mom hands me the spoon.

Nat sneaks up behind me and puts her arm around my shoulders. She kisses my cheek and whispers in my ear. "I want *all* the dish later, okay? No one gets this aglow unless there is some really good nookie going on."

I blush again. "It is a very happy time. I can't tell it more than once, so when Sara and Jenny get here we can find some time to hide out upstairs so I can tell you all at one time."

"Deal. Go. Stir. If the soup burns Mom will kill you."

"Fine." I turn back to the pot, stirring and smiling. RJ is the first guy I will have brought home to meet my family since I came back with Andres like a big stupid gift from duty-free fifteen years ago. Of all the guys I've dated—the longest being eleven months on and off with a strange guy who is the head of a local television studio, if you don't count Bruce—none of them have been good enough to bring home. With a family like mine—too intense, too many people who love one another fiercely, and too protective—it would be like running the gauntlet to bring home a casual guy; definitely not for the faint of heart. But I hope RJ will love it, and be loved by my family.

I grab Jeff and hand off stirring duty. I have a boyfriend I need to text right this minute.

Holy shit. I have a *boyfriend*. Happy New Year to me!

15

I'm hiding in my office. Patrick is on a tear about the shows getting boring, even though he signed off on all the themes and recipes for this week ages ago. But he keeps having second thoughts, wanting to revamp and tweak and take out recipes we thought were ready to go and replace them. He keeps wanting to work off the cuff, be spontaneous. It's making Bob crazy, Gloria has spent the better part of the week running out to shop extra new ingredients, and I have been ass-deep in the recipe files trying to work off of whatever lame-brained idea pops into his addled head.

"ALLLLLLLLLAAAAAAANNNNNNAAAAAAAAAAAA-AAA!!!" Oh crap.

My door flies open, and Patrick enters in a huff. "Where the fuck are you?"

"Um, Patrick, clearly, I am in my office. Researching frittatas. Because you decided you wanted to do a frittata episode instead of the quiche episode we were going to do later this afternoon. And if we are going to do that, you are going to need frittata recipes. Do you still want to do a frittata episode?" I know I am talking to him like he is a four-year-old, but since that seems to be the limit of his mentality at the moment, I can't really help myself.

"Don't be snide. I'm trying to keep us all employed here, and audiences are ficklc. That quiche thing was bullshit."

"Well, that may be, but since you didn't think it was bullshit when we planned it months ago, and just decided it was bullshit this morning, perhaps you can be a little patient with the rest of us."

"You're a smart-ass, you know that?"

"Better than being a dumb-ass."

"Cute."

"Yes I am. What is going on with you? You are crazier than usual. Is something up? Is Jamie not working out?" The new assistant we hired has been here almost a month, and so far, so good, but maybe he doesn't like her. Ever since Andrea left, he has been pouting. While we were in New York I gave him what-for. He said it was no biggie, he would apologize when we got home and all would be well. But by the time he called her, she had already taken the job with Emily and told him in no uncertain terms that he could take his apology and stick it right up his ass. Patrick had no problem being the one rejecting, firing, breaking up with, but he doesn't do so well on the other end of things. He dinged no fewer than eight potential assistants for everything from "having a weird piggy nose" to "being vegetarian" to "just smells like trouble." Jamie was my last hope, and luckily I think he had just gotten worn down and tired of not having help.

"Jamie's good. She's great actually. I've just got some stuff going on."

"Anything I can help with?"

"Not yet. I'll let you know. Just know that it isn't for nothing, you know? The show has to stay great, it has to keep growing. I can't just be some puffed head sleepwalking through frigging quiches."

"Okay. Whatever you need we'll figure it out, but it will

be better for everyone if you could come up with some clear directives and give us all time to adjust."

"Well, if I could, I would. You're just going to have to ride the ride, all of you. At least for now."

"Patrick, I hate to ask, but . . ."

"Yes, you can still leave early to set up for your party."

"Thank you. You'll be there? We're starting at seven, just simple open-house cocktail thing. Bennie would love to see you, and of course I'd really like for you to meet RJ."

"Of course, of course, I'll be there. You might as well get out of here. I think we're going to bag the third show anyway; it just won't be ready for shooting. But you'll still be in early tomorrow, right?"

"Yep, and don't forget I've got my first class on Thursday afternoon."

"Ah yes, the underwashed children."

"Underserved, Patrick. I'm sure they are plenty clean enough. And do at least try to tap into your inner Jamie Oliver before your master class with them next month, would you? You're going to have to at least make an effort to pretend that you care, that you want them to succeed, that you think they have what it takes to make it in the culinary world."

"And do they?"

"I think they probably do. On paper they certainly do, but I won't really know till I meet them."

"Fine. Okay. I'm going to try to make some magic out of this grilled-cheese thing we are shooting next. I'll see you later."

He leaves my office and I grab my bag and scoot out the back door so no one will catch me. I swing by the Merchandise Mart on my way home to grab Bennie, who has been shopping.

"Shall we go set up for this party?" she says, flopping herself into the car, plopping a large camel Birkin handbag in her lap. Yowza.

"Hello, *darling*!" I reach over and pet it gently. It feels like butter. "That is SO not a fake, you bitch."

"Oh, did you notice this little thing?" She is grinning ear to ear. "Alana, meet Baby. Baby, this is Aunt Alana."

"Where did you get it?"

"Giftie from happy client. Don't you just LOVE?"

"Love. So jealous."

"Yes, well, some of us have perfect boyfriends and some of us have lovely purses."

"I win."

"Yes you do. I cannot WAIT to meet him."

"And he, you."

We get to my place, which is already mostly set up for the party. I stashed the dining room chairs in the basement, so there is plenty of room to walk around the antique oak table Bennie and I found at a flea market last summer. The buffet on the side is decked out with warming trays for the hot items. Plates and napkins are all set. I did all the cold platters last night, so we just have to bring them up from the extra fridge in the basement. We're just doing champagne and sparkling water and Coke in little glass bottles, all self-serve. I hate playing bartender at my own house.

For a party like this, I do mostly cold nibbles, cheese platters and charcuterie displays, beef salami sticks and tall Grissini breadsticks in vases. A bowl of clementines. White-bean hummus and veggies. And on the side, for those who need something more substantial, a lemony chicken pasta casserole and my go-to salad, hearts of palm, celery, cucumber, raw zucchini, and artichoke bottoms with a creamy champagne shallot vinaigrette. I never do a lettuce-based salad on a buffet; it just gets all sad and depressed and wilty and you have to throw out any leftovers. This one stays fresh and crisp, and is just as delish the next day.

Bennie and I pull everything out, set up the buffet and the bar, put the pasta in the oven to reheat, catching up on her progress with Maria and her other clients.

"So," she says, helping me rearrange part of the living room so it will flow better for the party. "Who is coming tonight?"

"RJ, of course, Barry, Mina and her guy, Emily and John, Lacey, Patrick, Bob and Gloria said they would pop by. All my siblings are dumping their kids with Mom and Dad for a massive sleepover so that they can have date nights, but they are swinging by here to smooch you. And to do RJ recon for Mama and Papa, I'm sure."

"Maria told me she isn't coming after all, some awards ceremony?"

"You know Maria. All any charity has to do is say they want to give her an award, and she pulls out the sparkle and the checkbook."

"It's why we love her." Bennie laughs.

"Indeed. She did say if it didn't go too late she might stop by after, but you know she always intends to and doesn't."

"I promised that I would come find her when I got home to tell her everything. She is especially excited to hear about RJ."

"Well, I'm excited to hear what you think too!"

"Based on everything I've heard, and the sheer wattage of the glow coming off you, I have no doubt that I will love him. And where are we with the Bruce situation?"

Ooops. "I haven't told him yet." One of the problems with

a casual no-strings-attached sex thing is that if you find something real, you completely forget about the very existence of
your other dude. Especially if he lives nine hundred miles
away. Since Bruce and I have very little reason to be in direct
communication for work, I haven't really spoken with him
since RJ and I started to get serious.

"Back-up plan?"

"No, of course not. I'm not hedging my bets. I just feel like
he deserves me telling him in person, you know? I mean, we
are friends, and we've been hooking up for over four years.
I just want to handle this really well."

"But you are going to tell him."

"Yes, of course. He's coming here in a couple of weeks;
I figured I would tell him then."

"And you aren't worried about anyone else telling him?
Patrick for example?"

"Shit. I hadn't really thought about that." For a no-strings
thing, I forget what a tangled web it can be.

"Look, for what it's worth, if it were me, I would call him
and acknowledge that you would have preferred to tell him
in person, but that you also didn't want him to hear it from
anyone else. He'll respect that."

"You're right. I'll call him. Thanks, Ben, you're a lifesaver,
as usual."

"Just don't want anything to mar this time for you. I've
never seen you so happy, and I want it to be smooth sailing."

"You and me both!" My voice is upbeat, but it takes effort
to stay positive about RJ. I realize that I've never really had
much experience in grown-up relationships, and the more
I let myself care about him, the more danger I put my heart
in. I want to be giddy and throw caution to the wind and chat
with my girlfriends and family about how wonderful my life

is right now, but I can't. I'm suspicious by nature, I have a tough time really believing in the fairy tale, and the better things are with RJ, the harder I'm sure I will fall. I'm the host who always presumes no one will show up, the girl who doesn't trust the reserve in the gas tank and frantically fills up the minute the empty light goes on. Things fall apart. Things go wrong. And I'm usually certain that I'll be stuck in the middle of the maelstrom. I want to trust what I feel for RJ and what he says he feels for me. But it takes conscious effort. I shake off the creeping doubties that always sneak in, and finish getting ready for the onslaught.

When everything is set, we both sass up a bit, and pop a cork on a bottle of bubbly, toasting each other and our friendship. I've asked RJ to come a half an hour before everyone else so that he and Bennie can have a few quiet moments before the horde descends, and the bell rings right on the dot.

"God, you look beautiful," he says, kissing me right into my bloodstream.

"And you are very handsome," I say, taking in his crisp black slacks and lovely soft gray cashmere sweater. When he looks at me the way he is looking at me right now, it is easier to ignore the pit of the stomach reservations. Not eliminate them, but quiet them.

"And I am a vision of loveliness," Bennie says behind us.

RJ peers around me, and says, "Well, you certainly are at that!" He hands me a bag, and goes to greet Bennie. "You'll forgive me if I hug you. I feel like I know you already." He takes her in a full embrace, nothing hesitant or restrained.

I watch her melt. RJ gives great hug.

"Well, Alana, now you are in trouble, because I'm going to steal him from you."

"Bennie, with all due respect, there isn't a woman, living

or dead, who could turn my head from Alana, but I swear that if I were woo-able, you would be the girl to do it. I'm a sucker for a redhead with an Aussie accent."

Bennie blushes prettily, gentle pink rising in her porcelain cheeks, making her usually pale freckles go copper. She tosses her shiny hair, strawberry chestnut shot with deep auburn, and turns to me. "Oh, honey, you are in TROUBLE."

We all laugh, and head to the kitchen. RJ has brought some wines from his cellar, which he specifically tells me are for me and not to just put them out for the party. He pours himself a glass of champagne. "How is everything here? What can I do to be helpful?" he asks after we have dutifully toasted each other.

"I'm pretty close to done in here; why don't you two go hang in the living room and chat before the locusts descend."

He leans over and kisses me. "Will do. Come, you vixen from Down Under, I want to hear all about how you transformed this apartment, because I hear it was significantly fuller before you got hold of it, and frankly I can't imagine any more stuff in here."

"Oh, it was fine. I mean it wasn't fruit salad or anything, it just needed an update." She is so politic.

"It was a hot mess and she saved it and me. Now scoot!" I shove them toward the living room, not eager to hear how this story comes out.

My condo hadn't been so much decorated as it had been cobbled together. When I first bought it, I was moving from an apartment half the size, and was very concerned about getting it furnished completely. I spent my spare time at flea markets and consignment stores, and took a lot of wonderful hand-me-downs from Maria. I didn't have money for real art, so I bought a beautiful old antique book with hand-colored plates depicting classic recipes and old cooking equipment, took it apart and, with the help of some IKEA frames, managed to fill a lot of the wall space. In my travels around the antique stores of Illinois, I managed to acquire way too many small pieces, endless occasional tables, tchotchkes, and general household detritus.

Last summer, I had finally asked Bennie for help. She came in for a visit, and in three whirlwind days we edited, moved around, redressed. She took my whole condo, which was full of stuff, and made the stuff make sense. We shifted things around, and put many former treasures out in the alley for the next generation of young people in need of furnishings. By the time she was done, my place was still full, but more logically so. And there were some places for breath. I had confessed to RJ that, while my place seemed jam-packed with stuff, it had been reduced by nearly a quarter of its volume. He just laughed and told me that I would get the joke when I saw his place, which I did. While I lean Victorian, in the spirit of my 1906 stately stone lady, he stayed true to the Arts and Crafts sensibility of his little Ravenswood Manor bungalow. And while I have a lot more stuff, it is only because I have nearly three times the space. But where I have a lot of furniture and cooking and entertaining equipment, he has music equipment, gorgeous artwork, beautiful rugs. I have worked very hard not to imagine too much how our households might merge, but I am guilty of mentally redecorating my place with some of his stuff. Can't help it, I'm a girl, and we indulge in such madness.

When I finally come out to the living room, the party all ready for the rest of the guests, RJ and Bennie are chatting like old friends, much to my heart's delight. She winks at me, and I know they are bonding well. I sneak off to the bedroom, ostensibly to do a final primp, and call Bruce.

"Hello! I was going to e-mail you. Shall we hit Girl and the Goat when I'm there in a couple of weeks? I'll have to pull a favor to get us in, so I thought I should ask sooner rather than later."

"I'd love to have dinner there with you, if you still want to."

"Why wouldn't I want to? Oh, shit, what's up with Patrick that you couldn't fix?"

"It isn't a Patrick thing. Look, I was going to wait till you were here, to tell you face-to-face, but then I was afraid someone else might tell you and I thought you'd rather hear it from me, even if it is over the phone."

"That sounds serious."

"It's just, I've, well, I've met someone. And we've been spending a lot of time together, and I think he is going to specifically ask me to be exclusive and I'm going to say yes. And I needed to know that when I say yes, that you and I have already agreed that we are going to go back to a non-naked friendship."

"Alana, that is wonderful news and I could not be happier for you."

"Really?"

"Of course, kiddo. Look, I always knew you were a gift with an expiration date. And lord knows if I were cut out for a real relationship, I would have jumped through a lot of hoops to get you all for myself. And I know that I'm probably going to be really depressed about it pretty soon. But we always said we were friends and colleagues first, and so we shall remain."

"Thank you, Bruce, and thank you for everything you

have been and for being a very good friend. I'm glad that we get to keep each other."

"Me too. And I hope you'll forgive me if I say that I'm going to need some time before I meet him, but that I do want to meet him eventually. I really hope he's the one, Alana, you deserve it. And I hope if he turns out to not be the one, that you'll come back to me until you do find the one."

"It's a deal." But it isn't. Because I know that as great as my thing with Bruce was for its time, you don't come back after a guy like RJ. You are changed forever; your context is entirely different. I know that if RJ and I don't end up together, I won't ever be able to be with someone who is a placeholder.

"Okay, sweetie, then Girl and the Goat business instead of pleasure. I'll invite Patrick so there is an appropriate buffer and I won't be tempted to pounce on you. Maybe by next time I'll be able to invite your fella too."

"Ha-ha. Just remember, whatever you might feel isn't really about making a mistake with me, it's just because someone else has me; it isn't real."

"That is very sweet to say, and I appreciate your willingness to try to give me an out for being enough of an ass to lose you."

"Bruce, if either of us had really wanted or needed more from each other, we would have figured it out years ago. I think this transition will be much less onerous than you think it will be."

"All right, I'll focus on that. And don't worry, this will bring all kinds of interesting things into my therapy sessions."

"I do try to be helpful."

"So you do. Be well, honey. I really am very happy for you. I'll see you in a couple of weeks."

"Okay, bye, Bruce."

My whole spine feels longer and straighter. I come out of the bedroom, and see my man and one of my dearest friends, sitting on my couch and laughing and talking like they've known each other forever. RJ looks over at me and smiles, and I think, I really belong to him, and that it is finally starting to be the least scary thing I have ever felt.

Before I can get all the way over to the couch to join them, the doorbell rings and we are off to the races.

My night is a blur of mini conversations. I find that the two best things I can do as a hostess are to put out food and drink that don't need tending, and to be like a hummingbird, flitting from group to group for five to eight minutes at a time before moving on. Lucky for me, I have no worries about RJ; he fits anywhere, and everyone has been dying to meet him. So I spend a few minutes here, then a few minutes wherever RJ is, a few minutes there, then a few minutes wherever RJ is.

"Look at you," Sasha says, putting on Dad's accent. "One foot's here the other's there."

Alexei laughs and, not to be outdone, mimics Mama. "And here we thought you couldn't split them apart with water." He gestures at RJ across the room, where he is surrounded by Mina and Emily and Lacey.

"You can throw Russianisms at me all you want. I like that he doesn't need me to hold his hand in this shark pond."

"We're just teasing, Lana." Sasha puts an arm around me. "We like him."

"Yeah," Alexei says. "He seems really great. Happy for you, sis."

"Thanks, guys, that means a lot. Especially since he is coming to Shabbat next week. I'm glad you're getting a chance to meet him now, so he'll have a few friendly faces."

"Whose faces are friendly?" Jenny asks, sidling up to us, a little plate filled with food. Sasha immediately starts picking at the treats she has fetched. Sara is with her, carrying four glasses of champagne like a pro. I help her distribute them to the crowd.

"Hopefully all of yours, next week at Shabbat. If this is running the gauntlet, next week is the running of the bulls. I just want RJ to be comfortable."

"Look at him," Sara says, sipping her drink thoughtfully, and waving away Jenny's proffered plate. "He looks entirely at home."

Just at that moment RJ looks over and smiles and raises his eyebrow at us.

"He looks happy," Jenny says around a mouthful of prosciutto and fig. "And so do you."

"I am."

I kiss them all and flit away again, checking in on Bob and Gloria, who have no idea where Patrick could be, since he told them he would see them here. Gloria asks for the recipe for my salad dressing, and suggests that we talk to Patrick about doing a cocktail party episode. I wander over to check in on RJ, but the girls have him surrounded.

"Are you all behaving yourselves?"

"They are sharing some interesting stories with me," RJ says with a grin.

"Oh, no, you guys *promised*." High school stories, the worst.

"Hey, we promised not to bring PICTURES. And we didn't," Mina says.

"Yeah, never said anything about sharing stories," Emily adds.

"You're going to have to just leave us alone with him and

let the education continue." Lacey waves her hand at me like I'm some annoying fly.

"Do you need anything?" I ask him.

"Not a thing, sweetheart. All is well." I lean over and kiss him, and all three of the girls sigh loudly.

"Aw, shuddup. I'm allowed to kiss my boyfriend if I want."

Silence drops over them as if a record has been scratched. And then they all start saying "boyyyfriend," dripping with sappiness and innuendo. RJ puts his arm around me, and whispers in my ear. "I like the sound of that, girlfriend."

I wink at him and give him another kiss, and wander over to where Bennie and Barry are hanging out.

"He. Is. Dreamy." Barry sighs. "Do they make that model in gay?"

"He really is lovely, Alana," Bennie says. "You have not exaggerated in the least. And I frankly *love* the way he watches you when you can't see him. He has been hanging out with all your pals, but he knows at every moment exactly where you are."

"I'm a lucky girl."

And I am.

So very lucky.

Right up until the moment the phone rings.

"Come get me." Patrick sounds weird, and it is very noisy wherever he is.

"What? I can't come get you; I'm hosting a party for chrissakes. Take a cab, you big baby."

"Alana, listen closely. I'm at Larrabee and Division. And I'm not at the firehouse."

The only other thing at that location is a police station.

"Shit, Patrick. Have they booked you?"

"Not yet, but if you don't come here and help, they will for sure."

That fucking insane crapmonkey. I don't know what he has done, or to whom, and frankly I don't care. But I can't leave him swinging in the wind. "I'm on my way."

I pull RJ and Bennie aside and explain a bit. They offer to hold down the fort. I go to my secret cash stash under my bed and grab all five grand, hoping that I don't need it, but feeling better to have it with me. Then I think about going to a police station, and tuck it in my bra. Gotta be at least one benefit to schlepping around a pair of 38 DDDs—I can stash a country ham in here if I need to. I go to the freezer and take out a couple of the quick breads I was working on this week, a zucchini-walnut, and a carrot-apple, figuring that if he hasn't been booked, maybe I can make nice.

I whiz around the party claiming that the alarm has gone off at the studio and I'm on call, grateful that Bob and Gloria have already left and aren't there for the lie, and say I'll be back soon. RJ offers to come with me, but I don't want to drag him into this.

I fly down the expressway with anger seeping out of my pores. Why? Why tonight? I just don't understand him.

When I get to the station, I ask for the arresting officer of the stupid television asshole, and am met with a laugh, and a uniformed officer escorts me to a back room. Patrick is sitting in a chair next to a metal desk, looking ragged. There is a small bruise coming up under his left eye, and his hair is a mess.

"Hey," he says when he sees me.

"Hey yourself. What the fuck happened? Why are you here?"

"It's a long story."

"Bullet point it for me."

"I went home after work to change. I had a beer. I started to come over. I was sitting at a stoplight, and some prick in a BMW rear-ends me, then pulls around me and takes off, hit-and-run. So I take off after him. I chase him for a minute and then he goes to make that turn at Clybourn, and the Hummer and I don't corner so well, so I run up the curb and into the light pole. Where I discover that an officer has been following us. I really didn't hear the siren, I had the radio up loud. And instead of going after the schmuck who ran into me, he stopped, and decided to bring me in on suspicion of DUI, and reckless driving and who knows what else."

"Hi, you must be Alana," a voice behind me says. I turn around and see a short bulldog of a man, head shaved, three-day stubble, neck like an iceberg.

"I am. Has he been a terrible pain?" I'm dressed up, as cute as I get, and I'm not above using cleavage if it helps get Patrick out of a jam.

"Well, let's see. He left the scene of an accident, embarked on a dangerous high-speed chase through Lincoln Park, took down a light pole, and insulted an officer who was trying to help him. When we finally got him trying to explain his behavior, the officer smelled beer on his breath, which obviously complicates the matter again."

Good lord. We're in trouble. "Officer . . ."

"Detective. But you can call me Ryan."

"Detective Ryan . . ."

"Just Ryan."

"Okay, Ryan, are you going to book him? Not that I would blame you, it sounds like he has been a complete idiot, which isn't unusual as you can imagine, and I would know, I work with him all the time. But I will say that as big a putz as he is, he isn't a liar. So when he tells me that he had one beer, I believe him and I'm sure he blew under the limit." I'm pulling out every bit of everything I've ever learned from endless watching of police procedurals.

"We haven't decided whether to book him yet."

"Okay, good. So, I know the traffic camera at the intersection where he was hit will confirm that the other guy started it, not that it is an excuse, but even a public defender will claim that he was just trying to chase down the other guy so that he didn't cause more damage. And you know who he is, you know he can afford a big-time attorney, who's going to put on a show in court and make it seem like he is second only to Superman in protecting the public interest with no regard for his own safety, and that he had every intention of making a spectacular citizen's arrest. The media will eat the whole thing up, and trust me, the CPD won't come off as the good guys. So since you haven't booked him, and he isn't in the system yet, let me propose this. Leaving the scene of an accident is a misdemeanor. Even if you proved guilt, what could he get? A fine? Maybe a year probation if some judge wanted to make an example of him?"

Patrick starts to say something, and I put my hand up and give him a look that says he had better just stay the hell quiet. His open mouth snaps shut. I keep going. "And while both Patrick and I understand that there was the possibility of other people getting hurt, luckily for us all, that wasn't the case. How about this? You fill out the relevant paperwork and put it in your desk, including a complete statement from Patrick that he will sign, but don't enter it in the computer. Patrick is going to apologize to you, and to the other officer. Sincerely. And tomorrow he is going to call the media liaison for the police department, and offer his services for a pro-CPD campaign. For the next year, Patrick is your PR bitch. Want someone to film a video for you to use in schools explaining how important it is to work with the police? Part of that 'See something, tell something' thing you have going on? We'll film it in our studio. Need a place to hold a fund-raiser? Just pick any of his restaurants and he'll donate the space and the food. Need a stack of autographed cookbooks to give to everyone's wife in the precinct when there's been too much overtime? Done. I promise, if you don't get a call from your people tomorrow thanking you for being the genius who convinced a local celeb to get involved, you have my permission to file the paperwork and I personally will testify for the prosecution."

Detective Ryan looks at me, and then at Patrick. "You his girlfriend?"

"I'm his assistant. I'm way too smart and have too much taste and self-esteem to be his girlfriend."

"Good girl. What does he do to have a girl like you this much on his side?"

"He pays me enough that I can support myself and still have enough left to give money to my folks."

"But you are somebody's girlfriend."

I smile. "Yes, yes I am. And he is at my house right now hosting the party that was going on when this idiot decided to play city vigilante. My best friend is in from New York, and all my friends are at my place hanging with her and meeting my boyfriend, and I would dearly love to get back to them."

"Pity. If he ever lets you down, this boyfriend, I hope you'll call me." I'm getting a lot of that tonight. He hands me his card, and I wink at him. "Okay," he faces us both. "I like your deal. And you're right. He blew under the limit, so no DUI. And yes, I saw the damage to the back of his car, so I believe he was rear-ended. And you're doubly right; we'll get far more mileage out of using his fame to our advantage than going ahead with bringing charges. So, Mr. Andretti. We're going to do some paperwork and you're going to write and sign a complete statement, and once I'm satisfied, I'm going to lose that paperwork in my desk for exactly twenty-four hours. I'm going to release you into the custody of this lovely young lady, and she is going to ensure that I get a call about your new job as public spokesperson for the department, or I am going to file that paperwork and do everything in my power to see that they throw the book at you. And if you ever do anything this stupid again, I'm going to personally see that you regret it. Deal?"

Patrick looks up, contrite as a kid caught with his hand in the cookie jar. "Deal. Thank you, Detective, and I'm really sorry about the profanity. I was very upset."

"You swear like a ten-year-old girl. It didn't exactly make me blush."

"Thank you, Ryan. Really. Do you like zucchini bread? Or carrot?" I pull the loaves out of my purse and proffer them.

"I'll put them out in the break room, thanks; the team will really appreciate that." He hands Patrick a legal pad and a pen. "Write what happened, exactly, all of it, and sign and date it. I'll do the rest of the paperwork and see if we can get you out of here. Alana, would you like a coffee or a pop or something?"

"Water?"

"I'll bring you a bottle."

"Thanks so much."

"Hey, how about me?" Patrick looks up.

"Don't push it," Ryan says, and walks away.

"What a tool," Patrick says when the detective is out of earshot.

"Don't. Don't you speak to me right now. Just write your damned statement and do not say ONE WORD to me. I am so mad at you I could just spit. So don't be cute, don't try to play this off, just write the fucking statement and make it good so we can get the hell out of here. I'm going to call RJ and let him know what is going on, and see how the party is doing."

I leave him there, and run into Ryan in the hall. He hands me a bottle of water and points me to a side room where I can make some calls in peace.

I call RJ's phone, no answer. Ditto, Bennie. Finally I just call my house phone, and Bennie answers. "Alana's love castle."

"Hey there."

"Hey, what's going on?"

"Patrick isn't arrested, but there is still some paperwork to do. And then I have to take him home. I'm at least an hour out, probably closer to an hour and a half. How is everything there?"

"Great, actually. Maria did come after all, so she has RJ cornered, getting his complete life story. Your brothers left right after you did to take their wives to dinner and your sister and Jeff stopped by for a little while, but they just left as well. Denise and her charming John just got here a little while ago; she says to tell you that you did a perfect job with her cheese dip, and he brought a plate of the best bruschetta I've ever tasted. There will not be leftovers for you, I'm afraid; these locusts have decimated it already. And Barry and the girls are still here, but they are starting to talk about heading out, since it is a school night."

"How is RJ doing? I feel like such an ass for leaving."

"Don't. He's worried about you, but I think you could set him on fire and he would find it charming. He really loves you. And I think he feels really good that you were willing to leave him here with all of us. Like a mark of trust. Want to talk to him?"

"Please. And Ben, I'm so sorry your party got ruined."

"It only got ruined for you, honey, the rest of us are having a helluva time. Pity you're missing it. Hold on, I'll get RJ."

"Hey, baby, is everything okay?"

"It will be. He isn't arrested, so that is good."

"Why do I get the sense he isn't arrested because you are there?"

"Because you are a very smart man. I am so so sorry for abandoning you. I feel like a complete ass."

"You are a good friend and colleague, and all you've done is be the miraculous woman you are. As for abandoning me, you left me in your lovely home, with loads of good food and good drink and really fun people, all of whom have been very nice to me and fun to be with. I'm having a great time in spite of missing you."

"You are amazing. Any other guy would be pissed, or would have gone home."

"Well, whoever that other guy is, I hope I'm pulling solidly ahead in the running." He loves to tease me about my "other boyfriends," and I always play coy.

"You are leaving him in the dust."

"I liked being introduced as your boyfriend."

"Oh, you noticed that, huh?"

"I did. And even though I have always thought it was a ridiculous word, and I'm almost fifty, it sounds a little strange, but I like the sentiment very much."

"I liked saying it. I hope I'll be back in an hour or so, maybe a teensy bit longer, and I know it is a school night, so don't feel like you have to stay."

"I wouldn't dream of leaving here till I know you are home safe."

"In that case, feel free to plan on staying over if you like."

"That I like very much. Get home as soon as you can, my darling girl."

"I will."

It takes another hour to get everything settled at the station. I drive Patrick home in uncomfortable silence. When we pull up to his building, he turns to me. "I'm really sorry, Alana. I didn't mean to ruin your party, I really didn't. And I really did want to meet your fella. I know I'm a shithead sometimes, but it isn't intentional. And I really, really, *really* appreciate what you did for me tonight."

Sigh. I'm officially too tired to stay angry. "Patrick, you're nearly forty-two years old. You can't behave like a lightly damaged teenager forever. Trust me; your life will actually be more pleasant if you would just grow up a little bit."

"Yeah, I know, you're probably right. See you tomorrow?"

"Of course."

"Okay, then. Thank you, Alana. I really am very, very grateful."

"No problem. And Patrick? Not one complaint about anything the police ask of you for the next year. No whining, no trying to weasel out of anything. You will be gracious and warm and you will do every single thing they ask of you with a smile on your face, is that clear?"

"Yes, Mama Bear."

"I sent an e-mail to your PR team telling them about your new commitment to the Chicago Police as a personal cause, and let them know that they should be in contact with the media person there ASAP."

"Great, thanks. I promise, I'll follow up tomorrow."

"Yeah, you will, in front of me."

"Good night, Alana. See you in the morning."

"Good night, Patrick. And I'm glad you're not hurt. Please don't be so reckless with your driving; you're no good to me dead."

He laughs. "You're my sole beneficiary, Alana; I'm worth much more to you dead than alive." He gets out of the car and heads into his building.

I'm going to just presume that he was kidding. Especially because on a day like today, that little extra incentive might actually turn me into a *Law & Order* episode in the making.

By the time I get home it is nearly midnight, and everything is quiet. I open my door and walk inside. My house is pristine. I would never have known anything had happened here tonight. The furniture is back where it belongs, the kitchen and dining room spotless. I wander into the living room and see a sight that melts my heart. RJ is lying full-out on the couch, Dumpling splayed on his chest, both of them snoring deeply, in something that sounds almost like harmony. I walk over and kneel beside the couch, placing a hand on Dumpling's head, and kissing RJ's lips.

"Mmmm. You're back." He squints his eyes at me, and then smiles.

"Yes I am. And some magical fairies appear to have come to my house."

"Bennie and Maria helped me figure out where everything went. We just thought that you deserved to come home to a clean place."

"Maria? MARIA cleaned?"

"Well, sure, she helped. She helped pack up food, and then I washed and Maria dried and Bennie put stuff away."

"Maria doesn't clean. EVER. For anyone. You must have charmed her to bits."

"Well, I did try."

"And you appear to have charmed someone else here." I look down at Dumpling, who is semi-awake, and receiving rubs from both of us.

"Him is a good boy. We had a walk, we had some treats, Maria and Bennie gave him some snuggles, and then he and I had a good heart-to-heart talk. He peed on everything on the planet, but no poop. I figure you're supposed to know such things."

"Weird, he usually does have a nighttime dump. Probably just all discombobulated with the party and stuff. Speaking of which, should we go to bed?"

"Yes, please." I slide Dumpling off RJ's lap and onto the couch. Then I take his hand and we go to the bedroom, where I close the door.

We are kissing and undressing each other when suddenly RJ says, "Hey, I knew I won the lottery when I found you, but now there are cash prizes!"

Oops. Totally forgot about the five grand in my bra.

"Sorry, forgot that was there."

"Bail money in the bra. Classic." He laughs and hands the money over to me. I put it back in its hidey-hole, not even thinking twice about RJ watching, and turn back to him.

"Now, where were we?"

A while later, cuddled close in the dark, I tell RJ everything that happened, while he strokes my hair.

"What on earth would he do without you?"

"I have no idea."

"But you love it?"

I have to think about that for a minute. "I love a lot about
it. Do I love that he calls me in the middle of my life and
drags me into some insanity? No. But the normal parts of my
job are pretty fantastic. And the money is very compelling."

"What if the money weren't an issue?"

"Money is always an issue. I've got a mortgage here, a
mortgage on the Wisconsin house. And I give my folks money
every month."

"Wow, how much do they need help from you?"

"Well, their house is paid off, but there are still taxes and
upkeep. My dad's pension covers the basics, and they are both
on Medicare. But they have eight grandchildren with birthdays and Chanukah and graduations. And they try to go somewhere warm for at least a couple of weeks in the winter.
I bought them their car, and I pay the insurance on that. And
when something goes wrong in the house, I send someone
over and cover the bill. My brother Alexei manages their
money, their savings and such, so I just give him a small check
every month and he deposits it into their account. They don't
know how much I give them; they think it is just interest
and stuff. And anytime they need to take money out for
something, they ask Alexei if they can afford it and he says
yes, and if it taps into principle, I just write a check."

"Alana, that is so extraordinary. Why don't you want them
to know?"

"They'd never take it. They're too proud."

"And your siblings, do they all participate?"

"No, they can't. They all have decent jobs, but not insane income. And they also have all those kids with their lessons and clubs and new shoes every minute and college to save for and their own mortgages and stuff. Lucky for me, Dumpling doesn't need much."

RJ squeezes me tight. "You're just magical."

"Well, you're awful nice to come home to."

"Well, you feel like coming home to me."

I roll over and we kiss. "You feel a lot like coming home too."

And finally, after what feels like a forty-seven-hour day, there is sweet, sweet sleep.

When I get up, RJ is gone. I was so dead to the world; I hadn't even felt him leave. There is a little note on the kitchen counter.

Alana—

Thank you for:
Being you.
Finding me.
Having great friends.
Being a great friend.
Being in my life.
Letting me sleep over.
Having those eyes.
Calling me your boyfriend.
I'm a lucky lucky boy.

RJ

I jump in the shower and throw on my work clothes. I grab my coat and bag. "C'mon, Dumpling, time to go to Best Friends." In the car, I call RJ.

"You are quiet as a mouse; I didn't hear you leave at all."

"Well, I didn't want to disturb you; you had such a rough night."

"Thank you, sweetie, that is so wonderful. And I'm so glad that you had some bonding time with Dumpling, I think you guys have turned a corner. It was so nice to come home to see my two boys napping together."

"Yeah, about that, we might not be completely around the corner quite yet."

"Oh no, what did he do now?"

"Remember how weird it was that he didn't poop last night the way he usually does?"

Uh-oh. "Where?"

"My shoes."

"He pooped on your shoes?"

"He pooped *in* my shoes."

"*In* your shoe?"

"Shoes plural."

"BOTH of them?"

"Yeah, it was actually pretty impressive. Two little curls perfectly placed right in the center of the opening in both shoes. Pretty fancy shooting, Sheriff."

"Please tell me you noticed before you put your feet in there . . ."

"I did indeed. And he must have done it early enough that by the time I discovered it, it had dried out a bit and I could just shake the poop out. They're going to need a little disinfecting and deodorizing though."

"I will buy you new shoes."

"No need. It was pretty funny actually. And the stories are getting me good mileage with my clients. A lot of them are dog people, and they have come to love a good Dumpling story."

"You have the patience of a saint."

"Nope, just have the sense to know when I have a great thing."

"Thank you, honey. I'm pulling into the doggie day care now. I'll call you later?"

"I certainly hope so."

I turn to look at Dumpling, sitting on the seat beside me. "Seriously? IN his shoes? BOTH OF THEM????" Dumpling smiles at me, and I can't help it, I start to laugh.

16

I check and double check my mise en place. It's been a long time since I've been through something so basic, and I've never cooked with teenagers before. Luckily the demo kitchen here at the Cooking and Hospitality Institute is well-equipped, and today is going to be mostly about getting to know one another a bit. Maria has arranged for a van to pick the students up at their high school, and then take them all home after class. They arrive precisely on time.

I ask them all to take their seats, which I have assigned by placing a small paper tent at each of their places, names facing out so I don't mix them up. They file in, looking as nervous as I feel.

"Welcome. My name is Alana Ostermann. I am going to be one of your teachers this semester. In the kitchen, the title *Chef* is a mark of respect, and acknowledgment. I know that respect is important to all of us, so in this class we are all Chef. You will call me Chef or Chef Alana, and I will call you Chef in return. Today we are going to get to know one another a little bit, and introduce you to your equipment kits, and then do a little work. How does that sound?"

"Good," they all say in semi-unison.

"You can do better, please say, 'Good, Chef.'"

"Good, Chef." A little stronger, a little sassier this time.

"Excellent. Now I want to know a little something about

you. So please introduce yourself with your name, and what you think about cooking, and what you hope to do with the experience you are going to get here. Let's start with you." I point at the slight young man on the far left.

He is short, wiry, with slicked-back black hair and thin fuzz on his upper lip. He looks down at the table as he speaks. "My name is Renaldo. I'm the oldest of nine kids, and both my parents work two jobs, so I'm always cooking for my little brothers and sisters and I really like it most of the time. I have dyslexia, but we didn't know till last year, so my grades aren't good. But I never really thought of college anyway. My dad can bring me into his business, but I like cooking. So I thought this would be another thing to do."

"Thank you Chef Renaldo. Next."

A heavyset Latina who has a truly staggering amount of makeup on her round face and long corkscrew curls in an unnatural shade of orange says, "My name is Clara. As you can see, I love food." Her compatriots laugh, but clearly with her, not at her, so I let it go. "I love to cook at home, and I think I would love to cook for a living someday."

"Good, Chef Clara. Thank you. Next."

One by one we go down the line. Juan, an extremely tall, gangly boy in a walking cast, a former basketball star who had blown out his knee and had no way into college without sports. Mari, a teeny tiny firecracker of a girl with a long black braid, who admits to an obsession with food magazines, her own blog about cooking, and a desire to become a food stylist and writer. Helena, a spectacularly beautiful Indian girl who admits tearfully that her mother is very sick, and she started cooking for the family to help take the pressure off, and while she isn't entirely sure she wants a career in food, she does want to know more about what she is doing in the kitchen. Joseph, a handsome young African American kid with a puffed-up chest, who works part-time at his uncle's south-side diner, and who hopes to take over that business someday. He delivers his entire speech directly to Helena, who blushes, and I can tell this is either going to be a huge problem, or an adorable young love affair. Probably both, when I think of it.

Max, a bespectacled young man with pale skin marred by angry acne, looks horribly out of place. I remember from his application essay that he went to a chichi private school his whole life, but that his folks had divorced and then his dad's business went under and that was the end of alimony and child support and tuition money. His mom had moved them to a more affordable neighborhood, and he was in a regular public school for the first time. Clemente's student population is 63 percent Latino, and 34 percent African American, with 95 percent low-income households. For a white, formerly rich kid, it had to be an awful place to try to fit in. He admits that college is not the guarantee he once thought it was and that when he really missed some of the fancy restaurant dishes he used to take for granted, he decided to try to learn how to make them himself and discovered he loved to cook.

Aretha leads with announcing that she was named for the Queen of Soul, and is every bit an equal diva. Larger than life in every way, she says that she has an eighteen-month-old little boy at home, and she wants to make a better life for him. Her plan is to finish culinary school, open a soul food restaurant, and then get her own show on the Food Network and become a star, and have her restaurant become a national chain. And she indicates an intention to eventually marry Taye Diggs "when he is done with that white girl and ready for a real woman." Can't really blame her on that one.

I take them through their basic equipment, which the program has provided for each of them: An eight-inch chef's knife, and a four-inch parer. A sharpening steel and a set of whetstones. A good pair of tongs. A bandana, a chef's coat, and a stack of five side towels. I tell them a little bit about myself and my path to cooking and culinary school. Then we jump in with basic knife skills. They can all handle a blade reasonably well, some are better than others at keeping their fingers tucked in, but by the end of our three hours together we have some basic cuts that even Patrick would not be ashamed to use on air. Their homework for next week is to decide on a favorite recipe from their family, and to e-mail us the recipes so that we can bring in the ingredients for them to cook the dish for the group, and to practice their new knife skills with proper technique.

When class is over, I make sure to shake all of their hands and thank them for coming. They have blown me away and exhausted and exhilarated me in equal measure. I head over to Maria's, my head reeling with stories and moments and ideas. While taking on the actual teaching wasn't originally in my plan, as a member of the advisory board and planning committee, I realize that having this time in the trenches with the students is going to serve me and the program exceedingly well.

Melanie is already at Maria's, standing over the stove and stirring something that smells delicious.

"Hey, Alana!" she says over her shoulder. "How was it?"

"Wait, wait, *dios mio*, I 'ave to pipi. Do no' tell anything before I am 'ere!" Maria zips out to the powder room off the kitchen, and I sneak over to see what smells so insanely great.

"Zucchini pasta with chicken and lemon," Melanie says. "I'm using whole-grain linguini, and the zucchini is shredded in long strips the same size as the noodles. Half real noodles, half zucchini noodles, so everything twirls the same on your fork, but you halve the carbs and cut down the calories significantly." She grabs a tasting spoon and lets me taste the chicken, simmering gently in a rich lemony sauce.

"That is amazing. So light and fresh, but still depth of flavor."

"I love this recipe, especially in the winter like this; it just tastes like spring to me."

"Well, it looks amazing. I'd love to steal it for the new healthy cookbook we're working on."

"Sorry, I'm about to do a cookbook myself, and am going to need to keep it proprietary for the moment."

"Good for you! That is such a great idea. I bet it will be huge."

"We'll see."

Maria comes back into the room. "That smells incredible, and I am soooooo 'ongry."

She walks over to the wine cooler and pulls out a gorgeous bottle of Chablis, the perfect thing for the pasta, bright and crisp and mineral. She opens the bottle and pours three glasses, just as Melanie is stirring the pasta and zucchini strands into the chicken and sauce, adding some of the pasta water to smooth it out and sprinkling with Parmesan cheese.

Mel dishes up three shallow bowls with very rational portions of the pasta, or about a third of what I would serve, and brings them over to the table.

"To our new program!" Mel raises her glass.

"To changing the worl'." Maria clinks.

"To surviving the second class!" I toss in.

"Tell us everything," Maria says.

While we eat, I share the highlights and lowlights: watching them all get very excited about their new gear, and then watching Juan and Joseph immediately start to play fencing team with their chef's knives, completely freaking me out and immediately ruining the edge on both knives. Seeing Mari choose to partner with Max, clearly boosting his self-esteem. Watching Aretha and Clara bond as only big girls can bond. My heart going out to Renaldo when he asks if he can work alone instead of with a partner, and knowing that feeling of never being alone at home and just wanting something for yourself. Joseph and Helena making eyes at each other, and trading digits. Max watching Joseph and Helena sparkle at each other and looking dejected, while Mari watches him, equally sad. A crush triangle is never pretty, and we have a serious one abrewing.

"You fall in loaf and you see loaf everywhere," Maria says. "What about the cooking? Do you think any of them will benefit from this?"

"Sorry, I guess I did get a little wrapped up in the personal stuff. I think it is a shockingly good group, and they all seem to have a genuine interest in food and cooking. I don't know if all of them are going to want to go to culinary school, but I think they're all participating for the right reasons, and as a pilot group, I think we chose exceptionally well. I feel like the things that drew us to them in their applications became fully revealed in person, so it feels like they were pretty honest in their essays."

"That is awesome, Alana, and Kai says thank you so much for covering for him," Mel says.

"How is he doing?"

"Tired, but slllllloowly getting better. You know his partner, Phil, is the ultimate caregiver, so he is mostly working from home so that he can be there for Kai, and I'm delivering food every other day with immune-system boosters and lots of soothing soups. Our friend Nadia, who opened the wellness spa upstairs with our other friend Janey, keeps sending over their massage therapists and Reiki and acupuncture specialists, and our business partner, Delia, sends him caramel banana pudding and sweet potato pies, which I think are probably the best thing for him. He is very motivated to get better so that we all can stop fussing."

"Food people. We can't help ourselves. The need to nurture is within us."

"I need to get sick so I can 'ave carrrrramel banana pudding," Maria says.

We all laugh.

"So, I hear you have a fabulous new boyfriend, Alana. Maria says he is just a terrific guy."

"Yes, I do. And yes, he is."

"'E is sooooo sweet. I just loaf him," Maria says.

"Oh, the official Maria De La Costa stamp of approval. That is impressive," Mel says.

"I know. I think my friends all sort of like him more than they like me."

"I know the feeling." Mel laughs. "When I first brought Jonathan around, I thought all my people would be focused on how I was doing, and instead they all just fell madly in love with him, and I was like, Hello? How about me?" Mel recently got engaged to a great guy she met a couple of years ago. He's a personal trainer who, like Mel, went through a major personal transformation, from more than 350 pounds to a fit and trim 180. The two of them are insanely adorable together. They joke about just hanging in there to be eighty years old, and then never exercising again, and eating butter and fried food and pie all day.

"How are the wedding plans going?"

"Good. We're doing it in Maine, at Jon's family's summer house. Pretty small."

"Sounds perfect," I say.

"Mmmm, so, you and Arrrrre Yay, you will 'ave the small wedding?" Maria teases. "Bennie tells me you will marrrrry 'im."

"Well, I kinda hope Bennie is right." Ever since Andres, I never really thought of myself as a wife. I always thought of myself as more of a permanent-life-partner-living-in-sin kind of girl. But every time Bennie refers to him as my future husband, my heart skips a beat. Maybe I'm a wife kind of girl after all.

"Good for you. Have it all, honey. If you can manage it, have it all. I highly recommend it," Melanie says. And it sounds like good advice to me.

I'm almost home when my cell rings.

"Hello, beautiful."

"Hello, you. How was your event?" RJ had a sales meeting tonight after work, which he wasn't really looking forward to.

"Boring. Beer and wings do not a good dinner make."

"Melanie sent me home with a bucket of leftover pasta, wanna meet me at my place and have some?"

"Um, let me think. . . . YES! I'll see you there in about fifteen."

"Yay. I'll be there in five."

That makes me so happy. I didn't think I was going to see him today.

I get home and let Dumpling out for a quick pee. Then I go inside to heat up the pasta, and I'm just setting a place at the kitchen counter when Dumpling starts bouncing and barking.

I open the door and throw my arms around RJ's neck, kissing him passionately.

"Ouch," he says sort of into my mouth, and I pull back, seeing him wince.

"I'm sorry, honey, did I hurt you?"

"Wasn't you, my love. I wracked my back today."

"Oh, no, what happened?"

"I was going down the El steps this morning, and the woman in front of me tripped and started to take a header. So I instinctively lunged forward and grabbed her, but I was sort of twisted sideways, and I had my briefcase over my other shoulder, so I essentially took her whole weight on that one arm and something just popped."

The man is an actual superhero. "That is amazing; she could have really gotten hurt. How bad is it?"

He looks at me, and I know from his eyes that he is in a lot of pain. This is a man who was an All State linebacker in high school. He has had both shoulders operated on to rebuild them. All of his joints creak and pop when he exerts himself, and his ankles can slip out of socket just from his crossing his feet on the ottoman. He has a pretty high tolerance for pain. And I can see that he is really hurting.

"Its, um, very uncomfortable."

"My hero. Shall I fetch you a handful of Advil?"

"Please."

"Okay. And there is a big ice pack designed for backs in the freezer, lean on it."

I head to the bathroom and shake four Advil out of the bottle. I bring them back to him and he swallows them dry. "This cold pack is amazing. Why do you have it?"

"I threw my back out a few years back, so I know how you feel. It is so horrible."

"How'd you do that?"

Oy. "Not saving some damsel in distress, I can tell you."

"So, lifting with your back and not your legs? Overdoing the weightlifting at the gym? Picking up a niece or nephew?"

"A fork."

"A fork?"

"Yep. I was picking up a fork."

He looks puzzled. I plate the now-warm pasta for him, giving it an extra grating of Parmesan, and hand it to him.

"Was it some world-record enormous fork?" he asks thoughtfully around a mouthful of pasta and chicken. "Man this is good. Thank you, honey."

"Nope, a fork not unlike the one you have in your hand right now. In fact, that could be the very one."

He examines the utensil in his hand.

"Doesn't seem terribly threatening."

"It isn't. I dropped it on the floor, and when I was bent over to pick it up, I sneezed."

"You sneezed."

"I sneezed. Really hard. And popped something in my back. I was out of commission for a week."

He looks at me with a combination of sympathy and amusement. "My poor, delicate flower."

"I know. It was almost as bad as the time I broke my toe." Might as well share all the embarrassing injuries.

"Did you drop a fork on it?"

"Nope. Got into a hot bath, sat down, realized it was way too hot when I scalded my girl parts, and my leg shot out from under me trying to stand back up again, and I kicked the faucet." True story. I am the klutziest person on the planet. And I like a hot bath.

RJ laughs really hard. I love his laugh. "Ow, ow, ow, you can't make me laugh like this, it hurts too much. . . ."

"I'm sorry, honey." But I love that I can make him laugh like that.

I keep him company while he finishes his pasta, and then he goes to the living room and lies down on the floor. Dumpling wanders over, sniffs him, and curls up next to his shoulder, gently licking his head.

"Awww. He's trying to make you feel better." It is so sweet to see them.

"I know. So I'm going to try not to be grossed out." RJ winks at me, and lifts one arm up to pet Dumpling, who is apparently going to give RJ's head a thorough cleaning.

"Don't be grossed out by his love."

"It isn't his love really, it's more his breath."

"Ooops. Sorry about that."

"What did you have for dinner, hmmmm, handsome? Was it the dead warthog in Limburger cheese sauce again?"

"Ewww. It isn't that bad."

"And yet, it is." RJ slowly rises from the floor, wincing, petting Dumpling as he goes. "Okay honey, it's late, and I have to scamper home. But thanks for letting me come by for a bit and for giving me delicious dinner and making me giggle." He comes over and kisses me.

"Are you okay? Are you sure you don't want to stay?"

"The spirit is willing, love, but the body needs to be flat out and still. And you are something of a flopper. I have a little bit of work to do, have to throw in a load of laundry, and want to see the end of the basketball game, then crash."

This is true. I'm a side sleeper, and I do shift from side to side with regularity. I can see how that bouncing around would not be good in his current condition. "Okay." I walk him to the door. "But call me when you get home?"

"Will do."

Ever since that first date, whichever of us leaves to go home has to call the other so that we know we are safe. And if we aren't together, RJ calls before he goes to bed.

He kisses me one more time, and heads out.

I clean up the kitchen, take Dumpling for his last walk of the night, come back and get into my pajamas. I turn on the TiVo and play an episode of *The Killing*, an amazing police procedural that Lacey turned me on to, and which I am catching up on. The end credits are rolling when I realize that RJ still hasn't called, and he left well over an hour ago. I check my watch. Eleven fifteen. I check my cell, in case he called while I was walking Dumpling. Must have gotten caught up in the game. I dial his cell.

"Hey, this is RJ, leave a message and I'll get back to you."

"Hey, it's me, you forgot to call. I'm going to call your house phone."

I dial his land line. It rings and rings. Eventually it beeps.

"Helllllooooo? RJ? You there? If you are, honey, pick up. No? Maybe you're in the bathroom. Call me when you finish."

Just what a guy needs, his girlfriend announcing on his machine that she suspects he may be pooping.

I go to the kitchen and grab a Pamplemousse. I flip channels. I check my e-mail. Eleven thirty. I call his cell. It goes to voice mail. I try the house phone again. No answer.

Now I'm a little bit worried. What if he got into a car accident? I think of how much pain he was in, and the fact that his laundry is in the basement. What if he fell down the basement stairs? What if he went to pick up the laundry basket and made his back worse and he is now lying on the basement floor in pain and not near a phone? I take a breath. He probably just fell asleep with the game on. Eleven forty. I try the cell one more time. No answer.

"Dumpling, I can't take it. I have to go for a ride." My voice catches a bit, and I'm surprised by how upset I am, how worried. If something has happened to him, I just don't know what I would do. The very idea of him in pain or something being really wrong makes my whole stomach turn over.

I throw my coat over my pajamas and slip into my boots. I drive the two and a half miles to RJ's house, figuring I will just peek around to make sure he is okay.

His car is there. The lights are on. I get out of my car, and walk up the stoop and look in. I can't see him. I walk back around the side of the house and onto the porch. Not in the kitchen or down the hall. I try to peer in the basement window, but it is dark down there, which I figure is a really good sign, since if he had headed down to do laundry he would have turned the light on. So not writhing in the basement. I walk back around the side. The light in the den is on, but I am too short to see in the window and there is no shadow moving.

I take a deep breath. I call his cell. Straight to voicemail. I call his house phone. I can't hear it ringing in the house. Okay, Alana, don't be insane, he probably has his cell on vibrate, and something is obviously wrong with his house phone because you are standing right outside the window and you would hear it. He is asleep with the game on. Go home and he will never know you were here behaving like a stark raving lunatic. I turn to leave.

"Alana?" RJ is standing on his stoop, looking at me quizzically.

And I? Burst into tears.

He comes down the stairs, and puts his arms around me, shushing me. When he realizes I am not in pain, and nothing tragic has happened, he leads me inside, where I snuffle into a Kleenex and try to explain why I am there.

"I promise, I'm not insane, I just . . . You didn't call, and you didn't answer when I called, and your back was so bad and you said you were going to do laundry and I thought maybe your back went out and you were on the floor and . . ."

"Shh. Honey. I'm fine. I came home, and wanted to get the laundry in, started some work, fell asleep with the game on. Never heard the phone ring. I'm sorry I didn't call. But this is a little bit of crazy behavior."

"I know. I was just getting ready to leave. I wasn't going to ring the bell, I swear."

"Look, I'm tired, you're tired, and I think I do understand why you're here, and I'm going to assume this is just an anomaly and I know it comes from a place of caring. And I really am sorry I didn't call." But for the first time in our relationship, he is looking at me like maybe I'm not as easy and normal as he thought. And I realize that just like I have been secretly waiting for the other shoe to drop, for the magic to fall away, he might have been thinking the same thing. Actually, this makes me feel somewhat better. To know that maybe he is scared too, that he isn't so blithe about believing in our magic. I know that, as disappointing as my past relationships have been, his have been in some ways worse. We don't dwell in the past, but there have been some clues about a couple of his exes that imply a rough time. And knowing that maybe he harbors his own fears and trust issues makes me feel both less insane and the teensiest bit more confident in what we have.

"I swear this is not my usual. And you've forgotten to

call a couple of times before and I haven't come over. It was just because of your back, all I could think was that you were hurt and couldn't call for help."

He smiles at me the way you smile at a small child. "Well, it was sweet of you to worry and very rude of me to not call. I'll make you a deal; I'll try to remember to be better about calling, if you promise to not assume I'm dead if I forget now and again."

"Deal."

"Thank you for caring about me enough to be so worried and to come all the way over here."

"You're welcome. Thank you for caring about me enough to not break up with me for acting like some crazed stalker."

I kiss him, and he walks me to the door. "I would never break up with you for caring about me. And I don't think you're crazy."

"Okay." I feel like such a complete idiot, and just know that even though he is being kind and understanding, I've taken something of a step back in his estimation.

"Alana?"

"Yeah?"

He grins. "Call me when you get home."

"You bet I will."

And I do.

17

I open the oven at my parents' house and pull out the pans of chicken. In the other room, I can hear the buzz of my insane family as they compete to try to impress RJ with funny stories, details of exceptional children, and embarrassing tales of my youth. The whole gang showed up for this Shabbat, including Aunt Rivka and Uncle Eli. Luckily the cousins have scattered to the four winds, two on the West Coast, two on the East, and one in Amsterdam, so it's just the insanity of the immediate family. RJ claims that he is jealous, he just has his folks and sister and her family, and isn't able to really be close to his extended family in the way that my family is.

Nat wanders in to see if I need any help. "He is so freaking charming. Mama and Papa are eating out of his hand."

"I know, he's good-manned adorable."

"He really is. And he seems to just fit, here and at your party and with your friends and stuff. And you guys are so, I dunno, easy together. Do you think he's the one?"

I take a deep breath. "I do. I really do." I haven't dared say it out loud, but there it is, my secret joy and terror all in one.

She throws her arms around me. "Good for you, Lanuschka. That makes me very happy."

"Okay, okay, let me get this chicken organized, would you? Aren't there children to deal with out there?"

"Fine. You better be careful, mouth off too much and this family will vote you off the island and keep RJ instead." I swat her on the butt and shoo her back into the melee. But I can't keep from peeking down the hall; RJ is flanked by my parents, with my niece Lia in his lap. He is laughing at something she is whispering in his ear, and my folks are grinning ear to ear. My heart swells with pride to see him so connected already, and to hear from Nat that everyone approves. Not that I was worried. After the last schmegegge I brought home, the bar was very low. But it increases my joy to see how well RJ fits in.

I get the chicken out on a platter. I fluff the kasha varnishkes, sautéed buckwheat groats with little pasta bowties, and spoon it into a large serving bowl. Glazed carrots, steamed green beans, pickled beets. Rivka has brought the challah, as usual, and RJ brought wine. I'm discovering that when he says he has an interest in wine, what he means is that he has enormously vast knowledge, is so good that wine importers invite him to come on buying trips to France to help taste the wines and make notes to advise them on their purchases, and that he has a cellar so deep that it will outlive him. Tonight he has brought three magnums of a gorgeous Burgundy, and a bottle of port older than me. I mean, it's no unlabeled Polish vino, but it'll do.

I'm just getting ready to call everyone in for dinner, when the doorbell chimes. Who on earth?

I walk out to see who it is, and there it is, the only thing that could spoil this perfect night.

Patrick.

My mom is hugging him, and the nieces and nephews are jumping up and down and running around him. He is carrying a casserole dish, and has a huge Toys R Us bag over his shoulder. Jenny takes the food from him, while Sasha relieves him of the bag, and tells the kids they can have it after dinner, removing the temptation to the hall closet. RJ is standing back watching, and I immediately go to his side.

"Oy. You ready for this on top of everything else?"

He kisses the side of my neck, right under my ear. "Born ready, baby."

Patrick makes his way through the crowd and finally lands in front of us. "This must be the famous RJ."

"Hello, Patrick, it's nice to finally meet you." They shake hands firmly. I'm waiting for a black hole to open in the floor, or a break in the space-time continuum. But nope, nothing exciting. Just Patrick meeting my boyfriend, as if it is the most normal thing in the world.

"Mama . . ." I say, as she walks by.

"Vat? Is shabbas. Patreek ees alvays invited shabbas."

"Yeah, Alana. I am *always* invited shabbas," Patrick says, putting his arm around my mother and kissing her cheek.

"And yet, this week, no one mentioned it to me." I should have known Patrick would weasel his way into this dinner, especially when he overheard Gloria and me talking about how much she liked meeting RJ and telling me that the dinner would be great, especially now that he had bonded with my siblings at the party. Whatever. I'm not going to let it bug me.

Patrick's offering for the meal, short rib tzimmes, joins the rest of the items on the buffet, scarily perfect and utterly traditional, completely incongruous coming from someone who oozes Gentile out of his pores. Mama must be sneaking him family recipes now. Everyone walks down the line, entering the kitchen through the door from the living room and exiting out the other door to the dining room, plates full of delicious.

We are not a religious family. For us Shabbat dinner is just an excuse to get the family together. But we do say the three key prayers, wine, candles, bread, just to honor the tradition. Mama lights the candles. *"Baruch ata Adonai, eloheynu melech ha'olam asher kiddushanu bat mitzvoh tov vitzi vanu le chad lich ne'er, shel Shabbat."*

Papa breaks a piece off the nearest challah, the shiny mahogany crust of the braided bread giving way to soft yellow interior. *"Baruch ata Adoani, eloheynu melech ha'olam hamotze lechem mein ha'aretz."*

Mama looks around to see which of us will step up for the blessing over the wine. Suddenly, at my elbow, RJ says, "Shall I?" And raises his glass.

Mama nods.

"Baruch ata Adonai, eloheynu melech ha'olam, boray prei hagofen." His Hebrew is perfect, if somewhat strange spoken with the slight lilt to his voice, a tiny remnant of the Tennessee accent he has all but obliterated in his thirty years in Chicago.

Papa claps delightedly, and Mama grins. My siblings nod approvingly, and the kids at their end of the table giggle, but they don't really know why. Patrick, sitting on my other side, raises his glass to RJ, leaning over me slightly. "Showoff."

"Not bad for a shaygetz, huh?" RJ says, using the somewhat derogatory word for a Gentile man. "It's not my first rodeo." It's not Patrick's first rodeo either, he's probably been at a couple of dozen of these over the years, but he's never offered a prayer.

"You do very goot," my mom says.

"You can be shabbas goy!" Aunt Rivka says.

We all laugh, even Patrick, who must suddenly feel like the second cutest girl at the dance. I lean over to him and whisper, "I'm glad you're here. And I hope you get a chance to really chat with RJ."

"Alana, if you like him, I'm sure he's great. You don't need my blessing. He seems fine."

I'm not particularly sure why it hurts my feelings, but it does. Every single person in my life who has met RJ has raved, gushed, expressed personal delight at having made his acquaintance. Patrick's casual dismissal of "fine" really rubs me the wrong way. I'm about to call him on it, when RJ takes my hand under the table.

"Thank you for bringing me here." And my ire melts away. If Patrick has his head so far up his own ass that he doesn't want to make an effort to know this spectacular man, that is entirely his loss.

"Thank you for coming. And thank you for being."

"Being what?"

I lean over and kiss him. "Just being."

After dinner is over and we are all stuffed to the gills, Patrick retrieves the bag he brought and turns it over to the kids who tear into it with wild abandon, unearthing an endless trove of dolls and action figures and new games for the Wii. The gaggle of cousins dig in, finding something for everyone to get excited about.

The rest of us divide and conquer, some of us cleaning up in the kitchen, some getting the tables and chairs squared away, and much to my chagrin and delight, my dad, Patrick, Uncle Eli, and RJ step out on the porch for cigars. That should be fairly priceless. I begin to head in that direction, to save RJ if need be, but a hand on my arm stops me.

"Leave it, Lana," Nat says. "He's fine. That's a man who doesn't need anyone to fight his battles or protect him. You want him out there, and you want him out there without you. Trust me."

"I just . . ."

"Don't. He's great, honey. Leave it be."

When it is finally time to head out, RJ receives hugs, kisses, back slaps, and shoulder grapples from my entire family as we make our way to the door. He receives an open invitation to return from both of my parents, and each of my siblings has requested a double date with us in the near future. And Joshie breaks away from the Wii long enough to come running down the hall and launch himself into RJ's arms, whispering something very serious in his ear.

"You bet, buddy. That's a date."

"Thank you, Uncle RJ!" he says, and runs back down the hall.

"Uncle RJ!" Sasha says.

"What on earth did you promise my kid?" Alexei asks.

"He mentioned that he was sort of interested in art these days. I told him that a good friend of mine is a curator at the Art Institute, and that he can take us on a private tour of the stuff in the vaults."

"Oh, goodness, he would just love that," Sara says. "Thank you."

We head to the car, Patrick following along behind us.

"Nice to meet you, man," Patrick says as we get to the car, offering a firm handshake.

"Very nice to meet you as well, Patrick, I'm glad you were here." RJ shakes back.

"I'm sure we'll hang out again soon."

"That would be great."

"You're a lucky guy, my Alana is the best."

"Yes, she is." RJ puts his arm around me.

"Even if she does fart in her sleep," Patrick says, and my jaw hits the ground. He has just broken the barrier, referenced our one night together, and shattered the unspoken understanding between us to pretend that the incident never happened. And worse, he's done it in such a casual and insulting manner.

"Only rarely. And I think it's cute. Sort of musical really." RJ is unflappable. Luckily for me, I confessed about my error in judgment with Patrick during the trading of basic info about exes, with limited details, and he was totally cool about it.

Patrick seems a little thrown by the lack of reaction from both RJ and me. But I refuse to be baited.

"We should all have dinner or something one of these days. Patrick, you can bring, you know, whoever your agent sends for the evening," I say pointedly.

"Ha. Funny." But he doesn't look amused. He does rally, ever the smooth one. "Alana, my princess, have a great weekend, I will see you Monday. RJ, see you soon, I hope." He kisses my cheek, jumps into his new Escalade, and takes off.

"Think we should follow him to be sure he doesn't try to bust a drug dealer or take down a mob boss?" RJ asks.

"I think he is going to have to take care of himself tonight. I have more important things to focus on."

"Such as?"

"Such as making my fabulous boyfriend know how happy he makes me."

He opens the car door for me, and kisses me. "I'm up for that. Did he really just try to make me jealous about your one-night stand? Really?"

"I have no idea what the hell that was. Marking territory, maybe. I would imagine he is very threatened by you."

"Well, at least he didn't piss on you."

"That would have been a Dumpling move."

"Which is why he is having a sleepover!"

We ride back to RJ's place. Barry has Dumpling tonight. Considering his behavior of late, I couldn't risk bringing him to RJ's, even though he was invited. RJ has rugs worth more than my car, and I can only imagine what my crazy dog could do to one of them.

We settle into his den, and he brings in a couple cans of Pamplemousse, which he is now as addicted to as I am. We clink cans, and snuggle up. JP, his cantankerous cat, jumps up into my lap, purring like a kitten.

"That cat hasn't liked anyone since the first Bush administration. But look at him love you. How is it possible you were single, you wondrous woman?" he asks.

"I'm really really picky. What about you?"

"I had pretty much just written it off. Failed marriage, failed long-term relationships. I just thought, focus on work, friends, family, play my guitar, and head off into the sunset alone like a good cowpoke."

I look up at his sweet face. "I'm glad you didn't give up."

"I sort of had. But you brought me back." He leans in and kisses me. "You and Michael Chabon!" Apparently it was my listing *The Amazing Adventures of Kavalier & Klay* as the book I was currently reading that was the piece of the puzzle that finally got him to answer me on EDestiny. It's one of his favorite books, and he took it as a sign. "Falling in love with you is the best thing that has ever happened to me."

"And the best thing that has ever happened to me." I pause, and take a deep breath. "I really love you, RJ Oliver."

He smiles widely, and I can see that there are tears shimmering in his eyes. "Truly?"

"Truly, madly, deeply."

And nothing in the world has ever felt more utterly and comfortably true.

18

I gather the kids around me at the end of class.

"So, one at a time, what did we learn today?"

Joseph throws his hand in the air. I nod at him. "Well, we learned about food safety and proper cleaning and storage, and the danger of cross-contamination, so we really learned that my moms has been trying to kill the family for years." We all laugh.

"We learned about the differences between processed foods and whole foods," Max says. "And how it can be healthier to eat some real things like butter and olive oil instead of processed saturated fats like margarine and Crisco."

"We learned that if something is too spicy you have to drink milk or eat bread and not drink water, and that Helena has a mouth made of asbestos!" says Aretha, referring to the chicken vindaloo that Helena brought in as her traditional family recipe, in which the level of spice blew all our heads off.

Renaldo raises his hand. "We learned that you can take a recipe and make it healthier by replacing certain ingredients." Renaldo had brought in a rich pork stew that we lightened up by adding more veggies, trading out turkey breast for the pork, and just searing the chunks of meat in a little oil instead of deep frying them.

"Good, guys, what else?" I'm so proud of how far they have come in the past weeks, and so sad that this is my last class with them, since Kai is completely healed and finally has his energy back. It took him five weeks instead of three, and while I was sad for him and his slow recovery, I was selfishly glad for me, since working with these kids has been one of the most rewarding things in my entire career.

"We learned that the most important thing in a dish is balance of sweet, sour, salty, bitter, and savory, and that if you taste something and you don't know what it needs, you can go down that list and see if all those flavors are there," Juan says, getting the words out quickly. He has been a surprise superstar. I had written him off as a jock who was just going to be a little lost without the team, but his sports experience has made him a natural leader in the kitchen, and I can easily see him leading a brigade on the line. I gave him a copy of Gordon Ramsay's autobiography, since he also turned to cooking after an injury cut short a professional soccer career, and Juan read it in one week.

"We learned that Aretha makes the best macaroni and cheese on the planet," Clara gushes about her new BFF.

"And that Joseph can make an omelet in under two minutes," Helena says about her already ex-boyfriend. The whirlwind courtship flamed hard and fizzled quickly, luckily without much drama for the rest of us. He nods and winks at her, so maybe things aren't as off as I think they are.

"I learned that I am really going to miss Chef Alana," says Little Mari, pouting.

"Yeah, why you have to go, Chef?" Renaldo says.

"Aw, guys, I'll be back. But trust me; you are going to love Chef Kai. He's like a rock star. I was only ever a substitute teacher here. And I will be paying very close attention to each and every one of you as the semester goes on."

"We brought you something, Chef," Max says, offering up a wrapped package.

The lump in my throat threatens to choke me. "Aw, you guys . . ."

"Open it, open it!" Aretha says, impatient.

I carefully remove the paper to reveal a lovely linen binder. I open it up and it has eight sections, each labeled with the name of one of the students. When I flip to those sections I can see that each of them has written me a letter, included a picture, and several recipes from their families or of their own creation.

"It's a custom cookbook from all of us," Mari says.

"You guys, this is, without a doubt, the single best present anyone has ever given me. Thank you all so much. I love you guys." We end up in an awkward group hug. Finally from the middle of the pack, Joseph's voice.

"Damn, does it have to be all *Dangerous Minds* up in here?"

We all laugh, since the running joke these past weeks has involved all the classic "White Teacher Makes a Difference in the Ghetto" movies.

"Hey, Chef," Clara says. "What is your boyfriend doing for you for Valentine's this weekend, hmm?"

I blush. "He is making me dinner. And let that be a lesson to all of you, cooking for someone is an act of love."

"Don't you want him to take you out? Go somewhere nice for a fancy dinner?" Aretha says.

"All I care about is that we are together. And going out for a fancy dinner is not nearly as personal as the fact that he wants to cook for me."

"That's cool, I guess," Juan says.

"I think so. And I think each and every one of you has plenty of love to put on plates. So I want you to come next week knowing that I am passing you off to a truly amazing chef, and give him total respect. I'm going to be back in a few weeks when Patrick Conlon is doing his master class."

I give each of them a hug and a personal thank-you as they leave. I watch out the window to be sure their van is gone before I dissolve in tears.

The next afternoon, after a brutally slow workday where I can't focus on anything except the clock, RJ picks me and Dumpling up to drive out to the cabin for the weekend. It's our first whole weekend away, and I'm excited to show him my place and have a relaxing and romantic time. And I'm hoping that Dumpling will behave himself. It's been a couple of weeks since he did anything overtly awful, mostly he just tries to get between us when we are hanging out on the couch, and we still have to lock him out of the bedroom.

Well, he did eat RJ's laptop charging cord a couple of days ago, but that was hopefully just a little slipup.

We're halfway there when a smell that can only be described as the foulest stench on the planet wafts up into the front seat and slams my head back. Goddamnit.

"What. The. Hell. Is. THAT?" RJ says, opening his window, despite the freezing mid-February air.

"Oh, honey. I'm so sorry. Dumpling, um, juiced."

"It smells like a thousand dead crabs just washed up in this car. What the hell is juicing?"

Sigh. There is nothing sexy about this sentence. "Sometimes his anal glands relax and release their liquid. It usually happens when he is either excited or nervous. I'm so sorry. I'll find a pet store." I frantically search with my iPhone for something close by.

"Don't we just need a gas station?"

"It's better if we can pick up this enzyme stuff." I check my iPhone. "There's a Petco just off the next exit."

We head for the store, and I pick up a bottle of cleaner and a roll of paper towels, and proceed to de-funk RJ's backseat, grateful that at least he has leather interior. Fabric would have been done for. We get quickly back on the road.

"I gotta say, that is about the nastiest thing I have ever smelled. I feel like it's in my clothes."

"I know, it's just beyond awful. Luckily it doesn't happen that often."

"I guess. Is there anything to be done about it?"

"Well, he can go to the vet to have his glands expressed regularly."

"I'm in. I'll pay for it. How often? Once a month? Once a week? I don't care. Whatever the cost, it will be my treat."

"Aww, honey. You don't have to do that."

"If I'm going to live with that dog, I think I do."

In the past couple of weeks, RJ and I have admitted to each other that we both feel that we have found the person we are supposed to be with, and have started to refer to the life we want to make together as a thing that will happen instead of something that might happen. The biggest issue is that RJ loves his little bungalow, and his lovely neighborhood, and is getting his head around the idea of leaving them both to move into my place. It's only two and a half miles away, but for RJ it is something of a chasm. He recognizes that the space is an issue, and knows that if his place was as large as mine, I would be happy to live there, but I can't downsize at this point. He is, as he likes to say, getting his head around it.

"Tell you what, when you move in, I'll pay for the gland-expressing program."

"We'll figure it out."

And I know we will.

We get to the cabin and I give him the tour. It's a simple place: two bedrooms, two bathrooms, and one large room that encompasses kitchen, dining area and living room. A small screened-in porch, and a back deck that leads to the Puddle. I have six acres of woods, a little creek, and a shed for storing equipment and the outdoor furniture. We drop our bags in the master bedroom, and unload the groceries for the weekend. I'm unpacking the cooler when I see a card with my name on it.

"What is this?"

"Maybe a little Valentine."

"Can I open it?"

"You may."

I open the card, which has a picture of French fries on it and the words *My heart . . . my life . . . and one, maybe two of my French fries . . .* and on the inside, *All yours.*

"Awwww," I say as I start to read what he has written.

Alana—

By the time you read this we will be spending our first Valentine's Day together. Hopefully the first of many. While I know we both pooh-poohed the Hallmark holiday, I can't let a day that signifies how important one person can be in one's life go by without notice. No one has ever touched me at my core the way you have. I love being on this road with you, and I'm glad you finally caught up to me! I've never before felt that I was truly pointed in the same direction like I am with you. You had me at pamplemousse.

With all the love and like and admiration I could ever muster in this or any other life, writ large and amplified with the world's hugest megaphone.

Yours,
RJ

I throw my arms around him, wetting his cheek with my tears of pure joy.

"That is the sweetest, most wonderful Valentine ever, and I love you very much."

"I love you, baby. Thank you for making me the happiest man in the world."

Damn, that man is a good kisser. We abandon the kitchen for the bedroom, leaving Dumpling to his own devices in the front room.

After a post-romp nap, we emerge in bathrobes to a pouting dog and ravenous appetites. RJ gets to work in the kitchen on the dinner he is preparing, allowing me to sous chef. He seasons duck breasts with salt, pepper, coriander, and orange zest. Puts a pot of wild rice on to cook, asks me to top and tail some green beans. We open a bottle of Riesling, sipping while we cook, and I light a fire. The place gets cozy, full of delicious smells and the crackling fire. We ignore the dining table in favor of sitting on the floor in front of the fire, and tuck in.

"This is amazing," I tell him, blown away by the duck, perfectly medium-rare and succulent, with crispy, fully rendered skin. "Really, honey, it couldn't be better."

"Thank you, baby. That's a major compliment. And I have to say, I love cooking with you."

"I love cooking with you." And I did. I never once felt like I wanted to jump in or make a change, or suggest a different choice. I followed him as I would have followed any chef, and the results of trusting him are completely delicious, literally and figuratively.

We devour the dinner, demolish the wine, and lounge happily in front of the fire.

"I have something for you," I say, getting up to get his present.

"And I for you," he says.

I hand him a small bag, stuffed with tissue. He opens it and pulls out the book.

"*The Amazing Adventures of Kavalier and Klay*! It's our book! Thank you, sweetie."

"Open it."

He opens the front cover to reveal the inscription.

To RJ

Happy Valentine's Day. I'm glad to have had some small part in helping your soul mate find you. Here's to a lifetime of wonder and adventure together.

Michael Chabon

"How did you . . . ?"

"Emily knows his wife. Six degrees of writer separation. She helped me."

"That is amazing, sweetheart. Thank you so much."

We kiss. And when we part, there is a tiny bag in my hand. "And what is this?"

"Open it and find out."

I open the bag to discover a beautiful pair of earrings, little round hammered white-gold drops with one tiny diamond embedded slightly off center. They are simple and sub-tle, and just the perfect thing. "I love them."

"I went to that store you were telling me about, Virtu on Damen? The owner helped me; she said she knew this was a designer you like."

"They're perfect. Thank you so much. This is the best Valentine's Day ever."

"Yes, it certainly is."

We head back to the bedroom and snuggle in. RJ falls asleep quickly, and I realize I have a powerful thirst and have forgotten to fill my water bottle. I always keep a bottle of water next to my bed. A bottle, not a glass, since I have an irrational fear of a bug falling into an open glass and drink-ing it in the night. I never said I wasn't a crazy person.

I sneak out of bed and tiptoe down the hall, filling my bottle from the cooler in the kitchen. I can feel that the jug is almost empty and make a mental note to return it for a full one tomorrow when RJ and I are running around. I want to take him to this cool place full of rugs and textiles and interesting furniture, and maybe some antiquing in Rich-mond. And tomorrow night we are going for all-you-can-eat broasted chicken at Crandall's. Sunday there will be a hearty country breakfast at a local diner before heading back to the city. I drink half of my bottle of water, refill it to the brim, and tiptoe back to bed. I drink a little more water, and fall asleep.

I wake somewhat suddenly, and check the clock. It is only seven. But I need to get up. My stomach is churning. With all my stomach issues and the reflux and the whole ex-gallbladder thing, sometimes I get very nauseated. Usually it means I'm hungry. Sometimes it means I have to poop. Often it means both. I leave RJ sleeping, and since I don't think I have to poop, I sneak out to the kitchen, and eat half a banana. While I'm up, I throw a load of laundry in. The banana should settle things down, so I try to go back to sleep. But about twenty minutes later, I feel a terrible urge to go to the bathroom. Guess I chose wrong. I go to the other bathroom, so as not to pollute the one in my bedroom, grateful that RJ is such a sound sleeper. Terrific. Couldn't my bowels just be normal for our first weekend getaway? I'm pissed. And from what happens in the bathroom, it is going to be a long morning. I go out to grab some Imodium from my purse; I'm always prepared for this circumstance, and eat the other half of the banana. Then I go back to bed. But twenty minutes later, I need the bathroom again, and this time it is no longer lower digestive.

There is nothing in the world I hate more than throwing up. I would rather be in pain. Or bleeding—I have no problem with bleeding. But puking is just the worst thing on the planet. And nothing could make vomiting worse than trying to do it quietly up the hall from your fabulous sleeping boyfriend on Valentine's weekend. Unfortunately, this is the position I find myself in. On my knees, head in the toilet, trying desperately to throw up in the quietest manner possible and praying that I can manage it without crapping my pants at the same time.

Yes, I am that talented, and no, you don't want to know the details, but let's just say I owe a hotel in Turkey a bath mat.

I am somewhat grateful for the fact that banana pretty much tastes the same in either direction.

I'm rinsing my mouth out with the Listerine from the medicine cabinet, when RJ appears behind me.

"Hey. You okay?"

I look at him. I shake my head. "I appear to be sick. How do you feel?"

"Poor baby. I feel fine. How sick are you?"

"If you don't close that door, you will find out." He obliges by closing the door, and I lose it again. Ugh.

I rinse again and when I think I have at least some time before the next wave, I head out to the front room. RJ has dressed in a flash.

"Okay, what do you need? Gatorade? Saltines?"

"Probably both. I'm so sorry, honey. What a stupid thing to have happen. Are you sure you are feeling okay? This doesn't feel flu-ish; this feels more like food poisoning."

"Really, I feel totally fine. And we ate exactly the same things. Did you have anything I didn't have?"

"Nope."

"Aw, sweetheart, that's just the worst. Want a glass of water?"

"Please."

He walks over and grabs a glass, and starts to fill it from the cooler and then stops. "Hey, I'm pretty sure your water isn't supposed to be this color."

I turn and look at the glass he is holding up. It is a pale green.

"I think your water has gone off. When was the last time you were out here?"

It's been a couple of months since I was able to get here, and there were only a couple of inches left in the water bottle. That part of the kitchen gets some sun from the skylight, algae or mold or something must have grown in the bottle. Which I drank happily from last night. Oh, no.

I bolt for the bathroom, throw up, and then immediately

have explosive diarrhea. Fantastic. I have given myself water poisoning.

I come back out, carrying the deadly water bottle from the bedroom.

"Oh no, did you drink from there?" RJ says. I nod miserably. "Okay, here's some water from the tap." He offers me a glass that is blissfully clear, cool, and refreshing.

I flop onto the couch, and RJ tucks a throw blanket around me, and places the water on the table beside me.

"I'm going to make a list of what you need and then go out and get it, okay, honey?"

I nod. "I'm just mortified."

"Don't. You can't help getting sick. It's not like you did it on purpose. Let me take care of you."

"Okay. Um, Gatorade, something citrusy, and nothing blue or purple. Saltines. Maybe some chicken broth. Imodium. If you take a right at the head of the road and go straight about two miles you'll run right into a Walgreens."

"You got it. Will you be okay here for a little bit?"

"Yep. Thank you, honey."

Below me, an insistent bark. "Does he need to be fed?"

"Yes, please."

"C'mon, boy, how about breakfast?" Dumpling follows RJ to the kitchen, and I can hear kibble hitting bowl and dog hitting kibble. The buzzer goes off in the laundry room. I can hear RJ opening the door, and the unmistakable sound of wet laundry heading into the dryer.

"You don't have to . . ." I want to tell him he doesn't have to do my laundry, but unfortunately, I have to run to the bathroom again.

When I come back to the front room, I can see RJ out in the back with Dumpling. They are playing, and the sight warms my heart. I settle back onto the couch, and sip more of the water RJ left for me. They come back in, RJ carrying a blue bag. "Where do you drop these?"

"There's a can outside next to the front door."

He walks by, kissing my forehead. "I'm going to go get supplies and be right back. Dumpling, you take care of Mommy while I'm gone, okay, boy?" Dumpling jumps up on the couch next to me, and puts one paw on my thigh as if to say, I've got her, Captain.

"Thank you." I hate the tone in my voice. I sound so miserable and weak.

"I'll be back soon." And he is gone.

And that is when I start to weep. Because nothing makes me more miserable than being sick. But being sick with some one to take care of me for the first time in fifteen years, that is the best feeling in the world, and as miserable as I feel, I am also so very grateful to be able to let someone wonderful take care of me.

I doze off, but the sound of RJ coming back wakes me. Not only has he brought me both lemon and orange Gatorade and saltines and Imodium, but a stack of trashy magazines, a deck of cards, some old fashioned lemon drops, a crossword book, and a leopard-print Snuggie. I spend the better part of the day in and out of both the bathroom and consciousness. RJ watches television, does crossword puzzles, and finishes my laundry. By five o'clock it has been more than two hours since I threw up, and I think I can make it home.

"Will you be awfully disappointed to leave tonight?"

"Of course not, honey. I'm sure you just want to be home. I'll get the car all packed up."

The drive home is pretty quiet; I'm totally out of it. We listen to NPR, and I doze a little bit. When we get to my house he heats up some broth for me, and makes some dry toast. He runs out and picks up some sorbet, which goes down smooth and cold and sweet and is the perfect thing. The worst of it seems to have passed, but I still have that icky feeling that it could come back any minute.

"So, what's your pleasure, should I stay or should I go?"

"I'd love for you to stay, but I will totally understand if you want to go. This has been a bust of a weekend."

"Hey, not at all. I'm just so sorry you got sick. But if you're up for me staying, I would love to stay. And we can still spend the day together tomorrow; we can just cuddle up here and watch old movies."

"I'd like that. Thank you for taking such good care of me."

"It's my job. I plan on taking good care of you for as long as you'll let me."

"I plan to let you for as long as you'll do it."

"Good girl. I'm going to take this pooch for a walk. Do you need anything while I'm out?"

"Nope."

"Okay. We shall return. C'mon, boy, let's go for a walk!"

And this time Dumpling doesn't look back at me when RJ attaches the leash.

19

I arrive at Maria's house about twenty minutes late for the meeting with the At Our Core Foundation Board of Trustees, which is the arm of Maria's charitable organization that is in charge of the nutrition in schools program and the new culinary internship program. I hate being late. I always feel as if it makes me look scattered and unprofessional. As a result, I'm often early, since I give myself ample time to get everywhere. Sometimes I'm ridiculously early, which is why I always have books and such in my car, since frequently I have to sit and wait for twenty or thirty minutes until it is appropriate to actually show up for my appointments.

And I was, of course, completely on schedule to be here on time, except Patrick had a fit to pitch, and this time it was directed at me. I'd spent the weekend in New York with RJ, going to art galleries and meeting friends and spending time with Bennie and eating fabulously. We'd stayed at the Waldorf, shopped in SoHo, and eaten rice pudding from Rice to Riches for an afternoon snack every day. It was wonderful and easy and he showed me a New York I'd never seen. I'd patently refused to answer my phone, respond to inane stealth messages, or reply to e-mails. Not one thing Patrick tried to engage me in all weekend had any actual merit—it was all about what should he do about this woman he'd slept with once in LA who has now moved to Chicago and seems to think they should be spending a lot of time together. Or did I think that he should start working with a different personal trainer because he feels like he now knows what he has to say to his current one to get him to back off a bit, and maybe he would do better with someone new he would feel compelled to impress. Or why had I let him go so long without watching *The Wire*, which is clearly the best television show ever made. I ignored him completely for two and a half days, sending a quick note that I was in New York, and would be happy to chat Monday morning.

This did not go over well.

"Seriously, Alana, what the fuck?" He laid into me pretty much as soon as we were done taping for the day. "You get a boyfriend and suddenly you go off the reservation?" His tone when he says "boyfriend" is as dismissive as he can make it.

"Patrick, it was the weekend. I was out of town. Yes, with my boyfriend. Nothing you sent me had anything to do with work, so I chose to not interrupt my time away to offer you advice on women, working out, or your television habits. I'm allowed to have weekends, you know? We're heading into crazy time, we've got a guest shoot on *Today*, we've got the Charleston Food and Wine Festival, and we have to shoot next year's Thanksgiving and Christmas specials. We're balls to the wall for the next month, and I wanted to have a nice weekend away with RJ before he has to put up with my schedule going all wonky."

"Fine for you, but this is the job, Alana, you know that. This is not a nine-to-five gig."

"I'm aware of that."

"All I'm saying is that you have to call me back, respond to me. You had no way of knowing if there might not be some work stuff I would have wanted to go over with you."

"You're right, because nothing you sent me was about work. I'll make a deal with you. I will never ignore your messages or notes when they specifically mention work."

"Fine."

"Okay?"

"Okay."

"You going to tell me what this is really about?"

"Can't."

"Well, you'd better figure out how soon, because Patrick? This? It's not good for us. I don't want to fight, and I don't want you feeling frustrated with me. But there has to be space."

"Fair enough. Besides, it's not forever."

"Oh yeah, why is that?"

"Well, you know . . . relationships, this business. You said yourself, look at our schedule. You're like me, Alana; ultimately work will always come first. I mean, he seems nice, and I'm glad you're having a bit of fun, but eventually he'll leave, and you'll let him because our life is easier without complications."

I can't even believe he said that. Everyone in my life, everyone who loves me and cares about my well-being is so excited about my relationship with RJ. And here is one of the people who should be so happy and hopeful for me, and he is saying that the relationship is doomed to failure, and worse, that he is sort of biding his time waiting for it.

"That is a really shitty thing to say."

"It's just the way of the world. It's not personal. Fifty percent of marriages end in divorce, the stats have to be higher for non-legal dating things." He is so matter-of-fact, as if he isn't trying to hurt me but just speaking basic truths. "Hey, maybe you're the exception that proves the rule, but be real istic, the chances aren't great. It's just much more likely that you guys will hang out for a while and then you won't. I'm not saying it will be some ugly thing, I'm just saying that the odds are that this isn't forever. So I'm not going to get my panties in a twist about you slacking a bit for the time being. Boyfriends come and go; Patrick is forever." He smiles and rumples my hair.

"Patrick. Be careful. Because I have to say, if you ask me to choose, I might not choose you." My chest tightens, especially since I don't want to think about the possibility that he might be right.

"No one has to choose anything. Time will out. Besides, I've got you on contract for another three years!" He laughs, and I know I have to leave before I completely lose my mind.

"I've got to go, I've got a meeting. I'd prefer to not continue this conversation so that I don't say something I'll regret."

"Why? Are you on the rag?"

That's it. I have to get out. I give him a look that I hope is appropriately withering, and leave without saying another word, just turn on my heel and walk away. I hit traffic on the way to Maria's, and by the time I arrive, they are already under way. I sneak in and grab a seat. Mel winks at me, and Maria jokingly looks at her watch and raises an eyebrow. We hear reports from the charter schools, and Mel talks about the intern program and how great the students are doing. Maria asks about how things are going with trying to make inroads with the rest of the school system, and Rachel, the executive director of the Foundation, says that they have the support of the mayor and his wife, and some positive initial meetings with the teachers union. Various board members ask questions, which get answered, offer program advice, which is duly noted, and talk about fund-raising ideas.

My stomach is in knots. I can hear all of the wonderful things that the Foundation is achieving, but nothing really sinks in. All I can think about is stupid Patrick and his blathering. I have to try to squelch the fears that it brings up for me. RJ and I have been talking easily and blithely about forever. We talk about when we are going to live together, and he makes comments about things he likes in his soon-to-be-new neighborhood, since he reluctantly agrees that trying to cram us into his adorable bungalow would be the death of us both, and is still "trying to get his head around" the reality of moving into my place. I've offered to give it up and look for something new together to start fresh, but he says he does like my place very much and believes it makes a lot of sense to live there together. We joke about Lacey renting his house, since she has been getting the itch to move, and Jaxie would love his area, so close to a big park and with a lovely little backyard. We've talked about the trips we are going to take and the parties we want to have. We are hosting our first joint dinner party next week, a blend of his friends and mine, at my house. For the first time in my adult life I'm in a relationship where I feel completely myself, utterly at ease, and slowly letting go of my fears about the future. So why is it that there is a part of me that is struggling not to believe Patrick? I believe that the love I feel is real and permanent; it grows deeper every day. And I believe that RJ feels the same way. And he is completely supportive of my work and my schedule. At least so far. But then I remember that we've only really been together for four months, even though we had nearly a month and a half of meaningful communication before we met.

I shake my head. This is stupid. My parents met, got married, and emigrated to the U.S. in the span of three months.

Sasha and Jenny got engaged after dating for six months. Alexei and Sara spontaneously got married in Vegas when they were there for her college roommate's wedding after they had only been together just under a year. And yes, I married Andres after only three weeks, but we aren't really going to count that. I was young and dumb and in Spain and drinking a lot of Rioja. The bottom line is, when we fall for real, my people, we fall hard and fast. I don't want to play games or follow someone else's timeframe. Bennie and Barry both think that I am not crazy in the least to be talking forever with RJ. Maria thinks it is the coolest thing ever. Mina, Emily, and Lacey have a bet going as to when the proposal is going to occur, with a round of breakfast burritos at Lula on the line.

So why the fuck can't Patrick get with the program? Why does he have to be so negative? He has one divorce under his belt and no actual relationships since then. Suddenly he is the expert on love?

"Alana? Anything to add?" Melanie says.

Uh-oh. Crap. I really have not heard anything that has been said in the past five minutes. "Nope, I think that pretty much covers it." I hope they don't notice my cop-out.

"Good," says Rachel. "I think that does it. Thank you all so much for your work and for your input tonight, we really appreciate it. Thank you, Maria, for hosting. We'll see you month after next. The meeting will be at Melanie's new South Loop location. Alana, if you have a moment?"

Everyone chats a bit while gathering their stuff together, and I walk over to sit with Rachel.

"So, how do you feel about the new program?" she asks, sipping water and clearly relaxing a bit after having to lead the meeting, which is a little bit like herding cats. The good part about the board of trustees for Maria's foundation is that they are very engaged. The bad news is that they are *very* engaged, and it can often be difficult to keep them focused and to gently let them know that the staff actually knows what it's doing. They love to come up with big new ideas, and keeping them excited and motivated, and generous—while gently explaining that launching a city-wide cooking competition for kids with the grand prize being an appearance on Maria's show is not exactly connected to our mission of nutrition education—is a full-time and often thankless job.

"I think it is going great. I've spoken with Kai and he is very excited about how they are doing, and thinks that all eight of them will finish the program strong. He is fairly certain that four of them are likely to accept the scholarships if offered, and two more are on the fence. For a first run, I think that is pretty amazing."

"Kai said that the students really responded to you, and that the curriculum you all put together seems very manageable and replicable. He even thinks that you might be able to train regular classroom teachers in being able to run the program."

"We did try to create something that a passionate and skilled home cook could manage, since there are always a few of those on any teaching staff. We also think a talented culinary student would be able to teach it."

"Alana, I'm not going to beat around the bush. This program is prime for expansion, both as a program we run ourselves and a program we could teach to others who want to have it for their school. As you know, our mission is to have both deep and broad impact. We want the students in our programs to have more than just a surface experience; we want it to change their lives meaningfully. And we want to work with as many of them as we can. But we know that in terms of systematic impact, our best bet is to train teachers. If we work with a thousand students, we impact a thousand students, which is amazing. But if we work with a thousand teachers, we can impact as many as a hundred thousand students a year, every year those teachers teach. That is when we really start to see change."

I love Rachel. She is calm and to the point, but it is so clear how passionate she is about this work. I know that she works endless hours for minimal pay, but she seems so deeply rewarded by it all, I'm often envious of how completely her job seems to make her life richer.

"That is very exciting."

"We think so too. But if we are going to expand the direct program with kids and add a teacher-training component, then we are going to need a program director who can handle all of that. And we think you'd be the perfect person."

Wow. "Rachel, that is so flattering, but I don't think I would have the time to do it justice, even the little bit of work I did this time around was at about the limit of disposable hours that I could carve out."

"You misunderstand me, Alana. This isn't asking you to do more as a volunteer. We are offering you a full-time position. We can't begin to match your current salary or benefits package, and we know that. And of course we will completely understand if you have to turn us down as a result. But I have watched you at these meetings and I see the joy and personal fulfillment you have gotten from helping create this program, and I think that can be worth more than money. I've put together a packet detailing our offer." She hands me a thick manila envelope. "While it is full-time, it is probably still many fewer hours than you currently work. For now, you would mostly be working at home, but we will have an office for you at the Foundation offices. You would report directly to me, but would have a tremendous amount of autonomy to mold and shape the program the way you think it should be. Take some time to read through it, think about it, mull it over. We're just in the beginning stages of laying out what this program is going to look like, but we wanted to plant the idea in your head. Let's plan on meeting before the next board meeting to see what you think."

I stroke the envelope. It contains the possibility of a whole new life, which is in equal parts exhilarating and terrifying.

"Rachel, thank you, for even thinking of me. I don't begin to know what to say or how to respond except to say that I am very honored, and I promise I will give it serious thought."

"That's all we can ask. Why don't you and I plan on meeting at the Foundation offices about two hours before the next meeting to talk about this, and then we can go to the meeting together."

"Great."

"And in the meantime, please call or e-mail me with any questions the materials may bring up for you. I will tell you that we put together a salary and benefits package at the very limit of what the Foundation can manage financially. We have tried to honor that you would be taking a step back from what you are used to. So, unfortunately, there isn't wiggle room there. But if you have questions or concerns about anything else, please don't hesitate to ask. To a certain extent, the job will be yours to create from scratch, so there will be a lot of flexibility in that area."

"Thanks, Rachel. I will be in touch if anything comes up."

Rachel gets up and gathers her belongings. "For what it's worth, Alana? I was a six-figure consultant with partnership on the horizon when I left to take this job. But I was busy eighteen hours a day, my life was work and work and more work, and the work itself, while I was very good at it, never really fulfilled me that much. I don't wear the designer clothes or six-hundred-dollar shoes anymore, and the Spa at the Peninsula misses me a lot. I'm driving my current car until the wheels fall off, and I haven't ordered a bottle of wine over forty dollars in seven years. But I love my life."

"Thanks, Rachel."

"Thank you. No one will be offended if you turn this down, Alana. We know we are shooting for the moon here. And we'll be grateful for whatever continued support you can give. But take the money out of the equation and think about the life you want. The rest is just noise."

She winks at me, and walks away.

RJ is waiting for me when I get home, sitting on the couch with Dumpling watching the Cubs lose.

"This is the most welcome sight on the planet." I dump my bag and jacket by the door, and walk over to kiss my boys. RJ gives me a lingering smooch. Then he pours me a glass of wine from the bottle of Syrah he has open on the coffee table. I take a deep sip, letting the wine warm in my mouth, slipping smoothly down my throat. "Juicy and delicious, thank you."

"I thought so. How was your meeting?"

"Interesting . . ." I fill him in on the unexpected job offer.

"I'm really proud of you. That is so amazing, you must be very flattered that they would ask. And a big set of decisions you'll have to deal with. My last job was the same sort of out-of-the-blue offer, I know that it's a lot to process all at once. Do you think you're leaning toward wanting to take it, or would you rather stay where you are?"

"I have no idea. I know that it is certainly tempting on an emotional level. But I also know that it probably isn't realistic financially."

"What if finances weren't an issue?"

"It's always nice to say that, everyone thinks it helps in situations like these, but I don't think it does. Finances are an issue. They always are. Sure, if I were independently wealthy, I might jump at this chance to make a difference. But I'm not. I have responsibilities to my family, to myself. I own property. I hope to retire someday. I need to have a cushion of savings for when my car breaks down or, god forbid, I have a health crisis. The economy is in the toilet and I currently work in a volatile and ever-changing industry with very little security. And I'm not a kid." I take another sip of wine. "And to be honest, it's not like I'm miserable in my job."

"Not miserable being the same as happy?" It is a genuine question and not a statement.

I think about this for a minute. "I'd say that on the happy scale, I'm pretty happy at work. The team is a good one, and we like and trust each other. The work is as good as we can make it and no one is lazy or coasting, so there is a sense of pride. Not the same kind of pride as doing the good work of the world, but I do feel lucky to be a part of the shows and a part of the brand Patrick is creating. The hours are weird, and long, and erratic. But there is a lot of independence and my voice is heard."

"And the money is pretty great."

I laugh. "Yeah, the money is good. And as much as I do have that pull to be tempted by the do-gooder aspect of the Foundation job, I'm not ashamed to say that I like my lifestyle. I like that I can travel when I get the time away, that I don't worry about my bills getting paid, that I can help my family. I like the comfort of being able to splurge on a spa treatment or a great pair of shoes every now and again. I'm almost forty years old, and I have made a good life that I'm proud of, and there is certainly a part of me that feels very entitled to the perks of the money I work very hard to make."

"But?" He smiles.

I laugh. "Their FACES!"

"Those young people can break your heart, huh?"

"They are just about the coolest people I've ever met. And yes, I love the idea of being able to impact even more kids with this program. It makes my heart smile."

"C'mere." I put down my glass, and snuggle up beside him, entwining my hand with his. Dumpling scootches over, climbing half onto RJ's lap from the other side, and places a paw on top of our hands. "Ha! I think your boys are saying that whatever you decide, we are here for you."

"And I love you both for that."

I look up and RJ leans down to kiss me deeply. Suddenly there is a flurry of licking all over our faces.

"Okay, okay!" I push Dumpling away. "I can only kiss one of you at a time!"

"Me first," RJ says.

I take his face in my hands. "Now and always."

"That's good to hear." He kisses me again. "Now, about that almost-forty thing . . ."

"Yes?"

"How are the Alanapalooza plans going?"

"Very well, thank you."

"Everything set?"

"I think so. Patrick and I are taping Maria's show at the crack of dawn, but then I have the rest of the day off. Bennie is flying in, and she and I are doing a spa afternoon. Gil is giving me the whole restaurant for the party, and has come up with a killer menu. Naomi at TipsyCake is doing the cake, and it should be amazing."

"Mmm, cake. What kind of cake?"

"Almond cake with a layer of fresh apricot puree, white-chocolate-mousse filling, and vanilla buttercream."

"Oh. My."

"I know. Should be a killer party." We will be just the nearest and dearest for the celebration. Mom and Dad are hosting the usual big family birthday dinner on Sunday night prior to my birthday, so they offered to take all the grandkids for a sleepover so my brothers and sisters can have a night out. This kind of party isn't really up their alley anyway. Of course the girls and their significant others, Maria and Jefferson, Melanie and Jon, Kai and Phil. Bob and Gloria and their spouses. Barry and Bennie. RJ's friends from New Year's, who we have hung out with a bit, and who have become friends of mine. And Patrick, of course. The restaurant, Chalkboard, is the perfect place, a warm and intimate room, insanely great food. It will feel like a large dinner party, only I don't have to cook or clean up. I'm bringing my uber case of wine from Patrick to be the red of choice for the evening, and RJ asked to do the bubbly and white out of his cellar. It should be very grown-up and lovely, and exactly what I want.

"Anything else I can do to be helpful?"

"You can be my date."

"Of course!"

"You are all I need for my birthday. Everything else is just bonus."

"Thank you, baby."

Dumpling starts his sneezing and spinning routine, and

RJ and I get up to take him for a walk before bed. It is a beautiful spring night, you can finally feel the winter chill breaking, and I'm out for a stroll with my favorite boy and my favorite dog. And even though I can feel that the earth is turning and that there are major changes in the offing, for the first time in my life I just know that everything is going to be okay.

⁓

20

I have no idea where they are coming from," RJ says, batting the air at the huge, glossy black houseflies that are bobbing and weaving over his head. There are at least twenty of them here in his kitchen, and at least a couple in every other room in his house. "They are driving me and the cat mental. But I can't find the source, although clearly the kitchen is their favorite hangout." JP, who is chasing a particularly enormous fly, leaps in the air, paws akimbo, catches the fly in midair and then haplessly slams into the wall, releasing the fly again.

"He's very talented," I say, as the cat gets up, shakes off, and then tears down the hallway in pursuit of his prey.

"Well, at least he doesn't puke into my laundry basket." Dumpling stayed over here with me the other night and befouled a full basket of clean laundry in the worst possible way. Strangely, he and JP seemed to get along fine. After a few hours of looking at each other warily and walking in circles around each other, they finally settled in, Dumpling in his usual place between me and RJ, and JP on RJ's shoulder, and in the morning we found them happily snuggled up on the couch together.

"Can't argue with that. I'll pick up some fly traps and see if we can't get this place cleared out by the time you get back. If they don't work, I'll call Terminix. Consider me your

personal fly-removal manager." RJ is heading out this afternoon for a longish business trip, three stops on two coasts and
not back for five days. I offered to keep an eye on the mail
and feed JP in his absence. Made especially convenient as last
week I was ceremoniously presented with my own set of keys
to RJ's house. I immediately returned the favor, and we have
been spending about every other night together since, mostly
sleeping at my house since RJ's bed is the single most uncomfortable thing I have ever attempted to sleep upon. Hard as
a rock. I'm a squishy girl. I need a squishy bed.

RJ leans over and kisses me. "You are the most amazing
woman on the planet."

"True enough." I kiss him back.

"What are you going to do in my absence?"

"Miss you. Take Patrick to do his Master Class with the
kids and hope he doesn't pollute their impressionable minds.
Miss you more. Spend some more time thinking about this
job offer. And it is Girls' Night In tonight. Plus, you know,
missing you."

"Sounds very busy. You'll barely have time to miss me.
What are you thinking about the job offer?"

"I change my mind every ten minutes. I think, this is the
perfect thing, the absolute best thing I could do with my life,
the most exciting rewarding thing I could have as the final
act of my professional life. And then I think, I'm almost forty
years old, and it is a huge step backward financially, and
would mean an enormous change in my lifestyle, and am
I really ready to make that kind of sacrifice?"

"Good. That means that your mind is open, and you are
asking yourself all the right questions. And it's still very new;
you've barely gotten through all of the materials. Keep reading and keep letting the idea wash over you and just see how

you respond organically. Ultimately, the decision may be easier than you think."

"I keep waiting for a lightbulb moment."

"It will come. And whatever you decide, you have my full and unconditional support."

"Thank you, my love." I walk over and give him a huge kiss.

"Ask the girls tonight for their thoughts. And keep them away from EDestiny."

I look at him and grin. "I will. Besides, I completely erased my EDestiny profile ages ago. Permanently and irreparably."

"That's what I like to hear."

"C'mon, we should hit the road in case there's traffic."

"You know you don't have to take me to the airport, I could take a cab. Fully reimbursable."

"I want to take you. I'm not going to see you for almost a week, I need as much time as I can get." And the thing is, I really do want to take him. In spite of the fact that doing the airport run is the single most annoying thing on the planet. And regardless of the fact that his company would happily pay for his taxi. I don't want to lose any minutes with him.

"Well, I'm not going to argue with that. Let's do it!"

Luckily there is minimal traffic between his place and the airport and back, so the whole trip is under an hour. I stop at Home Depot on my way back and pick up some hanging fly traps, and a special nontoxic trap that says it's safe for the kitchen. I'll get them set up tomorrow on my way to work when I go to feed JP, and hopefully fix this new fly problem. I'm not a fan of bugs. I have Terminix on a monthly check-in program out at the cabin, and one sign of anything more major than the occasional spider or creepy thousand-legged bugs that are part of living in an older building, and I'm off to the basement cabinet where I keep cans of deadly for every possible crawler that could invade. But I've never had a fly problem. And I hate the way they career around so randomly, never in a straight line. They could bump into you at any moment. Ick. My phone goes off. I hit the hands-free.

"Hey, bro, whassup?"

"We've got some not great news on the parent financials front."

"What's going on?"

"You know how they have been talking about trying to do the Florida thing six months a year instead of two weeks?"

"Yeah, they said when they were ready that they would sell the house and get a small condo here and one there."

"Right. Well, they got a call from the people they've been renting from down there, and they have been thinking that they probably want to sell in the next six months or so. They like Mama and Papa, so they wanted to give them a heads-up on buying the place."

"What's the issue?"

"The issue is that there have been six foreclosures and three short-sales in a two-block radius of the house. The fact is, their place is worth about half of what it was worth four years ago, and the chances of it selling at all in this market are slim."

My stomach sinks. "How much are we talking about?"

"To buy the Florida place? It's not exactly South Beach. I think we can get it for 150, 170 max based on the info I got from the Florida real estate agent about the comps for that area."

"That's a lot more than I have ready access to, Alex."

"I know, kiddo, and I hate to even dump this on you, but

we are all on tightened belts right now, our investments and savings all took a huge hit in the crash, you know. . . ."

"Okay. Don't say anything to them; just let me think about things and I'll get back to you."

"Sorry, Lana."

"I know."

"How's RJ? Joshie hasn't stopped talking about that tour at the Art Institute. He now wants to go to Art School like Uncle RJ!"

"That's awesome. Give Sara and the boys a kiss from me."

"Will do. And, Lana, if it doesn't work it doesn't work. Don't do anything insane just to try to fix this for Mom and Dad. They'll be fine whatever happens."

"I know. I won't."

I get home, and take Dumpling for a quick piddle before settling in to write up the new recipes I tested over the weekend while I wait for the girls to arrive. But first, I shoot an e-mail to the guy who manages my finances, and ask how bad it would be for me and my future to try and make 150K liquid in the next six months. Can't wait to see how that goes over. It isn't like I haven't taken a hit myself in this crazy economy. I make a very good living, but it isn't millions. I've got two mortgages, two sets of taxes, two sets of housing upkeep, and only one income. I'm good about putting the maximum away every year in my retirement accounts, and not being overly aggressive or risky with my investments. I have trusts set up for each of the nieces and nephews, fifty dollars a month goes into each one automatically, to be handed over when they graduate from college. Plus the money for Mama and Papa. I try to put something from every check into short-term savings for vacations and unexpected expenses, and yes, the occasional spa treatment or household splurge. With the extra two hundred dollars a month I'll need to send to them now, that will pretty much wipe out the extra savings options.

The manila envelope from At Our Core is sitting on the table next to my laptop, and I look at it with a feeling of dread. I open it again. The offer letter is right on top. The salary is very generous by not-for-profit standards, and I know it is the limit they can offer, but it is still about half of what I currently make. It would put me in a lower tax bracket, so I would take home a greater percentage than I do now, and if I reduced my level of savings, my level of annual charitable giving, and significantly tightened my belt in terms of my lifestyle, cut the kids' trust deposits in half, I could just barely make my monthly nut. But there wouldn't be money for Mama and Papa. Not the way I currently handle things. I could sell the cabin, but that idea makes my heart break.

I think about the kids and how much I have grown to adore them in such a short time and how deeply rewarding the work has been. How much fun, how personally fulfilling. And Rachel's discussion of what is to come, to be able to leave a legacy. Something that is actually mine, as opposed to a bunch of television shows and cookbooks with someone else's picture on the cover. I seem to have forgotten along the way that just because I don't want to be scrutinized in the public eye doesn't mean it isn't nice to have public recognition of accomplishments.

But first, you sort of have to have accomplishments.

When I lay it all out for the girls, they are quick to jump on me.

"You have loads of accomplishments!" Emily says, smacking me playfully in the back of the head. "Dumbass."

"Great, thanks, that is very helpful," I say, wincing dramatically and rubbing my head.

"She didn't hurt you," Lacey says. "And she's right, you are a dumbass. You have your name on six *New York Times* bestselling cookbooks. In the credits of more than three hundred hours of pretty damn good television programming. You have helped to create a new program that has already changed eight lives, and you will be a part of it moving forward even if it isn't as the director. You have a family that loves you, one of the best dogs on the planet, and pretty spectacular friends."

"And a majorly dreamy boyfriend," Mina says.

"EXACTLY! Thank you, AND a majorly dreamy boyfriend." Lacey is triumphant.

"I get it, you guys, I do, but you know what I mean. This job would be a chance to really do something amazing with the next part of my life. Not just the career part. Regular hours. Dinner before nine. No middle-of-the-night drop-ins, no vacation-interrupting phone harassment, no having to leave parties to bail someone out of jail . . ."

"But still, you do love your job. And Patrick is endearing in his way. You wouldn't have stayed this long if you hated it. And since when is not-for-profit anything but overworked and underpaid?" Emily pipes in. "Maybe it would be regular hours to begin with, but as the program grows, my guess is you'll be right back to long hours. And without the compensation to cushion things."

"Oh, that is true. A woman who left us to take over marketing for a nonprofit now works at least twenty percent more hours than she did with us. AND no free chocolate." Lacey shudders at the very thought of losing her Willy Wonka pipeline of delicious, and passes over the box of caramels and marshmallows they've been testing. "Personally, I think you thank them for the offer and keep the job you have and keep volunteering. There is no shame in wanting to keep a lifestyle you worked really hard to achieve."

"I dunno," Mina says. "Alana has seemed extra happy since this program came along, and I've never heard her this excited to tell us about a show they were shooting or some cookbook as she has been to tell us about the kids and their progress. Money isn't everything. Besides, she isn't going to be a single-income household for much longer!"

"No way, guys, I can't let RJ play into this decision beyond whether it would be detrimental or positive for our relationship. But nothing financial. I know he and I keep talking about the moving in together and getting married and everything, but I can't do anything except assume that for the foreseeable future I am still very much a single girl and very much responsible for my own upkeep."

"I'm just saying." Mina shrugs. "Speaking of boyfriends, I have to go pick mine up. Alana, you'll make the right choice. Whichever you pick. You're lucky; there isn't a bad decision here, just a decision." She gets up and grabs her purse, kissing her palm to the room. "Toodles, bitches. See you all next time!"

"That girl is crazy. But she's right." Emily stands up and brushes the crumbs off her polo shirt, sighing at a midbosom hummus stain, and fluffs her golden curls. "You can't make a wrong decision, you win either way. And you'll figure out what kind of winning is most important to you."

Lacey calls Jaxie over, and waves away my attempt to make her take the rest of the chocolates. "Got to get back in fighting shape," she says, patting her belly. "Going back on Match this week." She has been between servicemen for a few months, I have no doubt that within the week we will start to hear about the latest uniform she is dating.

I put on Dumpling's leash and we walk out with them. Lacey decides to walk Jaxie along with me and Dumpling.

"What does RJ say about the job thing?" she asks, as Dumpling and Jaxie romp around in the grass out front.

"He's like you guys, totally supportive whatever I decide. And he keeps telling me that I can't make a decision based on money or helping my folks. He says that the economy has hurt everyone, they wouldn't be surprised to discover it impacted them as well, and they would respond accordingly."

"He's right, you know. The kids will be fine with a smaller trust from their aunt Alana, because they have your love and support and attention. Don't be ashamed to turn the job down and keep the comfort, but don't hesitate to take it if you think it is really what you want. The finances will figure themselves out."

"Thanks. I know it deep down. But I'm genuinely torn. I'm not unhappy at work, I'm comfortable there, I'm good at it, it's exciting and challenging in all the ways I like to be challenged without any micromanaging, and it gives me enough flexibility to participate in the At Our Core stuff on my terms. On the other hand, it has been a long time since I had a new kind of challenge, and my industry is notoriously fickle. From the moment you reach the top you are one bad season away from boring and underemployed. Think about how many shows we loved that annoyed us by season three. How many sophomore albums were grating and regrettable. You get to the third book in the trilogy and read it out of a sense of obligation instead of real joy. My fortune is tied to Patrick. He's at the top now, but it's a quick trip down, and when he falls he takes me with him. Provided he doesn't blow a gasket and fire me before then."

"You can't base any decision on what-ifs. Take the information you have, make the best decision you can, and live with it with as much happiness as you can muster."

"You're very bright, you know that?"

"I do, in fact."

"We both appear to have blue-bag duty to perform." I look over to where Dumpling and Jaxie are taking something of a synchronized dump.

"What is he doing?" she says, motioning at my goofy dog, who is pooping with one leg straight up in the air as if peeing on an invisible tree.

"Poop plié. He loves ballet."

"That dog is bizarre."

"I know." When the dogs are finished, we pick up the evidence, and walk over to drop the blue bags in the garbage.

"Good night, sweetie. Talk to you later," she says, heading for her car.

"Bye. Thanks for the pep talk."

"Anytime!"

Dumpling and I get home just in time for RJ's call. He's wiped out from travel and meetings, so we keep it brief. I send best wishes from the girls, and tell him that they have not made my decision for me. He laughs and tells me to not pressure myself. To just let it be what it is and try to let the decision make itself. I tell him he is very wise, and thank him for his counsel. He tells me that he loves me and misses me and sends love to Dumpling and promises to call tomorrow when he isn't so exhausted. Then he tells me to be sure to look under my pillow before I go to bed.

The front of the card I find there shows a diner scene,

and says, *I'll have the special.* On the inside it says, *That would be you.* RJ's note, in his usual scrawly handwriting says:

Alana—

Dreams don't come easy. Please don't lose sight of yours, especially the dreams you didn't know you were dreaming. You've done everything "right" and now you have to make some decisions. But that doesn't necessarily mean changing course. You'll get what you want, it's your nature. In the end, a harder struggle to get it will make it that much sweeter. I believe in you without hesitation, qualification, or any other "tions." I absolutely love you with all my heart, and I'm here for you however and whenever you need me. Let's help you together.

Love, RJ

I shoot him a quick e-mail to thank him for his lovely words and for his support. It feels so amazing to have him in my corner, to have someone who truly believes in me with such purity of heart. I pour myself a glass of port from the bottle we opened the other night, a 1985 Fonseca that is like drinking the smoothest, yummiest raisins on the planet. I run a very hot bath, toss Dumpling a bully stick, and lower myself into the water, sipping the warming wine and letting my stress begin to ease a bit. No sooner have my shoulders begun to unclench than my phone rings. It's after eleven. I've already spoken with RJ. Anything else will have to wait. I take a decent soak, and when I am appropriately pruny, I get out. I remember reading once that the best way to combat dry skin is to just stay naked after bathing and rub yourself with the water till it absorbs. It's a ridiculous exercise, but now and again I try it, because from November through April in Chicago, most of me looks like an elderly alligator. I am attempting this bizarre trick when suddenly Dumpling goes from sound asleep on the bathroom rug to bouncing and barking. Goddamnit all to hell.

I throw on my robe and go to the door.

"Alana-quintana! You look flushed." Patrick kisses the top of my head, and kneels down so that Dumpling can launch himself into the loving arms of the last man on earth I want to see tonight.

"Patrick . . ."

He wanders over to the kitchen, grabs a glass, helps himself to the last of the port, and opens the box of chocolates Lacey left, popping two into his mouth at once. "Alana, get ready, my love, my light, your life is about to change."

"Can I put clothes on before this change?"

"Of course. I'm raiding your fridge."

"Of course you are. I'll be back. Please don't give the dog any food, he's getting fat." Dumpling turns to glare at me in an insulted manner and then returns his attention to Patrick.

I leave Patrick talking to the dog and rummaging in my fridge and quickly throw on some clothes. Every bit of relaxation I had achieved is gone, and my shoulders are back up around my ears. For the eleventh time today the pendulum swings, this time away from Patrick and toward the Foundation job. I'm pretty sure Rachel would never show up in the middle of the night to raid my fridge.

I text RJ that Patrick has just arrived, and if he isn't asleep yet, he should feel free to call and save me. I wait, knowing that if he is up, I'll get a reply text quickly, since his phone is always at his elbow. Nothing. Crap.

I wander back out, and find Patrick doing the unthinkable. He is cooking. There are two placemats on the island, napkins and forks. He has found a dish of leftover pasta I made last night, linguine with chickpeas, pancetta, and toasted bread-crumbs, with torn basil leaves and lemon zest. He's put together a frittata, which he has cooked on one side, and is deftly flipping it over to cook the other side. On another burner, some of my marinara that I put up last summer sim-mers in a small saucepan. A pile of shaved Parmesan is on the cutting board, two plates sit at his elbow. Patrick never cooks for me. And certainly not at my house. Something is definitely up.

"To what do I owe the pleasure?"

"I felt bad. I know I've been really hard on you lately, and extra demanding, and I know I was sort of rude about RJ. Plus, you always cook for me, figured it was more than my turn."

"I just don't know what is going on with you. You've been insane and secretive and cranky. Let's put aside the business about RJ, which, frankly, wasn't rude, Patrick, it was mean and hurtful. Regardless, I can't support you if I don't know what the hell is going on."

Patrick slides the frittata onto a cutting board. "Okay, I deserve that about the RJ thing. I'm getting used to being the number-two guy in your life, and it doesn't suit me ter-ribly well." Dumpling butts his calf with his tiny head. "Sorry, buddy, number three." Dumpling harrumphs, sneezes, and flops onto the floor.

"Patrick, you just have to be honest with me. I know that we aren't exactly just employer and employee, but that does have to be the biggest part of our relationship."

"What if I want more?"

"What the hell does that mean?"

Patrick drops on one knee and takes my hand.

Oh . . . no. This cannot be happening. That would be too sappy rom com even for a sappy rom com girl like me. What on earth am I going to do?

"Alana, you know how much you mean to me." My heart drops into my toes.

"Patrick . . . don't. I mean I'm flattered, but . . . really, it's just not, I mean, you know . . ." He grins at me with the wickedest of twinkles in his eye. That bastard. I smack him in the head. "Get off your knees you unmitigated asshair."

"I can't believe you actually thought I was going *there*," he says, getting up off his knees, and laughing in a profoundly annoying way.

"You are a shithead."

He puts his arm around me and pulls me tight against him. "I am. And if ever I were going to make such a ridiculous gesture of romantic hooey, I know I could do a lot worse than aiming it in your general direction."

"Wow. Such flattery. You going to serve that or just let it perfume the air?" I gesture at the frittata.

"Good point." He walks back over to the cutting board, slices two thick wedges and places them on the plates. He dollops tomato sauce over each one, garnishes with cheese, and then hands me a plate and we head for the island.

"So," Patrick says, around a mouthful of frittata, "about this secretive business. There is something going on, which I have not been at liberty to share with you. Technically, I am still not at liberty, but I do hate when my little Alana is cranky with me, and I agree that it has been a particularly difficult and annoying time for all of us, so I'm going to trust you with something pretty big and you are going to have to keep it under your hat."

"Have you ever known me to spill a secret?" Damn, this frittata is freaking delicious. Never let it be said that the man can't cook.

"I have not. Which is why I'm going to tell you. You? Are looking at the new Warrior Chef on *Master Chef Battle.*"

"WHAT?!" *Master Chef Battle* is the Food TV parent network's answer to *Iron Chef America*, the major difference being that the opponents aren't limited to restaurant chefs. Caterers, home cooks, critics, celebs, even other television chefs—anyone can issue a challenge. And instead of one secret ingredient, there is an initial mini battle and the winner gets a one-minute head start in the pantry to have a slight advantage in choice of ingredients. They each have to produce a five-course meal that must include at least one dessert, and periodically during the cooking a buzzer will go off and the judge will issue an extra challenge or some twist. Each chef has one sous chef, and they have their own twists and turns during the course of the show. It's been doing insanely well in the ratings, since it taps into a more mainstream audience. All three of the initial Warrior Chefs have become major stars, and their on-air sous chefs now all have shows of their own and cookbook deals and their own fan bases. On-air sous chefs . . . Oh no.

Patrick watches the reality sink in. "Yep! That's right my little princess. Get ready for fame and fortune, because we are going to be the hottest team on television! First off, we're going to be undefeated forever, because we are unstoppable! My speed and your palate, your knife skills and my butchering, your insane ability to remember recipes, and both our gorgeous faces . . ." He takes my face in one large hand, squishing my cheeks together, and puts on a good imitation of my mom's accent. "Such a *punim*, we are going to be huge!"

My stomach turns over. This is my worst nightmare.

"And the best part? The money is RIDICULOUS! For both of us. Network money, baby, not cable. The show is already in syndication, and they air reruns every afternoon, so in addition to the per-show appearance fees, there will be residuals rolling in almost immediately. The cookbooks will get a bump, the other shows will get a ratings boost, and you, my soon-to-be star, will have your own show and your own cookbook deal within the year. And endorsement deals for both of us. Maybe we'll do a cookware line together. Seriously, Alana, I was talking to Jeff last time I was in New York, and his sous, Howie, just bought his parents a new house on Long Island. For CASH."

And that is when my heart breaks completely in two. Because I know in that moment that this opportunity is probably the difference between my folks being able to keep their house and have the Florida place for comfort in their golden years and scraping by with two weeks' warm vacation and barely enough money to sustain a decent lifestyle. The chance for me to secure my own financial future, not just year to year, but for the long run. I could keep the cabin. And maybe even do the big master bedroom project at home, make it roomier and more comfortable for RJ to move into.

"Aren't you going to say something?" Patrick looks like a little boy who has brought home a first-prize trophy, and I'm sitting here mute attempting very seriously not to shit my pants.

"Patrick, that is so great for you." My head is swimming. The very idea of being on camera makes me feel like I am about to vomit. I think about the blogs that are devoted entirely to people who make idiots of themselves on television. The candid pictures of television people in their least attractive moments. Any error captured forever to be YouTubed and Tweeted endlessly. Ever read the Food Network Humor blog? It's hilarious. Because it is about someone else.

"For us, kiddo, for us! That's why I've been so nuts lately about the show. The network has been watching footage and looking to see where we are headed and make sure the show is still on an upward trajectory."

"No, it all makes sense now, I totally get it. And it is very exciting for you . . ." But the kids. If I took this job I might not be able to have time to participate fully in the program, but I might be able to start a scholarship fund.

"US! Don't you get it? I could never have gotten this without you, hell, half the things they praise me for in these meetings are things that are your ideas. And now, we get to take this next step together. We're getting called up to the bigs, the show, the major fucking leagues! I'm the pitcher and you're my catcher. I'm Starsky and you're Hutch. . . ."

"I'm Turner and you're Hooch. . . ." I think that was my out-loud voice.

"EXACTLY! We're gonna be amazing."

"Patrick, I'm really grateful, and it is a wonderful opportunity, but I do have to think about it. I have to learn all the details and responsibilities and obligations, and I have to spend some time making sure it's right for me. I'm hugely excited for you, and I think they are damned lucky to get you, but I can't just say yes without knowing all the details and having some time to think about it." Why? Why now? Why not three months ago, when I could have just made a decision without this Foundation thing hanging over me.

"What's to think about? It's fabulous money. Between you and me, you're starting equal pay and perks to the other sous chefs; I made sure of that, so you'll be on equal footing. And it is ON TOP of your current salary and benefits! You're going to get a full-time assistant, to take some grunt stuff off your plate. And I'm telling you, by the end of the season you'll have a show of your own!"

"That's all great, Patrick, but it is possible I don't want a show of my own. . . ." A show of my own? That would be even WORSE. But maybe I could be the background person. How awful could it be? It isn't like it shoots in front of a live audience. And what would I care if a bunch of mouth-breathing bloghoos with nothing better to do than to poke fun at people on TV write some snarky shit about me on the intertubes? I could have a nice life, my parents could have a nice life, and I could still be involved in the work of the Foundation, maybe even become a board member.

"Well, it isn't a requirement. You can just be my right-hand gal, and still rake in the moolah! You might not get as big a cookbook deal without your own show, but for sure we'll get to do one together based on the stuff we make on the show. Alana, you're finally going to make the money you should be making, passive income, royalties, and bonuses, all the stuff you should have had for years but we couldn't manage. You should be insane with delight!"

"Look, Patrick, it isn't all about the money for me. I have to take a look at the whole picture, my whole life, and make sure that this is what is best for me." I think about Max. He said to me that in some ways, his folks losing the money and the house is the best thing that ever happened to him. He feels closer to his mom now. They shop and cook together and play board games instead of occupying different rooms in a massive house and eating meals in restaurants. He feels like he is a better person for living in a diverse neighborhood, going to a school with all sorts of different people. He likes that he can tutor some of his classmates, and that the friends he is slowly making feel very real to him. None of his pals from his former school have kept in touch. And while he still intends to go to college, he thinks he might be able to pay for it by working in the school cafeteria. And I have a piece of that. I have seen his spine get straighter, his skin clear up, his confidence increase. And I think he and Mari might be dating. Or hanging out and kickin' it, as Joseph would say. He is a different person from the one I met, and I had a part of that. That has got to be worth as much as a cookbook deal, doesn't it? Maybe more?

Patrick waves his hand at me. "You're insane. And you're tired, and this is a lot to process. In the morning, you'll be singing in the shower and praising my name to the heavens." He gets up, puts his empty plate in the sink, and tosses Dumpling a small chunk of frittata. "I'm going to let you get some rest. Everything is still in the planning stage. I'm waiting on my contract, and then we'll figure out a press release for that, and then get you squared away, so it will probably be a month or two before you get paperwork, but I wouldn't tell you if it weren't a done deal. And until it's all signed and sealed, MUM'S THE WORD!" He leans over and kisses me on the top of my head. "We're going to be the best team since Butch and Sundance, kiddo. Just stick with me, and I'll make you a star! See you tomorrow, honey. We'll see if we can't give those kids of yours a class to remember. They can say they knew you when!" Something tells me he doesn't remember how Butch and Sundance ended up.

He whistles his way to the door, tips an imaginary hat, and disappears into the night.

Dumpling wanders over and puts one paw on my knee.

"You know buddy, this week is just full of surprises."

Dumpling yawns and schlumps down into a dog loaf at my feet.

"Holy Frankenfuck, dog, I don't know what the hell I'm going to do. Except go to bed and think about it tomorrow." I look around at my kitchen and the detritus Patrick has left for me to clean up. "At least, I will once I finish the dishes."

21

Okay, lay it on me, what did you learn?" Patrick says to the class, who are all enraptured after a three-hour marathon session with him that has covered everything from knife skills to the importance of nutrition to how to pursue a career in television to how to use things you learn in the kitchen in the real world. He has been honest, charming, self-deprecating, and funny. He has not pandered for one minute, or talked down to them. He hasn't tried to use their lingo or show how cool he is. I'm prouder of him than I have ever been.

"Your best days are the ones where you work so hard at something you believe in that you are completely drained, but still can't wait to do it again the next day," Max says.

"Good. What else?"

"Cooking for someone should be giving them a gift from your soul," Mari says, looking sidelong at Max and blushing. Something tells me she has cooked for him recently.

"Absolutely."

"But good food is also a gift you give to yourself and taking the time to eat really good food that is really good for you shows that you respect yourself," Aretha says. She has lost a few pounds since starting with us, and I know it is because she is learning about making smarter choices.

"Food safety is like aircraft maintenance, always worth

the time and effort," Renaldo says, quoting one of Patrick's favorite quips, and making everyone laugh.

"Perfect!" Patrick offers a hand for a high five.

"There are more jobs than you can imagine in the food industry, and if we want a career, there will be one to match the things that most interest us," Helena says. Originally, I assumed that her being here was just about cooking for her family, but as the class has gone on, she has started to ask about restaurant management in a way that makes me think she might be thinking about a front-of-house position, which I think would be a great move for her.

"And if we want to run a restaurant we better be sure it's the only thing in life we want to do, because it is very, very hard work and very difficult to be successful." Joseph is more determined than ever to take over his uncle's diner, and I have every faith that he will do a wonderful job with it.

"Your kitchen is only as good as the lowest-paid person in it, and if that person is you, you have the whole place riding on your shoulders." Juan says this with pride. He recently started washing dishes at Nuevo Leon, a job I hooked him up with, and even though the work is sort of thankless, hearing Patrick say how important it is I know makes him feel good.

"We have to be willing to try anything once, especially the stuff that scares us." Clara may have changed the most of any of them. The orange plastic curls are gone in favor of her own gorgeous thick black hair, grown out to just below her chin, and pulled back with a simple headband. The thick makeup has been replaced by clean, clear skin with just a hint of blush, lip gloss, and mascara, the green contacts gone to reveal sparkly brown eyes. The flashy, tight clothes slowly disappeared, and today she is wearing a simple denim skirt and dark eggplant-purple shirt that flatter her voluptuous frame and caramel skin. Kai gave her a major makeunder, and the results are wonderful. She looks like a typical teenage girl, not jaded or world-weary, and seems to have gained some amount of comfort in her own skin. And she has been blowing us all away with her food, most of it traditional Mexican recipes from her grandmother and foods from other Latino cultures that she finds in cookbooks and magazines. I would not be surprised to see her become a powerhouse in the Latin food movement. She's going to meet Rick Bayless next week about a summer job, and I have every faith she will nail the interview.

"Alana? Anything they missed?" Patrick looks over at me.

I think hard and take a deep breath. "Life is also about balance, just the way recipes are about balance. When your recipe isn't balanced, it doesn't taste right. Too much salt, or too little can make all the difference. Lack of acid, too much bitter or sweetness, if you don't find the balance your food will never be all it can be. The same is true of your life. You need it all. Work that makes you happy and fulfilled and supports you financially. Family and friends to lean on and celebrate with. Hopefully someone special to share your life with, and a family of your own if you want that. Some way of giving back, in honor of your own blessings. A sense of spirituality or something that keeps you grounded. Time to do the things you need for good health, eating right and exercising and managing your stress. If you have too much of one and not enough of another, then your life isn't balanced, and without that balance, nothing else will matter."

All day I was sure that I would turn down the Foundation job. The financial downside is just too big to ignore. As much as I love the idea of working with kids, training teachers to empower them with our curriculum, having an impact on so many lives, the sacrifice is too much. Because the sacrifice isn't just mine. I can't just blithely go after something that feeds my soul to the detriment of my parents' lives. I was sure of it.

But now, after these past three hours, I'm up in the air again. When I'm here with these incredible young people, my heart just wants more. I want to see them grow and develop. I want to follow their paths. I've had a million ideas today about the program and things we could do, new programs we could start, and it jazzes up my blood and makes me feel all sparkly. The idea of being on *Master Chef Challenge* does not make me feel sparkly. It makes me feel nauseated.

"You guys have been amazing," Patrick says, "so I'm going to make you a promise. You continue on your path, and you have me in your corner. Provided you stay out of trouble and on the straight and narrow, you have access to me. If you need a job, I will find you one, either in one of my restaurants or on one of my shows or through someone else I know. Finish school, keep in touch, and if I can ever help you, I will."

The kids clap, and come over to get the cookbooks we brought them as gifts, signed and personalized. I watch Patrick with them. As awful as he can be, when he's like this, it melts my heart.

As we walk to our cars, Patrick has a spring in his step.

"Thank you for that, Patrick, really. And offering to help them with jobs and stuff, that was very generous."

"My pleasure. They seem like very cool kids."

"They are."

"And you seem really attached to them, and this program."

"I am." This would be the perfect time to tell him about

the job offer, to at least be honest with him that I'm strongly considering it.

"Just think, when you are up there on TV, all those kids are going to look at you and be so proud that you were their teacher. And girls everywhere are going to see you as such a role model. Child of immigrant parents, self-made, up by your bootstraps. You are an inspiring woman, Alana, and people are going to notice that."

I never thought of it that way. I've only ever thought about being in the public eye as something negative, something that invites criticism and ridicule and embarrassment. But he's right, the flip side of that is the possibility to inspire and educate and be a role model. I think of the girls I grew up with in my neighborhood, girls who figured their only options were housewife, hairdresser, or housecleaner. The really ambitious ones aiming for nurse or teacher. And all five of those are honorable and honest jobs. But what if they had some reason to believe they could do or be more? What if someone from our neighborhood had been on television? Would some of them have dared to dream bigger?

"Well, I'm still thinking about that."

"Yeah, yeah, think all you want. We're going to have such fun on this adventure. Thanks for today, it was awesome. I'll see you bright and early tomorrow at the studio?"

I jump in my car and head over to RJ's. I need to feed PJ and see if the fly traps I set this morning have done anything. I put eight of the long, curly hanging ones all over the house, and in the kitchen, and this weird trap that looked like a paper towel tube covered in ultrasticky glue, sitting in a base like a little square cup. I had to bait the trap by putting honey in the cup part. It was strange, but the package said that it was safe to use near food, and I hated the idea of the toxic kind in the kitchen.

I let myself in with my shiny new keys, and step inside, turning on the light. I love RJ's house. It looks like him. It smells like him. His beautiful Arts and Crafts antiques, the art, his guitar collection. It is warm and cozy and very much representative of who he is. I can hear loud mewling coming from the back of the house.

"I'm coming, JP. You can't be out of food already, I was just here this morning!"

As I go through the house, I notice that the fly traps seem to be doing their job; each one has at least three or four dead flies attached, and I only notice one live one flying around. And when I get into the kitchen I discover that the tube trap has hit the mother lode.

It has caught a whole cat.

JP is straddling the tube like a witch on a broomstick, and the thing is completely attached to his underside from his chinny chin chin to the pink starfish butt hole he is so proud to wave in people's faces. He is writhing in profound annoyance at this situation, all four legs stuck out straight and waving, unable to get any purchase or dislodge the offending item. He is also covered in glue and honey and dead flies.

"Shitshitshitshitshitshit." What the hell am I going to do? I grab JP by the scruff and toss him in the bathtub, and then call Barry on his cell.

"Hey, you! I just dropped your dog off, sorry I missed you."

"Help."

"What? What's wrong?"

"You have to come to RJ's. It's an emergency."

"I just left your place, so I'm not far, what's going on? Should I call nine-one-one?"

"No, I just, I'm having a cat problem and I need some assistance."

"Whew. Is he okay?"

"Mostly. He's caught in a fly trap."

"No, seriously."

"SERIOUSLY. Barry, just get over here. You remember the house? On Manor, just north of Montrose, Japanese maple in the front."

"I remember. I'm on my way."

I unlock the door and leave it ajar. Then I call the emergency vet. They tell me to try to remove the glue with some sort of cooking oil, but assure me the cat is in no danger. I have to ask the most embarrassing question.

"Is it possible his little butt hole could get glued together? The trap seems to be stuck in that area."

The nurse on the other end laughs. "I can promise you, even if there is glue there, he will clean it properly; there isn't really any danger."

"Whew. Thank you so much." I am just hanging up when Barry comes through the door like an avenging angel.

"What on earth is going on?" he asks, kissing my cheek.

"Look," I say, motioning to the bathroom.

Barry sees poor JP in the tub and begins to laugh.

"This is not funny, this is a disaster!"

He wipes his eyes, then grabs his cell phone and snaps a few pictures. "What? You are going to want this documented, trust me."

"Look, will you just help me figure this out?"

Barry puts down the phone, takes off his coat, and rolls up

his sleeves. He looks at JP, who glares at him as if to say, "Hey! Asshole! Want to give a cat a hand here?"

"As I see it, I should hold him still while you pull the trap off, and then we should try to clean him off."

"The vet's office said cooking oil might get the glue off his fur."

"You get the oil and the paper towels, and I'll hang here with Professor Sticky Pants."

I go to the kitchen and grab a roll of paper towels and a bottle of peanut oil that RJ uses for popping popcorn. When I get back to the bathroom, Barry is sitting in the tub, JP cradled against him, trap facing out. He has JP's rear end sort of trapped between his thighs, and is holding his upper body firmly by the scruff.

"This fellow appears to be rear-wheel drive only, so watch the claws as you get down toward the tender bits," Barry says.

I close the bathroom door behind me, figuring if he gets away he can't go far. The idea of him getting any of that ick on one of RJ's rugs or pieces of furniture makes me break out in a cold sweat. "Okay, here goes." I grasp the top of the trap firmly, and begin to pull it away from JP's body; he wriggles and mewls, but doesn't try to bite me or claw at me. This stuff is really sticky, so I have to go very slowly or I risk ripping out the poor thing's fur at the roots like the worst Brazilian ever. But eventually I get the whole tube separated from cat. Barry readjusts his grip, and I pour oil on the sticky swath down the cat's belly, and begin to gently use the paper towels to pull the glue off his fur. It's going well, but suddenly I hit a particularly stubborn bit, and pull a little hard.

JP yowls. Then Barry yowls as JP digs his claws into Barry's thighs and launches himself into the air. He lands on the sink, gives a mighty shake, spraying the whole little bath-

room, Barry, and me with a fine mist of peanut oil, and then
begins to run in frantic circles, and eventually cowers behind
the toilet.

You know how they talk about trying to catch a greased
pig? Greased cat is no better. Every time one of us grabs him,
he slithers right out of our grasp. Finally we throw a towel
over him, and use it to pin him down, and I work quickly to
get as much of the glue off as possible. When I'm satisfied that
he is fairly well degunked, Barry looks at me.

"So. Now that we used the oil to get off the glue, what do
we use to get off the oil?"

I hadn't really thought of that. But he's right, we can't just
let him loose all covered in oil, he'll ruin everything he
touches.

"Ever wash a cat?" I ask him.

"Nope."

"Well, we're going to have to. What should we use?
Shampoo?"

Barry looks down. "I think dishwashing detergent, isn't
it designed to combat grease?"

"You're a genius. Sit tight." I zip out to the kitchen and
look under the sink. Thank god. Dawn. It gets grease out of
your way. Says so right on the bottle. I also grab a small bowl,
figuring we'll need it for rinsing, and return to the bathroom
where Barry and I give JP a very thorough and, I'm sure,
uncomfortable cleaning. By the time we are done, Barry and
I are both wet and greasy ourselves, and the cat is damp
with some residual oil, but not enough for me to be worried
about the furniture. We give him an extra-special treat of a
can of tuna for his trouble and clean up all the paper towels
and the offending trap. I drape some towels on the places
I know he likes to sleep, the corner of the couch, his favorite

chair, RJ's pillow. JP, having decimated the tuna, jumps onto the couch right on the towel and begins cleaning himself frantically.

"Barry?"

"Yes, my sweet?"

"Will you help me do something the teeniest bit wrong before we leave?"

"Of course, what's that? Are we looking for his porn stash? Old love letters? Secret drug paraphernalia?"

"Of course not. It's just . . . well, there are a few pieces of his furniture that are going to look so good at my place, and I want to take some measurements to send to Bennie. You know, so she can start thinking about a plan for our eventual cohabitation."

Barry laughs. "Now that is some serious recon. I'm in."

We quickly do some measuring of my favorite pieces of furniture, a few rugs, some of the art, writing it all down on a scrap of paper, giggling the whole time and talking about redecorating my place. We check in on JP, who is still cleaning himself, but who seems ultimately none the worse for wear, and lock up the house.

"Pizza?" I ask as we walk to the cars. "On me."

"You got it."

Barry follows me back to my condo, and I put in an order at Giordano's for an extra-large extra-thin crust with extra sausage and double extra black olives. I am extra hungry and extra grateful.

When we get inside, Barry plays with Dumpling, who greets him as if they didn't spend the whole afternoon together, and I change out of my damp, oily clothes. I grab one of RJ's T-shirts for Barry. While he changes in the bathroom, I grab a couple of beers out of the fridge.

"Thank you," I say, handing Barry a beer when he comes back.

"Anytime. That's what friends are for."

We catch up, demolish the entire pizza, and I fill him in on my current employment conundrum, leaving out the *Master Chef Challenge* and just saying that I'm up for a major promotion from Patrick, which is close enough.

"Do you have any idea what you want to do?" he asks.

"I really don't. I completely go back and forth. One minute all I want is to let go of Patrick's craziness, and create the most amazing education programs. And the next minute all I want is to hand my folks the keys to their place in Florida dangling off a red ribbon. I wake up ready to face the financial challenges of working for a nonprofit, and go to sleep ready to face up to my own selfish needs and go for the bucks."

"What does RJ say about it?"

"RJ is in complete support of whatever I believe will make me happiest. And that is the thing. Even if you take my own creature comforts out of the way, I genuinely find it equally compelling to do wonderful things for those kids and to do wonderful things for my parents. On the one hand, I have it in my power to make my parents' final years more comfortable, to be able to help them both keep the home they worked so hard for here, and also spend the harsh winters someplace warm. On the other hand, I could have a role in moving forward both positive nutritional education and the culinary field, and help a whole lot of teachers get reenergized about what they're teaching, and a whole lot of kids dream a dream they didn't even know was dreamable."

"Wow. That's a lot of words."

Sigh. "I know. I have plenty of words and no concrete decisions."

"You know who you need on this."

"I know. But she'll be biased."

"Maria will be able to help you figure it out without pushing you in any one direction, even if she does selfishly want you to take the job with her team."

"She's out of town doing her road-tour shows for the next couple of weeks, but when she gets back Patrick is booked on the show, and we're having lunch after the taping. I can ask her then if I haven't figured it out on my own."

"Good plan. And now, my sweet, not that it hasn't been the most interesting night of the month so far, I have to take myself away."

"You are totally going home to tweet about our evening and slap those pictures of poor JP all over the interwebs, aren't you?"

"Completely. Shall I send you copies?"

"Absolutely."

Barry gives me a big hug and kisses both cheeks. "Don't overthink it, princess. Even if you flip a coin, that will be the right choice for you. And at the end of the day, make sure it's you making the choice . . . not your pals, not your boss or your former boss, not your fabulous boyfriend or your well-meaning siblings. You make this choice for yourself and know that everything will be fine in the end."

"Thanks, honey. And thanks for being my knight in shining armor tonight."

"Anytime you have a cat that needs greasing and then degreasing, I'm your gay."

While I clean up the pizza box and beer bottles, the phone rings.

"How's my sweet banana puddin'?"

"She is very tired. But very happy to hear your voice."

"How was your night? Do anything fun?"

"Well . . . the good news is that your fly problem is significantly improved. The bad news is that one of the traps was something of an overachiever . . ." I regale him with the tale of our fly trap adventure, which has him laughing so hard he is making dolphin noises. I do not mention the careful accounting of his belongings, or how well they are going to fit here at my place once I make room for them.

"Oh, honey, that is just the funniest thing I ever heard. And I'm so sorry my flies became such a project for you. How did your class go?"

"It was great, actually. Patrick was amazing with the kids."

"That must have been hard."

"In what way?"

"Well, on the one hand, I'm sure being with the kids made you want to think about the Foundation job, and seeing Patrick be great with them must have made you want to stick with him."

"Yeah. You hit it in one."

"I think you should take some time and try not to think about making a decision and just try to focus on the present. You're making yourself nuts. Give it time and don't put so much pressure on yourself to make a decision. You have nearly seven weeks before you meet with the Foundation, and probably at least that before you get a firm, quantifiable offer from the network. So maybe just wait till that starts to happen and have some real conversations, and then make a decision. You'll still have a whole month before you need to deal with the Florida thing for your folks."

He's completely right, of course. "Thank you for talking me off the ledge. You're right. I'm obsessing like this is a

decision I need to make today, and I don't. I can just let it sit
with me for a while and focus on what is real. Like getting
the recipes for the new cookbook cranked out and dealing
with the show."

"That's my girl."

"I'm thinking we should talk more about this whole
moving-in thing. I really hate spending nights away from
you."

"Look, baby, I know it makes the most sense, and I do like
your place very much, and I like your neighborhood very
much. But I have to process it all in my own time. It's a when,
not an if. And you just keep reminding me how much you
want me there; you know I can't deny you anything for very
long."

"I'll keep reminding you in as many good ways as I can."

"Okay. We'll talk more when I get home."

I hang up the phone and think about what he said, about
reminding him how much I want him here. And I smile as
I open up the computer.

⌒

22

100 Very Objective and Important and Totally Unbiased Quantifiable Reasons RJ Should Move In with Alana and Dumpling As (Reasonably) Soon As Possible, Approved by the Universe and 9 out of 10 Doctors and Anyone Who Knows Them

1. She loves him more than anything in the world.

2. Home to her isn't home anymore without him.

3. She has the comfy bed, even if he did finally upgrade the sad pillow collection.

4. The new pillows will really be happier on the comfy bed.

5. Dishwasher. Really good dishwasher.

6. Her laser precision for eliminating potentially harmful food-stuffs means never again a melty vegetable, moldy fruit, or questionable piece of meat will be in the house, and he can eat with total confidence and gastric impunity.

7. She is really good at paperwork.

8. TiVo.

9. She has multiple flavors of toothpaste to choose from. Yum!

10. *Her shower has really good water pressure.*

11. *She only really breathes comfortably when he is around.*

12. *No matter how crazy and busy and stressful things get, they would get to spend most all of their nights together.*

13. *MORE SEX!*

14. *There are a helluva lot more walls on which to display his gorgeous art collection.*

15. *When he has those random middle-of-the-night questions, she will be there to answer them.*

16. *Crosswords will get completed at a speedier rate.*

17. *Because after waiting their whole lives to find each other, spending unnecessary time apart is sort of criminal.*

18. *She has a really good DVD collection. Even if you ignore all the shit from the 1980s.*

19. *Her house is walking distance to the Blue line for all that pesky business travel. And still only a couple of miles from the Brown line for commuting.*

20. *Dining room can seat twenty at one table. It doesn't have to, but it can.*

21. *In case he needs to see a procedural, there are always plenty on deck.*

22. *The fact that the place is the littlest bit cold in the winter means much more cuddling!*

23. *Mutually much more convenient for delivery of adorable cards and love notes and little happy presents.*

24. She has the MAC Knives.

25. They would get to record a cute joint outgoing answering machine message. Provided she can remember how to change the message on the machine. Maybe they can just shop for a new answering machine.

26. She has two parking spaces, and the cars look so happy together.

27. Good, walkable restaurants, AND La Boulangerie! Mmmmm. Crepes.

28. Dumpling promises to try to be a good boy.

29. She will do everything humanly possible to make it a happy home for him, and will never forget to appreciate his sacrifice.

30. Two toilets, no waiting.

31. There is a farmer's market right at the end of the block that gets better every year. And does not give you a kitten when you ask for broccoli.

32. Lettuces would grow very well in flower boxes on back porch (provided Alana does not attempt to touch them or engage with them in any way).

33. With the downturned real estate sales market, rentals are at a premium, so there won't be any problem finding a good tenant at a nice monthly rent to be in RJ's place. Possibly even someone they already know who might be interested in renting. Hypothetically.

34. Oodles of floors on which to display his beautiful rugs.

35. No more having to say good night and then go away.

36. *More I love yous.*

37. *Dinner in PJs. After sex.*

38. *Showers together.*

39. *High ceilings/low overhead.*

40. *When RJ has to work at home, beverages and snacks and quick neck rubs can magically appear.*

41. *All that schlepping 2.4 miles between houses adds up when gas prices are this high.*

42. *More smooching.*

43. *It will be ENORMOUS FUN!*

44. *The front porch is a lovely place to sit and have a glass of wine and watch the people go by.*

45. *Now that all their friends are all getting to be friends with each other, there can be awesome get-togethers without having to schlepp equipment, and without anyone having to spend time putting their place back together alone.*

46. *Weekday mornings are less icky when you get a good-morning kiss from your favorite person.*

47. *What sounds better than "Our house"?*

48. *2.4 miles feels like 24,000 miles when she really wants to be with her baby.*

49. *We officially become the best EDestiny success story, without ever paying them a dime.*

50. *All the parents will be so excited, and they're not getting any younger.*

51. *Soul mates should be roommates. It's the law. Or should be.*

52. *Guest room! For guests!*

53. *Did we mention the enormous amount of lovin'?*

54. *Life maintenance becomes something to do together, not something that keeps them apart.*

55. *She gets ALL the cooking magazines.*

56. *She always hoped she would maybe find someone she liked enough to want to be a longtime partner and figured that would probably include separate housing . . . until she met RJ, who made her believe in and actively long for Marriage and Permanence and Full-Time Togetherness . . . because she loves him for who he is and for who she becomes when she is with him, which seems to be the best possible version of herself. Much to her delight.*

57. *She won't have to wait for his call to say good night! Much less annoying for everyone.*

58. *Even though he thinks she is always glass half full, when she looks at him, that glass is overflowing, and she knows in every cell of her being that it will only get better when they are 100 percent together.*

59. *She likes the sound of his rocking out in the other room, and can't really hear it very well from 2.4 miles away. Plus, she has enough space to create a full-time rock room, and his amps can go to eleven.*

60. *The cat will have a whole new neighborhood to terrorize.*

61. *If he doesn't move in with her soon, the terrorists win.*

62. *Many more opportunities for making each other laugh till they bust.*

63. *Pretty much everyone has now heard the romantic "how they met" story and, frankly, they are going to need some new material soon.*

64. *Makes eating healthy and making smart life choices much easier with full-time support. And in a pinch, that pint of ice cream or bowl of popcorn is much less damaging when you split it with someone.*

65. *She has really awesome towels. Like uber towels. Seriously.*

66. *He can reach the stuff on the high shelves.*

67. *Random acts of nakedness.*

68. *There are some people who will remain nameless who are going to lose the pool if he doesn't move in soon. People he likes. Whom he might want to win.*

69. *Because a love as big as theirs needs a lot of room to spread out.*

70. *If it is inevitable, it might as well evit.*

71. *They are so good at making a life together; making a home together is going to be a slam dunk!*

72. *She loves him more every second she knows him, and it is very inconvenient to not be able to show him all the time.*

73. *She has the big Boos Block, and it is just too heavy to move around.*

74. *They are way behind on breakfasts in bed, surprise weeknight middle of the night romping, and random Thursday champagne drinking.*

75. *She can't think of anything about living with him that scares her, potentially annoys her, or would be anything less than the best thing ever.*

76. *She always has plenty of Pamplemousse.*

77. *Netflix Instant Watch on the TV.*

78. *She could really use some assistance putting Patrick in his place on a more regular basis.*

79. *Republicans hate it when Democrats are happy, and what would be happier than more RJ and Alana time?*

80. *When you know that the reason you are on this planet is to love someone, you ought to be near them to fulfill that destiny as much as humanly possible.*

81. *All those times they think they need to remember to tell each other something, they can just turn to the other one and say it.*

82. *So. Much. Lovin'.*

83. *Much easier and cheaper to shop for groceries for just one kitchen.*

84. *The bathroom faucet at Alana's has really super-duper cold water all the time. Delicious and refreshing.*

85. *Those sheepskin rugs in her bedroom make winter mornings much cozier. Happy toes!*

86. *Not having a backyard means no more weeding, and no more guilt about not weeding! And whatever he loses in the "back-yard" is replaced with six acres of green! That he doesn't need to weed. Or feel guilty about not weeding.*

87. *Digging out cars from the snow is good exercise and character building at such a level that you hardly miss having a garage. And she already has a good cheap shoveling guy for the rest of it.*

88. *After-dinner walks around the Boulevard.*

89. *No TV in the bedroom means more reading, and that is always nicer lying next to your baby.*

90. *When he gets that middle-of-the-back itch he can't reach she will be there to scratch it.*

91. *Her place has a ridiculous amount of potential to be the dream home they build together. And it starts out pretty dreamy to begin with.*

92. *She has over a dozen types of vinegar. Mmm. Salads.*

93. *Her house has never looked as good as it does when he is in it.*

94. *She's pretty sure they aren't going to get that primo EDestiny SpokesCouple gig unless they are living together.*

95. *He is fulfilling his destiny of making all of her dreams come true, so adding this one to the list is his moral obligation.*

96. *She is pretty sure that the pants he is missing might just be staging a small protest because they want to live at her house, where she is far more likely to take them off him.*

97. *There is nothing more romantic than cohabitation.*

98. *She really does know what he is giving up, and loves him even more enormously for being willing.*

99. *Once he fully commits to and embraces the idea, he is going to get really excited about what the reality brings and may even enjoy the planning.*

100. *SHE LOVES HIM MORE THAN ANYTHING IN THE WORLD AND MISSES HIM LIKE MAD WHEN HE ISN'T AROUND AND LONGS TO MAKE A HAPPY HOME FOR THEM BOTH (when he's ready).*

Ready? How about now? No? What about now? Okay, then, soon? Ballpark?

This message has been approved by Barack Obama, People for a Loving Cohabitation, The Chicago Cubs, Official Members of the Team RJ Coalition, Purcell, Daryl Zero, BonSoiree, the Movement for More Smooching, The Logan Square Preservation Society, Serta Waking Hours Mattress, Willy Wonka, Café Fanny, Payton, Francis Urquart, Gene's Sausage Shop and Delicatessen, The Lucky Dog, Booker T, Rice to Riches, The Whole Family Ostermann, The Company Store, MAC Knives, Confreres De L'ordre De Pamplemousse, Rickenbacker, Herbes de Provence, Chantelle (Party of Three), Thomas Keller, TiVo, Jonnie, Jackson, Bacchus, Leo Kottke, Acme Bakery, Alex Chilton, The City of Paris, Littorai Vineyards, University of Illinois, the Letter M, People for More Banana Cake, Tom Colicchio, Honda/Acura, The National Pork Board, 60647, Richard M. Daley, The City of Montreal, Rev. and Mrs. Oliver, School of the Art Institute Alumni Association, Chicago Bears, The Waldorf Astoria, The Blue Line, Alana's Couch, Puma, Wines Ending in Slese, Jews and Crackers United, Church of Barry Gibb, Fender, NYT Crossword Puzzles, Alana's Potato Salad, The Town of

Uzes, EDestiny, The Order of the Polish Stonemasons, the Association for Burgundy Appreciation, and Thermomix.

You are the most amazing, ridiculous, fabulous woman on the planet," RJ says after reading my list with much laughter and the occasional "aww." I've picked him up at the airport and left my list in a card on his seat. I meant it to be a top-ten list, but I got a little carried away.

"I'm glad you're taking it in the spirit in which it is intended. I was worried you might think it a little much."

"I think it's hilarious and wonderful and you are wonderful for writing it down. I love it. And I agree with it. And I promise we will start making some plans very soon, okay?"

"Okay!" He takes my hand and kisses it.

"Guess that fortune cookie was right after all, huh?"

"Guess so." The first time we ordered in Chinese together, on maybe our sixth date, his fortune read, "Stop searching forever. Happiness is just next to you." Chills all around.

"Ooooh. Maybe we should have Chinese for dinner!" he says.

"That's a deal." And I head for home, the home that is currently mine, but soon, ours.

23

And why exactly do I need to look so sassy?" I ask Dana, one of Maria's producers, who has just had me sit down for hair and makeup.

She looks at me a little quizzically. "Because on top of everything else, Maria has all the kids from your program as special guests in the audience today, and she wants to do a photo shoot after the taping with you guys to use for the program annual report and other materials."

"She's very sneaky."

"You might very well say that. I could not possibly comment," Dana says with a wink.

At least I'm dressed well enough to have my picture taken. Bennie insisted this morning that I could not spend my birthday in cargo pants and a black hoodie, and said she would not set foot in the Peninsula Spa with me dressed like a skate punk. So out of my comfy work gear, and into a skirt and blouse I got, since no one argues with Bennie.

"Don't you look gorgeous, my little birthday girl!" Patrick flies into the room, kisses the top of my head, and plops himself in the seat next to me to get his makeup done as well.

"Thank you. You look very handsome yourself."

"My little Alana, all growed up and FORTY! Who would have thunk it?"

"Yes, I know, I'm forty, big whoop."

"It IS a big whoop. This is THE decade. When everything happens."

"Well, it is certainly starting off well." I'm not one of those women who freaks out about birthdays. I love birthdays. Any excuse for cake and presents is all right by me. And these odometer birthdays? The big, round numbers? Bigger cake, more presents. Whenever anyone in my family makes a comment about getting older, Mama just says, "Ess bitter zan alternateeve." Which is, when you think of it, very true.

"Hey, I need you to do me a favor," he says.

"Sure, what is it?"

"Well, um, Leesa was in town last night." Leesa Thorne, current British It Girl, who has been in Chicago off and on filming her first American movie, who had dinner at Conlon her first week in town and succumbed to the charms of our Patrick like so many before her.

"Bully for you, guv. Did you remember to bring doughnuts?" I don't know when or why the tradition started, but for some reason, on our crew, if you get lucky with someone new, or have a particularly robust evening with your significant other, you bring in doughnuts for everyone.

"Practically bought out the Doughnut Vault. But that isn't the issue."

"Yes?"

"I didn't really get a chance to work on the recipe for the demo today."

"Patrick! That's a new recipe; you've never done it before." It's one of Maria's favorite dishes, a Cuban pork and plantain stew, and it has a lot of steps. I've prepped everything; he mostly just has to explain what has already been done, chop an onion, toss everything in the pot, and then pull out the already finished dish that is in the studio oven. But still, it isn't the easiest.

"I'm aware. Look, I've read it, I think I can wing it, but I was wondering if you might Cyrano this for me, just in case."

Oy. Every now and again Patrick is somewhat less than prepared to do one of my recipes on camera. The first time it happened it was the fault of Tony Bourdain, Bill Kim, and a series of Jaeger bombs. He showed up to the studio completely hungover, and having not even read over the recipes for the first shoot. The sound tech popped a tiny earpiece in his ear, and hooked me up with a mic pack, and I talked him through it. It worked brilliantly, even if it did put my bowels in an uproar all day, and when the shoot was over he called me his Cyrano. We don't have to do it very often, but we do have it down to something of a science.

"Seriously, Patrick? CYRANO? On Maria's show? Are you fucking KIDDING ME?"

Maria flies in en route to her final walk-through. Patrick puts his finger to his lips.

"*Mi amorrrrrs*, I am so 'appy to 'ave you both herrrrre." She air-kisses my cheek, and walks over and squeezes Patrick's thigh. Then she is gone in a cloud of Chanel No. 5.

"Patrick, we're ready for you," Dana says, and he gets up from the chair, kisses Julie, the makeup artist, and rubs my shoulder.

"Break a leg, bossman," I say to his back. He waves over his shoulder.

"There, you are, gorgeous. And happy birthday," Julie says. She has done a beautiful job; I am as adorable as it is possible to be, even if it does have the goopy heaviness required for photographs.

"Thanks so much, you are a miracle worker."

"Okay, let's get you hooked up," says a sound tech, who wanders in with a mic pack.

Sigh. "Okey dokey." I take the mic and thread it under my blouse, handing the end to the tech who clips the pack to the back of my skirt and plugs me in while I attach the mic to my collar.

Verna, the stage manager, leads me to the wings, where I watch Maria do what she does so well. The show is divided into five acts, sort of like a play, designed to accommodate the four commercial breaks. The first act is the intro and basic interview, light and funny. The second act will be the more serious part of the interview, a little introspective and where she will try and make him cry. Act three will be the cooking demo. Act four will be the discussion of his participation in the intern program and a couple quick shots of the kids with maybe one or two of them commenting about their experience. And finally they will wrap up with some Q&A with the audience and say their good-byes.

Maria introduces Patrick, and the two of them fall easily into a bantering interview, with some quips and quotables on both ends. They know each other well, they are comfortable together on camera, and they pretty much ooze charm all over each other. During the second part of the interview, Maria delves into his past, his parents, and his playboy life-style. She gets him to open up a little bit, especially about his mother, and while she doesn't get the full blubber, she does get him to well up just enough for the camera to catch it. My heart breaks for him, and I am reminded once again how amazing my family is and how lucky I am to have them.

They get set up for the cooking demo during the commercial break, and I grab my notes to get ready to walk him through the recipe. I give him basic instruction, toss him some info about Maria having the dish as a child, and lead him step-by-step through the process. He is a rock star, smooth as silk, and before I know it, he is feeding Maria a bite of the finished stew, and she is rolling her eyes and mumbling things in Spanish. I take a deep breath and let my sphincter unclench. Always an adventure with Patrick.

They get settled back down on the couch for the third interview section, talk about the Master Class he did, and get great quotes from both Joseph and Clara. The kids look great, it is clear that they all got Maria-ed, new clothes and hair and makeup, and now I'm a little bit excited about this photo shoot since it means I'll get to see them for a few minutes before I have to leave.

After the kids are done speaking, Patrick turns to Maria and says with a grin, "Maria, I want you to know that I have been so moved by the work you are doing with these young people, and I had such a great time teaching that group over there"—he gestures at the students in the front row—"I want to make sure you are able to continue to do this amazing work. So I am creating an endowment for the culinary intern program for ONE MILLION DOLLARS!"

The place erupts, and suddenly a stagehand is delivering one of those enormous cardboard checks to Patrick and Maria.

"Isn't he amazing?" Maria claps delightedly, and I can tell this is a genuine surprise to her.

I look out at my students, and the guys are high-fiving and the girls are crying, and I can feel a lump rise in my throat. Patrick. I know that he is a celeb and has a lot of money coming in, but he's no George Clooney, making twenty million a movie. A million dollars isn't nothing to him; it is significant. For him to make a million dollars liquid is huge, I don't care what kind of tax break it will get him. My heart swells. They cut for the commercial break and Patrick walks the big check back over to where I'm standing.

"You're amazing," I whisper to him.

"You're not kidding. Look at the fine print." He points to the memo portion of the huge check. It says The Patrick Conlon and Alana Ostermann Endowment.

I'm flabbergasted. "Patrick . . ."

"Hey, I would never have gotten involved if it weren't for you, and I genuinely loved teaching those kids, even for just one day. I could have been any one of them, and I can only imagine what it might have been like for me growing up if there had been a program like this. I believe in it, and I know it will be great because you were and are a part of making it happen."

I reach forward and give him a huge hug. "Thank you, Patrick, thank you from the bottom of my heart."

And in a weird way, him endowing the program in both our names, acknowledging my role, it makes me feel a weight lift from my shoulders. Because I know that if I decide to leave him to work with this organization, he will genuinely understand and wish me well. And that if I decide to stay, I'm staying with someone who would not only make that kind of massive personal financial sacrifice, but would do it in the name of someone he knows would if she could, but cannot.

"Hey, we're a team, we're in all of this together."

Velma gives him the high sign and he kisses the top of my head and scampers back onto the stage for the next part of the interview. Maria facilitates some questions from the audience, Patrick fields a funny marriage proposal from a smitten woman in her eighties, and then she returns to sit with him on the couch. Then she asks Patrick what he has coming up.

"Well, Maria, I'm very excited to give you an exclusive on that."

"Rrrrreally? More excitement on top of excitement! We loaf a scoop, what is yourrrrr news?"

"I am officially going to be the new Warrior Chef on *Master Chef Challenge*!"

The audience goes nuts.

"Congrrrrrratulations, Patrick, that is wonderrrrful for you."

"Not just for me, Maria, but for someone we both know and love."

Oh. No. Everything slows down, and one by one things click into place.

The clothes, insisted upon by Bennie.

The hair and makeup, supposedly for a photo shoot.

The Cyrano schtick to get me in a mic pack. My stomach clenches up.

"Your former personal chef, one of the teachers in your program, the other name on the new endowment and my right hand, can't-do-it-without-her girl, Alana Ostermann, is going to be my official sous chef on the show!" Patrick actually gets up on the couch and does a full-on Cruise.

The audience is going crazy. I turn to my left where they have stashed the equipment from the cooking demo, and promptly vomit up my breakfast into the garbage can. Velma, cool as a cucumber, produces a bottle of water as if by magic, and leans over to whisper in my ear. "You can do this, baby girl. There are only seventy-five seconds left. You go out, you smile and wave, you sit on the couch. That is Maria out there, she loves you, and she will take care of you, just maintain eye contact with her and it will be over before you know it."

I take a sip of water.

"And she is here today with me, what do you say, everyone, want to meet her?" Patrick is milking this for all it's worth.

"Alana, come on out," Maria says.

My feet are leaden, but Velma gives me a little push and I robotically move forward into the bright light of the studio.

I have no idea what happens. I cannot remember one thing that I say or is said to me. I know that Maria asks me a couple of questions, and that the audience laughs at my answers in a way that sounds like they are not laughing at me, but think I am funny. I know Patrick keeps touching my shoulder and putting his arm around me. I know that I am smiling even though I'm filled with a combination of fury and nausea. But ultimately, Velma was right, I just keep looking into Maria's eyes and it is over quickly, and then I am offstage again. And then we are taking pictures, and all the kids are so excited and eventually my blood pressure returns to normal and my stomach stops doing jumping jacks.

"You werrrrre fantastic, I am so proud of you!" Maria says when the hoopla is finally done.

"How could you do that to me?" I whisper. "You know how I feel about being on television. How could you ambush me like that?"

And she looks at me and her whole face sinks. And I suddenly realize that she didn't know it was an ambush.

"He didn't tell you, did he?" I nod my head in Patrick's direction, where he is saying good-bye to the kids, who are buzzing around him like bees. "He told you I was on board." No wonder Dana looked at me like I was insane for asking her about my hair and makeup.

"Oh, honey, of courrrrrse he did. I would NEVER do that to you, not in a million . . ." Her beautiful brown eyes fill with tears.

"It's okay, Maria, he's an ass. I should have known it wasn't you."

"And on your BIRRRRRRTHDAY!" She wipes at her eyes with a handkerchief, and then launches into what I can only presume is a Cuban curse on Patrick's manhood and lifespan.

"Hey! My gorgeous ladies! Wasn't that fun?" Patrick glides in from the green room.

Maria turns on him with venom in her eyes. "No, Patrick, it is not fun to lie to me and upset my best frrrrriend on national television."

"What are you talking about?" He looks confused.

"Maria, don't. It doesn't matter. I have to go, I'll see you tonight." I give her a look that tells her clearly that this is my fight, that I need to do this for myself and on my own. She nods and I kiss her cheek. Then I turn to the man who completely swung my emotions from the highest to the lowest in the span of fifteen minutes. "Patrick, car. Now."

Maria's show always sends a limo for guests. We walk out to the underground parking garage, and I take deep slow breaths. We get in the car and the driver pulls out. I press the privacy button and raise the window between the front and back seat, and then turn around and sit facing him.

"How could you do that?"

Patrick reaches into the little cooler near him and grabs a bottle of water. "Do what?"

"Announce that I am going to be with you on *Master Chef Challenge*, make me come out on the show without telling me about it."

"I thought it would be a fun surprise, and the network

thought it was brilliant. And I didn't tell you because you would have said no."

It boggles the mind. "If you KNEW I would say no, why the FUCK would you think I would be okay with a freaking AMBUSH?"

"Look, the network knew I was going on the show and wanted me to announce it exclusively to Maria. I called and told Maria that we should introduce you as well, so that people can start to see us as a team. Maria said you had stage fright and she was surprised you were going to do the show, and I said not to worry, that you're a trooper and are on board."

"But I'm NOT, Patrick. I'm not on board. I told you I had to think about it, I haven't committed to do the show at all."

"But you are going to."

"I might not."

"Of course you will. Come on, Alana, of course you will. You'll never get a better offer. And now you've broken your television cherry and you can see it's no big deal. And that was with a studio audience, on *Challenge* you just have to be there with the crew and staff and judges."

He thinks he did me a favor. Like a parent teaching their kid to swim by chucking them into the pool. "Patrick, I want to be very clear about something. This was not a favor, and it wasn't about me. This was about you assuming that you'll always get what you want. That you are somehow entitled to have everything fall at your feet. But let me be clear. I have not yet committed to this show, and I have very grave concerns about what it would mean for me and my life. You can't just railroad over me, and you can't do things like you did today. It was thoughtless and selfish and enormously upsetting." I know I'm going cry, and I can't let him see it.

I have to stay grounded. I roll down the barrier and ask the driver to pull over at the next intersection. "Do me a favor, Patrick. Don't come tonight. You have done a great deal to ruin my birthday already, and it is going to take me most of the rest of today to try to ignore how furious and hurt I am by your disregard of me and my feelings."

"C'mon, Alana, isn't that a little dramatic? I'm sorry if I handled this wrong, but it isn't that big a deal. You know you'll be sad if I'm not at your party."

"Patrick, the best present you can give me tonight is your absence. You are very genuinely not welcome, and I can tell you for sure that if you do come, we are done. I mean it. I need a couple of days."

His jaw flops open, and I know that he finally realizes that I'm serious.

"I'm getting out here," I say to the driver, who gets out of the car and walks around to open the door.

"Alana . . ." Patrick starts, but I put my hand up.

"Don't." I get out of the car, cross the street and hail a cab. And to my credit, I don't start to cry until we are a block away.

Maria calls just as I get home, and I sit on the stoop to chat with her before I go in.

"Arrrrre you okay, *mi amorrrrr*? I feel just terrrrrrible."

"I'm okay, Maria, I am. I gave Patrick what for, and uninvited him to the party tonight. I just need some space."

"Good forrrrrr you. That son ov a beetch."

"Indeed."

"But you will be okay? I feel so awful that this happened on your birrrthday."

"I will be fine. If I let Patrick Conlon and his inane pranks ruin my lovely birthday then I am an even bigger idiot than he is. Bennie and I are going for a whole afternoon at the spa, and then the party is tonight, and nothing is going to ruin that for me."

"Good girrrrl."

"And don't trouble yourself, Maria, you couldn't know. I'm not at all angry with you or your team."

"I feel better. And you have a rrrrrelaxing day and I will see you tonight."

"Thanks, Maria."

"I loaf you, Alana."

I laugh. "I loaf you too."

I take a deep breath and open the door, waiting for Dumpling to come greet me before remembering that he is boarding overnight at Best Friends today so that I don't have to worry about walking him after the party, and so that RJ and I can have a quiet, romantic night and a good sleep-in tomorrow morning. I drop my work bag, go to the bathroom to clean off the television makeup and make sure it doesn't look like I've been crying. I shoot an e-mail to Rachel to let her know that despite what it might look like on television, I have not made any final decision about her job offer, that it is still my intention to meet with her next month to discuss it further, and that I am still giving it every consideration. I call RJ and fill him in, and he is perfectly disgusted on my behalf and asks if I want him to beat Patrick up. I laugh and say no, but he is in charge of getting rid of Patrick if he shows up tonight. He agrees to play bouncer if I need him to and tells me he loves me and will pick me and Bennie up at six thirty, and that he will do his best to help turn the birthday around. I tell him he already has, and then I head out to meet Bennie at the Peninsula, where I am sure that the masseuse is going to have her hands very full trying to unclench my back.

Lucky for me, nothing bad can happen to you at the Peninsula Spa. Bennie and I spend the afternoon in a festival of bliss. Tea and snacks in the relaxation lounge. Facials to make our skin glowy, body treatments to make our limbs silky, hot stone massages. Then a primpfest of mani-pedis and blow outs. By the time we leave, I feel like a new woman, and the stress of the morning seems like it happened a long time ago to someone else. My face is smooth and dewy, my body feels all loose and noodly and as soft as a baby's tush. My traditionally unruly hair looks like a Breck-girl commercial, shiny and smooth and bouncy. Bennie is staying at Maria's, but brought her stuff with her to get ready at my place. While we dress and put on our makeup, I chastise her for her part in the fiasco, but it turns out she didn't know either; she just genuinely thought I should wear nicer clothes on my birthday. I fill her in on the whole morning, the job dilemma, Patrick's ridiculous behavior.

"He thinks he's losing you and it scares him to death."

"Why would he think that? He doesn't know about the other job, and he clearly thinks that the show with him is a fait accompli."

"Alana. You know him better than anyone, and whether you want to admit it or not, he knows you pretty well himself. He can feel you pulling away personally and professionally. You're in love with RJ. Think he will still feel comfortable showing up in the middle of the night if he knows you aren't alone? Your family is in love with RJ—think he is going to feel as comfortable coming to holidays and family gatherings as a third wheel? And you didn't jump at the new job immediately; you said you had to think about it, and deep down, he knows that means you could say no. He must be insane with worry and fear."

"Why?"

"Because you are his best friend. And his partner. And he knows he is better with you than he is on his own. And his life without you would be chaos."

"The man is an idiot. And he's not my best friend."

"I didn't say he was yours, I said you are his. There is a big difference."

I think about that for a minute. And realize she is probably right. "It doesn't excuse his behavior."

"Of course not. But it does explain it."

"What am I going to do?"

"Tonight? Nothing. Tonight you are going to have a wonderful birthday celebration, and pretend that Patrick doesn't exist. You'll deal with it in a day or two."

"So I wasn't wrong to uninvite him?"

"No. And you shouldn't re-invite him. If you're going to salvage your friendship and your professional relationship, he needs to know there are consequences to his actions. Let him stew. Let him know that you will not tolerate this ridiculous behavior. It'll do him good."

"Okay. I wish I didn't feel so guilty about it."

"Well, you can't fix your heritage. Just try to ignore it."

She gives me a hug, and then the front door opens. "My wildest fantasy come true!" RJ says from the door, observing our embrace.

"Naughty boy, come kiss me," Bennie says, and RJ obliges. Then he turns to me.

"Wow. You are so beautiful." He looks me up and down, and then pulls me in for a delicious kiss.

"Hello, handsome boy."

"Hello, birthday girl. You ready for a party?"

"You betcha."

We head to Chalkboard, which is aglow with candles and

beautifully set. Everyone arrives, and despite my specific request for no gifts, there are bags and packages galore. The food is spectacular, people make lovely toasts, and I feel truly blessed and happy. I am getting ready to think about cutting the cake when I realize that RJ is suddenly not by my side. Figuring he probably went to the bathroom, I decide I'll freshen up myself, and head back down the small hallway that leads to the kitchen, bathrooms, and eventually out to the back garden. The back door is ajar, and I hear voices. Voices I recognize. I sneak down the hall to get closer.

"You just can't be here, man. Not tonight. You hurt her once today, and I'm not going to let you do it again. You're younger than me and in better shape, but have no doubt, I will kick your ass if I have to." RJ is calm, but clear.

"Look, I get it, I fucked up, and I know she's pissed, but I just want to apologize." Patrick sounds genuinely remorseful.

"I'm glad you know you fucked up, and when she's ready to talk to you, I hope that apology is a good one. But she isn't ready, and if you go in there tonight, it isn't about what is good for her, it's about what's good for you, and frankly, you cannot begin to fathom the magnitude of the fuck I do not give about what is good for you."

I have never wanted him more.

I can hear Patrick sigh. "Okay. I get it. You're right. I just, I love her, man, you know? And I really thought that the stage-fright thing was sort of bullshit, and I figured she would be fake pissed for a minute and then we'd be back to normal. I didn't really think it through, and I certainly didn't dream I would make her that upset or ruin any part of her special day."

"I think I know that, and I think Alana knows that deep down. I think she knows that the bigger part of you is the part that made that donation in her name and not the asshole who embarrassed her on national television. But you have to suffer on this one."

"Okay. Okay. I'll go. Will you just, um, give her this and tell her that I'm really sorry and I won't bug her, but when she is ready I want to apologize in person."

"Okay. I will. And thank you for coming to the back door and asking for me first and not just barging in on her."

"Hey, I'm a bull in a china shop, but usually not twice in one day."

I turn and zip back up the hall and into the bathroom, before my resolve fades and I open the door and invite the devil inside. I check my watch. It's been nearly fourteen hours. Officially the longest I have ever been furious at Patrick. And even though I haven't completely gotten over it, I know in my heart I already forgive him.

I pee quickly, wash my hands, freshen my gloss, and return to my party.

"There she is!" RJ says, walking over to join me and giving me a glass of champagne. "I'd like to be the last one to propose a toast, if I may. Six months ago this spectacular woman came into my life and made me the luckiest man on the planet. I pinch myself every day. And as much as I love her and am so glad she is in my life, I have also really loved getting to know all of you. She has broadened my life and heart with much more than just herself, but with her amazing friends and family. Alana, your first forty years made you into the incredible woman we all know and love. And I know I am honored to be along for the ride, and I hope that I can be a part of making the next forty happy and full of love. Thank you for loving me and letting me love you."

I can feel the tears go. RJ kisses me and hands me his handkerchief.

"And thanks to RJ for putting that shit-eating grin on her face these past six months!" my brother Sasha calls out. We all laugh.

"I just want to thank everyone for coming to help me celebrate today. I love you all, and I am so blessed to have you in my life. And especially I want to thank RJ. One year ago today I asked the universe to send me the person I'd been waiting for, so that I wouldn't spend one more birthday without him." I look at my wonderful man. "And I am so happy that the universe complied. I love you very much and you are my every birthday wish come true."

He kisses me, and everyone claps.

"And now, CAKE, for the love of all that is holy," I say.

The cake, as I knew it would be, is insanely amazing. And lucky for me, there is enough left over for RJ and me to take a chunk home. Gil brings out a round of Manhattan Milkshakes to accompany the cake, and I wonder why no one ever thought to put bourbon in a vanilla milkshake before. He is an evil genius. Once dessert is over, everyone trickles out, and the waitstaff helps RJ and me load my haul of gifts into his car.

When we get back to my place, we schlepp the gifts inside, and I kick off my heels.

"Sore feet?"

"Too much standing in cute shoes."

"C'mere." RJ sits on the couch and pats his lap for me to put my feet there, and he begins to rub them.

"Ahhhh. You are amazing."

"It's true, I am, because these things are sweaty and stinky! Peeeuuuuw!" He waves his hand in front of his nose.

"Cut that out!" I pull my feet back, knowing that it is not impossible that they are as he describes them. If I'm not careful I do have a tendency toward the funky feet.

"I'm just kidding. I love your feet." He leans forward and kisses the top of my foot.

"My feet love you back."

He pulls me to him and kisses me slowly and softly. "I love everything about you, Alana Ostermann."

"And I love everything about you RJ Oliver."

I get up off the couch and hold out my hand, and we head for the bedroom to explore this subject a little more in-depth. An hour later, snuggled up and sated, RJ whispers into my hair.

"Don't we maybe need more of that cake?"

I pop up. "And presents!"

"Absolutely."

We jump out of bed and throw on pajamas. RJ heads into the bathroom while I toddle out to the kitchen and pull out the chunk of cake and two forks. I bring the whole thing to the living room, where the gifts are piled on the coffee table. RJ comes out of the bedroom, grabs a fork, and takes a huge bite.

"Good lord that is the best cake ever."

I take a bite. So moist and delicious. "Naomi, she is a genius."

"Okay, shall I play Santa?" RJ asks, handing me a present.

"Perfect." I open one after another, amazed at how great my friends are. Scented candles and beautiful scarves. Cashmere lounging pajamas from Maria, who knows all about my melty Target Cashmiracle wear. A gorgeous antique jade bowl from Bennie. A sassy apron, gift certificates for spa treatments, a Kindle from my siblings. Bottles of wine and champagne.

Cookbooks and a pair of earrings and a new wristlet purse. It is quite the haul and I'm so touched by everything.

"Last one," RJ says, handing me a large box. "It's from Patrick. He stopped by the party."

"I know. I heard you guys when I went to go to the bathroom."

"Sneaky minx."

"You were wonderful and I so appreciate your taking care of that situation for me."

"Of course. For what it's worth, he knows he was wrong and he is very sorry."

"I know. But at the end of the day at a certain point you have to stop being wrong and then sorry and you have to start being aware of how your actions affect other people."

"I agree. Anyway, he promised to not call or bug you till you're ready, and just wanted to be sure you got this and that I told you that he is truly so sorry that he upset you."

I take the box and open it. That bastard.

"What is it?"

"It's a Thermomix."

"That crazy cooking-blender thing you were telling me about?"

"The very one." I've been coveting this piece of equipment ever since my last trip to Montreal when I found out that nearly every great restaurant there is using them. It is essentially a powerful blender that also heats, so it will cook your soup and then puree it. It can spin slow enough to make risotto or hollandaise, or fast enough to turn whole unpeeled apples into the smoothest most velvety applesauce you've ever tasted. They aren't for sale in stores or online; you have to go through a special independent contractor salesperson, and they don't sell them in the U.S. Also? They are fifteen hundred dollars, an expense that even I couldn't justify for a piece of kitchen equipment.

"I thought you can't get them here?"

"You can't. He would have had to go through someone in Canada."

"Wow. That is pretty amazing."

"Yeah."

"I'm starting to fully understand the whole not-staying-mad-at-him problem."

"He's Jeckyll and freaking Hyde. I loathe the part of him that pulled that stunt today, but the part of him that made that donation and tracked down this extravagant present for me that he knows I've been wanting forever, that part I love."

"Well, at least he has the good side. A lot of guys in his position don't."

"True enough. And speaking of enough, despite this very thoughtful and generous gift, I have had enough Patrick for one day, and I'd rather focus on you and this cake."

"Works for me!"

We tuck in and finish the cake, and then head back to the bedroom. On my pillow there is a box.

"What is this?"

"No way I was going to let Patrick have the last present of the night."

"Sneaky. I thought my party was my present." RJ refused to let me pay for the event tonight, saying it was bad luck to pay for your own party. Even with the super-duper friends and family discount, it was still expensive, and I was blown away by his generosity.

"Your party was your party. This is your present."

I open the card first.

Alana—

Happy birthday, my love. Thank you for letting me share this special day with you. Knowing you makes me better. Loving you makes me more complete than I ever hoped to be. Being with you makes me believe that anything is possible. I hope it's obvious how crazy I am about you, but it's more important that you know how much I admire you, respect you, and adore you. I admire your respect for others and the way you elevate everyone in any situation. I respect your intellect, your insights, and your intuition. And I absolutely adore your eyes, your smile, your laugh, and your ability to make me paralyzed with laughter at your humor. Alana, I love you and nothing makes me happier than thinking about us being together forever. And since every minute with you is extraordinary, and I hope you feel the same, I thought this might help keep track of them.

All my love and all my heart forever,
RJ

I immediately begin to cry. And then I open the box.

"I can't believe you remembered." Inside is the most stunning Bedat watch, which we had seen in a boutique in New York our very first trip. It has an unusual elongated shape, surrounded by diamonds. I had mentioned very briefly that someday when I was a grown-up I would have a gorgeous elegant watch like that. The whole thing had been maybe a thirty-second pause, and then we moved on. The fact that he even remembered I would want a watch, let alone the specific one I had seen, especially since it was months ago, just moves me as much as his unbelievable generosity.

"I pay attention."

"Yes you do. And it is perfect and I love it. And you are perfect and I love you. Thank you for being my birthday wish come true."

"You are very welcome."

We climb into bed and I turn out the light.

"Is it just me or did that cake give you a little bit of extra energy?" RJ says, rolling over toward me.

"Oh, my, you frisky boy. I'm going to ask Naomi what she put in there."

"What can I say, you inspire me."

"Lucky me."

Lucky, lucky me.

24

You can pick him up from Best Friends anytime before six. They have his leash, toys, poop bags, treats . . . everything you'll need. Here are bowls for water and food. I just leave the food bowl full, he will monitor himself. Watch the treats, and please don't feed him people food."

Patrick laughs. "I can't help it, he loves my cooking."

"Ha-ha. Seriously, no people food." After a couple of tense weeks, Patrick and I are almost back to normal. I waited two days after the Maria show debacle and then met him for breakfast before work that Monday. We had a long talk, and we both listened, and I think he really heard me. I explained to him about my stage-fright problem, and my fear of being in the public eye.

"I don't get it, Alana. You're so great with the students, you're great when you're in staff meetings or dealing with the studio crew, and I've seen you in a bar full of chefs telling the stories, commanding the attention. What is the deal with being on camera?"

I take a deep breath. "There are two problems. One is the stage fright. I've had it since I was a kid. All those silly scenes in movies where the kid freezes on stage trying to remember a line, or knocks over scenery, or throws up on his neighbor? All taken from my life. My general klutziness? Increases exponentially when people are watching. When I was six,

I knocked over the flagpole during an assembly. Onto the principal. Sliding his toupee off one side of his head. When I was eight? At the school-wide spelling bee, when it was my turn, I tripped over my own goddamned feet walking up to the podium, and slid on my knees over half the stage, dead-ending at the foot of the proctor, and when I tried to stand up, with the whole audience laughing at me, I went right UP HER SKIRT and we got all tangled and I knocked her over too."

Patrick laughs.

"IT'S NOT FUNNY. When I was thirteen I threw up in the middle of the school holiday pageant. Into the orchestra pit. And the piece de resistance: when I was in college, I sharted on myself during my final presentation for my Shakespeare class. Not just a public FART, a public SHART. Audible and then smellable to everyone in the room. So yeah, every time I think of doing anything with an audience, my stomach clenches, I break out is a Nixon-esque sweat, my heart races, and my bowels loosen. Because historically, when-ever people are watching, I'm at my worst. And in my life, with my insane family, sharing a room with Nat, the damn cousins in and out of the house all day, people were ALWAYS watching. No haircut, clothing choice, pound gained, boy dated, grade received went without comment from the peanut gallery. Everything I ever did happened under the watchful scrutiny of no less than a dozen people. I do the things I'm good at, and I avoid the things that are destined to make me a laughingstock. I keep my head down and take pride in what I do, and I know that if I do make a mistake, it is just my mistake, it isn't fodder for other people's amusement or discus-sion or opinions."

"But when you teach? You're so good with those kids . . ."

"It's different. It's quiet, it's what I know, I feel safe."

"Alana, I'm not asking you to go on *Circus of the Network Stars* for chrissakes, we're talking about *cooking*. It's what you know, it should be safe. Bruce would be producing, and you'd be there with *me*."

"And what if I become one of those idiots who is always dropping the sauce, and hacking off chunks of fingers, and not getting the food on the plate in time? What if I become one of those people everyone makes fun of?"

"So what if you do? Alana, if you do it right, we win, which we both know you would love. If you do it wrong, we make good television, and we still win because it will keep the show funny and entertaining and on the air. The people who know you, will still love you and be proud of you. And if you would just do what I do and laugh at the parts of yourself other people make fun of, they can't hurt you. Your family and friends, for everything they have seen you do, for every humiliation you have suffered in front of them, aren't they still your biggest fans?"

It's true, they are. It's also true that Patrick is the king of calling himself out for the stuff any tabloid or snarky blogger might say about his lifestyle, his dating habits, the way he dresses or any other fodder for disparagement. He owns it all publically, jokes about it openly in interviews and articles, and even brings it up in front of his staff.

"Yeah."

"I don't want you to do something that you genuinely don't want to do. But you are one of the most competitive people I know. You are always pushing yourself to be your best, and I've watched those shows with you, I've heard you say what you would do better or different, and I think you and I would kick some serious ass and not embarrass ourselves enough to not try. I think you should do the thing that scares you. Because only you can flip the script. And at the end of the day, if you can get past your fear? We would have a really good time AND make a bucket of money."

There is a lot of validity in what he says. But wanting to change my relationship with this particular phobia and actually doing it are two different things.

"Patrick, I appreciate that, I just, I still need some time to think about it, okay? I have a lot of other considerations, and I need to process it at my own pace."

"Okay. That's fair. But I can only hold off the network for another couple of weeks, and then you're going to need to make a decision. But I promise not to nudge you about it, is that fair?"

"Yeah. That's fair. And Patrick, thank you for taking Dumpling this weekend."

"I figured you and RJ deserved a nice, quiet weekend away."

Which we do. RJ and I have both been crazed at work. It's been hard enough to just find time to be together, and with him so stressed I haven't wanted to push him on the whole moving-in-with-me thing. I think he's finding it harder to wrap his head around leaving his place and his neighborhood than he thought.

"Seriously, Patrick, he's getting fat, keep the treats to a minimum and NO PEOPLE FOOD."

"Okay, okay, good lord, you'd think you didn't trust me."

"Don't even get me started on that."

"Fair enough. Look, I've got this. Let me have a weekend with my little furry buddy, and you have a weekend with yours."

"Very funny."

"Really, I hope you and RJ have a great time. I like him, you know, I really do. He is a terrific guy and he really loves you and treats you well. You have my permission to keep him."

"Thank you for your support."

"Get out of here and go have a great weekend and I'll see you Sunday night."

"Okay. Bye, Patrick."

I grab my bag and head home. RJ is sneaking out of work early so that we can get to the cabin before rush hour hits.

He arrives just as I am finished packing up. The drive to the cabin is uneventful and beautiful. Chicago is actually having a real spring this year, but underneath it you can feel summer coming. The air is losing its postwinter softness and the sun is burning hotter. Everything is lush and green, and when we get to the cabin it is actually hot enough to get into the pool.

We cook burgers on the grill, eat on the back porch, watch a ridiculous movie he has been dying to see called *Sharktopus*. Half shark. Half octopus. All killer. And, not surprisingly, the result of a government experiment gone awry and out of control. It is deliciously ridiculous. Plus fun to say. Sharktopus. Awesome!

We sleep with the windows open. The cool Wisconsin air is just the ticket, and we don't get out of bed till eleven the next morning. We hit a local diner for enormous breakfasts, and then go antiquing in Richmond. RJ buys a beautiful old coat rack, which he says will look great next to my front door. We spend the afternoon in the pool while two racks of ribs that RJ gave his magic rub to two days ago slowly smoke on the grill. I make my classic potato salad, and steam asparagus. RJ's ribs are the best I have ever tasted, no sauce, just the perfect seasoning and amount of smoke. We lick fingers and feed each other spears of asparagus and then delve into the frozen custard we picked up in Richmond for dessert.

After dinner we take a walk in the woods, stopping to sit and dunk our feet in the icy cold creek, still running high with all the recent rainfall.

When we get back to the cabin, RJ opens a bottle of champagne and says he has something for me.

"Present?"

"Yep."

I clap my hands. "Goodie! But I don't have anything for you. . . ."

"You might, you never know . . . wait there." He goes to the bedroom and returns with a slim package. Inside there is a fabric-covered book, and when I open it there is a picture of us that Bennie took on our first trip to New York.

"Awww."

I flip through the picture book. It is the whole history of our relationship, with pictures of us and funny captions. Pictures of our families and friends. Pictures of a can of Pamplemousse LaCroix, the cover of *The Amazing Adventures of Kavalier & Klay*, Oscar Wilde, and gougères. The pictures are funny and lovely, and the captions hilarious. I love that he would pull this together, this celebration of our time together. Then I get to a picture of us from my birthday party, with the caption *While this book might be at the end, you and I are at the Beginning. I love you more than I ever thought it possible to love anyone.*

I turn the page and there is a picture of JP, with the caption *I love this part!* and then a picture of Dumpling with the caption *Do it already!*

Do it? Do what? I turn to look at RJ, and discover him next to me on one knee.

I shake my hands in front of me. "Oh! Oh! Oh!" My heart races, and I'm sort of bouncing on the couch.

"Alana," RJ says, his eyes welling up with tears.

"YES!"

"I love you very, very much."

"YES!"

"And I've never been happier in my whole life."

"YES!"

He keeps telling me how great I am and how happy I make him and how much he loves me and loves us and I can't stop saying "yes" and finally he says, "Will you marry me?"

"Absolutely yes with all my heart!" And then I am in his arms and we are kissing and our tears are mingling on our cheeks and life is exploding with perfect.

When we finally stop laughing and crying, he reaches in his pocket and pulls out a small box. Inside of which is the single most perfect ring I have ever seen. A large center stone in a radiant cut is surrounded by a delicate line of diamonds on a thin platinum band with little diamonds all the way around. It is elegant and simple and beautiful and very, very me.

"Holy SHIT!" I can't help the words flying out of my mouth—it is a truly spectacular ring, with more sparkle and fire than I have ever seen.

RJ laughs. "I guess I did okay!"

"It's perfect."

"I'm so glad. Your sister and I had a good time picking it out."

"That sneak. She never said."

"I'm sort of amazed you didn't know, frankly, especially since everyone was in on it."

"Everyone?"

"Well, I asked your folks for their blessing . . ." He goes on to tell me about the whole secret adventure he has been on for the past couple of months, including having Patrick take the dog this weekend.

"You are amazing. I am the luckiest girl in the whole world."

We smooch some more, and go to the bedroom and make love, and whisper the word fiancée at each other in the dark, and look at my ring sparkle in the moonlight coming through the bedroom window. And then we get up to make a few key phone calls.

My parents are very excited. They said it was "as if a mountain has fallen off the shoulders" not to have to try and keep the secret anymore, and let me know that there is a surprise family dinner scheduled for Sunday night so that we can all celebrate together. My siblings tell me it is about time, and all the nieces and nephews yell congratulations at me and "Uncle RJ." I take a picture of the ring with my phone and text it to Bennie and Maria and Barry and the girls with the note, "I'm having a good weekend, how about you?"

We call RJ's parents, who we are scheduled to go visit in a few weeks, and I speak with them on the phone, and they seem warm and lovely and very excited for us and looking forward to meeting me in person.

We are just getting off the phone with them when it rings again. Patrick.

"I was just about to call you! I know you know, but yes, it is official, and we're very happy and . . ."

"Alana." His voice is rough, and very serious.

"What is it?" My heart sinks.

"There's been an accident. It's Dumpling. You have to come home."

25

Mi amorrrrrr." Maria floats into the sitting room at the Lake Forest Animal Hospital. "'Ow is he? Better?"

"Still touch and go."

Barry squeezes my hand.

"New recruits. I'm going to let you guys visit and head back. Call me if anything changes, okay?"

"Okay. Thanks for coming, I really appreciate it."

"Hey, that's my guy in there. I'll come back tomorrow."

He kisses my cheek, and then Maria's and heads out.

"So, tell me what happens?" Maria says, sitting in the chair Barry vacated. She was out of town for the weekend and just got back last night, and Bennie filled her in.

"According to Patrick, they were in the park, and he let Dumpling off his leash, which I do all the time. But this time Dumpling took off after a squirrel and before Patrick knew what was happening, he chased the thing right into the street and was hit by a car. Patrick got him to the emergency vet pretty quickly, where they were able to stabilize him enough to transfer him to here to Lake Forest, which is the best in the area."

"'Ow bad is it?"

"He lost the bottom half of his right rear leg, and his left eye, and he has some broken ribs. There was some internal bleeding, so they operated, and it seems to be fixed, but they say we will know more in a day or so." I start to cry for the umpteenth time in the past three days.

Maria puts her arm around me. "'E will be okay. That dog is the strrrrongest dog I know. And he is not rrrrrready to go yet. You have faith, 'e will be okay."

"I hope so."

"And 'ow arrrrre you?"

I laugh. "I'm a mess. I'm scared and heartbroken about my dog, I'm excited and happy about my engagement, and I'm completely up in the air about what to do about my career and I'm running out of time to make my decision."

"I cannot fix the dog, and the engagement doesn't need fixing. So talk to me about your careerrrrrr."

I explain about my being so torn between the job with her Foundation and the job with Patrick. I tell her about my parents' financial situation and my sense of responsibility to them. I tell her about my discussion with Patrick about my fears and how I should face them, and about my discussions with Rachel and Melanie, who both made huge career shifts that were less lucrative and more personally satisfying. I tell her about my discussions with RJ and his support of whatever I do, but also that I am afraid he will take on the burden of helping support my parents if I choose to take the Foundation job, and that I don't want him to feel obligated in that way. She listens carefully.

"Why are you so focused on the orrrrr?" she asks.

"The or?"

"*Sí*, the orrrr. This job orrrr that job. Money orrrr feeling good. Kids orrrr Patrick. Helping your parents orrrr helping young people. You keep saying *orrrr.* Not *and.*"

"Maria, that is the essence of this decision, it is one or the other."

"No. That is wrrrrrong-headed. Not *orrrr. And.* Both. All of the best things are AND, not ORRRR. Chocolate AND caramel. Peanut butter AND jelly. Bacon AND sausage. Salt AND pepper. Fish AND chips. Bread AND butter. You cannot make a decision, because this is no decision to make. One is not better than the other. They arrrrre both perfectly good on their own, but better together. So you have to figure out how to have BOTH. You have to ignore the ORRRR and figure out AND."

"I'm supposed to figure out having two full-time jobs?"

"I can't tell you what it looks like, but you have to figurrre out 'ow to have the benefits of both jobs, but in one job."

"That sounds like a magic trick."

"Not magic. You just have to think. It will come to you. But do not give up ANYTHING. Do not let anyone tell you that you cannot have everything. When they say choose either or, you say no, you choose BOTH. Bread AND butter, *chica.* Pan y mantequilla. Is better for you, and better for everyone. You will see."

"Okay, Maria, if you say so." But for the life of me I can't begin to think that she is right, or that there is any way to have what she seems to think I can have. One of the challenges when a lot of people in your life live a life that is sort of rarified, especially if money is never an issue and other people go out of their way to make sure they get what they want, it can be difficult to explain to them that the world doesn't necessarily work that way for everyone.

"I do. I say so." She slaps her hands together. Problem solved. "You call me if you need anything, *sí*?"

"*Sí*. Thank you for coming."

She holds my chin in her hand. "I am always herrrre for you, *mi amorrr*." She leans over and kisses me on both cheeks, and then leaves.

The vet comes out to talk to me. He is calm, professional, but honest.

"So, here is where we are. He is fairly stable, and was able to eat some food this morning and keep it down, which is a good sign. And we were able to get him up on his feet for a little bit and walking with some help, which is also important. He isn't entirely out of the woods, but we are much more hopeful today than we were two days ago. Ideally, we'd like to keep him here for one or two more days before we let you take him home. He's going to need some extra help as he gets used to the missing eye and missing leg, so don't move anything around your house for a while. I'll give you a referral to a local trainer who specializes in this kind of transitional training to help you both adjust to his new reality. We've sewn the eye socket shut, so it should heal fine, but until it does, he'll need to wear an eye patch to keep out dirt and possible contaminants. We have a nurse who can come to your house every other day to change bandages and clean the wounds, so you don't have to worry about that. And going to the bathroom is going to be a little awkward for a while, so be patient if he has accidents. We recommend that you create some sort of pen for him so that his movement is limited and you have control over what he gets into, especially if you are going to leave him alone. And the cone will be essential until the leg and belly incision have healed fully."

"Of course."

"Toward that end, we're going to put him on a restricted diet designed to keep his bowels moving easily so that he doesn't strain, which would be bad for his stitches from the surgery and be more difficult because of the loss of the leg."

I'm trying to be strong, but the tears are coming back. My poor little guy. The vet pats my knee reassuringly.

"I know it's a lot, but I do think he is going to make it and be fine. He is a tough little guy."

"Okay." I sniffle. "Thank you."

"Why don't you come back and see him for a few minutes before we give him his next pain med dose. And then you should go home, there won't be anything else you can do here tonight."

I follow him back through the doors, and he leads me to the area that looks sort of like a doggie ICU. I go over to the cage where Dumpling is lying against the far wall, a large plastic cone on his itty bitty head, white bandage on his new leg stump and across his belly, eye patch over his eye. I notice the little divot where a small piece of one of his fruit bat ears has gone missing, and various other cuts here and there on his tiny little sweet head. He rolls his remaining eye over at me, and even though he looks like hell, there is still a little spark in there.

"Hey there, little man," I whisper to him, and he turns to the sound of my voice, tail wagging feebly. He stands up awkwardly, using the wall to balance, and starts to move toward me. He stops, swaying a bit, and then the big cone just pulls his head straight down, landing flat on the floor on the cage, trapping his poor head. He slides forward in this odd way and then, when the cone hits the front wall of the cage, schlumps over on his side, cone flipping back up. I put my hand in the cage, past the cone, and he licks it. I scratch under his chin, and he pushes against me weakly, but surely, and I just stand at his cage and weep.

The ride home seems endless, and by the time I get there, I am completely exhausted. I barely make it into the house before collapsing on the couch and falling into a fitful sleep. I wake to the feeling of a soft kiss on my forehead. I peel my eyelids back.

"Hello, beautiful fiancée."

"Hello, handsome fiancé."

"How's our boy?"

My eyes fill up. "He's all battered and sad and the cone is too heavy for his tiny head."

RJ's chin begins to quiver. "What do the docs say?"

"They say he isn't totally out of the woods, but it looks better than it did a couple of days ago, and that we might be able to bring him home day after tomorrow."

"That's great. That's so great." RJ folds me into his arms.

"I need your help," I mumble into his chest.

"Anything."

I tell him about my conversation with Maria. About her insistence that the reason I can't make up my mind about my career is because I am looking at it wrong. About her concept of finding the AND.

"Well, she does have a point. Your pull to stay with Patrick and do this new challenge isn't just about money, but also about tackling an old fear that you might finally be ready to conquer. And the Foundation job is appealing for more than just your do-gooder impulses; it is also about having something of a lifestyle change."

"I know. She is right, I'm split down the middle because the cons for both jobs sort of negate, and I'm equally interested in all of the pros that remain."

"So what can I do?"

"I need you to help me figure out the AND."

RJ nods thoughtfully. "We will do it. But can I feed you first? I think you'll need your strength, and I have a suspicion that your lunch was out of the vending machine."

"Guilty as charged."

"Okay. Why don't you go wash your face and relax and I'll rustle us up some dinner. . . . Opart?" Our favorite Thai restaurant.

"Perfect."

"I'll be back in a flash."

He's barely out the door when the doorbell rings.

"Silly boy, what did you forget besides your key?" I say to the back of the door. But when I open it, it isn't RJ.

Patrick looks even worse than when we saw him at the emergency vet Saturday night. There are huge bags under his red-rimmed eyes, three-day scruff on his face, his hair is a mess.

"Hi," he says.

"Hi." I stand aside so that he can come in.

"I called Lake Forest; they said he's doing better."

"Yeah. Not out of danger, but if he continues getting better I can bring him home in a couple of days."

"I gave them my credit card, so make sure they don't try to charge you for anything."

"That's sweet, Patrick, but you didn't have to do that."

"Yes, I did. I just . . . Alana, you can't know how sorry I am. Please don't hate me. I just, I'm such an asshole and I know I'm awful and when RJ told me he was getting ready to propose and asked for my advice on how to do it, I just wanted you to have a perfect weekend, you know? And I thought, if I took Dumpling then you guys could be totally focused on each other. He was right next to me, and then he was gone and in a flash there was just the most horrible sound I've ever . . ." His voice breaks.

"Patrick. It wasn't your fault. When that damn dog gets fixated on a squirrel, there is nothing in the world that can change that. I've called him for ten minutes while he runs

clear to the other side of the park and back. He's never ever
gone anywhere near a street, which is why I always have him
off leash in the parks without even thinking about it, and you
had no reason not to do the same. You didn't do anything
wrong, this was just a horrible accident and I don't hate you.
I could never hate you." Which, as it is coming out of my
mouth, I realize is actually true. I open my arms and he grabs
me in a hard hug and I can feel his back relax a little. "I'm
sorry; I should have called you and said that sooner. I didn't
realize you were feeling so guilty." When we had seen him
Saturday night, he had mumbled apologies and snuck away
when we were in meeting with the vet and discussing options,
and since then he's left messages and I've texted him brief
updates, but we haven't spoken.

He sniffs and wipes at his eyes. "Okay then."

"Okay."

"He caught the squirrel, you know." He grins.

"No way."

"I think it's why he got hit, I think he got it and it made
him stop in the street. But the tail was in his mouth when
I got to him."

This makes me laugh for the first time since that horrible
phone call. Really laugh. And then Patrick is really laughing
and the two of us hold each other and crack up at the idea of
my poor, dumb dog lying in the street with his prey in his
mouth, thinking, "Got you, you bastard." Like some shot-up
cowboy whose last round found its mark.

"I'm glad you're here, Patrick. There is something we need
to talk about. Can you stay for dinner?"

"Yeah. I'm sort of starving."

"Haven't been eating much?" I feel so bad that he has been
beating himself up so much.

He looks at me like I'm insane. "No, I've been eating plenty, but lunch was like six hours ago." And, we're back.

I call RJ and ask him to increase our order to accommodate one starving chef, and then Patrick and I sit down on the couch. I tell him everything about the Foundation job, my being so torn. I'm honest with him about the things that job offers me that he doesn't, my need for some balance and boundaries, some normalizing of my life and schedule. I'm also honest with him about the parts of what he offers me that I don't want to lose. Then I tell him about Maria's concept of AND, and tell him that the best thing I can do for myself is to see if there is a way to achieve that, but that I wanted him to know that if I can't come up with a new plan, that the other job is solidly in the running. I tell him about my responsibility to my folks, and their financial problems. It may be the first time in all the years we've been together that I talk to him without editing myself, the first time I am completely open. And Patrick, to his credit, listens to it all. And more important, he hears.

"Look, Alana, you know that the idea of losing you makes me crazy. But frankly, I've been ready for it ever since that day with the onions when you stood up to me in front of everyone and put me in my place. Deep down, I can't believe you've put up with me this long, and after my asshat move on Maria's show, I'm completely shocked you didn't quit weeks ago."

"I probably should have."

"Probably." He grins. "But you love me."

I sigh. "Yeah, I guess I do."

"Okay, so if I have a chance to keep you and it means I have to figure out how to help you have everything you want, then I'm going to do that."

"That's very kind."

"Kind nothing. I'm a selfish bastard, and you know it. I won't find anyone like you, and so if I'm going to have to share you with RJ and your family and Maria's foundation and all those freaking kids, I will, because at least then I still get to keep you. Besides, it'll be a huge pain in the ass to have to change my will."

"You have to stop joking about that, or I'm liable to actually kill you one of these days."

His face gets serious. "Alana, you are as close to family as I have ever had. I'm not going to get married again, I'm not going to have kids. If I go first, it's all yours, kiddo."

"Oh, Patrick . . ." I am at a loss.

"Well, you know, unless you up and completely abandon me for a bunch of snot-nosed kids and some husband." He grins.

"All right. Then we need to put our thinking caps on, because I've been trying to think about this all afternoon, and I really don't know how to do it."

"We'll figure it out. And, Alana?"

"Yeah?"

"Your folks? They have been kinder and more supportive of me than my own parents ever were. Regardless of what you decide with your job, I hope you won't be too proud to let me help make sure they have what they need."

"Patrick . . ."

"Hey, we can do it however you feel comfortable. I can buy the place in Florida and tell them I need to do it for tax purposes because of the Miami restaurant, and that I need someone to sort of be the caretakers. Or I can buy their house here for enough that they can buy the place there, and then rent it back to them for whatever they can afford. I could do it through a fake corporation so they don't know it's me. Pretend I'm a developer buying up stuff for a possible future project or something. Or if you want to keep me out of it altogether, I'll just give you the money and you can handle it. But whatever happens, no matter what, your folks are not going to lose out on having a good and comfortable life as long as I am here, okay?"

"Thank you, Patrick. That means more to me than anything. And yes, it does make me feel better about not having to consider that part."

"Good."

The door opens and RJ enters with two huge bags. "I may have gone overboard."

I kiss him and relieve him of the bags, which are heavy enough to make me think he has ordered the whole menu.

"Hey, man." Patrick puts out his hand.

"Hey." They shake hands, and begin to catch up while I unpack the food.

Maria's voice rings in my ears. Both. AND. I look over at my two men. My boss and my fiancé. My lover and my friend.

And for the first time in forever, I think that the solution I need, for every part of my life is not only possible, it is right in this room.

Epilogue

⌒

"How was it?" RJ asks me, when I call from my car en route home.

"It was great. Everyone is on board and ready to go, the school signed off, the network signed off, we have all the legal paperwork back from the parents, and we start shooting in the late fall."

My first go at executive producing will be a new documentary series about the culinary internship program. We'll be following this year's group of twenty-four interns for the whole year. And this time, we are working with juniors, so that we have the possibility of keeping them for a second, more intensive year before they have to make a decision about college or culinary school. Last year's interns are each going to serve as a mentor to three new interns as well. We have master classes set up with amazing famous chefs from all over the country, a two-week culinary tour of Europe during their spring break, and I think Kai, as their primary teacher and mentor, is about to become the next great television star.

Turns out, once we really looked at it from every angle and then spoke with Maria and Rachel, my ultimate best value to the program is as an advisor, and using my background in television to create a way to bring light to the program on a national scale, hopefully encouraging other cities to create similar programs of their own. Patrick is also a new board member, and he was very cool about taking *Feast* and *Academy* off my plate to work on the new series, which Bruce, bless his heart, pushed through the process at the network as if it had been his idea, including going to bat for me as exec.

And to his credit, Patrick hasn't complained overmuch about my not working with him on his shows. After all, he still has me as his cookbook coauthor and as his sous chef for *Master Chef Challenge*. And since we are currently undefeated after our first five battles, he can't really complain. Plus, I found him a total rock-star replacement. Gerry was in my class at Le Cordon Blue, and after graduation she headed for Europe, where she did stints in Paris, Florence, Berlin, and Vienna before landing in Barcelona for the past few years. But then on a trip home she met a wonderful guy and realized that maybe Chicago would be a good place to be. She is brash and bold, and she and Patrick both speak the language of people who have spent time on the line in major restaurants, and that shorthand seems to be working well for them.

And lucky for me, I get a ten-thousand-dollar bonus every time we win, which is helping me pay back Patrick for the loan I took from him to buy my parents their place in Florida. I fibbed a bit and said I got a big signing bonus for my new job, and Alexei managed to convince them that I needed to buy more property anyway to help with my taxes, so between us, we convinced them that it was essentially doing me a favor. They bought it hook, line, and sinker, and I let Patrick float me the whole amount so that we could pay for it with cash, with the agreement that I would pay him back. He only said yes when I agreed to do it as an interest-free loan, refusing to make money on the arrangement.

Interestingly enough, the bonus checks have been the very

thing that has helped me manage my camera fright, since I know that fifteen wins means Patrick is paid off, so I put my head down and cook as hard as I can, and so far, so good. Other than one small flub, where I dumped an entire batch of ice cream base into the machine without closing the chute door first, thereby dumping the whole thing on the floor and down my front, I've been relatively competent. And most important, all of my bodily effluvia has stayed in my body, which is as good as I can manage for now. I'm still a little nervous, but usually by five minutes into the battles, I settle into a groove, and at the last shoot, I was even able to banter a bit on camera with Anne, the host. We'll see what the press and bloggers have to say when the episodes start airing. And Emily's editor is talking to me about maybe doing my first cookbook, which I'm actually excited about.

"I'm so glad the meeting went well. That is all just great, honey, I'm so proud of you."

"Thanks, baby. How was your day?"

"I sent the contracts off for the florist and the photographer, so that's the last of the wedding stuff I had to do, right?"

"Right."

"Okay, then we are all paid-up, so you are locked in, missy."

"I'm in." The wedding is scheduled for two months from now, a very small simple event, just fifty people for an afternoon ceremony and cake and champagne, and then our families and a couple important friends are having dinner that evening in the private room at MK, where my friend Chef Erick Williams has planned an insanely amazing seven-course tasting menu with loads of special touches. We had a great visit in Nashville with RJ's folks, and then they came to Chicago to meet my parents. You'd think they would have nothing in common, the Russian immigrants and the sixth-generation Tennesseans, the mostly non-practicing Jews and the Reverend and his wife, but within ten minutes of meeting, the four of them were like old friends, and RJ and I felt like a fifth and sixth wheel. I've been talking and e-mailing with RJ's sister, who is awesome, and we are so excited that she and her husband and RJ's nieces are all able to come up for the wedding.

"You'd better be. How close are you to home?"

"Five minutes. You?"

"I'll be more like twenty." The moving-in process, or the purge-and-merge as we've been calling it, has been somewhat slow, but steady. And as of last weekend, even though a lot of his stuff is still at his house, he is officially sleeping here every night, which is wonderful. As an engagement present Bennie is going to come visit in a couple of weeks to help us effectively come up with a new design incorporating both of our belongings.

"Okay. See you there. Love you!"

"I love you, honey. See you in a bit."

I get home and park, and open the door.

"Hey, buddy!"

Dumpling hops off the couch, where he and JP are curled up together napping, and he does his little tripod jitterbug over to me. He is surprisingly fast for a three-wheeler, and still manages to hop straight up and down in the air with joy, spinning and sneezing like his old self. He looks even sillier now that he has the stump and the eye patch. Technically he doesn't need the protection over his eye anymore; it has healed beautifully, but when we tried to throw it away, he dumped over the garbage, got it out and brought it back to us. We think he likes it as a fashion statement, and Maria had one of her wardrobe people make him a half dozen in different fabrics to match his mood. Today I have him sporting the one with the Chicago Bears logo. He's a Chicago dog, after all.

I go over to the couch and pet JP, who hisses and nips at me. He is not adjusting terribly well to being an indoor-only cat, but it is just not safe for him to go outside in my neighborhood; he'd be an ex-cat within a week, and after the drama of the past couple of months, we just aren't up for more animal emergencies. We are talking seriously about letting Barry adopt him, since he is on a quiet street and has a garden apartment with a fenced backyard. RJ wants to give him another couple of weeks to see if he turns around, but agrees that it would be the next best thing to have him close by and with a friend, instead of here and miserable.

Dumpling yips.

"Okay, okay, should we go out?"

He hops over to the door and grabs his leash.

We take a quick walk around the block, and run into Ollie, who has started lying down when he sees Dumpling so that they can visit without Dumpling having to try to stand up on his one rear leg, which he still doesn't really have the hang of yet. He tends to lose his balance and just tump over. It is very sweet. Luckily, all those years of that weird one-leg-in-the-air pooping is serving him well, and he is able to do his business without a problem. My little miracle boy.

We head back inside, and I toss him a chicken snack, and he flops down on the floor to eat it. My phone rings.

"Hey, baby, my hands are kind of full, can you come get the door for me?"

"On my way."

I wipe my hands and open the door. RJ is standing there, and in his arms is a wriggling French bulldog puppy of the most inexplicable color, almost pale honeyed yellow tinged with a sort of peachy pink.

"Oh my goodness! Who are you?"

RJ hands me the pup, who immediately starts licking all over my face and biting my ponytail. Dumpling tries to stand on his one leg to see what is going on, and falls over at my feet. RJ scoops him up and puts him face-to-face with the puppy.

"Dumpling, there is someone we want you to meet. We thought you might want a little sister."

Dumpling looks at the puppy, who leans forward and licks his face. Dumpling licks back. The puppy sniffs his ear and then with one move, snatches the eye patch right off his head and starts to chew it. Dumpling looks at me with his one good eye, head cocked as if to say, "We're going to have our hands full with this one," and then turns and licks RJ under his chin.

"I can't believe you did this! You are so sneaky."

"Well, we did talk about wanting to do it, and a guy at work breeds them for showing, but this one is off the allowable color charts."

"She does have a certain, um . . . Well, she's kind of, um . . ."

"Pink? Yeah. Some weird anomaly, and apparently, not good for the show circuit."

"But good for us."

"That's what I thought."

"What should we call her?"

RJ smiles. "I was thinking Pamplemousse."

"Of course. What else could she be?" I turn to the puppy, and gently remove Dumpling's eye patch, now slightly mangled and covered in spit, from her mouth and hand it back to

RJ, who replaces it on Dumpling's head. "What do you think? Are you our little Pamplemousse? Hmm?" She leans forward and licks my face and then nips the end of my nose. "I guess that is a yes!"

I put Pamplemousse down on the floor, and RJ puts Dumpling down next to her, and the two of them begin to circle and play. RJ puts his arm around me, kissing the side of my head and squeezing me tight to his side.

And this? Right here?

This is what happened.

The End.
        And happily ever after.

In the Kitchen with Alana and Friends

～

Bruce's Midnight Scrambled Eggs

SERVES 2

Alana knows that nothing keeps them coming ba... like g od company, good loving, and great food. Want to make ...neone swoon with a midnight snack or breakfast in bed? This dish will keep them eating out of your hand.

6 eggs

1 tablespoon cold water

3 tablespoons butter, cold or frozen

4 slices good sourdough bread, toasted and lightly buttered

4 slices prosciutto

1 tablespoon chives, minced fine

Salt and ground grains of paradise or other pepper

Crack the eggs into a bowl and beat well with the water. Using a microplane or other fine grater, grate 2 tablespoons of the butter into the eggs and mix so that the little pieces of butter are well distributed. Heat a nonstick skillet over medium heat, and melt the remaining butter in the pan. When the foaming subsides, pour in the eggs, and gently stir fairly constantly as the eggs cook. Turn the heat down to medium-low once you start to see large curds forming. Keep stirring the eggs until they reach your desired level of doneness. Place two pieces of toast on each plate, and top with prosciutto. Divide the eggs over the pieces of toast, sprinkle with salt and the ground pepper of your choice, and garnish with chives. For extra richness, you can add a couple tablespoons of crumbled goat cheese or Boursin herbed cheese to the eggs in the last minute of cooking.

Dulce de Leche Cheesecake

SERVES 8

If Maria ever doubted that Alana was the right person to be her personal chef, this cheesecake sealed the deal!

Crust:
   2 cups gingersnap crumbs
   3 tablespoons granulated sugar
   7 tablespoons unsalted butter, melted

Preheat oven to 375°F. Mix crumbs, sugar, and butter until you get a consistency somewhat like wet sand. Press into and about two inches up the sides of a 9-inch springform pan. Bake until it smells toasty and has browned a bit, about 9 to 12 minutes. Let the crust cool on a rack while you make the filling. Lower oven temp to 300°F.

Filling:

- 24 ounces cream cheese at room temperature
- ¾ cup dulce de leche (see note)
- 2 tablespoons flour
- pinch salt
- 1¼ cup granulated sugar
- 1 tablespoon vanilla
- 4 large eggs at room temp

In the bowl of a stand mixer with paddle attachment, or in a large bowl with a hand mixer, beat cream cheese, dulce de leche, flour, and salt on medium speed, until very smooth and fluffy, about 5 minutes. Add sugar and vanilla and beat until well blended and smooth. Add eggs one at a time, and beat just to blend. Do not overmix.

Pour filling into crust and smooth the top. Bake at 300°F until the center just jiggles, about 55 to 65 minutes. It will be slightly puffed around the edges and vaguely moist-looking in the center. Cool completely on a rack. Cover and chill for at least 8 hours before serving. Pie will keep for up to 3 days in the refrigerator or can be frozen up to a month. To freeze, put the unmolded, cooled cake in the freezer, uncovered until the top is firm and cold, then unmold and wrap in two layers of plastic wrap and one layer of foil. To thaw, place it in the refrigerator overnight.

Note: You can substitute caramel if you can't find dulce de leche.

Girls' Night Beet Bruschetta

SERVES 10 TO 12 AS AN APPETIZER

Girls' night in never tasted better. Open a bottle of crisp white wine, and get ready to dine and dish.

1 pound mixed golden and chioggia baby beets (see note)

2 tablespoons canola oil

3 tablespoons extra virgin olive oil

1 tablespoon orange zest

1 teaspoon fresh thyme leaves

¼ teaspoon Aleppo pepper

Salt to taste

1 baguette, sliced into ½-inch-thick rounds

8 ounces goat cheese at room temperature

2 tablespoons honey

Preheat oven to 400°F. Trim and wash beets. Toss with canola oil and salt and pepper, and put in a packet made of heavy-duty foil. Roast for 25 to 40 minutes until a knife goes in clean and beets are very tender. Let cool just enough to be handled, then using dry paper towels, wipe the peels off the beets. Chop peeled beets into medium dice, and toss with olive oil, orange zest, thyme, Aleppo pepper, and salt to taste. Mix goat cheese with honey and spread a thin layer on the bread slices, and top with a generous spoonful of beets.

Note: You can substitute red beets, but I find the flavor of these more subtle.

Mother-in-Law
Maple French Toast Brulee

SERVES 6 TO 8

Nothing will ruin a brunch faster than dripping maple syrup down the front of a favorite blouse. Keep family relations happy with this elegunt take on a breakfast classic.

1 loaf Challah or brioche, preferably one day old
1 pint high-quality French vanilla ice cream or frozen custard
4 eggs
4 tablespoons butter
Salt
3 tablespoons demerara sugar
3 tablespoons granulated maple sugar
½ teaspoon fresh ground nutmeg

Melt ice cream or frozen custard completely and blend with eggs and a pinch of salt. Slice ends off bread, and then slice into 1-inch-thick slices. Arrange slices in a casserole dish, and pour egg mixture over them, allowing it to completely soak into all the bread, about 10 to 15 minutes.

Melt half the butter in a nonstick skillet. Cook toast in batches until golden brown and crispy on both sides and cooked through, about 2 to 3 minutes per side. Transfer to a sheet pan. Brush the remaining butter on the tops of the cooked toast. Arrange a rack in the top of the oven, and preheat the broiler. Blend the maple sugar, demerara sugar, and nutmeg with a pinch of salt. Sprinkle the tops of the toast evenly with a thin layer of the sugar mixture, and put under the broiler, watching carefully as the sugar melts and caramelizes.

You might need to rotate the sheet pan to be sure all the sugar melts evenly. Don't let it burn! Alternatively, if you are comfortable with a blowtorch, you can melt the sugar topping that way. Serve immediately, or the crisp sugar top will lose its crunch.

———⌣———

Mama's Caraway Pelmeni

SERVES PLEHNTY

These traditional Russian dumplings are a great thing to make with your kids, no matter how old they are. Caraway adds a special Ostermann family touch.

½ pound ground beef shoulder
½ pound ground pork butt
1 onion, grated, liquid squeezed out
1 clove garlic, grated
1 tablespoon caraway seeds, ground to powder in a coffee mill
    or with a mortar and pestle
Salt and pepper to taste
2 cups flour
3 eggs
1 cup milk
½ teaspoon salt
1 tablespoon vegetable oil

Mix beef and pork well with hands, then add onion, garlic, caraway seeds, salt, and pepper. To make mincemeat more tender and juicy, add 2 to 3 tablespoons of water. The mixture should be moist but firm enough to shape into balls. Reserve in refrigerator.

Mix flour with eggs, milk, salt, and oil until a soft dough forms. Knead on a floured surface until dough is elastic. Your hands will know.

Take some dough and make a snake about 1-inch thick in diameter.

Divide into pieces 1 inch-thick. Roll each piece into ball, and then, using dowel, roll out thin, so that each is $\frac{1}{16}$-inch thick.

If you like perfect, take a glass or a cup and make rounds with help on the dough. We no like perfect look, just like perfect taste, but Martha Stewart, she not approve. Fill each round with 1 teaspoon of the mincemeat and fold into half-moons. Pinch edges together and connect the opposite sides, making sure there are no air bubbles or dumplings will explode. Pelmeni can be cooked immediately or frozen to be cooked later (you can keep them in the freezer for a long time). To cook pelmeni, bring water to a boil in a large pot. It is important to use plenty of water, so that the dumplings don't stick to each other. Salt water to taste like Caspian Sea. Carefully drop pelmeni into boiling water. Don't forget to stir them from time to time. Boil for 20 minutes. To serve, melt butter in pan and add some chopped onions. Cook till golden and soft. Add cooked pelmeni and get crispy on one side. Serve with sour cream, maybe some applesauce, or sprinkle with vinegar.

Chilled Pea Soup

*Insanely simple and delicious. A go-to for last-minute enter-
taining, perfect for summer get-togethers.*

1 pound frozen petite green peas (buy the highest possible
    quality here, not the place for generic)
Cold water
Salt and pepper to taste
Crème fraîche or full-fat greek yogurt
Zest of one lemon
1 tablespoon finely minced chives
2 tablespoons celery leaves (the pale yellow leaves on the inside
    of a heart of celery)
Extra-virgin olive oil for garnish

Place the peas, still frozen, in a blender or food processor. Add
cold water until it barely reaches the top of the peas; do not
cover, the peas should be poking their little heads out of the
water. Puree on high for 2 minutes until as smooth as possible. Strain through a fine strainer or chinois, pressing to get
all of the liquid out. Taste and season with salt and pepper.
Keep in the fridge. To serve, top the soup with a dollop of
crème fraîche or greek yogurt mixed with the lemon zest,
sprinkle with chives and a couple of celery leaves. Drizzle a
bit of olive oil over the top.

    Can also be served hot.

Melanie's Healthy Wheat Berry Salad

SERVES 8 TO 12 AS A SIDE DISH

Hearty and good for you, without sacrificing flavor. (For more of Mel's famously light dishes, check out her mini cookbook at the back of Good Enough To Eat *by Stacey Ballis, available at booksellers everywhere and your favorite online retailers.)*

1 cup orzo

1 cup wheat berries

1 large or 2 small pink grapefruit

1 teaspoon honey

1 cup tangerine or blood orange juice

½ cup extra-virgin olive oil

2 teaspoons champagne vinegar (or more to taste)

Coarse salt and freshly ground pepper to taste

3 tablespoons toasted slivered almonds

3 tablespoons fresh mint, chopped

A day in advance, cook the orzo in boiling salted water until tender. Cook the wheat berries in boiling salted water until tender. Drain and place in a mixing bowl.

Peel the grapefruits and cut them into segments or supremes. Add any collected juices to the tangerine or blood orange juice. Place the juice in a small saucepan and heat on high and reduce by half. Remove from heat and stir in honey. When the juice has cooled, add the oil and vinegar and mix well. Season with salt and pepper and add to the orzo and wheat berries. Toss well and gently fold in grapefruit segments, and refrigerate overnight. Just before serving, add almonds and mint. Correct seasoning and serve at room temperature.

Olive Oil Spanish Tortilla

SERVES 6 TO 8 AS A MAIN COURSE, 12 TO 16
AS AN APPETIZER

A quick visit to Spain, and delicious anytime.

6 to 7 medium potatoes, peeled and sliced ⅛" thick (I like
    yukon gold for this)
1 whole yellow onion, peeled and chopped in ¼" dice
2 to 3 cups of good Spanish olive oil
5 to 6 large eggs
Salt to taste

Put potatoes and onions into a bowl and mix them together.
Salt the mixture well. In a large, heavy, nonstick frying pan,
heat the olive oil on medium-high heat. Drop a single piece
of potato into the oil to ensure it is hot enough to fry; it should
sizzle subtly but not frantically. If you get a lot of bubbles, it
means your oil is too hot. Turn a nearby burner on a lower
heat and carefully move the pan over, let it cool and retest in
2 minutes. Once the oil is at the right temperature, carefully
place the potato and onions into the frying pan, spreading
them evenly over the surface. The oil should almost cover the
potatoes. You may need to turn down the heat slightly so the
potatoes do not burn.

You want the potatoes to slowly go golden brown while
the insides cook completely. If you notice a lot of browning,
turn down the heat more. When you can easily poke a potato
with a fork or break it in half with a spatula, it is cooked. Be
sure to test three pieces or so, in case you get the one piece

that is fully cooked. With a slotted spoon remove the potatoes and onions to a bowl. If you want, you can put them in a colander to remove more oil. While the mixture is cooling, crack the eggs into a large mixing bowl and beat by hand with a whisk or fork. Pour in the potato onion mixture. Mix together gently with a large spoon so that the potatoes don't break up too much.

Pour 2 tablespoons of olive oil into a small, 9- or 10-inch nonstick frying pan and heat on medium to medium-low heat. Once again, be careful not to get the pan too hot because the oil will burn—or the *tortilla* will! When hot, stir the potato-onion mixture once more and "pour" into the pan and spread out evenly. Allow the egg to cook around the edges. Then you can carefully lift up one side of the omelet to check if the egg has slightly "browned." You can cover the pan with a lid to help set up the top a little. The inside of the mixture should not be completely cooked and the egg will still be runny.

When the mixture has browned lightly on the bottom, place a large dinner plate or baking sheet upside down over the frying pan. With one hand on the frying pan handle and the other on top of the plate to hold it steady, quickly turn the frying pan over and the omelet will "fall" onto the plate. Place the frying pan back on the range and put just enough oil to cover the bottom and sides of the pan—approximately 1½ teaspoons. Let the pan warm for 30 seconds or so. Now slide the omelet (which is probably still a bit runny), into the frying pan browned-side up, using a spatula to catch any egg mixture that runs out. Use the spatula to shape the sides of the omelet. Let the omelet cook for 3 to 4 minutes. Turn the heat off and let the tortilla sit in the pan for 5 minutes. Serve hot or at room temperature.

Michelle Bernstein's White Gazpacho

SERVES 4 TO 6

Reprinted with permission from Michelle Bernstein's Cuisine
à Latina *cookbook, which you should buy because DAMN
her food is amazing and all her recipes work. I'm just saying.
If you want to taste Michelle's food, head to Michy's or Sra
Martinez restaurants in Miami.*

2 cups chopped, peeled, English seedless cucumber

2 cups seedless green grapes

1½ cups salted Marcona almonds

1 small garlic clove

½ shallot

1 tablespoon chopped fresh dill

1½ cups cold vegetable stock or broth

½ cup good quality extra-virgin olive oil (I look for one with a
    more buttery taste than peppery)

1 tablespoon sherry vinegar

2 tablespoons dry sherry

Salt and pepper to taste

Garnish:

    ¼ cup sliced seedless green grapes

    2 tablespoons crushed Marcona almonds

    1 tablespoon chopped fresh dill

Put the cucumber, grapes, almonds, garlic, shallot, dill, and
broth in a blender and puree until very smooth, about 2 to
3 minutes. With the motor running on high, drizzle in the
olive oil in a thin stream until the mixture emulsifies. Stop

the motor and taste. It should be smooth and creamy, if slightly grainy. If it is still a bit chunky, puree for another minute. Add the vinegar and sherry and puree on high for one more minute. Season to taste with salt and pepper.

Serve chilled with the garnishes.

RJ's Famous Banana Salad

SERVES 8 TO 10

1 cup white vinegar heated until very hot in double boiler
1 egg
¾ to 1 cup sugar
1 tablespoon flour
Pinch salt
2 cups Spanish peanuts, ground fine
Up to a dozen bananas, sliced in half lengthwise, and then
    quartered

Beat egg well and add sugar. Add flour and salt and pour hot vinegar over the mixture, placing back over double boiler to desired consistency. Dip banana lengths into dressing and roll in peanuts. Eat if you dare.

Whole Wheat Pasta
with Cauliflower and Walnuts

SERVES 2 AS AN ENTRÉE, UP TO 6 AS A SIDE DISH

2 heads garlic, top quarter cut off

6 tablespoons plus 1 teaspoon extra-virgin olive oil

1 head cauliflower (about 1½ pounds)

Table salt and ground black pepper

¼ teaspoon sugar

1 pound whole wheat pasta, like orecchiette or penne

¼ teaspoon red pepper flakes

2 to 3 tablespoons juice from 1 lemon

1 tablespoon fresh parsley leaves, chopped

2 ounces Parmesan cheese, grated (about 1 cup)

¼ cup chopped walnuts, toasted

Adjust your oven rack to the middle position, and place large rimmed baking sheet on rack. Heat oven to 500°F. Place the garlic heads, cut-side up, in center of a piece of foil. Drizzle ½ teaspoon oil over each head and seal the packet. Place it on the oven rack and roast until garlic is very tender, about 40 minutes. Open packet and set aside to cool.

While garlic is roasting, trim the outer leaves of the cauliflower and cut stem flush with bottom. Cut head into florets. Place the cauliflower in large bowl; toss with 2 tablespoons oil, 1 teaspoon salt, pepper to taste, and sugar. Remove baking sheet from oven. Carefully transfer cauliflower to baking sheet and spread in an even layer. Return baking sheet to oven and roast until cauliflower is well browned and tender, 20 to 25 minutes. Transfer cauliflower to cutting board.

When cool enough to handle, chop the cauliflower into rough ½-inch pieces.

While cauliflower roasts, bring 4 quarts water to boil in large pot. Add enough salt to make the water taste salty, add pasta; cook until al dente. Squeeze roasted garlic cloves from their skins into small bowl. Using fork, mash garlic to smooth paste, then stir in red pepper flakes and 2 tablespoons lemon juice. Slowly whisk in remaining ¼ cup oil.

Drain pasta, reserving 1 cup cooking water, and return pasta to pot. Add chopped cauliflower to pasta; stir in garlic sauce, ¼ cup cooking water, parsley, and ½ cup cheese. Adjust consistency with additional cooking water and season with salt, pepper, and additional lemon juice to taste. Serve immediately, sprinkling with remaining ½ cup cheese and toasted nuts.

Stephanie Izard's Roasted Cauliflower

SERVES 4

Printed with permission from Stephanie Izard of Girl & the Goat restaurant in Chicago, www.girlandthegoat.com. For more amazing recipes from Stephanie, and trust me, they are all amazing, check out her new cookbook, Girl in the Kitchen, *available at your local booksellers and your favorite online retailer.*

2 tablespoons olive oil

4 cups cauliflower, sliced

2 tablespoons water

1 tablespoon crunch butter (see the next page)

1 tablespoon pine nuts, toasted

    2 tablespoons pickled banana or Hungarian hot peppers (or half
        and half), sliced fine

    1 ounce Parmesan cheese, grated

    1 tablespoon fresh mint, torn

Garnish:

    2 teaspoons pine nuts, toasted

    2 teaspoons Parmesan cheese, grated

    2 teaspoons fresh mint, torn

Heat the oil in a sauté pan until it shimmers. Add cauliflower and cook, tossing and stirring until caramelized on all sides. Season to taste with salt. Add water to pan and cover to steam cauliflower until cooked, about 3 minutes. Add the crunch butter and toss to coat, then add the pine nuts and pickled peppers. Toss to combine and stir until heated through. Remove from heat. Add the Parmesan cheese and mint, toss to combine. Plate or platter as desired and garnish with pine nuts, Parmesan cheese & mint.

Crunch Butter

MAKES 1 CUP

    4 ounces butter, unsalted, softened

    1 garlic clove, grated

    2 tablespoons Parmesan cheese, grated

    2 tablespoons panko breadcrumbs, toasted

    Salt to taste

In a mixer fitted with a paddle attachment, combine all the ingredients and whip until light and fluffy.

Susan Spicer's Grilled Shrimp with Coriander Sauce and Black Bean Cakes

SERVES 4

Printed with permission from Susan Spicer, famous at her Bayona restaurant in New Orleans, www.bayona.com.

16 medium to large headless shrimp, peeled and deveined (preferably Gulf shrimp)
2 tablespoons olive oil
½ teaspoon chopped garlic (optional)
¼ teaspoon ground cumin
½ teaspoon ground coriander
¼ teaspoon cayenne pepper
½ teaspoon salt

Toss shrimp with olive oil, garlic, salt, pepper, and spices. Skewer 4 to a portion and set aside.

Coriander Sauce:

1 tablespoon shallots, finely chopped
½ teaspoon orange zest (no pith)
¼ cup orange juice
¼ cup white wine
2 tablespoons sherry wine vinegar
¼ teaspoon ground coriander
4 tablespoons butter, softened
2 teaspoons cilantro, chopped
Salt and pepper, to taste

In a small saucepot, or saucepan, place chopped shallots, orange zest, orange juice, wine, vinegar, and ground coriander. Simmer over medium heat until liquid is reduced to 2 to 3 tablespoons. While still hot, whisk in softened butter by the tablespoonful until sauce is emulsified (thick and creamy). Stir in chopped cilantro and season with salt and pepper to taste. Keep warm, but not hot.

Black Bean Cake:
> ½ pound black beans, soaked at least 2 hours, or overnight, and drained
>
> 3 tablespoons cooking oil
>
> 1 small Poblano pepper, chopped
>
> 1 small onion, chopped
>
> 1 teaspoon garlic, minced
>
> 1 teaspoon chili powder
>
> 1 teaspoon ground cumin
>
> 2 tablespoons honey
>
> 2 tablespoons cider vinegar
>
> Salt

Cook black beans in water until tender. Heat oil in a sauté pan and cook onion, peppers, and garlic over medium heat for 2 to 3 minutes and add to beans in pot, along with all other ingredients. Stir frequently until beans have absorbed water and start to break down. Season to taste with salt and drain the cooked beans, reserving liquid. Purée in a food processor. Purée should be dry enough not to stick to your hands and still moist enough that it does not crumble. If it seems too wet and sticky, spread bean paste onto a baking sheet and dry in a low oven until it reaches the right consistency. (If too dry, work in a little reserved liquid.) When cool, form beans into cakes, dust with flour on top and bottom and sauté in oil to crisp on both sides. You want the bean cakes to be heated all the way through but be careful not to scorch. Keep warm.

When ready to serve, grill, broil, or sauté the shrimp. Take off the skewer (or not) and top with the warm coriander sauce. Serve with a warm bean cake topped with a dollop of sour cream and a sprig of cilantro.

Sangre del Tigre

SERVES 4

This will kick your hangover in the butt, or just spice up your next brunch!

4 cups tomato juice

1 cup clam juice

2 tablespoons prepared horseradish

4 eggs, separated, whites whipped until frothy, yolks reserved

1 teaspoon Tabasco or other hot sauce

1 tablespoon juice from a jar of pickled jalapeños

1 teaspoon ground white pepper

1 teaspoon ground black pepper

1 tablespoon salt

1 tablespoon orange zest

6 ounces mezcal (can substitute tequila, but it won't be the
     same)

Mix all ingredients together with egg whites. Shake with ice and strain into glasses. Float an egg yolk on the top of each glass, and put two to three drops of Tabasco on the yolk with a sprinkle of salt. Either take the yolk with the first sip as a shot, or for the more squeamish, stir it in and blend well before drinking.

Raw eggs can put you at risk for salmonella and other food-borne illness. If you have access to the new "safe eggs," which have been pasteurized, use those, or if you have eggs from a source you trust, you will be fine. If you have concern about eating raw eggs, prepare the rest of the drink as is, and serve with a hardboiled egg on the side. The protein with the drink is part of the positive effects.

Maria's Pressure Cooker Flan

SERVES 4 TO 6

Once you have flan cooked this way, you'll never do it another way again. I warn you, this is so delicious and easy (you'll likely always have the ingredients on hand) you might end up with a small flan problem. I find the cure is, um, more flan . . .

4 whole eggs

1 can sweetened condensed milk

The same can filled with either ½ can regular milk and ½
    evaporated milk, or all regular milk no less than 2 percent

Pinch of salt

½ cup sugar

Beat all ingredients, except the sugar, together in a bowl.
Heat sugar with 1 tablespoon of water in a small pan. Let it
heat over high until you have an amber caramel. Pour the
caramel into the flan pan and, working quickly, twirl it
around to coat the inside of the flan pan with caramel. Let
set for a few minutes to cool. Pour the milk/egg mixture into
the pan and secure the lid. Put it in the pressure cooker with
a steaming plate at the bottom (to lift it slightly off the bottom) and add 2 cups of water. Bring the pressure cooker to a
boil and then reduce the heat until you get a steady *swish
swish swish*. Cook for 20 minutes after the *swish swish swish*
starts, take off heat, cool pressure cooker immediately by running cold water over it until it releases, take flan pan out, and
cool in refrigerator for several hours. Unmold flan into a serving piece with enough of a lip to catch the caramel, and serve
with the caramel spooned over.

Sara's Thanksgiving Mashed Potatoes
SERVES 12

*Don't wait for the holidays to break out this dish—make it
immediately, and with regularity. You will thank me later.*

6 pounds Yukon Gold potatoes, peeled and cubed

2 sticks butter, cubed, at room temperature

1 pint half-and-half, at room temperature

1 pint sour cream (may also use crème fraîche, Greek yogurt
    (full fat), mascarpone, softened Brie with the rind cut off, or
    soft goat cheese)

1 bunch chives, chopped

Salt and pepper to taste

Start potatoes in cold, heavily salted water over high heat, and bring to boil. Once boiling, cook 15 to 20 minutes until completely tender. Drain potatoes completely and return to pot over low heat to dry out slightly, shaking a bit, just a couple of minutes. Transfer potatoes to large bowl with cubed butter and mash with hand masher just to get started. Fill potato pot one-half full with hot tap water and put back on stove on high heat. Using hand mixer on medium speed, slowly add half-and-half until the potatoes reach just slightly stiffer than your preferred texture. Add half of the sour cream, and taste for tang. If you like more tang, add the other half; if not, season to taste with salt and pepper. Turn the heat down to low and hold potatoes, covered in the bowl over the hot water. Garnish with chives before serving.

Alana's Healthy Granola

MAKES 30 ½-CUP SERVINGS

(178 CALORIES PER SERVING)

Granola that is both delicious and actually good for you. It is a lot of ingredients, but dead simple to put together.

3 cups rolled oats

3 cups puffed millet cereal

½ cup barley flakes

½ cup toasted wheat germ

1 cup grape nuts cereal

½ cup flax seeds

1 cup shredded coconut, unsweetened

½ cup sunflower seeds

¼ cup white sesame seeds

1 cup raw slivered almonds

¼ cup chopped pecans

¼ cup chopped raw cashews

1 teaspoon kosher salt

1 cup applesauce

2 teaspoons ground cinnamon

1 teaspoon vanilla

¼ teaspoon almond extract

⅓ cup amber agave syrup or brown rice syrup

4 tablespoons honey

¼ cup light brown sugar

2 tablespoons peanut oil

1 cup golden raisins

½ cup dried cherries

Preheat oven to 325°F.

Mix all of the dry ingredients except the cinnamon, sugar, raisins, and cherries together in a large mixing bowl.

Mix applesauce, honey, agave, sugar, vanilla, almond extract, oil, and cinnamon in a bowl until well blended. Add to dry ingredients and toss together lightly until very well mixed.

Spread the mixture out on two greased baking sheets and bake in oven, turning over about halfway through baking and redistributing the granola evenly during the baking process (I find a bench knife works great for this).

The goal is to get it evenly deeply golden without burning. Depending on your oven, this is about 40 to 50 minutes. Watch closely when you get toward the end of the baking time, as it can quickly overbake! The granola is not at full crunchiness until it cools, so go by color. Should look toasty, but not mahogany.

Let granola cool completely, then mix in fruit. Store in airtight containers. This is my favorite mix of flavors, but feel free to substitute for different nuts, dried fruits, and other grains.

(Because of the reduced amount of both fat and sugar in this recipe, this is not a granola that clumps into clusters; it stays pretty loose. If you aren't as concerned about calories and want that more solid style, increase the light brown sugar to ¾ cup and the peanut oil to ½ cup, which should give you the clumping you want.)

RJ's Gougères

SERVES 8 AS AN HORS D'OEUVRE

Gougères may have been one of the things that helped spark RJ and Alana's romance, but you will have a romance of your own with the crisp, cheesy puffs.

1 cup water
4 tablespoons softened unsalted butter
½ teaspoon kosher salt, plus extra for sprinkling
1 cup all-purpose flour
4 large eggs, at room temperature
6 ounces grated Gruyère, cheddar, Emmenthal, or other nutty
    full-flavored cheese

Preheat the oven to 350°F if you plan to make the gougères right away.

Bring water, butter, and ½ teaspoon salt to a boil in a small saucepan. Place the flour in the bowl of a mixer, add the boiling water mixture, and mix with a paddle, if available (not a whisk), or use a wooden spoon in a bowl. Beat in eggs, one at a time, until the dough is very smooth. Add in the cheese and mix well until dough is thick and cheese has pretty much melted into the dough. Place the dough in a large Ziploc bag. I find this easier than the traditional pastry bag method. You can just cut off the corner of the bag, pipe the gougères, and then throw it away. If you prefer to use a pastry bag, feel free, just use a medium plain tip.

Line two large baking sheets with either silicone baking mats or parchment paper, and pipe the dough in small mounds onto them, in about 1-inch rounds, leaving an inch and a half of space between them. Sprinkle each with a few flakes of kosher salt and, if you want, some extra grated cheese. Bake 20 to 25 minutes, until golden brown and puffed about three times their original size. Don't open the oven door for the first 10 to 12 minutes, or they may deflate upon themselves. They will still be delicious, but not as pretty. Serve and eat IMMEDIATELY! Best when hot out of the oven.

If you want to freeze them to bake later, pipe the gougères as directed, sprinkle them with grated cheese (this will help them not stick to each other during storage), and freeze them overnight. You can then store in a bag for when you want them. To serve: Let the frozen gougères thaw at room temperature while you preheat the oven to 350°F (about 15 to 20 minutes). Sprinkle the thawed or refrigerated gougères with salt and bake 25 to 30 minutes, until golden and puffed.

New Year's Morning Banana Bread with White Chocolate Chips and Pine Nuts

MAKES 1 LOAF

You can use whatever mix-ins you like, but this basic banana bread recipe is a winner however you make it, even plain. Store your overripe bananas in the freezer and you'll always be able to make this delicious quick bread.

1 cup sugar

½ cup butter, softened

3 very ripe bananas, mashed

2 eggs

1¼ cups flour

½ teaspoon salt

1 teaspoon baking soda

½ cup toasted pine nuts

½ cup white chocolate chips or chunks

Preheat oven to 350°F.

Cream softened butter with sugar. In a separate bowl, beat eggs until smooth. Add mashed bananas to eggs and blend into butter and sugar mixture. Sift flour, salt, and baking soda, and fold into wet mixture. Fold in nuts and chocolate chips. Pour into greased loaf pan and bake 45 to 55 minutes until a skewer comes out clean. Cool on a rack.

Solianka Russian Beef Soup

SERVES 6

Adapted from Karena on allrecipes.com. A hearty soup for a winter's day.

2 ounces dried porcini mushrooms soaked in ¾ cup water until they have rehydrated and become tender, at least 30 minutes. Strain and reserve liquid.

½ cup unsalted butter

3 onions, chopped

1 cup cooked diced veal

1 cup diced ham

¼ pound kielbasa sausage, cut into 1-inch pieces

2 quarts beef stock

3 bay leaves

10 black peppercorns

2 dill pickles, diced

2 tablespoons capers

12 cremini mushrooms, sliced

1 28-ounce can whole peeled tomatoes

2 tablespoons tomato paste

1½ tablespoons all-purpose flour

12 kalamata olives

⅓ cup chopped fresh dill weed

¼ teaspoon dried marjoram

3 cloves garlic, minced

¼ cup dill pickle juice

1 teaspoon Hungarian sweet paprika

Salt to taste
Ground black pepper to taste
Sour cream and lemon to garnish

In a large dutch oven, melt half the butter, and when the foaming subsides, sauté the onions until they become golden. Add in all of the meats, and the rehydrated mushrooms. Add the stock and liquid from the mushrooms and bring to a boil. Make a bouquet garni by tying the bay leaves and peppercorns tightly in cheesecloth. Lower the heat and add the bouquet garni, pickles, capers, and fresh mushrooms. Simmer 10 to 15 minutes. Melt remaining butter in a skillet and cook the tomatoes and tomato paste for a few minutes, then add the flour and sauté for another few minutes. Add a cup of the soup liquid to the skillet and stir in well, then return pan ingredients to the soup pot. Add the olives, dill, marjoram, garlic, pickle juice, and paprika. Adjust soup's seasoning with salt and pepper; and simmer another 10 to 15 minutes. Remove pot from heat and remove bouquet garni. Adjust seasonings and serve with sour cream and lemon.

Denise's Cheese Dip

SERVES 8 TO 10

Chefs are great pals to have, especially when they share their recipes with you. Check out Denise's cooking school at www.flavourcookingschool.com.

4 ounces cream cheese

¼ cup mayo

2 to 3 tablespoons of Greek yogurt

2 to 3 tablespoons lemon juice

1 teaspoon smoky paprika

10 ounces grated cheddar

8 ounces fontina

4 to 6 scallions, sliced

¼ teaspoon red pepper flakes

Grate the cheese either by hand or in a food processor. Put everything into the processor and blend til it is diplike. Taste and adjust lemon juice, salt and pepper.

~

Cocktail Party Wiltless Salad

SERVES 6

1 can hearts of palm, sliced

1 medium zucchini, quartered, seeds removed, and sliced

1 small English cucumber, quartered, seeds removed, and sliced

1 heart of celery, chopped, including the leaves

4 fresh steamed or canned artichoke bottoms, sliced

1 cup frozen green peas, thawed

½ cup champagne shallot vinaigrette (see below)

Toss all ingredients together and serve chilled.

Champagne Shallot Vinaigrette

MAKES 1½ CUPS

Adapted from Michael Lomonaco.

¼ cup Champagne vinegar

1 tablespoon honey

2 large peeled shallots, chopped very fine (can also use
    4 tablespoons of prechopped shallots in a jar)

3 tablespoons Dijon mustard

¼ teaspoon salt

¼ teaspoon pepper

¾ cup extra-virgin olive oil

Combine chopped shallots with vinegar and honey in a small bowl and let sit ten minutes. Add mustard, salt, and pepper to the shallot mixture and blend well. Put into a blender, or use an immersion blender to blend smooth and then add oil in a thin stream until it is well emulsified. For a less creamy, more broken dressing, simply shake in a jar or shaker instead of blending. The dressing may be stored, covered, for up to one week in the refrigerator, but should be brought to room temperature before using.

Melanie's Zucchini Strand Pasta with Chicken

SERVES 2

Healthy, light, and full of flavor, this is a perfect dish all year long.

¾ pound dried linguini or other long-strand pasta, whole wheat
   is great here

1 pound medium zucchini

2 tablespoons olive oil

1 small shallot, minced fine (optional)

¼ cup dry white wine

½ pound boneless, skinless chicken breasts, cut into strips

¼ cup chicken stock

Zest and juice of one lemon

1 tablespoon butter

Pinch red pepper flakes, or more if you like it spicier

Salt and pepper to taste

1 tablespoon coarsely chopped fresh parsley leaves

2 tablespoons fresh chives, chopped

½ cup grated Parmesan

Bring a large pot of water to a boil and add salt. Add the pasta and cook until al dente, about 10 minutes (plan to reserve ½ cup cooking water).

While the water comes to a boil and the pasta cooks, cut the zucchini into long strands that mimic the pasta . . . I use a julienne peeler for this, just running it around the outside of the zucchini and not using the pulpy seed part. You can also do this on a mandolin, or make long julienne by hand.

(The idea is to be able to twirl the zucchini up with the pasta, but if you don't care, you can cut it into half moons, it will still be delicious!)

Heat oil in a large skillet over medium-high heat until hot. Add the shallot, and cook until translucent, then add the red pepper flakes. Add chicken and sauté briefly until light brown. Deglaze the pan with the wine and let reduce until almost gone. Add chicken stock, lemon juice, and lemon zest. Swirl in butter. Taste for salt and pepper. Toss in zucchini strands and then immediately add cooked pasta and combine. Add the cheese and herbs and enough reserved pasta water to ensure the sauce is smooth, and toss to combine well. Taste again for seasoning and add salt and pepper, as needed. Grate about 2 more tablespoons Parmesan over the top and serve at once.

Delia's Get Well Soon
Caramel Banana Pudding

SERVES 12

Adapted from The Magnolia Bakery Cookbook. *May not cure what ails you, but you certainly won't care!*

1 14-ounce can sweetened condensed milk

1½ cups ice-cold water

1 3.4-ounce package Jell-O Instant Vanilla Pudding mix

4 ½ cups heavy cream

1 12-ounce box Nilla Wafers

4 cups sliced bananas (4 small, or 3 medium)

1 jar excellent quality caramel sauce, or one cup homemade
   caramel sauce

1½ tablespoons sugar

Beat the sweetened condensed milk and water until completely smooth. Add in the pudding mix and blend for at least 2 more minutes, ensuring that there are no lumps. Put in a zip-top bag, press out all the air so that no skin can form and refrigerate for at least 4 hours, or overnight. Will hold for three days.

When you are ready to assemble the pudding, whip 3 cups of the heavy cream to stiff peaks. Whisk the pudding mixture to lighten it up and then fold pudding mixture into cream in two batches.

In a large, deep 4- to 5-quart casserole dish or bowl, layer one-third of the wafers, followed by one-third of the bananas, followed by one-third of the pudding mix. Drizzle on ½ cup of caramel sauce. Repeat the layers (wafers, bananas, pudding, caramel) two more times, ending at the pudding. Whip the remaining cream with the sugar to soft peaks and top the pudding with the whipped cream. Crumble 4 to 6 wafers to fine powder and dust the top of the cream with the cookie powder.

Let sit in the refrigerator at least 4 to 6 hours before serving, or overnight. Take the pudding out of the fridge about 30 minutes before serving just to let the chill dissipate.

Use the formula for exciting variations! You can substitute chocolate pudding and chocolate wafer cookies for a chocoholic version, or skip the caramel and do raspberries instead. Or keep the bananas and try melted peanut butter instead of caramel. Go exotic with fresh mango and gingersnaps. Once you have the basics down, it really lends itself to experimentation.

Kasha Varnishkes

SERVES 8 TO 12 AS A SIDE DISH

A classic bit of Jewish comfort food, and a great side dish for any braised meat with a gravy that needs sopping.

4 cups chopped onions, or more
1 cup rendered chicken fat or olive oil
1½ cups kasha (buckwheat groats)
Salt and ground black pepper
1 pound mini farfalle (bowtie) or other small noodles

Put onions in a large skillet with a lid over medium heat. Cover skillet and cook for about 10 minutes, until onion is dry and almost sticking to pan. Add fat or oil, raise heat to medium-high and cook, stirring occasionally, until onion is nicely browned, at least 10 minutes or so longer.

Meanwhile, bring a large pot of water to a boil. In a separate, medium saucepan, bring 1½ cups water to a boil, stir in the kasha and about a teaspoon of salt. Cover and simmer until kasha is soft and fluffy, about 15 minutes. Let stand, off heat and covered.

Salt the large pot of boiling water and cook noodles until tender but still firm. Drain and combine with the onions and kasha, adding more fat or oil if you like. Season with salt and lots of pepper and serve immediately.

Patrick's Frittata

SERVES 4 TO 6

*On the one hand, your boss showing up after bedtime is a real
annoyance. But if he can take your leftover pasta from last
night and make it into this? You are inclined to forgive him.*

1 pound spaghetti or bucatini

¼ cup small diced pancetta

½ cup bread crumbs

¼ cup extra-virgin olive oil, plus more for drizzling

1 cup canned chickpeas, drained and rinsed

1 teaspoon crushed red pepper flakes

¼ teaspoon ground cinnamon

2 tablespoons pine nuts, toasted

3 tablespoons grated Parmesan

Bunch basil leaves, torn into large pieces

¼ cup grated Parmesan, plus more for garnish

Salt and pepper to taste

10 eggs

¼ cup heavy whipping cream

1 cup marinara sauce

Bring a large pot of salted water to a boil. Cook the pasta
according to the directions on the box. Reserve ¼ cup of pasta
water. Drain the pasta.

Cook pancetta in a dry skillet until the fat is fully rendered
and the pancetta cubes are crisp. Remove the pancetta, leaving the fat in the pan. Add ¼ cup olive oil to the pancetta fat,
and add the pepper flakes, the cinnamon, and the chickpeas.
Add in the pine nuts and pancetta and sprinkle the bread

crumbs over the top, mixing over medium-high heat until the bread crumbs are toasted. Add in pasta, Parmesan and reserved pasta water. Season to taste with salt and pepper and stir in basil.

Eat half of the pasta for dinner. The next day, mix the eggs with the cream and blend with the leftover pasta. Cook over medium low heat in a skillet with 2 tablespoons olive oil until golden brown and almost set up. Slide the frittata onto a plate, drizzle the top with olive oil and flip it over back into the skillet to brown the other side and cook through. A knife in the center should come out clean.

Let the frittata rest for ten minutes before cutting into wedges. Serve wedges with a spoonful of marinara and a sprinkle of Parmesan.

Alana's Classic Potato Salad

SERVES 8 TO 10

Adapted from Cook's Illustrated, *and the best basic potato salad I've ever tasted. Might just get him to propose!*

4 pounds russet potatoes (7 to 8 medium or 5 to 6 large), peeled and cut into ¾-inch cubes

Table salt

4 tablespoons distilled white vinegar (can substitute white wine or rice vinegar)

4 tablespoons minced red onion (very fine)

½ teaspoon sugar

1 cup celery, chopped fine

6 tablespoons sweet pickle relish

1 cup mayonnaise

1½ teaspoons powdered mustard

1½ teaspoons celery seed

4 tablespoons minced fresh parsley leaves

½ teaspoon ground black pepper

2 large hard-cooked eggs, peeled and cut into ¼-inch cubes
   (optional)

Place potatoes in large saucepan and add water to cover by 1 inch. Bring to boil over medium-high heat; add 1 tablespoon salt, reduce heat to medium, and simmer, stirring once or twice, until potatoes are tender, about 8 minutes.

Drain potatoes and transfer to large bowl. Add vinegar and, using rubber spatula, toss gently to combine. Let stand until potatoes are just warm, about 20 minutes.

Meanwhile, in small bowl, put the minced onion and stir in one tablespoon of vinegar and a half teaspoon of sugar and let sit for ten to fifteen minutes, and then drain. Stir together celery, onion, pickle relish, mayonnaise, mustard powder, celery seed, parsley, pepper, and ½ teaspoon salt. Using rubber spatula, gently fold in dressing and eggs, if using, into potatoes. Cover with plastic wrap and refrigerate until chilled, about 1 hour; serve. (Potato salad can be covered and refrigerated for up to 2 days.)

Pamplemousse Olive Oil Cake

SERVES 8

Pamplemousse *is not just the best single word in French, but as an ingredient, grapefruit is underutilized and a wonderful surprise. Replace orange in nearly any recipe and see how it brightens things up. This loaf cake is perfect for brunch or afternoon tea, or as a hostess gift.*

1½ cups all-purpose flour

2 teaspoons baking powder

½ teaspoon kosher salt

1 cup sour cream

1 cup plus 1 tablespoon sugar

3 extra-large eggs

3 teaspoons grated grapefruit zest (approximately one large grapefruit)

½ teaspoon pure vanilla extract

½ cup mild fruity extra-virgin olive oil

½ cup grapefruit marmalade

⅓ cup plus one tablespoon freshly squeezed grapefruit juice

Glaze:

1 cup confectioners' sugar

1 tablespoon Campari liquor

2 tablespoons freshly squeezed grapefruit juice

Preheat the oven to 350°F. Butter a loaf pan well and line the bottom with parchment paper. Grease and flour the pan.

Heat the marmalade in a small saucepan with one tablespoon of the grapefruit juice until liquid, and set aside to cool.

Sift together the flour, baking powder, and salt into one bowl, and in another bowl, whisk together the sour cream, 1 cup sugar, the eggs, grapefruit zest, and vanilla. Slowly whisk the dry ingredients into the wet ingredients. With a rubber spatula, fold the olive oil into the batter, making sure it's all incorporated. Pour the batter into the prepared pan, drizzle the marmalade mixture around the top and swirl it into the batter with the tip of a knife, and bake for about 50 minutes, or until a cake tester placed in the center of the loaf comes out clean.

Meanwhile, cook the ⅓ cup grapefruit juice and remaining 1 tablespoon sugar in a small pan until the sugar dissolves and the mixture is clear. Set aside.

When the cake is done, allow it to cool in the pan for 10 minutes. Carefully place on a baking rack over a sheet pan. While the cake is still warm, poke some holes in the cake with a long, thin skewer, and slowly pour the grapefruit-sugar mixture over the cake and allow it to soak in. Cool.

For the glaze, combine the confectioners' sugar, Campari, and grapefruit juice and pour over the cake.

Read on for a sneak peek at another
delicious novel from Stacey Ballis

Good Enough to Eat

Available now from Berkley

Mashed Potatoes

The first conscious memory I have of food being significant was the Thanksgiving after Dad died. I was four. We gathered at my grandparents' house, made all the right noises; there was football on the television and a fire in the fireplace. But no one seemed to really be there. My mom was still nursing Gillian, and spent most of the day off in the guest bedroom with her. And the food was awful. Overcooked, underseasoned. I remember thinking that Daddy would have hated it. He loved to eat. It's what killed him. Well, sort of. The police found a half-eaten Big Mac in his lap after the accident. They assumed that he was distracted by eating when he ran the red light and into the truck. I remember looking at my family and feeling like Daddy would be so mad at us for not having a good time, for not having a good meal. And halfway through dinner my grandmother said, "Oh my god, I forgot the mashed potatoes. They were Abraham's favorite. How could I forget!" And then she ran off crying. And I thought, I'd better learn how to make mashed potatoes quickly or the family would completely disintegrate.

O kay, Mel, let's start with something good," Carey says. "What happened this week that was really great?"

I have to think about this for a moment. "Well, the store showed a small profit this week. . . ."

"Wow, that's like three weeks in a row, right?"

"Yeah. Not anything huge, but my accountant says that all we need is a trend. If I can do three more consecutive weeks in the black, we should be able to project the rest of the year's income. You know, since this is the slow season."

"Why slow?" Carey asks.

"Well, it's February. The New Year's resolutions to eat healthy and exercise have worn off, it's four degrees below zero, and everyone wants comfort food. Chicago in February is no time to run a healthy take-out establishment. No one wants to get out of their cars to pick up a decent good-for-you meal, they want stick-to-your-ribs fare and they want it delivered." I'm babbling.

"Well, then, I'm even more proud of you that you're doing so well in such a tough time." Carey is unflaggingly supportive. She's so much more than a nutritional counselor; she is like my life guru, friend, and therapist all rolled into one bundle of positive energy, and I'd never have gotten through the last three months without her. "But I'd like to hear about something good for you personally, not related to the business. Did *you* have anything good this week?"

"Well." I take a deep breath. "I threw out my bed. I just put it out in the alley, along with all the pillows and bedding, and went and bought a new one."

"Well, that sounds like fun! A little shopping spree for your new place, right?"

"Yeah. I mean, when I moved out it seemed logical to take the bed, since Andrew was staying at Charlene's." I hate having to say their names out loud. "But, I don't know, it just felt like . . ."

"Bad ex-husband juju in the bedroom."

"Yeah. Exactly. I got home from the store, exhausted, went

to go collapse, and couldn't bring myself to get in the bed. It was like his fucking ghost was in the fibers or something. And I know that he said he never brought her there, I mean they never did it in our bed, but still. I slept on the couch. In the morning I remembered that the nice woman who did all my window treatments had given me her husband's card. He's over at American Mattress on Clybourn, and she said that he would hook me up if I ever needed a bed, so I just went over there and picked out the tallest, biggest, squishiest, most indulgent bed they had. And then went to Bed Bath and Beyond to fit it out with down pillows and eight-hundred-thread-count sheets."

"That's awesome!"

"It was ridiculous. And I couldn't really afford it, but I felt like I couldn't afford not to either. Wanna know the weird thing? The bed is named Waking Hours. And at first, I wasn't really sure why Serta would name a bed that, since the point of a bed is supposed to be sleeping hours. Except that after the first night, I wanted to spend all my waking hours in it too!"

"And how has the sleeping been since?"

"Better. Much better. But I'm dreaming about cakes again."

Never fails. Stress or sadness, my dream life is all about food. When I decided to lose the weight two years ago, I left the law and went to culinary school, and then got a degree in holistic nutrition. That's where I met Carey. She was one of my teachers in the nutrition program. My store, Dining by Design, is a healthy gourmet take-out café, amazing food that is amazingly good for you.

But no matter how much I feel in control of my relation-ship with food, my subconscious craves the habits of my former life. The days when Andrew and I would eat spaghetti carbonara as a midnight snack after sex, when there were always cookies in the cookie jar and a cake under the glass dome in the kitchen. The days when food was celebration and joy and reason for living and cure-all. A substitute for two dead parents and a little sister who lives in London and rarely calls. A replacement for the children I never got around to having, and now don't have the energy, money, or husband to make feasible. A way to patch the holes created by a soulless job. A way to fill up that empty pit of hunger that seemed never satisfied.

"And how do you feel about these dreams?" Carey asks. "Are they still about denial, or are you getting to eat the cakes?"

Carey has been with me through everything, the hardest-to-lose last twenty-five pounds, the purchase and opening of the store, the surprising end of my marriage. She knows my dreams almost as well as I do.

"I don't get to eat the cake. I'm just in the room with the buffet, and the cakes are everywhere, and I'm loading up plates with every possible flavor, and putting them aside to take home, to eat in secret, but then there are people and I have to mingle, and then I can't find the plates I put aside. It's extraordinarily pathetic."

"Not pathetic. Natural. You're feeling deprived, physically and emotionally. It's February in Chicago, and your desire is for comfort food. And you're working very hard and going home to a place you haven't fully embraced as home yet. And you are probably a little lonely . . ."

"And horny." If we're going to be honest about it.

Carey laughs. "Of course, and horny. Will you do something for me?"

"You know I will."

"Get your butt over to Sweet Mandy B's tomorrow. Buy every flavor of their mini cupcakes that appeals to you. Go home, pour a glass of champagne, light a candle, and eat every one, slowly. Lick the crumbs off the plate; savor the different flavor combinations, the texture of the frosting. Eat until you are full, and then stop and throw the rest away. We have talked about this before; sometimes you have to eat what you crave purposefully so that you don't fall into a binge of fog-eating."

"I know. And I know I'm in a dangerous spot. But you're right, I do need to address the cake craving soon or I'm going to jump off the wagon and land in a vat of frosting and eat my way out."

It doesn't matter how much I know about this process, how much I am able to counsel others, being a compulsive overeater is no different from being an alcoholic or drug addict. The only difference is that you can avoid drugs and alcohol completely and you have to have a relationship with food every day for the rest of your life. It's actually the hardest addiction to live with. If you were an alcoholic and someone said to you that you were required to have a single drink three to five times a day every day, but were not supposed to ever drink to excess, or a drug addict who was required to take just one pill several times a day every day, but you're not supposed to ever take more than that . . . no one would ever make it through rehab.

"You're doing great," Carey says. "I'll send you an e-mail about our major stuff from today. Keep up the good work, and don't forget to call or e-mail me if you have any questions."

"Thanks, honey."

"Thank you! Great session today. I'll talk to you in a couple of weeks."

"Okay, Carey. Talk to you later."

I hang up the phone and stretch my arms above my head. I head to the bathroom, where I throw my thick, straight chestnut hair into a ponytail to get it out of my way. I wash my face carefully, my skin being my one vanity, and slide a lightly tinted moisturizer on, surprised as I am every day to find that I own cheekbones, and have only one chin. A coat of mascara on my lashes, making my slightly close-set gold-flecked hazel eyes look bigger. This is as cute as I intend to get today. I check my watch. Eleven a.m. A long day stretches ahead of me. I know I should love Mondays, my one day off, but they always scare me a little bit. Especially since Andrew left me on a Monday. I always wake up feeling like something bad is going to happen, like a Vietnam flashback. Tuesday through Sunday I'm up at five for a forty-five-minute workout, and am in the store by six thirty. By the time I open the doors at eleven, Kai and I have cooked in a frenetic burst of energy, and the cases are full of delectables.

Half Japanese, half African American, and only twenty-two years old, Kai was the star of our graduating class from culinary school. He has better knife skills than anyone I have ever seen, and a cutting wit to match. And along with Carey has kept me sane and functioning these past weeks. Not only did he come sit with me that horrible day, which he refers to as our Abominable Snow Day, but he also essentially did all the heavy lifting at the store for the first week while I walked around in a numb haze, burning things and giving people the wrong items. At the end of that week he came over after work, made me pack a bag, and forced me to move in with him and his boyfriend, Phil, a successful trader. Phil pays the bills, but is out of the house from about five in the morning till about three in the afternoon, which was why Kai could afford to take the job with me for essentially minimum wage, since it is only six hours a day, and only four days a week. On Tuesdays and Saturdays I have an extern from the culinary institute: every other month a new fresh-faced budding chef to train, currently a slightly dim thirty-year-old former dental assistant named Ashley who thought cooking would be more fun than poking around people's mouths all day, and forgot to find out if she had any real passion for food.

In the afternoons and on Sundays I have Delia, who lives in the women's shelter up the block. It's part of a job-training program they started with the local business owners. Delia escaped her abusive husband in Columbus, and a sort of Underground Railroad for battered women moved her to Chicago for her own safety. New in town, with no contacts, she has been living in the shelter for the past nine months. When she started taking over in their kitchen, the shelter volunteers recognized her love of cooking, and approached me about the program. I pay her minimum wage on weekdays and time and a half for the Sunday hours. She's a homegrown soul-food goddess who learned at her grandmother's knee, and it's been a struggle to hamper her desire to cook things in bacon fat, but she works like a dog and is a fast learner, and reluctantly admits that the food tastes good, even if she thinks the whole idea of cooking healthy is a little silly. "Sisterfriend," she says to me at least once a day, "at my house, it is going to be fried chicken like the good lord intended. None of this oven-baked-skinless nonsense."

All week long there is work to do from sunup till way past sundown, and lovely people to help. There are regular customers to catch up with, and new customers to convert, and bills to pay, and products to order, and precise cleaning to do to keep within sanitation regulations. Occasionally on

Wednesday nights there are cooking classes to teach, and on Friday nights there are special events. The other nights there are new recipes to test and perfect.

But Mondays. Mondays are long. Do the laundry. Change the sheets on the dream bed. Clean the condo that never gets very dirty since I'm at the store six days a week for sixteen hours a day. Go to the grocery store and make sure that the fridge is filled with washed and cut-up veggies, fresh fruit, yogurts, and cottage cheese and easy makings for salads and healthy snacks. Try not to think about what Andrew and Charlene might be doing. What sort of plans they are making, if they are talking about me, wondering if they have spent these last three months in a haze of sex and food and happiness while I have uprooted my entire life. Or rather, while they have uprooted it.

When Andrew finally confessed that it was Charlene he had fallen in love with, Charlene he had been sleeping with, it doubled the betrayal, made the humiliation exponentially worse. Charlene is the managing partner at the law firm where I worked in my former life as a medical malpractice attorney. The life where I made a substantial six-figure income, was married to the man I thought was my soul mate, and lived in a gorgeous brick house in Lincoln Park that was built in 1872, right after the Great Chicago Fire. The life where I leased a new BMW every two years, put fabulous designer shoes on my feet, and ate whatever my 289-pound self desired. The life where I had ridiculous amounts of energetic sex with a man who reveled in every soft curve of my ample frame.

Charlene was more than my boss; she was a friend. At about 275 pounds herself, she was my partner in crime, quick with a midday candy bar or cookie, the first to suggest an order of onion rings to accompany the after-work martinis. The one who celebrated every one of our wins and commiserated about our losses by taking us to lunch somewhere decadent, where we would order half the menu on the firm's generous expense account.

But when I decided to take control of my eating, to try to reverse the diabetes I had acquired, to ease the pain in my joints, to prevent further health issues and hopefully ward off a heart attack, Charlene pulled away from me. And when I left the firm to go to culinary school, she essentially dropped off the face of my earth. I tried to maintain the friendship, never preaching about my program or even suggesting she make changes herself, knowing firsthand that there is nothing more irritating than someone currently successfully managing her weight trying to get a fat person to drink whatever Kool-Aid is the flavor of the day.

I even tried to get together with her at nonmeal times so that she never had to listen to me order something healthy and feel pressure to do so herself. Because you know what sucks? Sitting across from little Miss Egg White Omelet with Tomato Slices Instead of Potatoes, when what you want is a stack of pancakes dripping with butter and syrup and a side of sausage. If you order what you want, you feel judged, and if you order something healthy, you feel like a phony, not to mention disappointed. I suggested spa dates instead, afternoon shopping, theater matinees. She found a million excuses to avoid me, and eventually I stopped trying.

You'd have thought that as I started to shrink, Andrew's ardor would have increased. After all, while there was less and less of me to love, what was there was more and more strong and flexible. We could have managed positions that would have been impossible before, but the smaller I got, the

less interest Andrew had in sex, and what had been a three-
or four-night-a-week habit dwindled first to once a week, then
every other week, then once a month. By the end, it had been
so rare I stopped keeping track. He supported me through
culinary school, helped me buy and open the store, and then
he left.

It was a month after he left me, at the final walk-through
when we sold our house, that I found out it was Charlene he
had been sleeping with for nearly two years. He left his phone
on the counter, and when it rang, I saw it was her on the caller
ID, and everything fell into place.

"CHARLENE?" I had screamed. "You've been fucking
Charlene?!?"

"Lower your voice, the real estate brokers are right upstairs."

"I don't care if the goddamned queen of goddamned England is upstairs. It's Charlene, isn't it?"

Andrew sighed, as if it were very inconvenient to have to
deal with me. "Yes, all right? Is that what you need to hear?
Yes. I'm in love with Charlene, I'm moving in with her. Please
don't be a drama queen about this."

"*I'm* the drama queen? You're the one behaving like you're
starring in some afternoon soap opera. Really, Andrew, you
couldn't have gone more cliché if you tried. It's pathetic."

"I had really hoped we could be friends, Mel, after all this
time, but you're making it very hard."

That was when I realized fully that I hated him. That I
hated who he was and what he had done to me and what he
had turned me into: some shrill ex-wife berating him in public, embarrassing herself more than him. I would not let him
turn me into the worst version of myself.

"Andrew, I don't think I want to be friends. In fact, I'm pretty sure that if I met you today at a party I'd not want to know you."

"Have it your way."

"Don't you worry. I intend to."

I'm not the only woman to lose her man, and certainly not the only one to lose him to someone she thought was a good friend. But I do believe I'm the only woman I've ever heard of who got thin, and then had her husband leave her for a big girl. If it wasn't so humiliating and hurtful, it would be almost funny.

So now, I focus on my new life. The life where I make barely enough to keep my head above water. The life where I'm divorced from the man I thought was my soul mate, who turned out to just be a lying, cheating piece of shit with a serious fat-girl fetish. The life where I live in a little two-bedroom condo in Ravenswood Manor, a quarter the size of my old house, but all I could afford to buy outright with my settlement from the sale of the Lincoln Park house, since with the cost of the business, I couldn't afford to carry a mortgage as well. The life where I drive a Honda, wear Crocs instead of Jimmy Choos, and eat the way a normal person is supposed to, while trying every day to quiet the demons in my head that crave butter and cream and sugar. The life where I am diabetes-free, fit, and strong, with a healthy heart and a prognosis of a long life, and every day hoping that I'm getting closer to believing it can also be a happy one.

I look around me, at the haven I've tried to create for myself. When I bought the condo, I'd done it fast, because I'd needed a place to be, and I couldn't stay at Phil and Kai's for-ever with my belongings languishing in storage. Andrew and I, being lawyers, knew exactly how to get around the legal issue of separation, signed affidavits that we had been living separate lives under the same roof, which unbeknownst to me, we had, and got the Chicago version of a quickie divorce the same week we sold our house. My broker luckily found out about the condo before it was listed, and I made a full-price cash offer. We closed within two weeks, and I moved in right away.

I purposefully attempted to make it a sacred, healing space. I decorated in shades of dove gray, silver, and ivory, with touches of robin's egg blue. I picked soft textures and natural elements: mohair on the down-filled sofa, chunky tables of waxed driftwood. I built on my collection of bird's nest–themed art, finding prints and small sculptures to scat-ter around, focusing on the symbolism. The work that goes into the creation of a simple and functional place of safety and comfort. The life-affirming message of making a nest. The life that might happen within.

I get off the couch and stretch, the warm light coming through the tall windows reflected in the wall of muted silver-leaf, a major splurge requiring two artisans to work for three days to painstakingly apply the six-by-six squares of delicate leaf and then burnish and seal the wall with a darkening agent, so that the whole thing glows like moonlight under a gossamer pewter veil.

I head to the kitchen, which had been the thing I fell in love with the first time I saw it, a bright space with stainless-steel appliances, treated concrete counters, white subway tiles on the walls and a subtle blue floor. It's a third the size of the kitchen in my former house, but economical use of space makes it a cozy place to work. Everything I need is within reach: my best knives on the counter, spices and herbs in a specially installed wall unit, pots and pans hanging overhead from a wrought-iron rack.

I need to shake off the morose thoughts, and nothing does that as well as testing new recipes. With Chicago in the throes of comfort-food cravings, I have been working diligently to find ways to create some healthier versions.

And today, what I need, what I want, is mashed potatoes.